Nick Garson had watched, with a sort of detached interest, as his hands had reached into his jacket pocket and pulled out his gun and started shooting at the man in the bulldozer.

It wasn't until the bulldozer crashed into the pit that Nick began to think that maybe this was something he could get in trouble for; so he tucked the gun back into his jacket and went back to his car, thinking that he would just be moving along back to Buffalo, leaving no one the wiser that he had ever been here.

There were still a lot of loose bullets on the driver's seat. He scooped them up before he sat down, and then watched his hands reload the gun. He wondered why they were doing that; maybe they were expecting to be called on to shoot someone else.

His two little friends were just sliding the clip back into place when he heard the sirens approaching. Somebody must have heard the shots and called the police. Bad hands, Nick thought. Bad, bad, bad! Loading the gun when they should have been helping him drive away!

The cop car came tearing in from the north, braked rapidly and stopped at an angle at the side of the road. Two policemen got out, looking around cautiously. They had their own guns out; he could see the weapons in their hands.

One cop reached into the cruiser and pulled out the radio mouthpiece and started talking into it, while the other kept his gaze flicking around the scene. They seemed quite wary. Reasonable, Nick thought, considering that there had been gunfire. Funny; he felt more like a witness than a perpetrator, as if he should run over to them with his palms in the air and say *I saw who did it, officers, it was these hands here!*

Of course, he wasn't about to do something crazy like that.

Also by James V. Viscosi

Available Now

Night Watchman
A Flock of Crows is Called a Murder
Long Before Dawn
Television Man

The "Strings" Duology
Shards
Ravels

Coming Soon

Father's Books

Anthology Appearances

New Traditions in Terror
edited by Bill Purcell
featuring "The 66th Vampire"

Crossings
edited by Megan Powell
featuring "Draw"

www.jamesviscosi.com

A Flock of Crows is Called a Murder

a novel

by James Viscosi

PART ONE:
DEMOLITION

1

QUENTIN FARMER STOOD ON THE grassy yellow bank and stared across the water. The March wind from the northwest was stiff and cold and right in his face, making him squint; it whipped the surface of the canal into tiny scalloped ridges, parodies of waves. The branches of the barren trees that lined the opposite bank shivered and shook and clacked together as if trying to keep each other warm.

He pushed his hands deeper into the lined pockets of his coat, out of the icy bite of the air, and frowned. He didn't like what he was looking at.

He tilted his head a little bit to the left. It didn't improve the thing's appearance any. Without turning around, Quentin shouted: "Nelson!"

Behind him, the sound of hammering started up again. A couple of his employees—locals, actually, but he had hired them to put this sign up and that made them his people, at least for the moment—were driving big posts into the ground. As the ground was still partially frozen this was not an easy task, but they looked big and vigorous and Quentin was confident they could pull it off. Once that was done, they would mount the billboard, which was currently face-down on the grass behind them; it said *Future Site of Canal Plaza* in bright red block letters and, in smaller blue script, *A Quentin Farmer Project.*

His assistant materialized beside him. Nelson DeGrace, clad in a trenchcoat nearly identical to the one Quentin wore, except that it was a lighter shade of grey and cost half as much, didn't say anything. He looked briefly at his employer, then followed his gaze across the waterway. "Ugly," Nelson said after a moment.

"*Ugly?*" Quentin said. "It's an eyesore. I can't have that sitting across from my plaza."

Nelson scratched the back of his neck. "You know what it looks like?" he said.

"What?"

"Looks like a great big cock."

The cold wind gusted. Dry clumps of cloud skidded wildly across the sky.

"Let's go take a closer look," Quentin said.

Nelson stayed at the bank as Quentin turned away from the old building, trudged back toward the car. The grass, still rimed with morning frost, crunched under his feet. His Jaguar was parked at the side of the road, near the bumpy access ramp that led down into the broad, bowl-shaped depression that housed the construction site.

From behind him, Nelson's voice: "Sir?"

Quentin stopped, looked over his shoulder. Nelson was still standing down by the water. He folded his arms and waited for his assistant to continue, which he did, after a moment: "I was just thinking. Place like that, abandoned, falling down … it's not going to have much of an access road. Do you really want to take the Jaguar?"

"Good point," Quentin said. He thought a moment, looked around at the available vehicles, and said: "We'll take the pickup."

"That belongs to one of your sign-putter-uppers."

"So we'll rent it," Quentin said.

As it turned out, the sign-putter-upper who owned the truck was more than happy to rent it to Quentin. As a bonus, he gave them directions to the old building. With Nelson behind the wheel and an eight-track in the player—an *eight-track*, for God's sake—they drove off, following the guy's instructions. They were supposed to find a dirt road off of River Street, a mile to the east, but the interloping Thruway made it necessary to overshoot their destination and then double back.

Fifteen minutes later—it would've taken forever for them to find it on their own; the locals were good for something after all—they came to a long, unpaved, overgrown track that lurched down a ridiculously steep slope, skirted the edge of a boggy, reedy field, and vanished into a band of trees a half-mile or so away. Nelson slowed and turned left, into the mouth of the road, where he stopped right on the lip of the incline. "Is this trip really necessary?" he said, staring down the hill.

"Just like a rollercoaster," Quentin said. "You like rollercoasters, don't you, Nelson?"

"Not particularly," Nelson said. "I like things nice and level."

"If the world were all level, where would I ski?" Quentin said. "Let's go."

Nelson stepped on the gas and they plunged down the hill, skidding on rutted tracks of half-frozen mud. The road turned slightly to the left, but the truck tried to keep going, down another stubby bank and into the marsh. From his window, Quentin could see the iced surface of the swamp between the reeds and splintered brown grasses. He found himself pulling on the door handle, as if that would move the truck back to the correct heading; but then Nelson wrenched the wheel out of the skid and the big vehicle yawed sideways, turned ponderously away from the edge, and bounced back onto the track.

They bumped and rumbled along the dirt road. Vegetation scraped and scratched against the undercarriage of the pickup; Quentin hated to think what that would have done to his low-slung street machine. The marsh went by on the right, flashes of crusted water visible through the matted shreds of vegetation. He thought he saw a rusting piece of machinery out in the middle of the bog; looked like the top of a tractor. A big fat crow was perched on the seat, huddled up against the cold, watching them.

They passed into the woods. Barren limbs crisscrossed overhead, dirty brown trunks crowded each other for space. Dead bracken sprawled and scrambled in the gaps between the trees. Off to the left he could barely see the high embankment of the Thruway, curving away from them. Even the interstate didn't want to be anywhere near this place.

The dirt road veered to the right, climbed a bit, and spat them out in a bumpy, sodden clearing right behind the decrepit structure. The discolored clapboard wall was only a few yards away. Nelson slammed on the brakes; the pickup lurched, coughed, and slid to a stop in the shadow of the building, scant feet short of hitting the place. He shut off the engine and said: "Well, that was fun."

Up close, the place was even more ruinous than it had appeared from across the canal. It looked like a church, Quentin thought; one that had sat, unused and forgotten, as its roof collapsed and its walls sagged inward and its stout round clapboard steeple tipped more and more to the east, eventually coming to resemble, as Nelson had pointed out, the semi-erect penis of a recumbent man. A spreading tree that poked through the roof at the opposite end from the steeple, forming the pubic hair of the massive member.

"How?" Quentin said. "How did we never notice this place?"

"Well, we've never actually been here before, sir."

"I know that," Quentin said. Then, after a moment: "Somebody recommended this site, didn't they?"

"Yes."

"Who?"

"I believe it was Garson, sir."

"Garson?"

"Nick Garson. One of the designers. Food court specialist. He said you could take advantage of low property values and the proximity of ——"

"I don't recall any mention of having to bulldoze a ruin across the way," Quentin said. He drummed his fingers on the dashboard of the truck, eyeing the row of high, narrow windows that ran like perforations along the wall. Most of them were missing their glass; crows roosted in the holes, hunkered down in the icy air. Like the one on the tractor, these seemed to be observing him, except he had the weird impression that they would be bursting into laughter any second like some mocking chorus: *Ha ha, fooled you, made you buy bad land!*

Oh yeah?

"Make sure it was Garson," Quentin said, "and have him fired."

Nelson said: "Are you serious?"

Quentin cocked his head, still looking at the crows, and said, "I didn't quite catch that, Nelson."

"I mean, he's very good," Nelson said. "They say no one can lay out restaurants like Garson does."

"They do, do they?" Quentin said. "Well, next time you see them —whoever they are—you tell them I can find plenty of monkeys to pick spots for Burger Kings and KFCs." Quentin got out of the car and walked slowly around the place, through frosted clouds of his own breath. It didn't look better from any of the angles. He paused on the canal side and watched his temps nailing the sign into place, almost directly across the water. It was about to happen: another Quentin Farmer project, about to come into existence.

He visualized the site as it would look after the plaza was built, the muddy, grassy depression replaced by a series of gleaming white concrete steppes, a multi-tiered shopping experience. Little shops and most of the eateries—he had decided they would go upscale here, no fast food joints or bogus Chinese places or pizza twirlers in red hats—would be on the highest level, farthest from the canal and the smell of boat fuel and fish; then stores, medium-sized to big ones, like you would find at an outlet mall; and then a promenade right down at the bank, with lights and benches and more shops, small ones; and entertainers in booths, and canoe rentals, and trees in concrete pots, and maybe more restaurants, quirky little bistros with French-sounding words in their names. It was going to become a cultural center in the Selden Falls region; people were going to say, *There's so much more to do here since Quentin Farmer built his plaza!*

And across the water from all this, there would *not* be a large, degenerate, vaguely phallic ruin sitting in the tall weeds with a tree growing through its roof. There just wouldn't.

The old building creaked and groaned in the wind. Quentin gave it an unfriendly glance over his shoulder, and noticed that this side, too, sported a row of high, narrow apertures, although there was no crow population. He found that mildly odd, since these windows were in the lee of the building, out of the wind and right in the sunlight. Surely crows liked to be warm, just like everything else?

He noticed Nelson approaching across the flattened yellow grass. He was just slipping his cellular phone into his pocket. "I expressed your feelings about this place to Jones's office," he said.

"Why not Jones himself?"

Nelson shrugged, and said: "Racquetball."

"Christ, doesn't that guy do anything else?" Quentin said.

"I'm sure he does, at least occasionally," Nelson said. "Anyway, they promised to put the message right on his computer screen."

Quentin nodded. Simon Jones, the mayor of Selden Falls, was desperate for this development, and had bent more than one ordinance to keep things going smoothly. Not by any specific request, of course; all it generally took was a sigh and a comment about how unfortunate it was that they couldn't do such-and-such because of some absurd law enacted by so-and-so, years ago, when things were different. "Good," he said. "I would hate to see the development thrown off track by something as silly as a broken-down old barn with a steeple on it."

"That's what I told them," Nelson said.

Quentin glanced at the building. It hadn't vanished during his conversation with Nelson, so he said: "What about Garson?"

"Sir?"

"The guy who picked this spot. Is he gone yet?"

"I thought I would give you a little while to think it over."

Quentin looked at Nelson with one raised eyebrow.

"Or I could just call personnel now," Nelson said, retrieving his phone.

When Simon Jones got back from his racquetball date and went through his stack of messages, the one from Quentin Farmer was not among them. So when the phone rang later that afternoon and he had a brief conversation with Kevin Kowalski, Simon's racquetball opponent and the chairman of the Selden Falls common council, the mayor assured him that everything was on track with Mr. Farmer's very important development, which was going to be the linchpin of the town's economic revival and thus of great concern to the careers of all those involved in local governance. They chatted about other things; then Kevin went away happy, and Simon went away happy, and he stayed happy until he was getting ready to leave that evening and happened to roll his chair over a yellow slip of paper on the floor of his office.

Simon Jones carried the message from Quentin Farmer's assistant to a special common council meeting convened that night, with the suggestion that they find out who owned the land the old building stood on and, if it turned out to be the city, make arrangements to have the dump demolished immediately; and if not for the intercession of Jane Trott, council member and amateur psychic, they would have agreed immediately.

He didn't realize at first where Jane was going, when she stood up and started asking questions, like: "Does anyone know what this place used to be?" And, when no one did: "Well, I think it looks like a church, don't you?" To which there was a general mumble that may or may not have been assent. Then she said, "We need to think very carefully about what we're doing here." And then she sat down.

Jane was quiet after that, and Simon hoped her contribution to the evening's discussion was finished. But as it turned out, she was horrified by the thought of knocking down what she believed to be a church—even a decrepit and abandoned one—without a proper ritual, whatever that was; and when she spoke up again later in the evening it became obvious that she had been silent merely to give the other members a chance to demonstrate their own opposition to the idea, which they had failed to do. "I can't believe you're all so ready to go along with this," she said, interrupting Simon as he was going over the importance of once again accommodating Mr. Farmer. "You have no idea what might be unleashed. All the accumulated spiritual energy, let go just like *that!*" She snapped her fingers, apparently to emphasize the fashion in which the spiritual energy would be let go.

There was a momentary silence, and then Simon said, "Yes, well, I think we're all willing to risk a little spiritual backlash to help move this project along."

And Kevin Kowalski said, "Better than a voter backlash any day." This got a laugh from the other council members.

Jean O'Connor, sitting on Jane's right, said: "If we let superstitions stop us from doing what we can to help the town, why, we're no better than cavemen."

Jane said, looking at Jean, "First of all, let me just say that I've *been* a caveman and I find your comment arrogant and insulting." She turned to address the council in general. "Second of all, there's a procedure to demolishing churches, and I think we need to follow it." Jane paused, then added, with a sidelong glance at Jean, "If we don't, we're no better than fascists, going around and knocking stuff down willy-nilly."

Simon wondered if she knew what the procedure was; he doubted it.

"We aren't fascists," Kevin said. "We're a democracy. Let's take a vote."

Which Jane Trott lost, eight to one. She looked at all the other raised hands, then got up and stormed out.

"Democracy in action, people," Kevin said, as the meeting began to break up. "Beautiful, isn't it?"

Jane Trott left the council meeting resolved to get the ritual done herself, before the council had a chance to act on its decision. The problem, as she discovered when she tried to do some research on the place's denominational nature, was that information about the history of Selden Falls ranged from spotty to nonexistent. The building which had housed the old city hall and library had burned down twenty-six years earlier and taken a lot of records with it; the Historical Society had shriveled up years ago from lack of funding, and its archives had vanished; and the town just wasn't important enough to have information about it stored in other places.

She wasted three afternoons trying to find out what manner of cleric she needed to call in to perform the task, and ended up on Friday with no more of a clue than she'd started with; and then she ran out of time. She found out—from the paper, no less, not even from Simon or one of the other council members—that Sunset Construction had been retained to demolish the place on the upcoming Monday. The only thing standing between the old church and destruction was Saturday, Sunday, and Jane.

So she decided she would do the job herself. As a psychic—even an amateur one—she figured she was qualified to sense the character of the place and find the appropriate way to disarm its spiritual power before the common council and the mayor set it loose with a bulldozer and a wrecking ball.

The very next day, she went out to shut the place down.

"They just don't get it, Calvin," she told her husband, as she turned off River Street onto the overgrown track that led to the church. The ruts were deep and muddy but her Jeep churned easily through the muck. To their right the high grasses of the wide marshy field, crushed by the winter snows, were starting to turn green again. The trees weren't budding yet, but they soon would be. "I mean, sure, it's just an ugly old building. It's not the building *per se* that worries me. It's the energy." Bump bump bump along the track. "You get that many people together all concentrating on the same thing, it *charges* a place, you know?"

Calvin grunted noncommittally. It was a Saturday morning and the only charge he was interested in was strong black coffee. He certainly couldn't work up any level of concern over the fate of some broken-down old church at the edge of a swamp. They were supposed to have been going grocery shopping today; she hadn't unveiled this little side mission until they were well away from their house. He glanced at the dashboard clock; by the time they got to the supermarket it would be mobbed. But such were his fortunes since he'd married his slightly wiggy amateur psychic.

Jane said: "It's not that I think it's *dangerous* or anything, but we need to do this right, don't you think?"

Grunt.

"Exactly," Jane said. She parked in front of the place, in a wide, flat area of scraggly crabgrass and weeds and tufted mounds, facing the old building. Across the canal, the signs of imminent construction were obvious: large heaps of dirt, bright orange machinery, a sign angled to point at the Interstate advertising Farmer's soon-to-be-built plaza. The man moved fast, Calvin thought; none of that had been there earlier in the week.

"I mean, we don't want to start a big project jinxed because we did something stupid right at the beginning, do we?" Jane said.

Calvin didn't even bother to grunt this time. Continuing to eyeball the heavy equipment across the water, he concluded that Farmer's backhoe had sunk up to its axle in mud. That would take a while to pull free. He wondered if the machinery was from a local contractor or if Farmer had trucked it in.

"Of course we don't." Jane shut the engine. "You stay here, I'll probably just be a couple of minutes. I'm going to start by probing a little bit." She got out of the car, went to the threshold of the church, and stood in front of the crooked doorway for a moment with her arms spread. Calvin watched her. This was her antenna position, when she was trying to pull in all the signals, down to the weakest. If a hamster had ever died in the church, in her antenna position she would claim to sense it.

After a few seconds she dropped her arms and went inside. Calvin turned on the radio, came into the middle of a call-in show. They seemed to be talking about the latest political scandal in Washington. Because he didn't feel like finding something better, Calvin leaned back in the seat and closed his eyes and concocted responses to the calls. He thought his were much better than the ones the host and her guests came up with. After a while he got kind of cold, so he started the car and turned on the heater; then he got kind of warm and turned it off. Then he got bored with the show, so he shut the car and got out and started poking around the grounds.

Wasn't a single straight wall left, he thought, looking the building over. The entire structure was sagging in several different directions, with the steeple pointing opposite to the general slouch. Upon reflection he decided the thing looked less like a church than it did an old barn to which someone had attached a tower. He bent over to examine the foundation. Looked like the place sat on a slab; ground was probably too mucky for a basement. He straightened up, rapped on the wall. A clapboard came loose and clattered to the ground in a swirl of aged paint flakes, revealing wormy, rotting wood beneath.

Wouldn't take much to knock this place down, Calvin thought, nudging the board with his foot. A good stiff wind would probably do it. As if in answer to this thought, the wind kicked up suddenly, and he heard timbers groaning as the air pushed them. But it didn't look like the place was going to collapse just yet; and after a moment the wind dropped and the groaning died away.

He stepped back from the building, eyed the tiny little windows that ran high along the walls. Most of them were broken; the ones that were left weren't even stained glass, they were just clear wavy panes. What remained of the roof was shingled with grey slate, stained and mossy with age and decay. And, of course, the big tree poked up from the end opposite the steeple. Calvin scratched his head and looked at the tower and tried to figure out why everybody thought it looked like a cock. He didn't; he thought it just looked like a tower and a tree. People had overactive imaginations, he decided. His wife not least among them.

He circled all the way around the place, ended up near the front door. Jane still hadn't come out. He stepped onto the cracked and pitted square of flagstone that was set into the earth in front of the gaping entrance. The rock was damp, like everything else this time of year, and the far end had sunk deeply into the ground. He wondered if it had once been elevated, like a patio, or a place to park carriages, or the floor of a porch. He couldn't tell. Like the building itself, the flat piece of stone could have been lots of things.

He stood awhile on the tipped slab of rock and eyed the church and wondered whether or not he should go in after his wife. Jane hated to be disturbed when she was doing her psychic shtick, but it had been considerably more than the few minutes she had estimated; she might have fallen or something. More than once, her clairvoyant episodes had ended with her wandering around in a daze or babbling nonsense or simply unconscious. She said it was the power of the energy flowing through her, said it was too much for the frail vessel of her psyche; by which, he had at length figured out, she meant her brain. He had to agree; she *did* get herself a bit too worked up sometimes.

He edged to the hollow doorway and looked through. The inside of the old church was pretty dim. Calvin stood in the doorway and stared into the gloom and waited for his eyes to adjust. When they did, he found he could see the whole interior of the building, but he couldn't see Jane. Maybe she was behind the tree, which grew at the far end of the hall, sprouting just in front of what looked like an altar-type area; or maybe she was up in the loft, directly overhead. He thought about calling her but didn't; he might disrupt her concentration, with dire consequences. That's what she told him, anyway. She had sat him down one time and run through a list of all the bad things she thought could happen if he interrupted her while she was channeling. Stuff like losing control of her astral projection, whatever that meant; or giving spirits a chance to take over her body; or causing her to miss a crucial section of her vision; or blah, blah, blah. It all sounded impressively bad, but he was more concerned about being relegated to sleeping on the couch. So he kept quiet, and took a small step into the church.

The old bare floor was spongy beneath his feet; the air smelled of mildew and wet plaster. The boards creaked and groaned as he walked slowly from under the loft, into the big main room. Rotting benches lined the center aisle, covered with moss and slime and fallen bits of plaster; closer to the tree they were buried under the wreckage of the collapsed ceiling. The windows were slanted upward, so the illumination that came through them shone onto the ceiling, like footlights. What was left of the roof was sharply peaked, supported by massive crossbeams running right to left, from which smaller timbers branched out and formed a series of Vs against the sides of the roof. The ancient whitewash was heavily water-stained. He could see up into the tower, which opened in a round hole at the peak of the roof; it seemed to have once been accessible from a narrow wooden catwalk sticking out of the opening, running along beside one of the beams to the wall, then curving over to end at the loft. There wasn't much left of the catwalk, just a handful of moldering boards and a series of jagged holes where its supports had been. He would hate to have been the one to climb that thing, Calvin thought. Quasimodo clambering up to ring his bells.

He walked slowly up the aisle, stopped where the debris from the roof began, right at the base of the tree. He could see a pinprick of sun through the tangled branches of the barren tree, seemingly caged within the thick, twisted limbs. They were all tangled up with each other, interlocking, growing every which-way. Weird-looking thing. Kind of on the grotesque side, actually. He wondered if it would look better once it had leaves on it. Doubtful, he thought.

He eyed the junk that blocked his progress to the altar. No way was he clambering over that stuff. No way Jane had, either. She claimed that in one of her past lives—all of which she remembered, thanks to hypnotic regression therapy, or whatever she called it—she had been a mammoth hunter during the ice age; but now she didn't even like to get dirt under her fingernails, so he could be confident she hadn't scaled this decrepit heap of rubbish. Especially not in her go-to-market clothes.

So where was she?

He turned around. The door was a speck of brilliance in the gloom of the far end of the church. The scallops of light from the upturned windows shone weirdly up the scarred, discolored walls. For the first time he noticed the water stains on the ceiling, ripply, twisty marks in wild patterns that made his eyes hurt; he looked away from them, but the dull throb in his eyes moved into his head, and he began to get an itchy, crawly feeling in his skull, like those wormy stains had gotten inside his head and were shivering and squirming and twining around each other.

It was time to call Jane and get them both the hell out of here.

Before he could do that, though, a massive apparition appeared across the ceiling overhead, in the delta of light that seeped through one of the windows. It was a great flapping thing, a monstrous bird.

For a few seconds he suffered the illusion that he was seeing an actual physical creature, a carrion bird that might carry off a school bus; but it wasn't real, it was just a shadow, a trick played by his imagination and his headache and the angle of illumination. He watched the shadow shrink, and shrink, and finally a big black crow hopped into view at the edge of the window, its head flicking this way and that.

Looking for the trespassers.

Jesus Christ, Calvin thought. The crow didn't give a damn who was here. He was getting as bad as Jane. He opened his mouth to call her, but before he uttered a word the crow started cawing. The window channel must have acted like an amplifier or something, because this was the loudest crow Calvin had ever heard. Its coughing, hacking call seemed to rattle what was left of the windows, seemed to shake his teeth in their sockets. *Caw! Caw! Caw!* Looking straight at him, like it was talking to him personally. Issuing instructions maybe. *Hey, you, get out of here!*

It stopped after a few seconds, watched him for another heartbeat, then spread its wings and flapped out of the window and swooped toward him. Calvin almost raised his arm in front of his face, but didn't; and the crow didn't sweep down to attack him, it just banked upward and fluttered into the tangled limbs of the tree, where it proceeded to preen itself with an utter lack of concern about his presence. Apparently it had said its piece and lost interest.

Calvin found himself wandering up the center aisle again. He suddenly realized he still hadn't called Jane, so he yelled her name. It echoed hollowly in the big, empty room. Behind him he heard a loud flapping of wings as the crow took flight. He couldn't resist a backward glance, to see if it was flying at him; but it wasn't. In fact, it was gone. Disappeared.

And then he felt a hand clamp onto his shoulder and he whirled around and Jane was standing there looking at him. Her eyes were wide and glassy, her hair was a little bit tousled, her sweater and jeans had a dirty brown smear along the side, like she'd been lying down somewhere. She had an odd expression on her face, as if she were trying to figure out exactly where she had seen him before. He recognized the look; she often had it when she was coming out of one of her episodes. "Jane?" he said. "You okay?"

She let go of his shoulder, took a step back, nodded. She didn't take her gaze off him. Her expression was changing, from confused to predatory.

"You find out anything?" he asked.

She shook her head. Her lips twitched in a little smile.

"Can we go now, then?" That wasn't good, he thought; she would pick up the edge of nervousness in his voice, and he didn't want to have to explain why it was there. But she didn't say anything; she just shook her head again.

And slowly reached up to begin unbuttoning her sweater.

One of the few things Calvin found agreeable about his wife's psychic forays was that she sometimes came back with an extreme case of the hornies, for reasons she had never been able to adequately explain. They'd done it in the forest outside a friend's cabin, in supposedly haunted houses, in more than one cemetery. Usually it was fun. But *here*, in this smelly, rotten, moldering old building, with light that played wicked pranks and weird marks on the ceiling that got inside your head and crows that screamed at you like an angry landlord?

He would fuck her in a cemetery, but by God, he wouldn't fuck her here.

She had gotten her sweater open; she had a white tee shirt on underneath it, through which he could see her black bra. She was tugging at the sides of her shirt, pulling it out of her pants. Had to stop her now, before she went any farther.

Calvin stepped forward and grabbed Jane's shoulders and spun her around and hustled her out of the church. All the way back to the Jeep she kept trying to kiss his neck and bite his ears, and he kept having to scold her and push her off. But by the time he was driving the car back up the soggy track that led to the main road, she had recovered enough self-control to sit still and content herself with massaging his crotch through his pants. It was certainly distracting, but not as much as a blow job or something, which would probably have ended up with them hugging a tree.

He would definitely have to ask her what she found at the old church that had gotten her so worked up. It didn't seem like good sticky fun, this time. Still, he drove Jane home instead of to the grocery store as they had planned. She was in no condition to shop; and besides, why waste such an agreeable state of mind?

2

SATURDAY MORNING, QUENTIN FARMER RETURNED to Selden Falls. He once again stayed in what he'd been told was the best hotel in the area, a three-story Holiday Inn not far from downtown; and even though the place hadn't been remodeled in twenty years, and the rooms smelled like cobwebs, and the staff seemed to consist of three or four people who put on different uniforms to perform different functions, it really *was* the best, for God's sake. He'd have to build his own hotel, if only to have an acceptable place to stay when he came to visit.

From his room on the top floor, Quentin really couldn't see much of anything. Just the parking lot and the hotel pool, covered by a green tarp that still had filthy snow in it, and beyond that a wall of trees between them and a marginally well-kept subdivision. The room had a balcony but there wasn't any point in sitting on it, not with the air so icy and the sky crusted with clouds, and nothing to look at but asphalt and vinyl and the roofs of cars.

Because daylight interfered with the display on his laptop computer, which sat on the desk in front of the window, and because he didn't want to be observed, however remote that possibility was, Quentin had the mustard-brown drapes closed. He was checking out the local Internet provider's page, which contained many spelling and grammatical errors and a proliferation of unnecessary punctuation. Quentin was not impressed, but he followed the links to various local businesses and attractions. He wondered how many of them were profitable. Most weren't much better than the provider's page, and he soon got bored and started to wander.

The door opened and Nelson came in. He was in a room down the hall, but he had a key to Quentin's room; he always had a key to Quentin's room. The key situation was not reciprocal; this was because Nelson never sent Quentin on errands.

"Oh, it's just wonderful to be back in beautiful Selden Falls," Nelson said.

"Construction's going to start soon," Quentin said, not looking up. "I need to be here, and that means you need to be here." He signed off and shut down the computer. "So what's up?"

"I talked to Jones. Demolition of the old church is set to happen on Monday."

"Good. I knew they would be reasonable."

"Yes, sir. Desperate people can be very accommodating."

"That's why I like doing business with them." Quentin slipped the laptop into its leather carrying case. It was really the most marvelous thing, that case; it had pouches for disks and pockets for extra batteries, stiff slots for PC cards and padded bags for cables. Plus it was really, really expensive, and looked it. "What about that crackpot councilwoman? Will she be any trouble?"

"Simon says to let him worry about her."

"Oh, that makes me feel so much better." Quentin stood and carried the bag to the closet, where he left it on the floor as he took his coat off the hanger. "You see, Nelson, this is why I came back. Because *something* is going to go wrong."

"Like what?"

"I don't know," Quentin said. "I just have a feeling."

"Whenever I get feelings, I watch CNN until they go away," Nelson said. He eyed Quentin's activities. "Are we going somewhere?"

"Yes," Quentin said, slipping into the coat. "I want to find out more about this area. Let's go to the mall."

Nelson said: "The marketing people prepared a report on—"

"I read the report. Now I want to go to the mall and do some people-watching. That tells me things a report doesn't." Quentin picked up the laptop bag and slung it over his shoulder. The long strap was adjustable and had a soft pad to cushion it against his shoulder so it wouldn't chafe. "Are you coming?"

"Let me get my coat," Nelson said.

* * *

Nick Garson sat at his kitchen table and stared out the glass door at the woods a few dozen yards away. His wife also sat at the table, on the side to his right, watching him watch the woods and occasionally drumming her fingers on the table.

"I still can't believe it," Nick said. He lifted his glass, noticed it was empty except for foam and yellow droplets, and put it down again. "Fired."

"Sue him," she suggested.

"For what? What would I sue him for?"

"I don't know. Age discrimination."

"I'm only forty-two, Lois." He shook his head. His glass was leaving rings on the polished tabletop. "I mean, so there was an eyesore across the canal. I never noticed it. You can't see it from the Interstate, for God's sake, it might as well not be there. I never *stopped* in that town. I don't even remember its name."

"Selden Falls," Lois said.

Nick made a face.

"See, you do remember it."

"Of course I remember." He put his finger on the edge of the tall glass, tipped it back and forth, watching the droplets run down to the bottom. "He's the one who bought the land without sending someone to look at it."

"I guess maybe he figured you had already done that," Lois said. "Since you recommended the spot and all."

"I don't get paid to do that."

Lois stood up. "Well, now you're not getting paid to do anything. How long has it been? Three days? Are you going to start looking for a new job ever?"

"All he's got to do is knock the place down. Is that so hard? Do I have to get *fired* over that?"

"You know how he is," Lois said. "Or did you not really believe all the stuff you used to tell me about him?"

"I should go talk to the little freak," Nick said after a moment. "Make him listen to reason."

"If you do, don't call him a little freak. It'll prejudice him against you."

Nick judged that enough drops had accumulated in the bottom of the glass to merit trying to get another swallow out of it. He did so, but it was barely enough to get his lips wet. He shook his head. Ginger ale wasn't what he wanted now anyway. Why did they never have beer?

"So are you—"

"Let me make a phone call," Nick said, standing up. He went to the telephone and dialed one of his former colleagues, from whom he learned that Quentin had returned to Selden Falls earlier in the day for his usual pre-construction visit. In theory, this consisted of ingratiating himself with the locals, finding out more about the area, scoping out potential tenants, that sort of thing; but it was common knowledge that he actually went out to the sites and performed mysterious rituals involving sacrificial victims from the mail room, which was why they had such a high turnover down there.

"So he's gone," Lois said, when Nick told her of Quentin's trip. "You can't talk to him anyway."

"I can drive there," he said. "It's only six hours or so."

"You have to go to the unemployment office," Lois said. "You can't keep mooning over this job."

Nick shook his head. "Farmer's an idiot," he said. "I'm the best food court man he's ever had."

"I guess he's willing to chance finding another one."

"I'll talk to him. I'll go to Selden Falls and get my job back." Nick pushed the glass away, but miscalculated and knocked it over. It rolled in an arc across the table and fell off, hit the floor base-first, bounced, fell over, and came to rest against Nick's foot. He reached down and picked it up and put it back on the table. Lois, looking out the back window, didn't seem to have noticed. But it was a sign, Nick decided, just a small one, that if he did go to Selden Falls and find Quentin Farmer, he could get his old job back.

"There's a deer in the backyard," Lois said.

Two signs, Nick thought. That clinched it.

For the last few days, Simon Jones had been rather less happy than before reading the message from Quentin Farmer's assistant. It wasn't that he was afraid the project was going to get derailed, not over something as dumb as a church that looked like somebody's penis; but he was worried that Jane Trott might do something particularly nutty on Monday when the bulldozers showed up. He wouldn't put it past her to shackle herself inside the church and sing *Age of Aquarius* for the news crews, for instance. So he decided to drop in on her and see if he couldn't convince her that all this enthusiasm about the old dump was misplaced.

The first time he went by her house, she wasn't home. Suffering a premonition, Simon drove to Quentin Farmer's soon-to-be construction site and walked down to the bank of the canal. Sure enough, her mud-splattered Jeep was sitting in the lot across the water, half-visible behind the old building. He wondered what she was doing. Planting bombs and tripwires, maybe, or trying to commune with the long-departed worshipers who used to congregate there, assuming the place had actually been a church.

He often wondered how she had managed to get elected to the common council. Well, this was her first term and—he hoped—her last. Maybe she'd be obliging and shoot herself in the foot during the next campaign, talk about how she was on the common council in Pompeii just before the eruption and try to draw a parallel to the demolition of this old place.

The fact that a lot of people hoped for the same thing to happen to Simon made him feel a little bit uncomfortable, and he skulked around the site feeling slightly ashamed of himself until she came out of the church, being dragged along by her husband, Calvin. He didn't think he'd ever heard the man string three words together in a sentence, but maybe he didn't need to. Maybe he and Jane communicated telepathically.

At the moment, actually, it looked like they were communicating hormonally; she was all over him, like she wanted to pull him down and hump him right on the hillock. Jane Hot-To-Trott, Simon thought. Too bad he hadn't brought a camera; he could've leak photos to the press in the next common council election. Oh well. He watched them get into the Jeep; her husband practically had to beat her off with a stick. But she finally sat more or less still and they drove in a sharp little circle, out of the lot.

Simon returned to his own car, near the road. He hadn't dared pull too far into the site, because the ground was all chewed up and horribly muddy. He would be glad when all this grass and scrub and stuff was replaced with Farmer's plaza. The artist's renditions he had seen had been very impressive: an ivory-white promenade against the dark water of the canal, misty globes of light along the promenade, people laughing and walking and sitting at tables listening to musicians. Stores. Commerce. Boats piloted by wealthy tourists docked along the waterfront. They didn't get many pleasure craft on the canal, but maybe if there was something to attract them they would take the time to explore this little spur off the Erie, spend a day and a dollar in Selden Falls. Quentin Farmer said they would, and he should know, Simon thought; he had built a dozen places like this and had a pile of money to show for it, and you didn't get a pile of money if you didn't know what the hell you were doing. Plus the communities he had built in were generally happy with the results: increased trade, visitors from other towns and villages, tax revenues, jobs.

And, of course, reelection for government officials.

He drove slowly, giving the Trotts time to get home, if that was where they were going; and when he reached their house, the Jeep was indeed parked in the driveway, leaking clods of mud onto the pavement. He pulled to the side of the road and got out and walked to the front door for what he hoped would be a quiet, productive little talk with Jane Trott.

The councilwoman whom the mayor sought was currently being pleasured on the kitchen table by her husband. When the doorbell rang, neither of them was inclined to get up and answer it, either the first time or the second.

Bing-bong went the bell, for a third time. Calvin continued to ignore. The cat padded through on its way to its water bowl, paused to observe the spectacle with a critical yellow eye, and continued on its journey.

Bing-bong.

Silence, except for the sound of the cat's tongue lapping up the water, and Calvin's tongue lapping up something else. Jane fastened her fingers onto his head and squeezed.

Pound pound pound.

Calvin looked up and said, "Guess I should see who that is." Jane shook her head—she still wasn't very talkative—but Calvin went to the sink and washed his face and said, "Come on down. We can pick this up later."

Again, she shook her head.

God, but she was in a mood. "Just stay in here, then, and I'll get rid of whoever's there, okay?"

No response at all this time. He left her in the kitchen, went through the dining room to the front door. He looked through the peephole they had installed after Jane was elected to the council—just in case any would-be assassins came knocking—and through the fish-eye lens, he saw Simon Jones, his head all distorted so that it resembled a shoe.

Calvin opened the door. "Afternoon, Mayor," he said.

"Hello, Calvin," Simon said. "I need to talk to Jane."

"Can't right now," Calvin said.

"Why not?"

Calvin tipped his head toward the interior of the house. "In the bathroom," he said.

"I'll wait."

Calvin shook his head. "Be a while," he said softly, leaning toward the screen. "Female troubles."

Mayor Jones raised an eyebrow. "Female troubles," he repeated.

"Right."

"Why do I not believe that?" Simon said.

Calvin shrugged. "Because you're a politician and you don't believe anything unless you read it in a poll."

"All right, well, let me just remind you that your wife is also a politician," Simon said. Then he added, "I didn't see any female troubles when you two were at the church."

After a moment Calvin said: "Been following us?"

"You weren't home earlier. I guessed where you were." Pause. "So can I talk to Jane or not?"

"Call her office for an appointment," Calvin said, and he closed the door. As he walked back to the kitchen Simon started ringing the doorbell again, so Calvin turned it off with the switch next to the basement door. Jane was pretty much where he had left her. The cat was sitting on the counter grooming itself. He shooed it off and it ran into the other room, tail straight up in the air like a flagpole.

"Mayor wants to talk to you," Calvin said, as he resumed his interrupted duties.

* * *

Quentin and Nelson walked slowly through the mall, not actually going into any of the shops, just looking them over. Nelson wrote down the names of the places Quentin thought might be lured to the plaza, and he also wrote down the names of the ones that Quentin wouldn't let in no matter how much they begged. After they'd made a complete circuit of the mall, they sat at a more-or-less clean table in the food court. Quentin took out his laptop and slid it over to his assistant, who started typing the list into the database, which Quentin didn't know how to use.

As Nelson typed, Quentin took another look around the food court, wondering if familiarity would improve his opinion of the layout. He doubted it. The place had scads of aesthetic problems, starting with the fact that it was dim and drab as a tomb. Its totally inadequate illumination came from banks of fluorescent bulbs in the ceiling, and from the occasional semi-opaque skylight; the floor was made of muddy-brown hexagonal tiles, which didn't lighten things up any; the few fountains and planters they had passed were nothing special, just nondescript rocks with water flowing over them or wads of mossy, dark-green ferns surrounded by chocolate-colored bricks, respectively. Dark, dark, dark. Place looked like it had been built by mole-men. Hadn't they ever heard of *glass*? Or *marble*? Or even *pink granite*, for God's sake? Everything was earth-tone, like a burrow.

Quentin said, "All this place needs is a crypt and it'll be all set."

"What?" Nelson said. The overhead loudspeakers, living up to their name, were blaring tinny instrumentalized pop at a level that made normal conversation all but impossible.

"I said, all this place needs is a crypt and it'll be all set!"

Nelson laughed and said loudly, "Shop and visit grandma at the same time."

"Exactly." Quentin thought for a moment about the commercial prospects of the concept, then shook his head. "Nah," he said. "Too tacky."

Nelson shut down the laptop and snapped it closed and slid it back to Quentin, who tucked it into its little leather bag. He had it hanging over the back of his chair and was sitting back against the strap so he could feel if someone tried to steal it. Nelson announced that he was going to the bathroom, and wandered off in search of it.

A few minutes after Nelson left, Quentin noticed a disturbance in a store not far from the food court. It was a computer software outlet, from which a teenage boy was being ejected. Quentin watched as the cashier gave the kid a shove out into the mall, then turned around and went back inside. The boy, not evidently dissuaded, attempted to re-enter the store and was expelled again, but this time he got kind of tangled up in his baggy pants—the zipper of his jeans was at his knees—and fell down. His backwards baseball cap slipped off and was kicked away by a passing group of habited nuns who didn't pay the slightest attention to the brouhaha.

As the teenager got to his feet again, a cop—a real one, gun and everything, not one of those powerless rent-a-cops who used to haunt shopping malls—swept by Quentin, heading for the store. Quentin watched as the big grey-suited officer loudly harangued both the boy and the clerk, attracting the attention of passing shoppers and most of the people in the food court, even the nuns.

An elementary school kid hurried past Quentin's table, away from the software store. He was wearing the teenager's hat.

Nelson missed most of it; by the time he returned, the cop was talking to just the clerk, the boy having departed from the scene. Nelson came from behind Quentin and took his seat; he looked at the table, then at Quentin, then said: "Where's the laptop?"

"What?"

"I said—"

"I heard you." Quentin lifted up his expensive leather bag. The flap that came down over the top was unbuckled and the case was far lighter than it should have been, but he reached into the laptop's compartment anyway.

Gone.

"I keep telling you, sitting on the case that way isn't safe," Nelson said.

Quentin glared at him. "I'm sitting here and I'm thinking, *Do I need to hear Nelson say 'I told you so' right now?* And do you know what the answer is?"

"I wonder if that little show was staged to distract everyone while someone stole your computer."

That sounded like a plausible theory. "I was wondering that too," Quentin lied.

"It sure got my attention," Nelson said. "I could've seen your computer get stolen from my angle, if I wasn't watching that kid make a fool of himself."

The cop who had intervened in the matter under discussion was just passing their table on his way back to wherever he had come from; Quentin hailed him and he stopped. The officer was big and round, with a black mustache that looked like it was made of wax and a belly that looked like it frequently received samples of the goods available in the food court. Scanning the area as if on constant watch against those who would threaten the peaceful shopping experience, never meeting Quentin's gaze, the cop said: "Yeah?"

"My computer was just stolen."

The cop looked at him then. "Your computer?" he said.

"That's right. It's—"

"You brought a computer here and set it up and someone stole it?"

Quentin stared at the officer. He heard little choking sounds from across the table: Nelson trying not to laugh. After a moment he said, "It was a laptop computer." He lifted up the case, held open the empty compartment where his portable had been. "It was in here."

"Oh, sure," the cop said. "One of them little ones."

"Yeah, a little one."

"How much do them things cost?"

"It varies," Quentin said. "This one was about four thousand. Anyway—"

"Four thousand *dollars*?"

No, four thousand plump chickens, Quentin thought. God save him from morons. "Yes. Dollars. Anyway—"

"My boy's been asking for one. Wants to, what does he call it, surf? His ma says he just wants to look up dirty pictures."

"Well, kids do like computers. Which reminds me, mine was just stolen. Can I tell you about it?"

The big cop blinked at him, then said: "Go ahead."

So Quentin told him all about the computer: what it looked like, what brand, what year. The cop listened and nodded, not writing anything down; apparently he was storing all the information in his head. Scary thought. When he was done with the description, Quentin said: "I was thinking that disturbance you just took care of might've been staged to distract everybody while the kid's accomplice stole my computer."

"Oh, I doubt that," the cop said.

"You do?" Quentin said.

"Yeah."

"Why?"

"That was my boy Jasper. Jasper Junior," the cop said. "He's a good kid."

"Oh?"

"Yep."

"You don't think it's at all possible that your boy—the one who's been asking for a computer, and who just got kicked out of a software store—might've decided he could get one faster by stealing it?"

"Hey," the cop said, sounding annoyed. "Don't go around accusing people of things without any evidence. Jasper's a little bit rowdy sometimes, but he's not a thief."

Quentin drew a breath, held it, let it out. "Okay," he said. "Can I fill out some kind of a report, please?"

"Sure."

"Super. Where do we go for that?"

"Police station."

Pause. "I can't file a report here, with you?"

"Nope. Used up the last form when some kids cracked open *Space Invaders* or something down in the arcade last week. I haven't gotten any new ones yet. But if you got anybody you want arrested, you just let me know."

Quentin ran a hand through his hair. He wondered if it was greying as fast as he thought it might be. "Can we get directions to the police station?"

"Sure thing," the cop said. "Got a pen?"

Once Jane was finally satisfied, Calvin Trott had a moment to reflect on the day's events. He sat in a chair at the kitchen table, idly squeezing his dozing wife's foot and thinking about the crow that he had seen. He didn't know why he should be thinking about the crow, of all things, but he was. He didn't like the way it had looked at him.

He let Jane's foot drop and went to the refrigerator and got a beer. He cracked the can and took a long, deep drink, then put it on the counter. Jane was sleeping, it looked like. Sleeping right there on the kitchen table, head lolling to the side, idiot smile on her face. He wondered which of her personalities he had just finished humping. Didn't really matter, he decided. For this particular purpose, they were more or less interchangeable.

Damn, but that place was creepy. Calvin had always thought of himself as a practical man, but maybe some of Jane's nuttiness was starting to rub off on him. The water stains, the gigantic shadow, the feeling—he still couldn't shake it—that the crow had been talking to him, telling him something, warning him off. Even the way Jane had looked at him when she'd finally turned up, like he was a tasty morsel she'd found, had given her playfulness in the church a sinister edge.

Calvin took another slug from the can. Jane didn't like him to drink beer this early in the day, but he figured he had earned it.

Her eyelids fluttered open and she looked at him. She smiled and rolled onto her side; her big breasts fell out of her mostly-unbuttoned blouse. She said, "Well, well, well. Did the Hun enjoy his conquest?"

Jane had this thing where he had been one of Attila's warriors in a past life. How she knew all about *his* past lives, when it had taken months of regression therapy to learn about her own, was beyond him; but it was really just a game, more or less, one that usually came up after sex. Especially rough sex, such as they had just finished up.

"So what about the church?" he said.

She rolled onto her back, gazing serenely at the ceiling. Jane had no troubles at the moment. "What about it?" she asked.

"Knocking it down."

"Oh," Jane said. "We surely can't knock it down. There's unfinished business there." Calvin cocked an eyebrow. Because she was staring at the ceiling, she didn't see the gesture and he had to clear his throat to get her to look at him. When she did, she sighed and said, "Oh, Calvin, I'm getting a vibe from you."

"What kind?" he said, though he knew perfectly well.

"You know what kind."

He shrugged, just a little bit.

"It blocks me when you get like this," she said. She was back to looking at the ceiling. "All I get is this negative black stuff all over my psyche."

Calvin wondered if he should suggest Windex. Instead he had another slug from the can.

"We have to stop him," Jane said. "Simon, I mean. He can't do this."

Calvin was thinking that bulldozing that place would be the best thing for all concerned. Take out the crow, the water stains, the shadows. "If he does?"

"Trouble."

"What kind of trouble?"

"I don't know. But *something* will happen."

Something will happen. That was a pretty safe thing to say. "So what are you going to do?" he asked. He figured he knew, but he might as well hear her say it.

"Well," she said, "he can't very well knock down the church if there's someone in it, can he, Calvin?"

Calvin hesitated, then said: "Don't."

"Don't? Don't what?"

"Don't go back there." Pause. "Leave it alone. Let them knock it down."

She smiled. "Did you get a vibe while you were there, Calvin?"

He said nothing.

"I know it's dirty, creepy, and run-down," she said, "but it's safe enough. It knows I'm on its side. I could feel it. You're not sensitive, you just make your judgments based on what you see with your eyes. I saw it on a deeper level."

Calvin shrugged. Who was he to argue with the psychic?

Jasper Shoemaker Junior, having been bounced from the mall by his old man, took a circuitous route through the parking lot to arrive at his friend Oscar's van. Oscar was twenty-five, and worked at the hardware store down the street from Jasper's house, and didn't have many friends his own age. Actually, as far as Jasper knew, he had no other friends at all.

Jasper went up to the sliding door on the side and rapped on it twice. Oscar's face appeared in the window, and a moment later the door slid back to admit Jasper to the cavernous interior. As he entered the vehicle—it wasn't one of those mini-vans, it was a full-blown, road-clogging, child-stealing-sized van—Oscar settled back onto one of the middle seats. He had Quentin Farmer's laptop balanced precariously on his knees.

"So how's it look?" Jasper asked. "New?" He slammed the door shut and the van rang with the crash.

"Pretty new," Oscar said. "Not banged up. Think it's top-of-the-line?"

Jasper snorted. "They're outdated as soon as you buy them," he said. "But that doesn't mean they aren't expensive. Turn it on, let's see what it's got." He stood behind Oscar to watch the machine go through its boot-up procedure.

"What do you think it's worth?" Oscar asked.

"Couple of grand, at least."

"More than I make in a month," Oscar said.

"That's because you aren't *educated*, Oscar. Nobody's going to pay you good money just because they like you." Jasper drummed his fingers on the back of the seat. "I wonder what kind of screen it has. That makes a difference."

"How can you tell?"

"Not sure," Jasper said. "Did you grab the manuals?"

"No, man, he was sitting right on the strap. I was lucky I could get the computer out without him noticing. I couldn't go digging in the bag like I was looking for boogers."

The computer finished booting up and dropped them into some sort of security program. The background picture looked like a corporate logo, but it wasn't one Jasper had ever seen before; a big Q with a picture of the globe inside the letter. The watchdog program was asking for a user name and password; the default sign-on was *Nelson*. Must be the name of the former owner, Jasper thought.

Oscar looked at the screen for a minute, then said: "What do I put in for a password?"

"How should I know?" Jasper said, irritated that the guy had had the nerve to put security on his computer. Like he thought the mall was crawling with thieves or something. "Try just typing *Nelson*."

Oscar tried it. He didn't get in. "Doesn't work," he said.

"Yeah, I figured that was too simple," Jasper said.

A pickup truck went by in front of them. It had yellow lights—currently flashing—mounted on the roof of its cab. Mall security. They didn't worry Jasper much, except that they could block in the van and keep them there until the real police arrived.

After the truck had gone by, Jasper went up in front and peered out the window. The security vehicle was tooling along, not very fast, watching out for trouble. He looked over his shoulder at Oscar. "Let's get out of here," he said. "We can play with the computer at your apartment."

"You drive," Oscar said. He was busily punching the computer's tiny keys with his big fingers. "I want to keep trying."

"I'm not driving this thing," Jasper said. "It's like driving a fucking shed."

"It is not," Oscar said.

"Just shut it off and get up here."

Grumbling, Oscar turned off the laptop and snapped it closed. Jasper moved to the passenger seat. Oscar handed him the computer, then settled down behind the wheel and started the van. With a great fanfare of grinding gears and creaking metal, they trundled out of the parking space. There was a metallic *crunch* as the van clipped the bumper of a sedan parked next to it, but Oscar just kept going.

On their way to the exit they passed the wide glass doors that opened onto the food court; the little guy whose laptop they had stolen was standing at the curb, hands in the pockets of his expensive coat, looking up at the sky, ignoring the coming and going of other mall patrons. The wind blew his wispy blonde hair around his head. Jasper watched the guy for as long as he could, which was until a Jaguar pulled up in front of him and he got in.

Chauffeur-driven Jaguar, huh? He was richer than he looked.

They drove up the access road and he lost sight of the guy, so he turned around in his seat and patted the laptop's hard black shell. They had taught its owner a lesson today, he thought; taught him that he couldn't make loads of money off other people's work and not expect to pay some kind of penalty, to give something back. When you looked at it that way, stealing the computer was, like, a public service or something.

Gave Jasper a warm feeling inside, to be morally instructive like that.

Maybe next time they should take a shot at the Jaguar. That would be even more instructive, wouldn't it?

Quentin Farmer stared out the window as they drove to the police station, wondering who had stolen his laptop. He still liked Nelson's theory that the kid had staged the ruckus as a diversion, whatever big old Officer Shoemaker said. In his experience people were typically blind to the shortcomings of people close to them, which was why he avoided making friends; he needed to know exactly where everyone else stood on the moral spectrum.

It was his own fault he'd lost his computer, though. Nelson was right: he shouldn't have left it dangling over the back of his seat. There were crooks everywhere, even in a podunk town like Selden Falls. Especially here. What was there to do for a living, besides work at Wal-Mart or McDonald's or a dairy farm? Steal and fence, that's what.

The thing that worried him the most wasn't the loss of the computer, or even the loss of the data; there wasn't that much stuff on the hard drive that wasn't backed up. What was of greatest concern was the pictures.

He'd *meant* to delete those files, he really had, but then Nelson had interrupted him and he'd had to shut down quickly, and then he'd decided to go to the mall, figuring he could take care of them later. And now somebody might see them and—not knowing what a stand-up guy he was—they might draw all the wrong conclusions about him.

He found that he was clenching his fists, and relaxed them.

Nelson glanced at him and said, "Don't be too upset, sir. You can buy a better one for less money, and we have backups of most of the data."

"I know," Quentin said.

The police station was a squat brown building nestled in a stand of pines on the outskirts of town. Nelson parked the Jaguar in an isolated spot near the edge of the lot, away from other vehicles and the trees, right next to a pile of dirty snow that glistened in the sun. Quentin got out, and Nelson got out, and they both went into the building.

Five minutes later, they came out again. Nelson was carrying a box full of complaint forms and directions back to the mall; Quentin was fuming. "Officer on the scene needs to investigate," he muttered. "The only thing he's interested in investigating is the bakery."

They got back in the car. As Nelson started the engine, Quentin took the box away from him, removed one of the forms, and started filling it out. By the time they got back to the mall Quentin had finished the form and was finishing up a conversation with the answering machine at the mayor's home. "I'm not pleased about this," he said, though that had been adequately demonstrated both by the tirade preceding the statement and by the fact that he had left a message himself instead of having Nelson do it. "Call my assistant when you get in. I believe you know the number." He clicked off his cellular phone and stuck it back in the glove compartment. "I swear, Nelson, these people are *trying* to piss me off."

"I'm sure Simon will be happy to help," Nelson said. "Maybe he'll even fire somebody for you."

Quentin looked at him. "Is that a reference to Garson?"

"No, sir," Nelson said. "I wasn't even thinking of him."

"Good." He folded the complaint into thirds and slipped it into the inside pocket of his coat. "Come on, let's go find that cop."

Simon Jones wasn't at home to take Quentin Farmer's call because he was playing racquetball with Kevin Kowalski. They discussed the possibility of Jane Trott's doing something nutty at the old church, something involving handcuffs or chains or some other device; Kevin concurred with Simon's fears and suggested moving up the date of demolition. As if to illustrate the validity of his idea, Kevin proceeded to trounce Simon even more badly than he usually did.

The gym was just a few blocks from city hall, so on his way back Simon stopped at his office and called Henry Fontana, owner of Sunset Construction and one of his early political allies. "Henry," he said, in his best Happy Mayor voice, "what's happening?"

Pause.

"That's great, Henry, great. Love a good birthday party. What? Balloon animals? No, I don't know how they do it, they must teach it in clown school. You're the one who's in construction, you can't figure it out? Listen, Henry, what I'm calling about is that old church off River Street. Any chance your people could start on it tomorrow instead of Monday?"

Pause.

"I know it's a weekend, I know it's short notice, but this developer is leaning on me ... I can't afford to blow this project, you know how much we need the jobs. Ever since Bowes moved their factory to South Carolina things have been ... What? ... Well, uh, I can certainly recommend that, but in the end Mr. Farmer will pick whatever construction company he wants and the signals I've gotten are that he'll use his own people. He's got the leverage, you understand. What? Sure, I'll hang on."

Simon held the phone away from his ear as a highly off-key chorus of *Happy Birthday To You* was sung at the Fontana residence. Then he brought it back as he heard someone pick up the receiver on the other end. "Hello? Henry?"

Pause.

"Who's this? Is this Freddie?"

Simon listened for a moment, then said, "Well, happy birthday. How old—six, huh? It's all downhill from there." Pause. "Sure, I would've sent you a present if your daddy had told me about the party. What? ... Where would you keep a pony, kid? In the garage?" Pause. "Hello? Henry? Thank God. I almost got committed to a pony for your son. I have enough trouble meeting the demands of my constituents without buying them farm animals too. So, are we on for Sunday? I can cut you a check right now."

Pause.

"Great. That's terrific, I mean it ... How much? Jesus God, Henry ... Yes, I'll pay it. I'm writing the check now." He wasn't. "Nine o'clock? In the morning, you mean? Yes. Okay, I'll bring it over and give it to you there ... Of course I will! The city always pays its bills." Pause. "Well, I wasn't mayor then. Okay? Right. Right. Okay. See you tomorrow."

He hung up.

"This project had better be worth it," Simon said to the air.

When Nick Garson, driving along on the interstate, passed the site he had recommended to Quentin Farmer, he craned his neck to see if he could spot the old church that had gotten him fired. And yes, he could see a dark shape through the trees on the side of the canal opposite the development, but only because he was looking very carefully and there weren't any leaves in the way; and even so, he couldn't tell what it was. Could be a country club as easily as an abandoned building.

The exit for Selden Falls was a few miles past that spot, and when he got off the interstate the first thing he did was stop at a gas station and ask the flannel-clad guy behind the counter what the best hotel in town was. The clerk exchanged glances with the girl he'd been chatting up—high school girl, by the looks of her, although the clerk was definitely never going to see the inside of a classroom again except possibly with binoculars—and then said, "I don't know. Motel 6 maybe."

"No, Red Roof" the girl said.

"Red Roof's closed," the clerk said.

"It is?" The girl sounded surprised.

"Yeah," the clerk said. "Roof caved in after that last big snowstorm, remember?"

"Oh, yeah," the girl said, with obvious sudden recollection. "Guess it's the No Roof Inn now, huh?"

The two of them giggled. Nick wondered if they were high or something. "Can I borrow a phone book?" he asked. The clerk reached under the desk and handed him a directory, which he took to the counter in front of the hot dog machine. He opened it up on the blue Formica and flipped to the yellow pages.

"Don't get that all greasy," the clerk called. Nick nodded, though he couldn't imagine who would give a damn if the phone book at a gas station was greasy. He flipped through the listings, reading the headings: *hospitals, hot house builders, hot tubs, hotels and motels*. There it was. He stared, aghast, at the multiple columns of listings. Who would have thought a little town like this would have so many places to stay?

The clerk said something and the girl giggled. Nick didn't look up; he was trying to imagine where, if he were a repressed neurotic dictatorial little freak, he would elect to stay.

He did look up a little bit later, as he brought the phone book back to the desk with another question; but the clerk and the girl had both disappeared. The little three-pack boxes of condoms (*Ultra-thin! Ultra-sensitive!*) swayed slightly on the rack, and a door behind the counter which had previously been open was now shut. Nick stood there a moment, then walked out of the convenience store with the book and got into his car and drove away. Through a lengthy period of trial-and-error, he found his way to the future site of Canal Plaza and parked at the side of the road above it. The access ramp was in place, a wide muddy slope down to the grassy depression that would soon be transformed into a shopping bonanza. He had already started working on the layout of the top level, for God's sake; Quentin couldn't fire him now.

He could see the church much better from here. And—oh, Lord, it looked like somebody's dick. No wonder Quentin had flipped out. Everyone knew what a prude he was; no Playmate or *Sports Illustrated* calendars were allowed in cubicles or offices, no racy screen savers were permitted on corporate systems. The corporate handbook proclaimed that this was to maintain a "professional, non-offensive workplace," but everyone knew the real reason was that Quentin had no functional sex organs. Quentin's assistant Nelson had probably had to tell him the church resembled a penis; it was common knowledge that when Quentin urinated he did not look down. In fact, he didn't even hold it himself; Nelson did it for him.

Nick dug in his glove compartment for a pen, found one, and went through the list of hotels and motels in the phone book. He crossed off the ones that weren't chains, because Quentin probably wouldn't trust them to give him a proper level of service unless somebody had recommended it to him, and Nick doubted that anyone Quentin knew had ever spent much time in Selden Falls. This eliminated the majority of the accommodations. Then he crossed off the Red Roof Inn, which was closed, leaving a Howard Johnson's, a Holiday Inn, a Motel 6, and a few others. As an afterthought, he flipped to the bed and breakfast section of the yellow pages; there was only one of those. Apparently the Selden Falls area was not big with the country inn set. He decided he would try the hotels first; he didn't figure Quentin for the bed and breakfast type.

His targets selected, Nick closed the phone book, leaving the pen in it so he could find his place again. He put the book on the passenger seat and sat there for a minute looking at the old building; then he got out of the car. He stuffed his hands into the pockets of his jacket—it felt like it was about thirty degrees colder here than it was back in Buffalo—and walked down the uneven earthen ramp to the site.

Earth-moving was ready to begin any time. Massive heaps of dirt and gravel dotted the field, baby mountains growing from the high grass; parked among them was the machinery. A bulldozer, a roller, a backhoe that had sunk into the muddy ground. Somehow the equipment had been parked in a proprietary way, as if declaring that they owned the clay, the stones, the sand. It kind of creeped him out, the way they were lurking. Monsters waiting for their chance at mayhem.

He walked down to the water and stood directly opposite the old building. The sun was above and behind it, glaring over the place. Nick shaded his eyes with his hand and looked at the place.

Over this he had gotten fired. Over *this*. What the hell kind of executive could be so petty, for Christ's sake?

An oily-looking chunk of cloud stumbled in front of the sun, throwing a shadow across the earth; and that was when Nick noticed the crows. An entire flock of them, sitting in the tree that grew out of the roof of the old church, darkening its limbs and branches like malignant black buds.

After a moment, he realized they were looking at him.

He shook his head, told himself to stop being a goof. They were *birds*, for God's sake. Birds. Dumb, harmless, useless birds.

That were staring at him.

"Stop looking at me," he told them.

Silence.

No, they weren't going to stop looking at him; so *he* stopped looking at *them*, turning his gaze to the water. He watched clouds whip across its surface, reflections of the unstable sky. The bullying wind shoved the big cloud away from the sun and a tide of light swept over him. He looked up then, back at the old church; the crows had gone, leaving the barren, vacant limbs to click and crack against each other.

He stayed there a few minutes, watching, wondering where all those birds had gone. They hadn't flown away; he would have heard the wings. It was as if they had sprouted with the shadow and evaporated with the sun.

Weird.

When he went back to his car and started it, he was surprised to see he had been standing down there for nearly an hour. It certainly hadn't felt that long. He took another look at the site and the equipment and rubbed the back of his head, which was starting to throb. Stress-induced migraine coming on, he thought. Just what he needed. But after he drove away, doing a U-turn and heading back down the hill, under the Thruway bridge—there was a sign there that said it was under construction, though he saw no evidence of such activity—the headache receded like threatening clouds retreating in a sudden wind shift. Thank God. Another migraine was the last thing he needed.

After the bridge, he came to a fairly major intersection; he could tell because it had two gas stations. He stopped at one and took his stolen directory to the pay phone and called the hotels he had circled. He got lucky: Quentin was in the Holiday Inn. The girl he talked to wouldn't give him Quentin's room number, so he had her transfer his call to it; but the phone just rang and rang and rang and he gave up. Quentin must have gone out.

Nick called the hotel back and got directions to it.

After all, he would need to spend the night somewhere.

Oscar Kincaid lived in a cramped, dingy rat-hole of a place in the same building as the hardware store where he worked. There were eight tiny apartments on the top two stories, each with its own unique character; Oscar's place, for instance, was directly above the dryer outlets of a Laundromat that shared the ground floor, so his screens were usually coated with lint, and if he had the windows open for any length of time his kitchen and living room began to smell like fabric softener. No matter how long it had been since his clothes had been washed, Oscar typically smelled April-fresh.

In exchange for a reduction in his staggeringly high rent, Oscar did building maintenance; and when he and Jasper arrived there were several notes taped to his door. Jasper read the increasingly urgent notes over Oscar's shoulder; all of them were from Apartment G, upstairs, whose toilet wouldn't stop running. The guy made it sound like the world was ending, Jasper thought; somebody call the President, the can is overflowing!

Oscar ripped down all the notes, crumpling them into one big wad of tape and paper. Grumbling, he opened his door, collected a toolbox that looked like it had once fallen all the way down a mountain, and said he would be back in a minute, leaving Jasper Junior alone with their prize. He took it to the couch and sat down with it, but after a few minutes of guessing passwords he was shivering inside his jacket and his fingers were getting numb. The only heater in the apartment was in the hallway off to the right, which led to the bedroom and bathroom; it was not unlike the central corridor of a submarine, only much, much shorter and somewhat narrower. There wasn't much in the way of airflow through it, so the warmth just sort of accumulated there unless you did something to distribute it. Oscar kept a fan in the door of his bedroom, blowing the heated air that way; Jasper turned it around to face the living room. Then, because it would take a while to work—the apartment was tiny, but so was the heater—he took the laptop through the swinging door to the kitchen.

He stopped short on the discolored linoleum and sniffed the air. Fabric softener. The window was open a crack, that was why. He tried to shut it, but it wouldn't budge. Even though the kitchen was, other than the hallway, the warmest room in Oscar's apartment—no part of it was more than three feet away from the gas oven—Jasper returned to the living room and sat down on the couch. Five minutes next to an open window in Oscar's place always gave him a splitting headache; he'd deal with the meat-locker temperature until the fan took the edge off it.

He put his feet up on the chipboard coffee table, rested the computer on his lap, opened it, and resumed guessing passwords. None of them worked, so he put the thing down; then he thought of another one, but it didn't work either. Frustrated, he powered the thing off.

Ho-hum. This was rapidly becoming boring.

Despite his limited income, Oscar had a new television set. He had lost the remote already, but there were several old pool cues in a rack on the wall that served admirably as replacements. Jasper took one down and prodded the power switch with it; the television crackled to life. A talk show. Guys whose girlfriends are hookers, Jasper thought. He hopped through the channels. Nothing much on. He ended up back at the talk show and watched it for a little while. The girls had nice boobs, he thought, even if most of them were chunky and kind of sleazy-looking.

He finally got bored with this offering and turned the television off, leaving the pool cue on the back of the sofa. The smell of the laundry was fainter in the living room, but it was present and starting to make him feel light-headed. He went out of the apartment and upstairs, stopping in front of the door labeled *G*. He heard the sounds of water trickling and Oscar cursing. The carpet seemed kind of wet.

Okay, this was going to take a while, he thought.

He went back down to Oscar's place and left him a note that he was going home and that Oscar shouldn't destroy the computer before they got a chance to crack the password. Then he took his jacket and headed outside. It was starting to get late; the sky was deepening toward purple, the air was sharpening its wintry bite. It was only a mile or so to his house, but by the time he got there Jasper was shivering again, and wishing he had worn his heavier coat. His dad's truck was in the driveway, in front of his mother's little car; he wondered when they were going to get a vehicle for him so he could stop relying on Oscar to take him places.

His father was sitting on the couch watching the news; he only grunted when Jasper said hello, but as he walked by on the way to his room, his father said: "Hold it."

Jasper stopped.

"Did you stage that thing at the mall today so your friends could steal a computer?"

"No," Jasper said.

"You sure?"

"Dad," he said, "I think I would know if I stole a computer."

"Okay," his father said, turning his gaze back to the television. "I believe you."

Jasper hesitated, then said, "Why? Did somebody accuse me of something?" He hoped his voice didn't sound unsteady.

Jasper Senior didn't look away from the screen. "Yep."

"Who?"

"Little guy. A businessman. Quentin Farmer's his name."

"Never heard of him."

"He's the one building a place by the canal. Rich jerk. Don't worry about him."

"I won't," Jasper Junior said, going into the hallway.

3

THE BIRTHDAY PARTY WAS FINALLY over. The little gremlins had all gone home. Henry Fontana sat on the floor in the kitchen and surveyed the wreckage of his dining room and wondered, not for the first time, why they always had to have these parties at their house instead of at some nice kid-friendly restaurant.

Paige bustled by with an armload of shredded wrapping paper; Freddie had ripped into his presents like some sort of six-year-old fiend, turning their dining room into a slaughterhouse for gifts.

Paige looked at him sitting there and said: "If you're not going to help, you can at least get out of the way."

"Sorry." Henry pulled his legs in beneath him. She trundled by and began stuffing the paper into an enormous shopping bag from the mall. He pinched her bottom as she bent over to do it and she swatted his hand. He waited five seconds, then pinched her again.

An explosion rumbled out of the living room, followed by Freddie's voice shouting, "Oh, drat!"

Paige looked at Henry over her shoulder. "Notice how he's played every game except the educational one," she said.

"He'll get to it," Henry said.

"He left it on the kitchen table."

"He's working up to it." Henry stood, stretched. "You ever seen that old place off River Street?"

Paige shrugged. "Sure. Looks like a barn."

"The mayor is itching to have me knock it down."

"So knock it down," she said.

"He wants me to do it tomorrow."

"So do it tomorrow."

"I quoted him three times the usual rate and he didn't even argue." She looked at him. "Are you complaining?"

"No," he said. "Just curious why the big rush. I mean, I know that Farmer guy wants it down, but what's one more day?"

"I don't suppose you bothered to ask him." She brushed by him and began collecting discarded gift boxes from the table.

"Well, no," Henry said. "It was the middle of Freddie's party, I didn't think of it."

"I wouldn't worry about it. It's an election year, that always makes politicians flake out." She found the game their son had disdained to take with him— it was buried under a heap of ribbons and torn paper—and handed it to Henry. The box had pictures of suit-wearing bears cavorting amid gigantic three-dimensional numbers and letters.

"I guess," Henry said. He put his index finger to his lips and tapped gently. After a moment he said, "Well, if I've got to knock it down tomorrow, I should go take a closer look at it, right? Find out exactly what I'll need."

Explosion from the living room. The birthday boy shouted, "Jesus Christ!"

"First," Paige said, "go explain to your son that even though his father lets him watch movies where people curse and swear and blow things up, it doesn't mean it's okay for *him* to curse and swear and blow things up. All right?"

"Paige," Henry said gently, "it's just a game."

Paige processed this statement and sent it back to him as a glare of sufficient intensity to physically push him into the living room, where six-year-old Frederick was using his brand-new video game device to charge around some dimly-lit dungeon, laying waste with heavy ordnance to anything that moved and quite a few things that were standing perfectly still and hoping to avoid attracting attention. Henry watched this go on for a while; the romp ended when dark, scaly arms suddenly appeared from the sides of the screen and wrapped around the hero—if that was what you wanted to call a psychopath with a gun—and, with deft motions of taloned fingers, sent copious amounts of blood spurting across the shabby corridor. The screen turned a sickening shade of crimson.

"Fuck!" Frederick shouted. Then he clapped a small hand over his mouth and looked over his shoulder, apparently to determine if anyone had heard him. When he saw Henry his eyes became very wide and he opened his mouth as if to say something; but Henry cut him off.

"Did we buy that game for you?" he asked.

Frederick shook his head slowly.

"Where'd you get it?"

"Came with it," Freddie whispered.

"Can I take a look at it?"

"Okay." Never removing his gaze from his father, Frederick slowly turned off the system and ejected the game. He delicately returned the disc to its jewel box and handed the whole thing up to Henry.

"Thanks," Henry said. He gave Frederick the bear-decorated box that had been left on the dining room table and said, "Carry on." Then he went back into the kitchen.

Paige had gotten the table cleared of debris and was wiping it down with a sponge. He showed her the game he had appropriated. The instruction manual, which faced out through the front of the jewel box, featured a large burning pentacle and a demonic face glowering from the darkness beyond. She made a face and speculated on better uses for technology.

"Yeah," Henry said. "Neat pictures, though." He took his coat off the rack next to the door to the garage and put it on. He slipped the game into one of his pockets.

"Got a flashlight?" Paige asked.

"Uh-huh."

"Well, have fun."

"Will do."

As he opened the door, electronic-sounding music began playing from the living room. It was shortly joined by electronic-sounding footsteps. Henry peeked into the living room and saw that Frederick was playing the bear game, guiding a small, fuzzy teddy wearing a blue suit and a hat through a landscape of gigantic numbers, letters, and geometric shapes. Like a weird but innocuous drug-induced hallucination, Henry thought, watching as circles and triangles fell out of the sky.

He waved goodbye to Paige; she waved back.

As he shut the door there was a squishing sound from the living room, and Frederick yelled: "Oh, hell!"

Nick Garson sat in one of the small straight-backed chairs in the lobby of the Holiday Inn and continued to pretend to be reading a small leaflet detailing the attractions of the Selden Falls area. He had actually read through it once; it helped explain why the town was so pathetically eager for Quentin's investment. But the leaflet was only five pages long, including pictures, and he had been pretending to read it for the last hour and fifteen minutes, so he was starting to draw questioning if not suspicious looks from the desk clerk.

Well, he was a guest, and he could sit in the lobby if he wanted to. So there.

The front door opened. Nick looked up. Just an older couple shuffling across to the elevators. He went back to the brochure.

Selden Falls was settled by John Selden in 1804, he read. *The falls for which it was named collapsed one hundred years later, forming the rapids that still flow through Selden's Falls Park.* Yeah, he pretty much had that memorized. If he were ever on a game show and Selden Falls was a category, he would surely clean up.

The door opened again and Quentin Farmer stalked into the lobby. Nick had never actually met the man, but he had seen him around, of course; and nobody else would have Nelson DeGrace hurrying along after him like a puppy.

Quentin was talking into a cellular phone; he sounded really pissed off. "I'm not happy, Simon," he was saying. "I'm not happy at all. Not even a little bit."

Nick stood. He wondered who Simon was; some other poor sap about to get canned, maybe. Quentin swept by without even looking at him, and Nelson blew right past too; but Nick said his name as he passed and he stopped, then turned around. "Yes?" he said.

"It's Nick Garson," Nick said. "Remember me?"

Nelson looked at him over the tiny round lenses of his sunglasses. "What are *you* doing here?"

"Simon," Quentin said. "It's not that I can't buy another laptop. I can buy ten laptops. That's not the point." Quentin lifted the phone from his ear and glared at it and put it back. "It's the data, Simon. The *data*."

"I came to ask for my job back," Nick said.

"I don't like getting blown off by cops," Quentin said. "They're public servants, aren't they? I'm the public, aren't I? Hello? Is this making sense to you?" Pause. "Sure, I'll hang on."

"Not a good time," Nelson said. "Believe me."

Quentin had by now reached the elevator, and had apparently realized that Nelson wasn't with him. He looked their way and said loudly, "Nelson, who are you talking to?"

"No one," Nelson said, moving hastily to stand in front of Nick. Since Nelson was half a foot taller and considerably broader, he hid Nick more or less completely. "What's Jones got to say?"

"The idiot mayor is calling the idiot police department to find out why they gave me the run-around," Quentin said. "I'm waiting for him to—hello? Yes?" Pause. Nick didn't move from behind Nelson, but he could feel a sudden stiffening in the air, radiating from Quentin Farmer.

"Can't *find* it?" Quentin said.

Nick thought he saw frost starting to form on the chrome runner of the front desk. The girl behind the counter suddenly discovered that she had something to do and vanished through the swinging door in the center of her little area.

Nelson muttered: "Oh, God."

"I complained to the cop at the mall," Quentin said, with elaborately precise enunciation. "He sent me to the police station. I complained to them. They gave me forms—like I'm their delivery service or something—and sent me back to the mall. I complained to the *same cop* and gave him a form. And now they can't find my complaint? They have no *record* of it? Is this the way you people do business? Is this the sort of protection my plaza is going to receive? Because if it is, I'm going to have to rethink a few things." Nick heard him snap the flip-phone shut, the cellular equivalent of slamming down the receiver.

"Talk to him tomorrow," Nelson said, out of the corner of his mouth. "Call me. Room 338."

The elevator door opened. Quentin snapped: "Nelson. Come *on*."

Nelson went. Nick turned around quickly, buried his face in the brochure, and didn't look up until he heard the elevator close, when he slowly checked to make sure they were gone.

Yeah, he thought. He would wait, and talk to Quentin tomorrow.

The phone rang while Jasper Shoemaker Senior was about to come, and he couldn't interrupt *that*; so it took him a while to pick it up. It didn't help his concentration any that, after the first ring, his wife started yelling from the bathroom for him to pick up the phone; after four rings she yelled again, only this time she called it the *goddamn* phone. By that time Jasper had gotten himself more or less cleaned off, hastily wiping up the mess and stuffing the tissues into the wastebasket; but when he picked up the receiver he realized he still had some goo on his hand and had smeared it on the plastic. So there he was with one hand on the phone, one hand holding up his pants, and no hands left to do up his belt or clean off the telephone. He glanced at the bedroom door, hoping he had locked it, then said: "Hello?"

A raspy voice said: "Is this Jasper Shoemaker?"

"Yeah," he said. "Who's this?"

"This is your *boss*, Shoemaker. Remember me?"

"Shock Treatm—uh, Mr. Shockton?"

The knob of the bedroom door turned partway and stopped. After a momentary silence it began to rattle.

"That's right, Shoemaker." Paul Shockton was operations director of the Selden Falls police department. His nickname was *Shock Treatment* because that was what his subordinates thought he needed. "I just took a call, at home, from Mayor Jones," Paul said. "You familiar with Mayor Jones?"

The knob stopped rattling. His wife commenced rapping on the door with her bony knuckles. It was very loud. "Noreen," Jasper Senior called, "I'm on the phone, for God's sake."

"I asked you a question, Shoemaker."

"Open the door, Jasper!" Noreen shouted. "I'm out here in a towel!"

He stood there, paralyzed by this two-fronted assault.

"Shoemaker!" Paul yelled.

"Jasper!" Noreen yelled.

"Of course I know who the mayor is," Shoemaker snapped into the phone, accidentally using the tone of voice he had intended for his wife. He realized his mistake immediately; maybe if he hung up right away, the words would be cut off before they reached Shockton.

"I'm so sorry," Paul said, with excessive and forced politeness. "Am I interrupting you?"

"Jasper, let me in!" Noreen shrilled.

"Of course not, Mr. Shockton," Jasper said. Then, out of the other side of his mouth, he said: "Shut your trap, Noreen!"

"Sounds like a wonderful home life you got there, Shoemaker," Paul Shockton said. "Sadly, things at the police department are not so idyllic at the moment. Mayor Jones is very unhappy about the treatment our organization afforded to Mr. Quentin Farmer. Apparently he had some difficulty getting cooperation from the department. Mr. Jones is very worried about the impression this may have left on Mr. Farmer regarding the law enforcement environment in our area."

"Jasper, let me in this instant!"

"Christ, Noreen, give me a minute! This is an important call!"

"Oh good," Paul said. "You *do* realize that. I was starting to wonder."

Noreen gave the door a good swift kick—at least, that was what it sounded like—and then Jasper Senior heard the bathroom door slam shut. He sighed. No peace for him for a few days.

"Shoemaker? You there?"

"Yeah," he said. Then: "Yes, sir."

"I have your undivided attention now?"

"Yes, sir."

"Good. I made a few calls, Shoemaker, to the staff that was on duty around the time Mr. Farmer came to file his complaint, and your name came up. Repeatedly. In fact, Mr. Farmer was so impressed with your performance that he personally mentioned it to the mayor." Pause. "Now, did Mr. Farmer submit a complaint form to you?"

He had. It was in the truck somewhere. Jasper Senior had intended to file it, but had forgotten. There was so much to do at the end of a shift, and he'd been dying for a Danish. "I think so," he said.

"You think so. Well, that's a good start. Where might it be?"

"I'll have to look for it."

"There's an idea. I'll meet you at the station in a half-hour and we can look together."

Jasper felt compelled to make some sort of argument in his defense. "Mr. Shockton, I don't know if you've met this Farmer guy, but his attitude—"

"I don't care, Shoemaker!" Paul Shockton never missed an opportunity to shout, and he took full advantage of this one. "I don't care if he pantsed you in the food court. I don't care if he ate your doughnuts without permission. I don't care if he dropped his shorts and told you to kiss his hairy ass. Am I making myself clear?"

"Yes, sir," Jasper said. Oh, the misery.

The doorknob started to rattle again, more gently than before.

"See you in thirty minutes." Shockton hung up.

The bedroom door opened and Noreen stood there in her towel, rollers sprouting from her head like some weird sticky fruit, a bent hairpin—she must've used it to open the lock on the bedroom door— in her hand. She straightened up, staring at him.

"My boss was on the phone," he said.

She said nothing.

He showed her the receiver. "He's gone now."

"And that's why you have your pants down?"

"I—"

"And your best buddy hanging out?"

Jasper Senior looked down at himself, but couldn't see his best buddy around the curve of his belly. "It's—"

"I better not see any of those sex line numbers on our phone bill again this month," she said.

Henry Fontana drove a tiny little compact car because, after piloting great lumbering hunks of metal during the day, he liked the change of pace. However, as he perched at the top of the precipitously-inclined dirt road that led to the old church, he began to wonder if maybe he shouldn't go get the bulldozer instead.

He unfolded himself from his vehicle and eyed the descent before him. Twenty degrees, maybe more, mud all the way. He could drive down it, sure, but he had no idea if he could get out again. Simon Jones had said the road was in pretty rough shape, but he hadn't mentioned having to drive down a semi-cliff to get to it.

He could see the twin ruts running off toward the forest, dark lines through the grass. It looked like maybe a half-mile to the trees, and then God knew how far to the actual building itself. He could walk it, he supposed, but he didn't really want to. It was a cold, dark, windy night, and this was undeveloped land. Could be wild dogs running around out there. Or ghosts. Seemed like the kind of evening they would like.

The bent, broken grasses and cattails rippled in the marsh to the right of the access road. Henry didn't feel any breeze at the top of the hill, but that didn't mean there couldn't be wind down there, right? Or maybe it just hadn't reached his position yet; the movement had started off near the forest and it was coming his way like an advancing shockwave or the rolling of the tide. He stood there with his hands in his pockets and watched the weeds come to life, rustling against each other with a faint whispery sound, the leading edge of the motion coming closer and closer, and—

A crow cawed, very loudly, right behind him. Henry jumped, slipped, fell in the mud, and proceeded to slide down the rut to the bottom of the embankment. He lay there on his back a moment, sky above him, the stars visible behind a faint frosty patina.

If Paige were here, she'd be at the top of the hill laughing her ass off. Stuff like this never happened to Paige.

He stood up. His coat hung heavily on his back, caked with thick brown muck. Dry clean only, he thought; marvelous. He looked up the slope toward his car, which was still running. He could see the crow that had startled him, perched on the open driver's side door like it owned the vehicle, looking up at the moon, cawing its pointy little head off.

The wind gusted, coaxing hollow sounds from the trees that surrounded him. The muddy track stretched out before him, running just to the right of the woods, vanishing into the forest wall hundreds of yards away. The grass in the marshy field to his right waved and rustled. He thought again about walking out to the old building; but his flashlight was still in the car. Besides, did he *really* want to venture up this unknown road, on foot, at night?

The crow shut up abruptly; but instead of silence, the night was full of the scratchy sound coming from the marsh grasses. They continued to thrash wildly, this way and that, as if under a powerful down-draft. Henry didn't feel a thing; the gust of wind had died away already, leaving the air still.

So what the hell was going on in the swamp?

Henry looked up at his car again. The crow was picking at the weather stripping on his door, tearing it off in little shreds. "Hey, cut that out!" he shouted. The crow looked down at him briefly, then went back to work. And his voice sounded so loud, so sharp, he very nearly clapped his hand over his mouth, just like Freddie had done, and for the same reason: he was afraid somebody had heard.

And then he noticed that there was something wrong with the stars.

It was a subtle thing; if he hadn't looked up at the car, he probably wouldn't have noticed it. But the pinpricks of light in the night sky were dull and flickery, as if there were some sort of dusky filter between him and them. He stared up, trying to figure out what it was, trying to trace its borders. Was it a cloud? Was it smog?

Neither, he thought. Too low to be a cloud; too much in the country to be smog. And besides, if his eyes were not deceiving him, it was *moving*. He had discerned a form to it, a shape: the shape of a vast dark translucent bird, hovering over the swamp, staying in place by the steady beating of its wings. Which was ridiculous, of course. A phantom bird the size of an airplane, flapping away to keep itself stationary? Absurd.

But the marsh grasses thrashed in time with the downward motion of the wings, didn't they? And didn't he feel something after all, some breath of motion in the air, some faint cobwebby stirrings against his face, his hair?

He looked up at the gigantic shadow hovering overhead. Bulbous eyes looked back, darker than the night above and around them. Black spheres, hollow and rotten.

Simon could keep this job, Henry thought.

He turned away—away from the swamp, away from the thing in the air above it—and started climbing the hill, his feet slipping on the damp grass between the two muddy ruts. The crow stopped pecking at the weather stripping and looked at him with its bleak, blank eyes, eyes like smaller versions of the massive orbs that stared down from above. It started to make a little noise in its throat, a soft, rhythmic cry, as if it were calling to something.

Calling to the shadow up in the air.

"Shut up," Henry hissed.

The thing ignored him, of course, kept right on warbling. Henry could *feel* the thing that hovered overhead, thought he could hear its wings flapping in sync with the sounds the crow was making. It stopped abruptly, though, and looked at him, and then fluttered into his car.

Great. Now he'd have bird shit all over his steering wheel.

At the top of the hill, he looked back over his shoulder at the sky. The thing was still there, still fluttering, still watching. Jesus. What was Simon getting them into?

He turned around, faced his purring car.

Froze.

Curving down from above was an arc of darkness, like a corrupt rainbow. It was behind his car, a curtain of smoke, catching the red of the taillights and glowing like lava.

A wing, he thought. A wing from the shadow. It was reaching down, touching his car. As he realized what it was, the engine revved high and the front tires spun in the slick, muddy ruts. Henry tried to bolt out of the way, but his feet slipped and he fell and began, again, to slide down the hill.

The car leaped forward.

The headlights tracked across his vision, leaving red streaks inside his eyes.

The impact knocked him down the hill, back beneath the shadow.

Jasper Shoemaker Senior, his best buddy safely ensconced in his pants, walked quickly out to his big truck. The temperature was dropping and his breath made little clouds as he exhaled, which the wind snatched and blew away. He climbed into the cab and started the engine, then switched on the overhead light to look for Quentin Farmer's complaint. He thought he had left it on the seat, but it wasn't there. He opened the glove compartment; he didn't see the complaint, but he had left his gun in there again. Shit. He removed the gun and slid it under the seat, then riffled through the papers which had been underneath it. No form.

Then he remembered the chewing gum.

Oh, no. Please, God, don't let him have done that.

He leaned over so he could see into the garbage sack that hung from the passenger-side window crank. There was a crumpled-up piece of paper on top of the pile inside it. He removed this paper and carefully unfolded it; he could see the green wad of spearmint hiding in its center, kind of like one of those lollipops with the gum inside, which was, in fact, where this particular piece had come from.

He got the paper more or less flat and smoothed it out on the seat of his truck. The gum was stuck right on top of Quentin Farmer's signature. Jasper Senior rubbed the bridge of his nose with his thumb and visualized himself assigned to guard the city dump throughout the steamy summer months. Feeling extremely sorry for himself, he put the truck into reverse and backed out of the driveway.

Twenty minutes later, he went into the police station through the back entrance. Shockton's car wasn't in the lot yet, thank God; he might have time to salvage the situation. To this end, Jasper obtained a blank complaint form and a clipboard and sat down in a remote corner of the locker room to copy Quentin's complaint. Fortunately he had printed everything, so there wasn't a lot of fancy style to copy; Jasper would have thought a rich businessman like Farmer would be the type to write with lots of flourishes and curlicues and stuff, but no, he'd used block lettering throughout. Easy to imitate.

Every once in a while, one of the guys on the night shift would wander by and look over his shoulder at what he was doing. He never looked up or spoke to them or told them what was going on, but invariably they would start giggling. Apparently word of Shockton's rampage through the department had gotten around.

One of the observers lingered longer than most, not giggling, just watching him copy the rather lengthy description of the stolen item. Why Farmer had gone into such excruciating detail, Jasper had no idea; just to make his life that much harder, he guessed. He was forced to improvise a bit in that section, because stray tendrils of gum had obliterated strategic words; he threw in a few computer terms he had heard somewhere. Then he imitated Quentin's signature as best he could, what with the big hunk of aromatic goo squashed across it.

Done. He slumped forward; the churning in his stomach ratcheted down a notch or two. He was finished, he had a complaint he could pass off as the original.

Then the guy who had been observing him knelt down and said, in Paul Shockton's voice, "That was very good. Can I have the complaint now?"

Oh, shit.

Jasper slowly handed Shockton the copy he had made. The chief was wearing a dress shirt and a tie and smelled like baked chicken. His face was red as rhubarb pie.

"And the original also, please."

Jasper gave him that, too. Shockton held it by the corner, as if he thought the gum would crawl up the paper and fasten itself onto his hand if he got too close to it. "I assume this is *your* gum," he said.

Jasper nodded, reluctantly.

"Is this what you do with all the complaints you receive?"

Jasper slowly shook his head.

"Just the ones from influential businessmen, huh?"

There seemed to be no safe way to answer that question, so Jasper Senior didn't.

"The mayor was very keen to know exactly who gave Mr. Farmer the run-around," Paul Shockton said. He gave the crumpled complaint a little shake. "I was *going* to tell him it was a departmental fuck-up. Sort of take the rap myself, you know? Protect the men."

"And women," said a voice from somewhere in the locker room.

Shockton's face turned a tiny shade redder. He said, loudly: "Is anyone eavesdropping on my conversation with Mr. Shoemaker?"

"No, sir," came a chorus of unseen voices.

"Sir?" Jasper said. His voice came out a squeak.

"What is it, Shoemaker?"

"What're you … uh, what are you going to do to me?"

Shockton grinned. His lips were paler than the rest of his face, and his teeth were white. "I need the weekend to think about it," Paul said. "For now, why don't you just go on home and imagine it?"

4

SIMON JONES ROLLED OUT OF bed at seven o'clock Sunday morning. By seven-fifteen he had showered, shaved, and eaten a slice of untoasted bread for breakfast. He chased that feast down with coffee left over from the previous night, reheated in the microwave. This initiated a scorching protest from his stomach, which a handful of antacid squelched. Once all that had been taken care of, he threw on jeans and a sweatshirt and gave the sleeping Roland a kiss goodbye, then swarmed down the front stairs, grabbed his briefcase off the floor, and hurried out into the chill of the morning.

Inside the briefcase was a city check for an ungodly amount of money and a contract that Henry Fontana was going to sign, although Henry didn't know it yet. It wasn't even seven-thirty as he pulled out of the driveway, meaning he would be at least an hour early for the appointed meeting with Henry; but he had this desperate fear that Jane Trott would already be at the church, chained to the rafters like some deranged Mary Poppins, ranting from her perch to the local news organizations about spiritual energy and psychic backlashes and claiming to have been Jesus Christ in a former life and Lord, was he appalled at their churlishness.

He shuddered and tried not to think about it and drove much too fast all the way to River Street. When he reached the dirt road that led to the old church, he pulled onto the shoulder and parked next to the steep entrance.

What was that?

Something gleamed from the cattails and rushes that grew in the marshy bog at the bottom of the embankment. He got out and went to the edge of the slope and peered down into the swamp, and realized that he was looking at the rear end of a little car sticking up from the muck and vegetation. And damned if it didn't have a yellow and red bumper sticker that said *Sunset Construction*.

The mayor went closer to the edge of the hill, and that was when he saw the body at the bottom of the incline. It was a man, lying on his stomach.

Oh, no.

Simon stumbled and skidded his way to the bottom of the hill and tried to get a look at the corpse's face without touching anything, but in the end he had to lift the head with the toe of his shoe.

Henry Fontana.

Simon took a step back and rubbed the back of his neck and looked up at the pale blue sky. Christ, this was going to slow down the demolition, wasn't it?

He heard a groan, and figured it was himself. He was a wreck. Quentin Farmer was running him so ragged he didn't even know what he was doing.

Then he heard another groan, and this time he realized that it came from Henry.

Simon knelt down and carefully felt Henry's wrist for a pulse; he couldn't feel one, but was probably doing it wrong, and anyway he could see the shallow rise and fall of Henry's back. He dropped the wrist and stumbled up the slope to his car and dug his cellular phone out of its bag.

The first call he made was to the hospital.

The second call was to the cops.

The third call was to Henry's house. The phone rang and rang and rang, and then a sleepy female voice came on the line and said, "Hello?"

"Paige? It's Simon. I—"

"Oh, hold on, Simon." He heard some noises, then her voice—distant and indistinct—calling, "Henry! Henry, where are you?"

She thought he had gotten up before her, Simon realized, so she must also think he had gotten home after she went to bed. Boy, was this news going to be a shocker.

At length she came back on and said, in a slightly more conscious voice, "Henry isn't here, Simon. Maybe he went to get ready to knock down that church of yours."

"Well, actually, that's where I'm at," Simon said. "Um … are you in bed?"

Pause. "What kind of a phone call is this, Simon?"

Oh, for the love of God, Simon thought.

"Because my understanding was you liked guys," she said.

"Paige, are you sitting down?" he said.

A second, longer pause. "Why?"

"Will you please just answer me?"

"Okay, yeah, I'm sitting down. What's the matter? What happened? Where's Henry?"

A siren in the distance. That was quick. Simon was very impressed by his own importance.

Paige said: "Simon?"

He said, "Sorry. Henry's here. He's unconscious. He … uh, he seems to have run over himself."

There was a moment's silence.

Then Paige Fontana started to giggle.

Nick Garson got up early, awakening from a nightmare involving men from the bank and the keys to his house, and found he couldn't get back to sleep. So he watched early morning television for a while, an infomercial for this plastic convection oven thing with snap-on height extenders. Every time the host took something out of the oven, the audience broke into applause, like cooking was this new process that they had never seen or heard of before. Maybe they'd been flown in from some distant tropical island especially for the show. Then he thought, no, they'd be on their hands and knees worshipping the thing; which was what he was supposed to be doing, watching them.

The telephone rang. He muted the infomercial and picked up the receiver. It was Lois. "You talk to him yet?" she asked, after the greetings were out of the way.

"Not yet," Nick said. "I saw him last night but he wasn't in the mood to talk."

"No?"

"He was in the mood to kick ass and take names."

"Well, did he say anything?"

"I told you, I didn't talk to him. Nelson warned me off."

"Who's Nelson?"

"His assistant."

"Oh," she said. "The one who holds his dick for him."

"Lois, please," Nick said. On television, the infomercial host removed a glistening chicken from the oven, which had by now been stacked high enough to engulf a watermelon edge-on. The audience must be swooning, Nick thought.

"You're going to talk to him today?"

"I'll try," he said. "I'm supposed to call Nelson and find out what kind of mood Farmer is in."

"Well, good luck. Either way you're coming back tomorrow, right?"

"Right. Hey, Lois?"

"What?"

He was looking at the screen. "Do we need an oven?"

Every Sunday, Jasper Shoemaker Junior's parents packed him into the car and schlepped him off to church to save his soul. He never followed along in the book; he didn't sing; he didn't say the stuff he was supposed to say; in fact, he didn't participate in any way whatsoever, other than warming the pew with his butt. But every week, they subjected him to an excruciating hour of boredom. How did his old man put it? A little morality wouldn't kill him.

Today his parents—who seemed not to be speaking to each other again—had a wedding to go to, which they spent the entire morning getting ready for, even though it didn't start until five or six in the afternoon. Jasper Junior said something to the effect of don't they have a mass at weddings, and his mother snapped that the people getting married were Episcopalians so even if they did it wouldn't count. Then she launched into a protracted complaint that apparently the happy couple didn't realize people had jobs to go to on Monday morning, and how inconsiderate they were, and why couldn't they get married on a Saturday or at least earlier in the day so people would have a chance to recuperate, blah blah blah. She was so shrill it was harder than usual to tune her out; when she finally wound down, Jasper decided to keep his mouth shut for a while.

So there they were at church, both his parents dressed up for this wedding that wasn't going to happen for like six hours. His father was on the left, big and round in an aging sport jacket, like a powder-blue marble; his mother was on the right in a bright floral dress, like a walking photograph of a flower garden. Jasper Junior was between them, in a faded rugby shirt and jeans with paint stains all over them. He hadn't been doing any painting; he was getting in on the ground floor of a new fashion trend. Despite the coolness of his own attire, though, he was sitting between Disco Fever Man and Earth Mother and he just wanted to die of shame.

The priest was an old dodderer who looked like he should be clutching a walker instead of a podium. He often got lost during his sermons and had to turn to the altar boys for assistance. Today's homily was especially meandering, because he had apparently gotten his notes mixed up with the ones for last week. His pontification about a strip joint up near the airport—he was opposed, of course; didn't want there to be anything fun in the area—segued into a previous lecture about some biblical whore and how her situation was applicable to modern life. Jasper Junior slouched on the bench and thought: Send that whore my way, father, and I won't need to go to the strip joint.

When it was finally over, he didn't go to the car with his parents; he told them he wanted to walk home. His father just grunted and his mother ignored him. So now they weren't talking to *him*, either. Just as well; they rarely had anything interesting to say.

He watched them walk back to the car, side by side but not touching, like they were miming an invisible wall between themselves. He shook his head and went the other way, down the sidewalk, still damp with runoff. Today's events had reinforced his decision that he was never going to get married; nope, he would just play around until he got too old to attract reasonably acceptable women, and then he would invest in a big pornography collection.

He crossed the street at the bottom of the hill. The rains of early spring had washed away the white salt stains, but the roads were still gritty with sand. Along the curbs the winter runoff formed a miniature beach, sodden leaves and broken twigs and dirt and other debris which had been buried for the last three months. Every year the melting snowbanks revealed their contents, like one of those candles with prizes embedded in the wax. Usually there was nothing good, although once he had found a scuffed purse that contained usable money and credit cards; Oscar had scanned them, but they had been canceled. Another time he'd come across a skin magazine still in its plastic wrapper. The purse and credit cards had gone into the river, but he still had the magazine; his pornography collection was underway.

It was a lot warmer than yesterday; he could walk with his jacket unzipped. The air was clear and the sun shone so brightly it forced him to squint. Jasper wished he could remember what he had done with his sunglasses. To his right, between the sidewalk and the road, the sad remnants of once-mighty piles of snow formed a filthy, decaying mountain range. He kept one eye on it, but there was nothing of interest being revealed by its recession. Just gum wrappers and pencils.

He went by the Laundromat that gave Oscar's apartment its scent. The door was propped open with a cinderblock, letting warm, lemony air billow out. Jasper Junior walked beneath the blast from the dryer vents, then had to pick lint out of his hair.

Unlike many of the small shops in the neighborhood, the hardware store was open; the owner had figured out some time ago that people worked during the week and liked to shop on Saturday and Sunday. Jasper peeked through the front window, surveying the situation. Oscar sat on a stool behind the counter, watching yokels pick through displays of hammers and nails and screws of various sizes. Jasper slunk in, sidled over to a rack of sunglasses, and plucked off a pair that had tiny round blue lenses, the kind he'd seen rock stars wear on television. He surreptitiously ripped off the tag, scraped the UV sticker off with his thumbnail, and put them on. Then he trotted to the counter and said, "Oscar, what up!"

Oscar glanced at him. "Hi," he said. "Where'd you get the glasses?"

"Wal-Mart."

"Wal-Mart? Why didn't you buy them here? We sell that kind." Oscar shook his head. He always took it as a sign of disloyalty to shop at chain stores.

"Wal-Mart had them cheaper." Jasper took off the glasses and slid them into his pocket, which was when he noticed that Jasper had the stolen laptop balanced on his knees behind the counter. "Jesus, Oscar," he whispered. "What are you doing with that thing down here?"

"Nothing," Oscar said after a moment.

"You want to get caught? Put it away before—"

Jasper Junior broke off as a guy in a Caterpillar hat came over with a bag of nails and a compressed-air gun for driving them. As Oscar rang them up he said, "Got a project, sport?"

"Paneling," the guy said.

"Yeah? You check our remodeling guide? Just tell us what you want and you'll have it in four weeks, tops." Oscar produced a massive tome from under the counter. While he was doing this, the computer started to slip off his lap and Jasper had to lunge and grab it. Oscar didn't seem to notice, but the customer gave him an odd look, as if to say: Why are you reaching into that guy's crotch?

"So what can I order for you?" Oscar said.

"Home Depot's got what I need in stock," the guy said. He wrote Oscar a check, gave Jasper another suspicious look, and left.

"See that? There's no loyalty." He shook his head. "Home Depot's got it in stock," he said in a falsetto. He closed the book with a resonant *whump*. "Never mind that he's got to drive forty-five minutes to get there."

"At least he bought the nails and stuff here," Jasper said.

"There's no margin on all that," Oscar said, whatever that meant. Ever since Hiram had added *Assistant Manager* to Oscar's name tag in lieu of a raise, he'd been talking such nonsense.

When the customer was safely out the door, Jasper said, "You have to be more careful with this. You almost dropped it. Nobody's going to pay us for a busted laptop."

"I *am* being careful," Oscar said.

Jasper shook his head. Oscar clearly could not be trusted with delicate equipment. "You know the guy we boosted this from? He's Quentin Farmer."

Oscar said: "Quentin who?"

"Farmer. The guy building the plaza on the canal?"

"Oh." Oscar obviously had never heard of him.

Jasper looked around. There was a woman looking at garden implements way at the back of the store, but no other customers he could see. "Open that thing up," he said. Oscar complied. The display was dark, but when Oscar tapped the space bar the security screen popped up. Jasper had him change *Nelson* to *Quentin*. The machine accepted the new name, but still wanted a password.

"Okay," Oscar said. "Now what?"

Jasper thought a minute. Maybe Quentin Farmer obsessed over his car. "Try *jaguar*," he said. It hadn't worked when the user name was Nelson, but that didn't mean it wouldn't work now.

Oscar tried it. It didn't work.

The lady started heading their way, carrying a spade, and Jasper made Oscar close the computer and slide it under the counter, just in case he started reaching for anything. She wanted to pay for the implement with a credit card. Oscar told her there was a minimum purchase amount for credit cards and she was under it. The lady argued, Oscar stayed firm, and she told him where he could stick the spade and said she would buy it at Sears.

"See what I mean?" Oscar said after she had left. He looked reproachfully at Jasper as he picked up the spade and stood it on end behind the counter. "They just march out to the chains."

"We need to find out more about this Farmer guy," Jasper said. "So we can guess his password."

"Why don't we just sell the stupid thing?"

"We can't sell it if we can't even *use* it," Jasper said.

"Why not?"

"Would you buy a computer from somebody who didn't know their own password?"

"Sure I would."

"Well, that's because you don't know anything," Jasper said. "I explained all this before. We want to be able to pretend it's *our* computer."

"Oh," Oscar said. Then, after a moment: "Why?"

"We'll get more money for it if they think it's ours," Jasper said. "Use your head."

"Is that how it works?"

"Of course that's how it works! Think about it for a minute. It's stolen, they know you're desperate to unload it, right?"

"Right," Oscar said. "I guess."

"You following me now?"

"Yeah." Oscar was silent a moment, then said: "But we don't have any manuals or anything. Won't whoever buys it want manuals?"

Jasper Junior hadn't thought of that. He considered the matter, then said: "Well, we'll say someone stole the case, and it had all the manuals in it."

"Why would somebody steal just the case and not the computer?"

"Because they didn't know the computer wasn't in it, that's why." Jesus, Oscar could be dense sometimes.

"Okay," Oscar said. "So how are you going to find out stuff about him?"

Jasper Junior scratched his head. "I don't know. You think they'd have something about him at the library?"

"Maybe," Oscar said.

"They got magazines at the library?"

Oscar thought a moment, then said: "Probably not. Don't they just have books there?"

Jasper shrugged. "I've never been to the library. Where is it?"

"Across the street," Oscar said.

Jasper bent over so he could look through the window. "That's the fire house," he said.

"No, man, the library's upstairs. See the door on the right?"

Oh, yeah, there it was: a narrow door with a tiny sign that may have said *LIBRARY*. Jasper said: "How are you supposed to see *that*? I would've gone there lots of times if I knew where it was."

"Uh-huh," Oscar said.

"I'll go over there now. You keep that thing hidden, okay?"

"Okay. Jasper?"

"What?"

"Library's closed on Sundays," Oscar said.

Simon Jones watched as the tow truck attempted to pull Henry Fontana's half-drowned car out of the marsh. What he had thought was an ambulance had turned out to be a police car, which was now parked by the side of the road, lights flashing like crazy, ensuring that every passing motorist craned his or her neck to see what was going on, creating a huge bottleneck on River Street. It didn't help any that the television van was parked at an angle on the shoulder, confirming for everyone that there was news in progress nearby.

Simon glanced at Henry. He hadn't been moved, but the cop had covered him with a thick, stiff-looking blanket. He seemed to be at least semi-conscious; every once in a while he would speak, but none of it had been coherent. Something about birds and shadows. At least, that's what it sounded like.

The tow truck's wheels spun wildly, shooting mud all over, like they were being shelled by muck artillery. The clods flew through the air, splattered wherever they hit. Simon edged a few paces away, just in case.

Henry said, "Whummibid?" The cop was off to one side writing in his notebook and didn't appear to be paying any attention to anything that came out of Henry's mouth.

Simon's phone trilled in his hand. He fumbled it open. "Hello?" he said.

"Mayor Jones?"

Christ, it was Quentin Farmer's assistant. What did they want now? "Yeah," he said. "Hello, Mr. Nelson."

Pause. "I keep telling you, Nelson is my first name."

Simon rubbed his forehead with the back of his hand. "I know. I'm sorry. It's been a long and stressful morning."

"We can see that," Nelson said. "We're watching it live on television. Mr. Farmer is very interested in what happened out there, Mr. Jones."

Of course he was, Simon thought. Mr. Farmer was very interested in everything. Mr. Farmer was a regular Curious Fucking George. "The police will investigate the accident," Simon said. "All I can tell you is—" He jumped and bit himself on the tongue as a large and earthy chunk of mud smacked into his right shin. "Thyit!" he exclaimed.

"Mr. Jones?"

His tongue was bleeding, he could taste it. "Yeth, I'm here," he said. Damn, that hurt! It was swelling too. "A big piethe of mud jutht hit me."

"Why are you talking like that?"

"I bit my tongue right where I make an *eth*," Simon snapped. "Look, I'll call you back, okay?" He hung up without waiting for Nelson to answer.

An ambulance arrived in a whirl of lights and squeaky sirens. The back door popped open and a gaggle of EMTs tumbled out and started preparing their equipment. The news camera swung around to point at them. Simon watched for a moment, then returned his gaze to the tow truck that had injured him. It looked like now the driver was pouring gravel or kitty litter or something under the tires, to give the big vehicle more purchase. The cop was still making notes. Christ, how much could there be to write down? Simon put his hands in his pockets and attempted to look in charge of the situation. He edged toward the police officer and surreptitiously eyed his notebook. It contained doodles of pistols and a grocery list.

Please, God, Simon thought, don't let the camera pick that up.

The tow truck driver got back into the cab, and the tires started spinning again. Gravel sprayed from beneath them like antiaircraft flak, pinged and bounced and ricocheted all over the place. Simon cursed and shielded his face and wondered if Henry had survived out here all night only to be killed by shrapnel from the stupid rescue operation. But the added traction did the trick; with a tremendous, soggy slurp, the little car finally popped free of the sucking mud that had held it down. The tow truck lurched ahead, jerked the subcompact forward and sideways. The driver's side door was open and it flopped around like a piece of dead skin. Simon and the cop retreated as filthy water poured out of it.

A black clod washed out and landed right at Simon's feet: a huge, dead, sodden crow. Its feathers protruded at crazy angles, its wings were bent and stiff, its black feet stuck up in the air. Smelled awful, like something that had been wrapped up in plastic and left in the refrigerator for too long. Simon looked up. Yes, the camera was right on him and the cop and the mossy dead bird. Simon just knew that his grimace was going to be gracing every television screen in Selden Falls on the evening news.

The cop said, "Poor man's chicken." Simon successfully fought the urge to smack him.

The EMTs came swarming down the hill, but one of them slipped and they lost control of the stretcher. Simon and the cop scrambled to get out of its way as it careered down the slope, bouncing along beside the tow truck, rushing toward them; but it clipped the rear bumper of Henry's car and flipped over before reaching their position. The dead bird got caught beneath it and was squashed, popping open like a weird black-plumed tomato.

The EMTs arrived momentarily to right their runaway stretcher.

Simon felt his stomach turn over as one of them scooped up the ruptured bird with his bare hands and tossed it into the grass at the edge of the marsh. Simon hoped to God the guy would put on gloves before he went to work on Henry.

As the tow truck surged up the hill, tires spinning like mad, mud shooting every which-way, the hospital crew loaded Henry onto the stretcher and belted him in. Simon followed them back up to the roadway. The onlookers had cleared a path for the tow truck, and now it was trundling off to the police station, yellow lights flashing. Henry's car left a trail of marsh sludge behind it. The paramedics loaded Henry into the ambulance and then it pulled away, siren wailing, and passed the tow truck farther up.

The cop came up the hill, carrying his notebook. The reporter from the television station went after him. Yeah, Simon thought as he got into his own vehicle; go ask the cop questions. He started the engine, then was distracted by a *tap tap* on the driver's side window. The reporter from Channel Six was leaning over and smiling perkily through the glass; behind her, the big cameraman had his lens pointed right at the car. They had given up on the cop pretty fast, hadn't they?

Simon rolled down the window. "Just a few quick questions, Mayor Jones," the reporter said. She was a new one, though she had the same airbrushed, capped-toothed look as the last four. She was blonde, of course, but Simon could see dark roots.

"I'm not really ready for a newth conferenthe—"

"Was Mr. Fontana here on your instructions? Was he doing work for the city?"

"Mithter Fontana wath going to do thome demolithon for me today," Simon said. "Excuthe me." He dug a tissue out of the glove compartment and, keeping his back to the camera, dabbed at his tongue. The tissue came away all bloody. For God's sake. He showed the tissue to the reporter and said, "Ath you can thee, I'm bleeding. Call my offithe for a thtatement later." He rolled up the window. The reporter tapped on it again. He glared at her, but she motioned for him to roll it down and he did so. The crank felt like it was stuck in cement. "Yeth?" he said.

"Is it true that Quentin Farmer is going to sue the town over a stolen computer?"

He stared at her, aghast. "Where'd you hear that?" he said.

"Thank you," she said, straightening up. The camera turned away.

"Hey!" he shouted. They were already heading over to the news van. He got out of his car, stood up. "Hey … no comment! No comment!"

"Thorry, thport," the cameraman said over his shoulder. "We're live."

Simon slumped against the front fender and thought: Shoot me now.

He crawled back into his car and watched in miserable resignation as the pretty reporter was chauffeured away in a car while the rest of the crew packed up the van and the spectators drifted back to their vehicles. The cars began to drive away; the news van was the last to leave.

Then a red Jeep screeched to the side of the road and stopped, Jane Trott behind the wheel.

Simon rubbed his forehead. God, he needed an aspirin.

She got out and stood there a moment, looking at the watery hole Henry's car had left behind; then she came over to the passenger side of his car. After a moment he reached across and unlocked the door and she got inside.

"Hello, Simon," she said.

"Jane," he said.

"Got yourself some trouble, huh?"

Simon shrugged. "I'll deal with it."

"The church isn't going to let you knock it down. Not without a fight."

Simon pressed his palms into his eye sockets. "Did you come here jutht to make crathy talk at me? Becauthe I'm not in the mood. I'm really not." She raised an eyebrow at him and he said: "I got thtartled and bit my tongue, okay?"

"Something's there, Simon." She looked past him, out his window, at the distant row of trees that screened the church from view. "I went and stood inside it. I felt it. It knows what you want to do. It's aware of what's going on around it."

"Then it thould know it'th thtanding in the way of progreth," he said. "But tho are you, and you don't care either."

"I'm not opposed to Mr. Farmer's project," she said. "I don't care much for the vibe I get off the man, but his plaza would be good for the area, I'm sure."

"Then why are you fighting me over that thtupid building?"

She shook her head. "You don't get it. You won't listen, will you?"

"I will if you thtart making thense."

She pressed her pale little lips together and tipped her head at the marsh. "This wasn't an accident, Simon. It was an attack. If you keep it up, it'll happen again. And again. And again."

"Ith that a threat?"

"No." She looked at him with an almost pitying expression. "No. I'm just telling you what I felt when I was inside the church, that's all." She opened the door and got out. "Be careful, Simon," she said before she shut it. "Be very careful."

He stayed in his car and watched her walk back to her Jeep. She settled in behind the wheel and looked at him for a while, but he didn't move until she had driven away.

After Channel Six had wrapped up its live coverage of the surgical removal of Henry Fontana's car from the swamp, Quentin turned to Nelson and said: "I don't think I've ever had a project go quite like this before."

"It *has* been an unusual couple of days," Nelson said.

"The mayor sounded like Daffy Duck."

"I think you mean Sylvester the Cat."

Quentin was silent, staring at the switched-off television. "Cute girl," he said after a moment.

"Who?"

"The reporter."

"Oh." Nelson shrugged. "They all look cute on television. I think they manufacture them in a factory in California."

Quentin said nothing. He thought about how the camera had zoomed in close on the reporter's face. It was a nice face, open and pleasant, eyes blue as the sky, framed by wisps of soft-looking blonde hair, red pouty lips. The sort of face you could open up to—or that could open up to you. Quentin rolled onto his back. The ceiling was a pale shade of off-white, and as if it were a movie screen, he began to see images on it. The reporter in a bustier and stockings and fuck-me pumps, kneeling on the floor at his feet and giving him an interview, using his cock as the microphone, with a subtitle that said *Patty Chalmers live at Quentin Farmer's hotel room.*

The telephone rang. Nelson picked it up and said: "Nelson DeGrace." Then, after a moment, he began to speak in a low voice. Personal call, Quentin thought. He sometimes forgot that Nelson had an existence beyond mere assistantship. He didn't pay any attention to the conversation; he rolled off the bed and wrote down the Channel Six call letters and the reporter's name on Holiday Inn stationery, so he wouldn't forget them. Then he got the phone book out of the dresser between the double beds.

Nelson had stuck a bookmark in the restaurant section of the yellow pages. Quentin looked the listings over, made a face. The area had no decent ethnic places. He'd have to make sure he had at least one real polyglot in the plaza to make up for it.

He flipped to the television stations and found the listing for Channel Six. Its headquarters were in downtown Selden Falls—such as it was—in someplace called the Max Building. He glanced at Nelson; his back was turned and he was saying that now was not a good time for something. Quentin didn't bother to wonder what.

He cleared his throat.

Nelson said: "I have to go. Call back later."

He hung up the phone. Quentin presented him with the yellow pages and said, "Call this station. Tell them I want to set up an interview with Patty Chalmers."

"Who?"

"The reporter we were watching." Pause. "Tell them I want to talk to her first. Feel her out. Maybe over dinner. She can pick the place."

Nelson said: "This is the peroxide blonde who just bushwhacked the mayor?"

"That's right."

"Why on earth do you want to talk to her?"

Quentin said: "My name keeps floating around out there but nobody really knows who I am or what I'm doing. I need to come across as more sympathetic, instead of some faceless developer pulling all kinds of strings behind the scenes. You know? Squash rumors like I'm going to sue the town. That's not good publicity." He glanced at the television. It was still turned off; Patty was still gone. "I need to get some positive exposure."

As Nelson reached for the telephone he said, "Well, I'm sure she'll give you the exposure you're looking for."

When visiting hours ended, Paige left her husband sleeping peacefully under the influence of heavy-hitting painkillers. The doctors—he had been assigned three of them, for some reason: Clark, O'Shea, and Sullivan, all with the same specialty—had been very keen on the drugs, telling her exactly what they were called and how wondrous their effects would be, like they were trying to sell her a supply for her own personal use or something.

Perhaps due to those marvelous narcotics, Henry still hadn't regained consciousness, and the doctors couldn't say when he would. He had suffered exposure and a dislocated shoulder and two broken ribs and a concussion, but they hadn't detected any skull fractures or pressure on his brain or any of a host of other unpleasant-sounding complications. She wondered why they had even told her about the various injuries they said he didn't have. Maybe to make her feel so relieved, she'd pay their bills without a squeak.

She stopped by Henry's parents' house to pick up Frederick. Henry's father was working in the garden, clawing at the earth with a wicked-looking three-bladed implement. He saw the car and waved to her. She tooted the horn as she went by, smiled widely, and said through clenched teeth: "Yeah, you old goat, we all love each other, don't we?"

By the time she got to the door, Joe Fontana had come out of the garden and was standing near the door. He looked rumpled and sweaty and tired, but his eyes were bright and hard and flicking between her face and her breasts. And she wasn't even wearing a particularly tight outfit today, for Christ's sake. "How's Henry?" he asked. "Is he awake?"

"No," she said. "He's sleeping."

Joe shook his head. He and Florence had been in Henry's room for a little while, until the doctors had instructed them to leave. Too many people breathing the air, they said. Paige had bitten back the urge to suggest that maybe this was due to there being three doctors present. "Any word what happened?" Joe asked.

She shrugged. "We probably won't know until he wakes up and tells us."

"God willing," Joe said.

"God had better be willing or I'll kick his butt," Paige said. Then: "Where's Freddie?"

"Florence has him," Joe said. "Inside." He opened the door for her and stood out of the way.

"Oh, no, after you," she said.

"I'll be in soon. I need to put some things away."

So Paige climbed the stairs to the living room, knowing full well he was back there staring at her ass. She didn't hear the screen door bang shut until she moved out of his range of vision.

Horny old coot.

There was no one in the living room, so she headed into the kitchen. Florence Fontana was mixing cookie batter under Freddie's watchful gaze. "What are we making?" Paige asked, coming up behind them. "Chocolate chip?"

"Uh-huh," Frederick said.

Florence looked at Paige over her shoulder, shrugged, and went back to churning the dough.

"Is Daddy okay?" Frederick asked.

"Yes, honey, he'll be fine."

"Doctors." Florence shook her head. "Leeches and bleeders."

Paige wasn't sure if she was referring to their technology or their billing practices, but it was always safer just to agree with whatever the old lady said. "Yeah."

"Why three doctors? Why not just one? They'll just argue with each other and do nothing."

"More money for the hospital," Paige said.

Florence grunted, then said: "Are you staying for dinner?"

"I don't—"

"Or at least until the cookies are done?"

"I'll pick them up tomorrow," Paige said. Then, with sudden inspiration: "I need to be home in case the hospital calls." This excuse had the advantage of being perfectly true.

"Good idea," Florence said.

So Paige bundled Frederick up in his spring attire and herded him down the steps. Joe was just on his way in and gave the boy a hug goodbye. He sent Paige off with a peck on the cheek and a very slight pat on the behind.

She walked away quickly, before the desire to rip his arms off became overpowering.

By the time the evening news shows came on, Nick Garson had decided he probably wasn't going to be talking to Quentin Farmer any time soon. He'd wasted an entire day sitting in his room, periodically telephoning Nelson, but it had somehow never been the right time; he was starting to think that he was being stonewalled. Part of Nelson's job, after all, was to run interference for Quentin. Maybe Nick had been witnessing the man's blocking skills in action.

Consequently, he decided to bypass the assistant and go directly to Mr. Farmer himself. The problem was, he still didn't know what room Quentin was in. Nobody would tell him; Nelson wouldn't spill it, and the hotel had a policy against giving out room numbers, and Quentin apparently never ever answered the phone. Nick thought about the situation for a while, then got out the room service menu, selected something suitably expensive, and called the front desk. "This is Quentin Farmer," he said, pitching his voice several degrees higher than normal. "I'd like the surf and turf dinner sent up to my room, please."

After a momentary pause the voice on the other end said, "Yes, sir. Do you want it sent to your room, or to Mr. Garson's room?"

"What?"

"Well, you're calling from Mr. Garson's room, so—"

"Oh, I see. No, send it to my room. Thanks." He hung up quickly. He hadn't realized they could tell what room he was calling from. That was bad; if Farmer got a bill for room service he hadn't requested and called the front desk and found out where the order had come from, it wouldn't help the Nick Garson Re-Employment Effort any. He thought for a little bit longer, then called the front desk again and said, in his normal tone of voice, "This is Nick Garson. Mr. Farmer just ordered room service from here. I want you to bill it to me, not to him."

"Yes, sir, Mr. Garson," said the voice on the other end.

"Could you tell me how long it'll be?"

"About thirty minutes."

"Thanks." Nick hung up. He looked at his watch. Rather than wait in his room, he decided to go right to the third floor—Nelson's room was up there, so he suspected Quentin's was as well—and stake out the corridor. But when he got there, there wasn't anywhere to hide; it was just a long, straight hallway, closed at either end. No corners, no alcoves, not even a big potted plant like in all the movies. So he went into the stairwell and propped the door open with his foot and kept an eye on the elevators, several yards away.

After an hour or so, the elevator doors *dinged* open and the room service tray trundled out. Over the course of that hour there had been no signs of life from any of the rooms; Nick had seen livelier mausoleums. He watched what door the room service girl—who looked suspiciously like the maid—went to, then came out of hiding and walked up the corridor.

She was on her third series of knocks when he approached her and said, "Hi. I'm Nick Garson. Mr. Farmer ordered from my room."

She looked at him with heavy-lidded eyes and little evident interest.

He added, "He's in Mr. DeGrace's room now. 308."

She made a face, turned the cart around, and with exaggerated slowness, pushed it to Nelson's room. Nick followed. Nelson opened the door after the first knock, looked at the cart, then at the girl, then at Nick. "What's going on?" he said.

"Dinner," Nick said. He gave the maid a dollar. She took it delicately, said something about being able to retire now, tucked it into her apron pocket, and stalked off.

"Pleasant girl," Nelson said, watching her go.

Nick pushed the cart into the room. "Consider this a bribe," he said.

"I'm a vegetarian," Nelson said as he shut the door.

So Nick ended up eating the thirty-dollar meal himself, sitting on the edge of Nelson's bed with the tray balanced on his knees. It wasn't all that bad, once he scraped the blackened bits off the steak. The other major component of the dinner was a smattering of small, round, somewhat charred niblets that resembled miniature scallops but tasted like garlicky erasers.

"I'm not stonewalling you, if that's what you're thinking," Nelson said, as he watched Nick eat. "Quentin has been having a bad couple of days."

"Yeah?" Since he hadn't yet leveled any accusations, Nick wondered why Nelson would feel the need to say he wasn't stonewalling unless he really was.

"Yeah."

"Well, he can join the club," Nick said, taking a large bite of steak.

Nelson said: "Just imagine how long that'll be sitting in your colon."

"Will it still be there when I finally get to talk to Quentin?"

"Yes, as a matter of fact," Nelson said. "Call tomorrow. I think he'll be in a very good mood tomorrow."

"Why? Where is he?"

"He's out on an interview with a reporter. Don't ask for details." Nelson leaned back in his chair and folded his arms. "Just trust me. Tomorrow, Quentin Farmer will be a very contented man."

"So what does Quentin Farmer *want*?" Patty Chalmers asked, fixing him with eyes like disks of blue ice. They were in a dim corner of a restaurant deep in the forest an hour or so northeast of Selden Falls. It was right on the shore of a reservoir, and had a wide deck that extended over the water. He could see both the deck and the reservoir through a wide, many-paned window behind Patty's head. The moon was reflected in the rippling water, and there was still snow, crystal white in the twilight, covering the wooden slats and edging the lake with ivory. Very romantic, Quentin thought. Picturesque. Probably did a lot of business for weddings and anniversaries. He wondered if the owners were interested in acquiring a partner.

She blinked the ice chips at him, waiting for an answer. He smiled and took a sip of wine and said, "That's a pretty broad question. What does anybody want?"

She said, "Well, I want you to agree to that interview."

"I might," he said. "We'll see how the evening goes. But you don't want to blow all your questions now, do you?"

Patty shrugged slightly and traced the lip of her wine glass with a crimson-nailed finger. "I don't mind blowing a few things now if it gets me what I want later."

Quentin cocked an eyebrow at her. He took another sip of wine and—when he could trust himself to open his mouth without embarrassing himself—said: "Where'd you get the idea I was going to sue the city over my computer?" he asked.

"It was just a rumor," she said.

"You made Simon look pretty foolish."

"It's his own fault. He shouldn't be mayor if he can't answer questions."

"Maybe not," he said. "But he's my ally in building the plaza. I would hate to see his effectiveness compromised."

She looked at him blankly.

"I'm asking you to lay off him," he explained.

"Oh," she said. Then, after a moment: "He doesn't like girls."

Quentin rubbed the back of his neck and wondered if she was putting him on. He said, "What I mean is, tossing out left-field questions like that doesn't help either one of us." Then, just in case she thought he meant himself and her, he added: "Simon and me, I mean."

"It doesn't?"

"No," Quentin said.

"It's just television."

Quentin began tapping the side of his head. "Yeah, but it's *news*," he said. "People watch it expecting information. They expect the information to be true. You ask Simon if I'm suing the town, and for a lot of your viewers becomes a fact, regardless of what he says."

Patty said: "Oh."

The blank look was back. He said, "Am I getting through here?"

She shrugged and took another sip of wine.

Quentin said: "If I give you an interview, who's going to write the questions?"

"My boss."

"That's a relief," Quentin said.

As they drove home later that night, Quentin behind the wheel of his Jaguar, the air heady with the scents of leather and expensive perfume, they came upon a group of deer nibbling the tall grass by the side of the road. Patty gestured for Quentin to pull over, which he did. The deer stood just outside the range of his headlights and watched them with glistening green eyes.

He felt Patty's hand slide into his crotch.

"We never decided if I would get that interview," she said.

"That's true," Quentin said.

She crawled over and unzipped his trousers. Her hair smelled like apples. The deer wheeled and bounded into the forest, but Quentin wasn't paying them much attention at all. He was concentrating on the moist things happening just below his waist.

He didn't pay much attention when a car pulled up alongside his Jaguar, either.

At least, not until somebody inside it flicked on a floodlight.

5

Jane Trott rose from her bed like a gossamer spectre, her nightgown luminous in the darkness. She swirled into the bathroom, turned on the shower, shrugged out of her garment and stepped under the spray. She lathered herself up, face to feet, scrubbing hard with good, strong soap, washing away the traces of sleep, the clinging wisps of spirit that came back with her every morning when she awoke. Her dreams weren't like the dreams of other people; they took her through strange realms of altered consciousness, shadowy worlds populated by the phantoms of the dead and the yet-to-be-born, and the discorporate projections of others like her, and the whirlpools of psychic force that the superstitious knew as *demons*. Her dreams were journeys to remote times, distant places, where she learned things that weren't meant to be learned, where she saw what others couldn't see.

Tonight, in her dreams, she had gone to the old building by the canal. Her spirit had risen from her body and the place had drawn her, called to her; she'd traveled through the topsy-turvy halls of sleep to arrive outside it, at the very gate of the old church. It had been utterly black inside, a midnight maelstrom, trying to pull her inside; she had resisted, had wrenched herself away, but only with the greatest effort. She remembered what she had seen within the sagging walls: a deep, dark hole, a pit able to swallow up everything Simon could throw at it, and more. She could still hear the echo of its breath, a sound like distant wind tearing through hollow trees.

She had thought that, with Henry Fontana temporarily out of the picture, she had some room to maneuver. Now she knew she didn't.

The church must still feel itself immediately threatened; why else would it have intruded on her dreams, summoned her to come and witness its power? It was a plea; it was a warning. *Stop him or else.*

She turned off the water, stepped out of the shower, dried herself off, padded back into the bedroom where Calvin slept like a stone beneath the thick blue sheets. He wouldn't awaken, not if the roof caved in and God himself came through the hole and tapped him on the shoulder. She turned on the light in the walk-in closet and let it spill out into the bedroom, and she could *feel* the light on her, touch it almost, slippery photons sliding across her skin. That was her heightened state of awareness, her mind fully alert, neurons firing through parts of the brain that most people never even knew existed, let alone used.

She stepped into the closet. It smelled of cedar and freshly-washed clothes. The two scents swirled together in the air, the cedar pale orange and prickly, the detergent rainbow-hued with fuzzed edges. Just like in the television commercials, Jane thought, when the woman took the laundry out of the dryer and the colorful aroma rose from it like steam from a freshly-baked pie. The person who had made that advertisement must be psychic too.

When she emerged from the closet, she was wearing dark slacks and a black sweater. Guerrilla gear. In her pocket was a set of gleaming steel handcuffs, which she had taken from the colorful little box on the shelf above her shoes. She didn't take the key. If she had the key on her, she knew from experience, they would find it on her and use it to unlock the manacles.

She stole to the bed and kissed Calvin's forehead. He would never approve of this; he thought the whole thing with the church was loopy, and dangerous. But that was all right. He was asleep and he couldn't stop her.

When she went outside, it was snowing, just a little bit. Big fat puffy flakes that landed like feathers on the earth. A pillow fight in heaven. She blew on the windshield of her Jeep and the snow skittered off it. She climbed in, started the engine, gave it a little time to warm up. Get the oil flowing. After all, you didn't hop out of bed and run a marathon. She waited until warm air started blowing out of the vents before she drove away.

When she left the driveway, the eastern sky was just starting to redden with the approaching dawn; by the time she reached the old church, the horizon was a palette of infectious colors, red and orange and yellow, and the snow had tapered off as the clouds were pushed away by a wind from the south. She parked the Jeep almost exactly where she had the first time. Across the canal Quentin Farmer's site lay waiting, heaps of dirt and gravel giving it that anticipatory, unfinished look common to land that had been condemned to development.

She got out. The air was chilly and the wind was brisk. A flock of crows occupied the crown of the tree that grew from the roof of the church; they brooded in silence, black pustules on barren limbs. If they were aware of her arrival they gave no sign of it. She stayed a moment, watching them, thinking that she had never them there before. She wondered if they were real—physically speaking—or some sort of manifestation visible only during the dark hours between dusk and dawn, if they would disappear as the rising sun cleared away the tattered shreds of night.

One of the crows stirred, chattered at the sky. Sounded like any other crow she had ever seen. Natural birds, she thought, with a fragmentary disappointment.

She went to the front door of the church, peered into the dimness inside before entering. She listened to the floorboards squeak under her tread. They were warped and peeling, damp with age and dark with corruption. She wondered what she should cuff herself to. The benches were old and rotten, too easily cut or ripped apart; most of the woodwork was in a similar state of decay. She had to attach herself to something sturdy and, preferably, integral to the structure of the place. Something they couldn't just cut down. Probably the most solid item in the church was the tree, but it didn't have any suitable surfaces.

She went to the old door on the right, which opened onto stairs that led to the choir loft overhead. She climbed the steps, listening to them groan and protest; they were old, they were tired, they didn't want this kind of treatment anymore. Well, she thought, it was this or be demolished, and the stairs could take their pick.

The choir loft was mostly bare. The roof arched up over her head, with the hole for the steeple just a few yards forward from the loft; the splintered remains of a catwalk branched from beneath it like some sort of shriveled umbilical cord. A thick banister ran around the lip of the loft; she rapped it with her knuckles and found it surprisingly solid. Almost suitable, but made of wood and thus too easily cut. She folded her arms on the edge of the wall and surveyed the interior of the church. From up here she could see the whole layout, even past the wreckage where the roof had fallen in. The altar was still there, a big stone tablet resting on wide supports at the far end of the place. It didn't have any distinguishing features of whatever faith had once been practiced there.

What was that?

Something protruded from the top of the altar, right in the middle of it. A black ring of some kind. Thick. Iron, maybe.

Weird, but it might do.

She went back down the stairs, walked slowly up the central aisle. She wasn't trying to tune the place in, but she could feel the emanations rising up around her, radiating like heat from all around. The atmosphere was incredibly charged, even after all these years of abandonment and decay; it amazed her that everyone who came here couldn't feel it. The energy wasn't focused, it wasn't directed; at least, not right now. But it had been when Henry Fontana had come, and it would be the next time Simon took a shot at knocking the place down. And even if he succeeded, that wouldn't be the end of it; oh, no. Power like this didn't just go away. It would change its form, it would change its direction, but it wouldn't disappear. Maybe it would shift from defensive actions to offensive ones, bring the fight right to Simon's office downtown. *You want to knock down my home?* it would say. *How about I knock down yours?*

She reached the wreckage of the roof. The tree grew from the heap, a few yards away. The rubble was stained and mossy and moldering. She looked up. Through the tangle of limbs she could see the sky, which had lightened to blue, and the myriad shapes of the crows in their roost. They were motionless as stones; they might as well be part of the tree. She felt herself wondering, again, whether or not they were really there; but at the moment, that wasn't her concern, was it?

She skirted the central part of the fallen roof, tackling the climb near the right-hand wall where it wasn't piled so high. The fingers and palms of her gloves got all damp and filthy as she made her way along the wreckage—it had long since settled into a stable, if uneven, surface—toward the altar. When she was close enough, she jumped to it.

Landed.

The energy streaming up from it nearly blew her off again.

She expected it to lift her coat, to billow her hair, it was so strong; but that was a common neophyte mistake, assigning physical power to a purely psychic force. She walked gingerly to the stone tablet, feeling as if she were tiptoeing across blazing sand. She heard whispers around her, echoes of long-forgotten ceremonies and rituals, and had to force herself to block them out.

The table was made of thick, rough-edged slate, similar to the flagstone outside the front door of the church; the supports were the same material. She gave the thing a shove and it didn't budge; it wasn't bolted down, but even so it didn't seem inclined to go anywhere and they wouldn't be able to remove it without difficulty. The tablet was so large that she couldn't reach the center to test the ring, so she hopped up onto it and scooted across to the eye and flicked it with her finger. Solid iron, without a trace of rust. It was bigger than she'd thought; it looked like she could put her fist through it. She dug the cuff out of her pocket and attached it to the loop of iron, gave it a tug. Solid. Very solid.

She snapped the other end of the handcuff to her right wrist.

There, she thought; now let them try to carry her away.

She lay back on the tablet and looked up at the ceiling. The whitewash was stained and streaked with brown rings and curves, marks where water had come through over the years.

Her eyes widened.

Was it just her, or were the stains *moving*?

She had to be imagining it. *Had* to be. How could she have missed such a direct manifestation when she had been here before? She stared up at them, watching muddy ripples slowly swirling around each other, forming patterns and shapes, letters almost. Writing, after a fashion; or maybe pictograms.

She needed to be able to interpret this, she thought; it was an attempt to communicate. The church was trying to talk to her. But she would never be able to make sense of it. Not by reading the ceiling, anyway.

She closed her eyes.

"I'm here to set you free," she murmured. "You sense that, don't you? Just let me in, and I'll open the doors for you."

The energy in the stone beneath her changed, shifted, softened. She felt an icy thrill run up her spine, a sexual charge almost, as it enfolded her and caressed her and warmed her against the icy air. The spirit of the church was inviting her in, and she sank down into it, searching for the source.

Outside, the wind kicked up, blowing through the trees with a sound like great wings flapping.

Paige's clock-radio clicked to life in the middle of the morning show. The two DJs were engaged in a massive bout of hilarity at someone's expense, but she had missed the identity of today's victim. Paige rolled onto her back and blinked at the ceiling; sunlight was filtering strongly through the drapes. Must be a nice bright day outside, she thought.

"Okay, okay," the second DJ said. "So he runs himself over, and then—"

Hey—they were making fun of *Henry*! She was the only one who was allowed to do that! She punched the *off* button and made the DJs go away. Then she rolled out of bed, yawning, blinking away the graininess in her eyes. Her robe was in a puddle on the floor near her side of the bed; Paige picked it up and slipped it on, tightened and tied the belt. She wandered unsteadily into the living room, bouncing off more than one wall on the way. A blinking red light in the corner caught her attention: the answering machine, still flashing the message she hadn't rewound last night. It was Simon Jones, saying "Sorry, Paige, I have to give the contract to somebody else. I need it done right away and Henry never scheduled it with his people. I know you'll understand."

Yeah, she understood Simon pretty well, she thought. She pressed the rewind button this time. Bye-bye, Simon.

She opened the curtains and the morning sun poured in through the windows and the sheers, lighting up the room. Except there was a long, fuzzy shadow across the floor, being generated by an angry red slash across the window.

What on earth?

She went to the window, peered at the stain minutely. It looked like *spray paint*.

She went to the front entrance. The newspaper was crumpled between the storm door and the inside one, folded and bagged; she picked it up and brought it with her as she went down the driveway to take a look at the front of her house.

The air was crisp but the sun was warm, melting the remains of the night's frost, turning it into dew. Eden Avenue was quiet, no cars in motion at the moment; steam drifted from chimneys, the smell of wood smoke laced the air. Birds, newly returned from warmer climates, twittered in the trees that dotted the yards, budding but not yet bursting into leaf. It looked like the dawn of a beautiful day.

Not the kind of morning when you would expect to see *BURN IN HELL* scrawled across the front of your house in fire engine red.

It started on the porch, next to the front door, the letters getting smaller as they went along, the way they did when you were writing something and the end of the page began to approach and you realized you'd misjudged the available space. The words had been sprayed without regard to things like windows or shutters or ivy; the lettering went right across the wide picture window of the living room, across the trellis and its dormant vines, right over the bedroom window within feet of where she had been sleeping. And whoever had done it had left the paint cans in a heap next to the porch.

Was that a gesture of contempt, or just sloppiness?

Paige went back into the house, locked and chained the front door behind her. She left the paper in the living room on her way to the basement, where they still had leftover paint from when they had done the house last year. She found it under Henry's workbench: two cans, one partially used and one unopened. She grabbed the open can and a brush and a stirrer and went back upstairs.

Frederick had come into the living room while she was in the basement, and had assumed his usual position on the floor, playing a video game, one in which he had to make falling blocks fit into openings. Paige liked that one herself, and it had the added quality of not making Freddie curse like a sailor. He looked at her as she came in and said, "Mommy, can I have pancakes today?"

"Not today, sweetie," she said. "Today's a cereal day. Play your game." She opened up the newspaper and spread it out on the floor and put the can on it. She prised the lid off with the stirrer and began mixing the paint, so rapidly that some of it splashed out.

"Are you painting?"

"I just have to touch something up."

"Oh," Freddie said. Then, after a moment: "I had a dream last night."

"You did?"

"Uh-huh. I dreamed there was a man looking in my window."

Paige froze. The paint sloshed thickly, then was still. "A man?"

"Yeah. He tapped on the window with his finger."

Frederick's room faced the back of the house. She hadn't thought about the back. It was surrounded by a privacy fence for the pool, chain link with diagonal slats of wood through the mesh. It was difficult to scale the fence—the slats made it difficult to get a toehold —but a determined person could do it.

"I thought he was a vampire," Freddie said.

She started mixing again, even more furiously than before. She'd do the front first, before all the commuters started going to work; then she would check the back. "What'd you do?" she asked.

"I got up and closed my curtains so I couldn't see him anymore."

"Why were they open in the first place?"

"So I could look at the moon."

Of course. Didn't everybody want to look at the moon while they slept? "And then he went away?" she said.

"Uh-huh."

Paige decided the paint was mixed enough. She put the lid on it and told Frederick not to touch it, then went back to her bedroom and threw on sweats and one of Henry's shirts. She also grabbed his camera. When she returned to the living room Frederick was on his hands and knees sniffing the can of paint. She scolded him and he scuttled back to the video game. She hefted the paint can, headed for the door. "I'll be back in a little while," she told Freddie. "Then maybe I'll make pancakes for you after all."

"Okay," he said.

She hurried onto the porch. A big old sedan was going by, the driver gawking at her house. It was Mr. Kosciusko from up the street. God, this was going to be all over the neighborhood. She ran to the edge of the yard and snapped five quick pictures of the house, then ran back to the porch and popped open the can and started painting over the graffiti.

A half-hour and ten cars later, she was finished. It was an imperfect cover-up, but it would have to do for now. She collected the cans of spray paint—they weren't empty after all, they were full, as if the guy had intended to do the entire house but had been interrupted—in a paper bag and brought them into the house. Her sweats and Henry's shirt were splattered with white paint.

Frederick was sitting in the recliner talking on the cordless phone. "Uh-huh," he said. "Uh-huh. Yes. Here she is." He held up the receiver for her to take.

"Freddie, what have I told you about answering the phone?" Paige said.

"Not to do it," Frederick said.

"So how come you did it anyway?"

"It wouldn't stop ringing," he said.

"You don't answer the phone no matter how long it rings. Okay?"

"Okay," Freddie said.

"Okay." She took the phone cautiously. Maybe it was the hospital, with news about Henry; but she had a premonition that it wasn't. "Hello?" she said.

"Did you get my message?" a calm and pleasant male voice said.

"What message? Who is this?" she said.

"The message I left on the front of your house," the man said. "I know it wasn't news to you—that you're going to burn in hell, I mean —but I thought your neighbors would want to know."

"What the hell are you talking about?" she said.

"I found your husband's demonic paraphernalia," the man said. "It's no use denying it or playing dumb. God sees you, and God knows you, and I know God."

"Give him a message, then?" Paige said. "Tell him to stop hanging around with losers like you." She switched off the phone.

A few seconds passed, and then it twittered at her. She pressed the button and said nothing, just listened. After a moment the same voice —agitated now, without that phony pleasant veneer—said, "The carrion birds will pick the flesh from your bones, bitch."

She turned it off again.

Then she turned it back on and called the police.

* * *

Simon Jones went to the office early, and didn't see the morning paper.

He needed to locate a contractor to replace Henry Fontana's company, and fast. He'd tried to convince the office manager at Sunset Construction to send a crew out, but she wouldn't do it without Henry there to sign off on bumping their other clients, which he hadn't done before his accident. Freed of any obligation to wait for Henry to get better, Simon returned to the Rolodex to find someone else.

This turned out not to be as easy as he had hoped. There were a good nine or ten contracting companies in the book, but none of them would do the job. Lewis Smith of Akins Construction laughed and told him they couldn't possibly get out there any time before April. Ian Quill of Hutchinson Demolitions said, in a clipped British voice, "You'll have to give us more notice than that, sport." Nobody answered at Home and Garden Earthworks Incorporated. And so on, and so on, and so on.

His secretary poked her head into his office and told him hello and asked him if he had read the paper. He didn't answer her—he was listening to a recording tell him that the number for the seventh company on his list had been disconnected—and when she came in and pointedly left the paper on his desk, he didn't look at it.

The last call he made was to Karl Castle of Kastle Konstruction. This company was not at the bottom of the listing, but he had dealt with them before and didn't like them. As he dialed the phone, Simon wondered how much business Karl could get with a name like that. It looked either overly precious, like he had little teddy bears in overalls operating the equipment, or suspiciously Communist, with Bolsheviks instead of bears.

Then he got Karl on the phone, and Karl quoted him a figure twice as high as Henry's to get to the church any time in the coming two weeks. Definitely not Communist, Simon thought, but those teddy bears had one hell of a union.

While Simon and Karl were haggling, Kevin Kowalski showed up. He was also carrying a copy of the paper, and he looked about ready to burst into flames. Simon began to think maybe there was something in the paper that he needed to read, though he suspected he wasn't going to like it. "Hang on a minute, Karl," he said. He covered the mouthpiece with his hand, even though the phone had a perfectly functional *mute* button, and he looked up at Kevin and said: "What?"

"Have you seen this?" Kevin asked, waggling the paper at him. He was in a suit and tie and was wearing his ID pin from the hospital.

"Not yet. I've been on the—" Simon broke off as Kevin tossed the paper at him. It unfolded as it flew and landed face-up on Simon's desk, sending important scraps of paper billowing every which-way. "Damn it, Kevin, can't you see that I'm—oh my God."

From the other room Simon heard his secretary say, "I tried to show it to him but he wouldn't listen!"

"Oh my God," he said again.

Kevin folded his arms.

Simon stared at the headline: *Developer Caught In Sex Act With Reporter.* Below that was an article that Simon couldn't read without his glasses. Two pictures were in the sidebar; one was of Quentin Farmer, the other of a woman. And not just *any* woman; it was Patty Chalmers, the reporter who had ambushed him by the side of the road while they were rescuing Henry.

Simon dropped the phone on his desk and buried his face in his hands. "Tell me what they were doing," he said.

"Oral. Deep throat, from what I hear."

"Oh, God," Simon groaned. "Charges?"

"Indecency."

"Oh, God."

"He also offered the arresting officer a thousand dollars to let them go."

Simon, temporarily stripped of the ability to speak, managed a little whine.

"He made bail, of course," Kevin said. "So did Patty."

"Did he bail her out himself?" Simon asked, hoping for something to salvage what would surely be a public relations disaster. At least if Quentin had sprung the girl, they could maybe play it up as gallantry or something.

"Nope. Her husband did."

"Her *husband?*" Simon banged his forehead several times against his desk, then looked up at Kevin. "Who caught them?"

"An off-duty cop coming back from a wedding reception." Kevin checked his watch. "Read the article, Simon. I have work to do. So do you." He left and closed the door, not quietly.

Simon picked up the receiver and said, "I'll get back to you."

Then he read the article.

Then he called Karl back and told him that if he and his teddy bears could be at the church that afternoon, they had a deal.

Karl upped the price, but he got the contract.

Jasper Shoemaker Senior sat in a chair that was too small for him and watched Paul Shockton look out the window at the pine trees. Jasper had come in for his shift at the mall and the sergeant had ordered him to go to Shockton's office on the second floor, which was not a good thing to hear under any circumstances and especially not after what had happened last night. Paul had been sitting behind his desk when Jasper had entered; when Jasper sat down, Paul got up and turned his back on him. Ten minutes later, Shockton hadn't said a word, hadn't shouted, hadn't even acknowledged Jasper's presence. It was really kind of disconcerting.

Jasper said: "I'm supposed to be at the mall in five—"

"You aren't going to the mall," Paul Shockton said, not turning around.

Well, that was good. He had gotten a response. It was better than sitting there looking at Shockton's clenched butt beneath the tortured fabric of pants he would never admit were too small for him. But it did raise an ominous question: if he wasn't going to the mall, where was he going?

"You set it up real nice, didn't you, Shoemaker?" Paul said. It sounded like he was talking without moving his jaws.

"Set what up nice, Mr. Shockton?"

"I mean, you *could* have just busted Mr. Farmer and his, uh, friend. But that wasn't enough for you. You had to bust him and call the newspaper about it." Pause. "That was the really brilliant thing. Farmer is humiliated, the mayor is humiliated, I get my butt chewed out, and you cover your own ass, because if we reprimand you it looks like we're in Farmer's front pockets sucking on his tits. A great plan, Shoemaker, really. I'm amazed you thought of it."

"I was just doing my job."

"Yeah. Of course you were. We can all sleep better knowing you're keeping the streets safe from the likes of Quentin Farmer."

"He tried to bribe me."

"Of *course* he tried to bribe you." Paul turned around. His face was the color of cherry cough syrup. "He's a wealthy businessman. That's how they respond to trouble." Pause. "Why didn't you take it?"

"What? I take a bribe, *I'm* the criminal."

"Oh, spare me," Shockton said. "What do you think all that free food at the mall is? You think they give you that stuff because they *like* you? We're just talking scale here, Shoemaker. They give you food; he gives you money. What's the difference?"

"I caught him breaking the law."

"*Everybody* breaks the law," Shockton said. "You know that as well as I do. Sometimes you have to look the other way." He plopped into his chair. "I don't know what your vendetta against Farmer is, but lay off it, Shoemaker."

"Are you suggesting I shouldn't arrest him if I see him doing something illegal?"

"I'm suggesting that, for some reason, you are prejudiced against Mr. Farmer, starting with his stolen computer and ending with his cock in that reporter's mouth." Paul rubbed his nose. "Look. Bottom line. Simon is leaning on me *very* heavily to make sure you don't cross paths with Quentin Farmer ever again. There are not many ways I can do that and make it stick. I can fire you. I can suspend you." He held up a hand to forestall the objections Jasper was about to raise. "Don't think I can't find grounds, because I can, even if I have to manufacture them. But I don't want to do that. So here's what's going to happen instead: I'm pulling you from the mall and putting you in a car, and I'm putting the car on the Dudley-Maxwell-Yoxall beat."

After a moment Jasper said: "The slums?"

"Economically depressed area," Paul said.

"I haven't been down there in sixteen years!"

"I'll put you with somebody who knows the area." Paul looked him over. "Somebody who can get out and chase vandals while you call for backup."

"So let me get this straight: you're giving me a crappy assignment because I busted Quentin Farmer and refused to take a bribe?"

"You know I'm not going to answer that, for Christ's sake," Paul said. "Dismissed."

Jasper sat still a moment, then heaved himself out of the chair and toddled out into the hallway and down the stairs. He headed into the men's room, went into a stall, closed the door, and sat down. Then he took a small tape recorder out of his jacket pocket, stuck a headphone plug in the appropriate jack, put the tiny speaker in his ear, rewound it a bit, and pressed *play*.

Shockton's voice, tinny but unmistakable, came out of the device: "—leaning on me very heavily to make sure you don't—"

He clicked it off.

Yes, that would do nicely.

A very polite policeman came and talked to Paige Fontana and wrote down everything she said. He took the spray paint cans she had collected, and after he had left and his squad car had disappeared down the street, her telephone rang. She let the machine pick it up, and listened to a man's scratchy, thick voice say, "Pick up. I know you're there." She listened to him breathe for several seconds. Then he said: "You can't hide behind your machine. The police can't protect you. I'm going to—"

She pulled the phone jack out of the answering machine.

"Mommy? What's that man talking about?" Freddie said.

"I don't know, honey," Paige said. "I think he must be crazy."

"When I was talking to him before, he said Daddy was going to go to hell."

"I know he said that, Freddie," she said. Frederick had described the conversation to the policeman. "But it isn't true."

"How do you know it isn't true?"

"Because Daddy's not a bad man," she said. She wanted to say: *If anyone is going to hell, it's the guy on the phone.* She didn't, though; she didn't need to get into an discussion of Good and Evil with her six-year-old. "Go get washed up. We have to go visit your father." She sent him out of the kitchen with a swat on the behind.

After he had gone, she made herself a cup of coffee and sat down at the dining room table and tried to figure out why they were suddenly the target of some nut's attention. Maybe it was because of Henry's association with Simon's administration. Mayor Jones had been elected in spite of his sexual preference; he could hardly have lost, running against an incumbent who was a convicted felon and, at the time of the election, under indictment for raiding the city treasury to pay for an apartment for his mistress. However, Selden Falls was not, overall, a friendly place for homosexuals, or anyone else who strayed too far from the established norms. This was an election year, so maybe, somewhere, some right-wing fringe preacher was inciting his flock against the mayor.

But still, why target *her* house, *her* family?

The telephone rang again, making her jump. It chirped once; it chirped twice. She hesitated, then lifted the receiver and said: "Hello?"

It was the hospital.

And suddenly the phone calls and the graffiti didn't matter anymore, because Henry was awake. Relief knocked the locks out of her knees and she sank down into her chair, sobbing and giggling at the same time, thanking the caller again and again and again until he finally said, "I really didn't have anything to do with it, but you're welcome."

She hung up, and then she called Henry's parents and told them the news; and she called her parents in Seattle and her sister in Detroit, waking them all up; and she called Henry's brother in Burlington, waking him up too, because he was between jobs and had no reason to rise early. She promised each of them that she would call back later with details. By the time she was done, she had completely forgotten about the morning's events.

Freddie came into the kitchen and she picked him up and told him his father was awake, and he said good, with an air of nonchalance that came from never having expected anything else. She sat him down with a bowl of cereal while she showered and dressed, and then they left for the hospital.

By then, the euphoria had worn off enough for her to remember to set the deadbolts on the doors.

Quentin Farmer scowled at the morning paper, with its pictures of him and Patty and the lengthy article comparing him to various politicians and Hollywood celebrities who had also been caught with their sex organs in the wrong places. He wondered if he could sue. Probably not, because they didn't say anything that was explicitly untrue; still, he made a note to have Nelson call his lawyers and have them look into it. That would have to wait, though; right now Nelson was fending off calls from the local media. Quentin was just praying the story wouldn't get picked up by any of the nationals.

Somebody knocked on his door. Couldn't be Nelson; Nelson had a key, and wasn't afraid to use it. Quentin got up and tiptoed to look through the peephole. If it was the press, Holiday Inn was going to have a very irate guest on their hands.

It didn't appear to be a reporter; it was a small, kind of nebbish-looking guy with a hook nose and thin brown hair and a shirt and tie that matched neither each other nor his pants. He didn't have a notebook or a camera or a microphone; maybe he was a decoy. Didn't matter, really, Quentin thought; he certainly couldn't be expected to open his door to someone he didn't even know. Especially when he had a *Do Not Disturb* sign hanging on his knob. The only people who could possibly be so uncivil as to ignore a *Do Not Disturb* sign were lawyers and reporters, and unless they were working for him he didn't want to talk to either. He took out his cellular phone and called Nelson. Busy.

He waited a minute to see if the guy would go away; instead he knocked again. Quentin called Nelson again. Still busy.

The guy knocked *again*, even louder this time. How rude. You would think after twice not getting an answer, he would get the hint. Quentin called Nelson once more, and got through this time. Nelson's weary voice came through, kind of crackly: "Quentin Farmer's office, Nelson DeGrace speaking."

"It's Quentin," he said. "There's some guy knocking on my door. Stick your head out and see if you recognize him."

"Hang on a second." There was a pause, and then Nelson came back on. "That's Nick Garson," he said.

"Who?"

"Nick Garson. The guy who thought the canal would be a good place for a plaza. Remember?" Pause. "The man you fired?"

"The *food court guy*?" Quentin said.

"Yes."

"The *food court guy* is knocking on my door? What the hell is he doing here? How did he find me?"

"I don't know," Nelson said. "He probably wants to ask for his job back."

Garson knocked again. *Pound pound pound.* Quentin said: "Get rid of him."

"Why don't you just talk to him?"

"What's to talk about?" Quentin said. "He's history. End of story."

"But—"

"Get *rid* of him." Quentin clicked off the cellular and stomped around to the far side of the bed, sat down on the edge. Talk to Nick Garson? Yeah, sure. He had criminal charges over his head, and a missing laptop full of stuff nobody should ever see, and a derelict building that nobody could seem to knock down, and he was going to sit down and talk to the guy who had caused this entire mess in the first place?

Actually, that might not be such a bad idea, he thought; he could vent his frustrations on the guy, then kick his ass out the door.

That would be a good stress-buster, but he decided against it. With his current luck, Garson would grab a gun and start shooting, and the fun of shouting at him just wouldn't be worth it.

Nick Garson was so intent on pounding at Quentin's door that he didn't notice anyone coming toward him until he felt a firm grip on his shoulder. Then he whirled, afraid that hotel security had come to eject him; but it was only Nelson, standing there with a glum look on his long face.

"Give it up, Nick," Nelson said.

"What? Why?"

"He won't see you. He's in a terrible mood."

"You said he would talk to me today. You said he'd be a very contented man."

"Well," Nelson said, "that was before he … uh, have you seen the paper? Or the morning news?"

"I slept through it," Nick said, although *sleep* wasn't exactly the right word for the condition he'd been in. He had thrashed around all night, unable to get comfortable: the covers had been intolerably hot and scratchy, but when he threw them off the air had quickly become freezing; the pillows had been stiff and prickly, poking his cheeks with spiny broken feathers; strange noises—loud rustling sounds, shrieking bird calls, thumping and fluttering right outside his window—had kept jolting him awake. He had finally sunk into a fitful, restless sleep around four o'clock and had stayed that way until after ten.

Nelson eyed him for a few seconds, then said: "Well, his evening didn't turn out quite like he planned."

"Can't you get him to talk to me?"

"I'm afraid not. I tried, Nick. He won't see you." Nelson shrugged. "I doubt he'll *ever* be willing to talk to you. He associates you too much with the problems he's having on this project. He—"

"Well, that's just great. He's cranky and I'm out of a job. Is that fair?"

Nelson sighed. "I can't help you, Nick."

"Come on, Nelson."

Farmer's assistant shook his head. "Just go home. There's nothing more you can do here." And Nelson turned his back on him and walked slowly up the hallway. Nick watched him leave, the broad expanse of back, the long stringy hair, walking away.

"Nelson," Nick called.

He kept going.

"Nelson!"

"Go home, Nick," Nelson said.

He went into his room and shut the door.

Nick Garson stood alone in the hallway, waiting for Nelson to come out, to say he had thought of something, he knew how to get Nick's job back; but it didn't happen and he finally went back to his room and called his wife at work. She said: "I *told* you you were wasting your time out there. You were crazy to even think Farmer would—"

He hung up on her.

He stood up and looked out the window. The sun was bright, the sky was clear, and he didn't have a job. But there *had* to be something he could do about this situation.

There *had* to be.

Paige fairly ran through the hospital, drawing dirty looks from nurses and envious ones from patients in wheelchairs or shuffling along on their walkers. None of that mattered, though, because she was on her way to see Henry and Henry was awake.

She slowed down when she got to his wing, slowed even more as she approached his door. She was starting to get nervous. After all, he had hit his head; what if he wasn't quite right anymore? What if he was a little bit funny? What if he didn't recognize her?

What if she was getting herself all agitated and he turned out to be fine?

She took a breath, and walked into his room. Henry's bed was against the outside wall, near the windows; she walked through his roommate's territory and around the dangling green curtain, and there was her husband lying in a tangle of tubes and wires and hoses.

His head tilted and his eyes found her. For a second, she was afraid there was no spark of recognition there; but then he smiled and said, in a hoarse voice, "Hi, hon."

"Hi yourself. How do you feel?"

"Like I got run over," he said.

Only one of the three doctors—O'Shea—was present, making notes on Henry's chart. He said, without looking up: "You did get run over."

Paige said, "You look like a car engine, with all those tubes and stuff."

"Vroom vroom," Henry said. He chuckled, or tried to, but it came out a ghastly rasping, sucking sound. Having a cannula up his nose was probably responsible for that.

"Making automotive noises isn't on the list of things you should do right now," O'Shea said.

Henry made a face at the doctor, then glanced up at Paige and whispered, "Have you met Dr. Giggles?"

"Yeah," she said. "I met his associates Larry and Curly, too."

Henry started to laugh, but it collapsed into a soggy-sounding cough. The doctor asked him if he thought he had fluid in his lungs, and Henry said if he hacked any up O'Shea would be the first to know.

"I think I'll schedule another chest X-ray, just to be safe," O'Shea said. "Don't want you going pneumonic on us." The doctor departed, clipboard in hand.

Henry said: "I've had so many X-rays I should be developing super powers any time now." He started squinting at Paige.

"What're you doing?" she said.

"Trying to see through your dress."

"Oh, that can be arranged." She undid a few buttons and flashed her chest at him, then quickly buttoned it up again.

"Thanks," he said. "I needed that."

Paige squeezed his hand. "I'm glad you're awake."

"So am I."

"So what happened?"

"It was dumb," Henry said. "You would have laughed your ass off if you saw it. I got out of my car and slipped down the hill. I was climbing back up when the car popped into gear and came at me."

That was essentially what the police thought had happened, and why they had impounded the car. They were looking for mechanical glitches, she told him. He said, "Maybe they'll fix my muffler while they're at it."

"Simon pulled the contract for the church," she said.

Henry shrugged, then winced. "Ow."

"You okay?"

"Ribs," he said. "I'm not surprised. About the contract, I mean. He's in an awful hurry. Any idea who'll be doing it?"

"Nope."

"Just as well. Bad land down there. Mucky." Henry lay quietly a moment, then said: "How're you holding up?"

"Okay." Paige had decided not to tell him about the phone calls and the graffiti. There wasn't anything he could do about it when he was flat on his back in the hospital, and it would only worry him.

"Where's Freddie?"

"With your folks. They'll be over later."

Suddenly, in a strong, clear voice, the man in the other bed launched into a rendition of *New York, New York*. Paige jumped, but Henry only chuckled and said, "He does that. You get used to it."

The song went on for a few bars, then stopped.

Paige said: "Always the same song?"

"Oh, no. This morning it was *Be Our Guest*, and before that something I didn't recognize. The nurse told me it was from *H.M.S. Pinafore*. It woke me up, but she said Gilbert and Sullivan puts her to sleep."

Dr. Clark came in, carrying the clipboard that O'Shea had exited with. If she hadn't seen them all together once, Paige would have thought her husband's three doctors were really all the same person, throwing on disguises in the linen closet down the hall. Dr. Clark greeted Paige, then said to Henry, "I see we've got you down for more chest X-rays. While we're at it I'm going to recommend one more cranial, just to make sure nothing untoward is going on in that head of yours." He hung the clipboard on a hook beside the bed and left.

"Another forty dollars down the drain," Henry said.

"So," Paige said, "*is* anything untoward going on in that head of yours?"

"Not sure," Henry said. "Maybe if you unbutton your dress again there will be."

"Oh, no." Paige slipped her hand under the covers, let her fingers walk across his stomach toward his waist. "I have a better idea."

And before long, Henry was being untoward all over the place.

Jane Trott lay on the altar with her eyes closed, still trying to get a feel for the spirit of the church, still trying to communicate. The energy flow kept distracting her, though; it was the most interesting sensation, like someone was lightly running a feather up and down her naked body. Never quite enough to take her over the top; when her pulse would quicken, when her breathing would become rapid and shallow, the sensation would stop until she came away from the approaching orgasm.

The spirit of the church was teasing her.

Despite the distracting attentions of the feather, she kept exploring, chasing the constant, eddying currents of stale, trapped power. It was difficult to get hold of any solid impressions; the vagueness she had sensed about it went all the way to its core. It was really rather strange. In her experience, spirits were usually pathetically eager to communicate. She really couldn't figure out why this one should be different.

"Can't hide from me forever," she murmured. "Show me, tell me, let me in."

She hadn't done all that much psychic investigation; she had checked out places for friends who thought they were living in haunted houses, she had gone into old graveyards to figure out who was buried in unmarked plots or beneath stones whose lettering had weathered away. Little stuff, but not much different from this, really; just a question of scale, of intensity. None of it was like they made out on television, where you went into the haunted house and were immediately assaulted by vengeful ghosts with freakish supernatural powers, or where voices whispered clues at you from aging walls—

What am I bid?

She opened her eyes, looked around. The church was still and silent. No phantoms bobbling through the air, no half-formed spirits trailing ectoplasm in dribbles across the floor. But she had definitely heard something; maybe the place had read her thoughts, and was teasing her with parlor tricks. At least it was a response, an attempt to reach her; it knew she was there, it knew what she was doing. There was no reason for it to keep hiding, then, right? It had revealed itself. It was time for them to communicate.

She pushed and pushed, and the swirling psychic currents suddenly snapped into patterns, into a tableau spread out before her. She had dropped right into the middle of something that had happened here, something that had generated tremendous spiritual energy and been launched into eternity.

And then the feather brought her to the edge again, distracting her. She was dimly aware of the echo from the past, of voices, but it was hard to pay attention to it with the place brushing her between the legs like that. She was there, but only on the periphery.

It sounded like she'd come into the middle of an auction. She heard a huckster's hollow, empty voice echoing from the ages: *What am I bid for this china closet? What am I bid for this wardrobe? What am I bid, what, what, what?* And the same voice answered every time, though she could never make out what it said, exactly. Just mumbles, murmurs.

The energy kept at her. Oh, it was even better than Calvin's tongue.

The huckster: *What am I bid for this land, this farm?*

And a whisper, right in her own ear: *What am I bid for the body of this woman?*

The feather brought her over the brink, and she cried out, twisting and writhing on the altar; but the orgasm went sour suddenly, turned into a spasm, a sickening lurch deep in her stomach. She smelled candle flames, she caught snatches of a prayer to something dark and ancient, she heard the rush of great wings and a monstrous shriek, like the call of some gigantic bird. It hit her like a shockwave and swept her away, pushed her back, back into the present time, the present day, away from the auction and the teasing feather. But as she went she heard one last thing, one last sentence flung into the maelstrom that filled this place. A new voice, a voice she hadn't heard before, reminiscent of the huckster; but rolled into the words was a shrill and spiky tone, an echo of the cry that had sent her flying away.

The voice said, *What am I bid for the life of this girl, this girl, flesh and blood of the one we hate?* And an answering chorus of cries, a frenzy of them, cries like the raucous cawing of a flock of crows.

And a long, high, dying shriek split the vision and tore it to shreds.

Jane opened her eyes. The room seemed fuzzy around the edges and she had to blink it away. Blink, blink, blink. She shook her head, tugged on her handcuffed wrist. Tug, tug, tug. She wasn't going anywhere; she had seen to that herself.

She had been terribly, terribly wrong. This was *nothing* like the Johnson's cabin, *nothing* like the unmarked graves. This place was conscious, and it was wicked, and it was more powerful than she. She'd been rooked, she'd been used; and now, oh, God, now the place's attention was focusing on her, *right on her.*

She heard a fluttering of wings, and something alighted on her knee. It was one of the crows, a great fat one, with puffy black feathers and a beak the color of charcoal. It perched on her and stared at her with eyes like glistening drops of jet-black paint. She thought of the thing she'd heard, the wings, the cry; she shuddered at the thought of the feather that had stroked her. This was one of the children of that *thing.*

She shook her leg, but the crow dug in tighter with its black feet and kept its gaze right on her. She reached forward and swatted it with her hand. It nipped her with its beak, drawing blood. Two crimson drops fell onto the old grey stone altar, landed with a sound like glass globes breaking. She cried out and slapped the crow, backhanded it, knocked it away. It took flight, circled around, landed on her right shin and started pecking at her ankle. She lunged and grabbed it around the head with one hand, and jerked its body around like a New Year's noisemaker, snapping its neck; and she threw the feathery corpse away.

But then another one landed on her shoulder.

And another one landed on her back.

And another one landed on her leg.

And suddenly the entire flock descended on her, broad black wings flapping against the sunlight that streamed in through the shattered roof, sweeping down from the great grey tree that spread its limbs like veins against the sky. She flailed at them, beat them with her hands, swirled her coat at them. But there were more, and more, and more, and she couldn't even see the church through the fluttering mass of their bodies. Their beaks stabbed and nipped and tore, their hoarse, harsh cries jangled the air. She found herself screaming at them, screaming, screaming for them to stop, but they kept coming, piling on her, biting her, smothering her.

Fiery panic took over, seized control of her body, made it jump off the altar. Her handcuffed arm brought her up short; the manacles weren't about to let go, she'd bought them small on purpose. Her attempt to escape left her with one leg dangling off the thick stone, the rest of her flat on it, still covered with crows, slashing and shredding with their black needle beaks. She screamed and twisted and yanked on her arm, again and again and again, feeling the unyielding metal cuff dig into her flesh, feeling blood course down her arm; she didn't stop, even when the tempered steel began to clack against the raw bone of her wrist.

And then one massive crow forced its way through the flock, landed right on her chest. It was flecked with white, a hoary crest, patterns like frost across its wings. Its eyes were pools of ink, vast and bottomless. It cocked its head and looked at her, a cool and appraising look. Intelligent. Aware.

The other crows fell still and watched the white one.

Jane, her body a mass of cuts and punctures, blood seeping from a hundred wounds and oozing from the shredded skin of her wrist, stopped struggling and lay still as the panic burned itself down to ashes, under the appraising gaze of the gigantic crow.

This was it. This was the manifestation. The other crows might be ordinary birds, ordinary creatures under the control of that *thing*; but not this one. This one *was* the thing.

Blood trickled into her left eye, the only one that was still where it belonged. She blinked the crimson smear away, felt her right lid plow through the ruined, oozing jelly that she had once used to see. As if responding to this motion, the avatar spread its wings and stretched itself up and split the air with a raucous cry. Its wings fluttered madly; the wind from its flapping was rank and stale and sour.

It drove its long sharp beak straight into Jane Trott's skull.

The penetration was cold, as if from a freshly-used ice pick. It lanced into her brain, and even though she knew there were no nerve endings up there, nothing to sense what was happening, she could feel something, *something*, oozing out of the crow's mouth and spreading through her cranium. Spreading, congealing, a frosty glaze inside her head. It made her dizzy, made her feel like she was spinning.

She expected to die immediately, but she didn't.

The crow beat its wings, pulled back from her. A few drops of bright red blood dribbled from its beak. Jane immediately felt something cold and viscous ooze out through the hole in her forehead, slowly slide down her face, through the ruins of her right eye, out again. It flowed past her nose, into her mouth. Her tongue flicked at it reflexively. Salty, with a tang of sour iron.

She flopped back against the altar. The twisting stains in the ceiling had come together in the form of a gigantic bird. The crow hopped onto her stomach, worked its claws on her black sweater, made happy little burbling noises from its bloody beak. Her guts churned, felt like they were being pulled up her throat and out her mouth. She smelled blood in the air, tasted it on the back of her tongue. She coughed, and felt bubbles of it rise in her esophagus, and couldn't swallow them down again.

And then some of the stains started to *leave* the ceiling, sagging down from the aged plaster, pulling loose with a sound like sucking mud and hanging there like vines.

The old barn was full of the sound of massive wings flapping. The air rushed this way and that as the stains pulled free. She had awakened the thing, the wretched spirit, that she had heard in the past; and it was using her to climb into the present.

Jane closed her eyes, and thought of Calvin.

6

The speakerphone on Simon Jones's desk chirped, and then his secretary's voice came out of it: "You have a call on line seven."

"It's not the press, is it?" Simon had prepared a statement, which in effect said that he didn't condone Quentin Farmer's personal activities but his development was still important to the local business climate; he had faxed it to the local media organizations, and that was the extent of the contact he wanted with the story.

"It's Karl Castle."

"Oh, okay." Simon picked up the phone and said, "Simon Jones."

"Simon. Karl here."

He sounded like he was shouting into a bucket. "I can hardly hear you," Simon said.

"I'm on a crappy pay phone at a crappy gas station on River Road."

"You're out there. Excellent."

"Yeah, we're out here, but things aren't excellent," Karl yelled. "There's a problem."

God, but Simon was getting sick of problems. "What's going on?"

"Somebody's car is at the church."

Simon suddenly developed a sick feeling in the pit of his stomach, like he'd swallowed a handful of bad gelatin. "What kind of car?" he asked.

"Huh?" Karl said.

"What kind of car?" Shouting now, like he was disciplining a child over the phone.

"A red Jeep."

Christ. Jane Trott's car. She had probably found some dark corner to affix herself to. Maybe she had climbed into the rafters, the little monkey. He should've posted a police car outside the place. He should call them now and send them to drag her to the pokey. But no, he thought; the media monitored police radio, they would hear about it. God, what a zoo that would be. *Councilwoman chained to condemned building; film right now!*

"What should we do?" Karl hollered.

"Sit tight," Simon said. "I'll be there in a few minutes."

"Fine by me," Karl said. "You're paying us by the hour." He hung up.

Simon grabbed his coat and was out the door.

Fifteen minutes later he was parking in the lot of the old church. To start the demolition, Karl had brought out a bulldozer and a backhoe; both were sitting idle in the high grass off to the left, between the lot and the trees. The flatbed that had brought them was parked on the side of the road, back at the beginning of the driveway.

As Simon got out of his car, Karl Castle approached. He was wearing black pants and a dress shirt and a tie—clip-on, Simon thought—as if he had stopped by for a little demolition on his way to the office. "Hiya, Mayor," Karl said. "How's it hanging at City Hall?"

"I don't remember agreeing to pay you an hourly rate," Simon said.

"You don't?" Karl scratched his beard. "That's funny. I'm sure you did. Well, we can settle it while you're here."

"I'm not giving you any more money," Simon said. "I'm already way over budget on this thing."

Karl laughed. "You don't even *have* a budget on this."

"Yes I do. I'll send a copy to your office."

"Right," Karl said. "I'll be waiting for it."

"You do that." Simon eyed the church. "So did you find anyone inside?"

Karl gave him a blank look, and said: "We didn't look."

"What?"

"We didn't look. We're not getting paid to poke around a dangerous ruin. We're getting paid to knock one down. Anything going on inside the place is your problem, not ours." Karl folded his arms, as if daring Simon to tell him differently.

The longer this went on, the more Simon was reminded of why he didn't like doing business with Kastle Konstruction.

He turned away from Karl and walked to the front door of the church. A rank, musty smell wafted from it, the odor of damp and decay and neglect, awakening again after having been frozen down all winter. He just didn't get why Jane Trott was so anxious to save the place. Psychic energy, spiritual backlash. Hokum-pokum. The place was deader than a nightclub at six o'clock on a Monday.

He glanced back. Karl and his helpers were gathered around the bulldozer, smoking cigarettes and laughing about something. Yeah, he thought, no need to help the mayor search the rotten old church for the deranged councilwoman or anything.

He went inside. The floor stuck to his shoes. Old paint of indeterminate color clung to the boards in patches, like remnants of skin flaking off an old skeleton.

Simon grimaced. That wasn't the sort of image he needed to think about.

He stopped only a few paces in, looked around. He couldn't see anyone. "Jane!" he shouted. His voice echoed throughout the church. There was a momentary silence, a startled hush; and then he heard a great thrashing of wings, and saw a cloud of crows rise from some distant point in the cavernous building, black fluttering shapes pulling themselves up through the hole in the roof to settle in the tree that grew from the floor. They cawed quietly to each other, as if they were having a conversation about him.

"Jane, it's Simon!" He looked around at the mildewed walls, the sagging floor of the loft that bowed down overhead. Ahead of him the main section of the church was vast and dim, pierced by shafts of light that found their way through the twisting branches to shine weirdly on the vacant rows of rotting benches.

He really didn't want to have to search the place. Karl was right: it was a ruin, and it was dangerous. Jane Trott *deserved* to have it fall on her. He went into the main part of the building and stopped behind the row of benches on the right. He sniffed the air, detecting traces of a faint and unpleasant coppery smell. The crows burped and chattered rhythmically; it seemed like they were trying to speak. He took a few steps farther in, stopped. He could see up into the tree, where the birds had gone; except there weren't any crows there. The gnarled limbs were barren and vacant.

Simon rubbed the back of his neck, which was starting to get a nasty, itchy, prickly feeling to it; his ears seemed to be plugging up on him, his sinuses seemed to be slowly filling. The calls of the invisible birds resonated in his ears, began to sound like a chant: *Selden Selden Selden Selden.*

Selden? That was ridiculous. Crows didn't say *Selden.*

He shook his head, swallowed, trying to clear the pressure in his head; but it increased instead. The floor seemed to be tilting beneath his feet, tilting and spinning. The coppery scent had grown into a miasmic stench.

He had to get out of here.

He stumbled toward the entrance, or thought he did; but he ran up against the trunk of the tree instead, the rough, cool bark scraping his hands and face. He clung to it for a moment, long enough to feel the wood begin to ripple under his fingers, shiver and convulse like it was getting ready to split open and unleash a torrent of squirming insects. The bark turned gummy in his hands, his fingers dug into it; the wood seemed to be turning into a column of rotten pink flesh, bloody and rancid. His cheek stuck to it when he pulled his face away. Made his stomach churn; made him want to vomit up everything he had eaten, ever.

Selden Selden Selden.

He raised his head, sighted up along the pillar of meat, and saw through the hole in the roof a winged shadow looming over the church, like a great, black bird; and he knew, somehow, that all this was going on inside his head, and was coming from that shadow.

Then Karl Castle's voice boomed from behind him. "Hey, Mr. Mayor!"

And just like that, it all went away: the shadow, the pressure, the chant. Simon found himself up against the tree—and that was all it was, a tree—hugging it, clinging to the bark with his fingers. He pushed himself away from it, looked back toward the entrance. Karl was a silhouette against the square of light.

Thank God. Thank God.

Karl said: "What're you doing to that tree?"

"I tripped," Simon said. He was drenched in sweat beneath his clothes, icy cold inside his jacket. His knuckles hurt; he looked at them and they were bleeding where he had scraped them on the bark.

"You were hanging onto it for a good five minutes," Karl called. "You hurt yourself?" Although he didn't sound overly concerned, Simon thought, he at least had the courtesy to ask; but then he added: "Or did you find a knothole?"

Simon said: "Are you going to help find Jane, or are you going to stand there heckling?"

"Actually, if something doesn't happen soon, I'm going to head out."

"Thanks so much. Just hang on a little longer, okay?" He leaned up against the tree—sideways, so as not to give Karl any ideas—and gave his temples a quick massage and waited for any lingering effects of his attack of the willies to abate. His arms and legs felt wobbly, his head hurt a little bit, but other than that he felt better in a few minutes.

The metallic stench still hung in the air; not as strong as it had been during his delusional episode, but quite noticeable. He moved away from the tree, climbed partway up the heap of debris, until he could see the platform beyond.

"Oh my God," he said.

From behind him, Karl said: "What?"

Simon didn't answer. He stared at the splash of color in the midst of the aging whitewash and the earthy tones of wood and rot and mold; a mass of crimson stretched out on a pallet of stone, a wad of gore, a human-sized blood clot. Something that may have been an arm stretched out toward the middle of the tablet, a silver link glistening between it and the dark ring in the center of the stone.

A handcuff.

"What'd you find?" Karl said, sounding interested in spite of himself.

Simon still didn't answer. He thought of the crows he had startled when he had called Jane's name.

And this time, he did throw up.

Nick Garson didn't know what he was going to do.

He knew what he *should* do: go home, face Lois, start looking for a new job. But instead of performing those completely appropriate activities, he was driving aimlessly around Selden Falls, making lefts and rights onto streets that went God knew where, trying to think of how he could make Quentin Farmer talk to him. That was all it would take. If he could just make the little freak sit down and *listen*, he could get his job back. It wouldn't be so hard. It wouldn't take much convincing.

But Nelson ... how was he going to get through Nelson? That was the hard part.

After a while, he noticed that he had gotten into sort of a seedy area. Many of the houses were boarded up, many were burned out shells, all were decrepit; and there were lots of wide, empty lots where tall grass—flattened and yellowed from winter snow—grew unchecked around piles of rubble and debris, heaps of masonry and timber and roofing. From the condition of the inner city, he would've thought he was in a town much larger than Selden Falls.

By now, he was totally lost. Hoping to make his way back to less unfamiliar territory, he began following graffiti-covered signs for the Thruway. Hell, maybe when he got there he would just hop on it and drive back to Buffalo, like he should have done hours ago. Except that along the way, he passed a little store with a smashed newspaper vending box on its front step and windows that were barred on the inside, and a big sign in the middle of the window said that everything was on sale, and a smaller sign in the bottom right-hand corner of the window said, in neat black lettering, *GUNS*.

Nick turned around in an abandoned gas station up the street, drove back to the shop, and pulled over to the side of the road. He got out and headed into the little store; he came out again ten minutes later, followed the directions the shopkeeper had given him, and found the automatic teller machine that he had just been told about. It was inside a small, seedy grocery store, and the owner gave him all kinds of evil looks as he took money out of the machine. Nick considered buying something, just to placate the little man, but decided the owner could fuck off, because when was the last time anyone had ever done anything to placate *him*?

He returned to the gun shop with a hefty wad of cash, and came out a half-hour later with his new .38 safely tucked away under his coat. He hadn't bought any ammunition for it, even though the shopkeeper had assured him that any round he chose would blow nice big holes in whatever he was aiming at. He really had no desire to fire the thing. He had selected it because it was the biggest, scariest-looking gun the man had, not because he intended to shoot it.

He was just going to point it at Quentin Farmer's face until they were done talking.

Simon Jones leaned against the hood of his car and watched the paramedics wheel Jane Trott's body out of the old church. They had her under a bloodstained sheet so the observers—who now consisted, in addition to himself and Karl Castle's crew, of photographers from the local paper and a film team from Channel Six, not live this time, thank God—couldn't see the damage to the corpse.

But *he* had seen it, hadn't he? Right up close, he had seen it. They could hide her under a sheet, but he still knew what she looked like: skin and meat flayed right down to the bone, muscles and gristly bits left strung out where the crows hadn't finished ripping them loose.

Just thinking about it was making his stomach heave again.

"You all right, Mr. Jones?" the cop asked.

"Yeah," he said, drawing and holding a deep breath. "Yeah. Sorry." The police officer—Grady-something, or something-Grady; Simon was having an awful time with names lately—was interviewing him about the circumstances of finding Jane's body. To his relief, this had so far kept the reporters away from him. He didn't want to talk to the press just yet. He could just imagine how quickly they would stray from the topic of Jane Trott's sad demise to the matter of Quentin Farmer's apparent inability to keep his pants zipped.

"You were saying that Mrs. Trott didn't want this building demolished," Grady said.

"That's right," Simon said, watching the paramedics navigate the transition from the front hall of the church to the sunken step out in front. "She kept saying it was loaded with psychic energy and needed to be purged. I was expecting her to try something like this, but ... I didn't think we'd have to remove her with a spatula, for God's sake." After the words were out he realized how flip he sounded and, with a nervous glance at the reporters, added: "Please don't quote me on that."

"Sure," the cop said.

They had gotten the stretcher out of the church; now it was clacking along the tilted flagstone. The only sound came from the wheels, squeaking and clicking. Simon eyed the paramedics; a couple of them had also been in the group that came for Henry the day before, and he was pretty sure one of them was the guy who had picked up the squashed crow. He was scowling and shaking his head like he was being buzzed by a mosquito. Simon wondered if that was what he himself had been doing when he'd had that attack in the church. Must be some kind of fumes in there, he thought.

Yeah, that was it. Fumes. Fumes and stress.

The stretcher hit the lip of grass where the sunken patio ended, and Simon suffered a flash of déjà vu from the day before, a sudden foreknowledge that the stretcher was going to tip over. He watched in awful anticipation as its front wheels dug into the soft earth. The guy who had picked up the dead crow just kept pushing, like he didn't even notice they weren't moving anymore. The stretcher turned sideways; the others tried to right it, but the one in back didn't stop pushing, and suddenly the gurney half-jumped into the air like it was on a spring, tipped over and spilled Jane Trott's bloodied body from beneath the sheet, onto the cold, soggy ground.

Someone gasped. One of Karl Castle's men made a gagging sound and turned away. Grady said: "Jesus." Simon was silent; he couldn't help but stare at his erstwhile nemesis. She had been reduced to a ragged, pockmarked thing, her flesh poked and torn and shredded, the one remaining eye staring bloodily at the sky from a socket whose lids had been torn off. A neat round hole in her forehead oozed a glistening stream down her face.

The newspaper photographer's camera clicked furiously; the cameraman from Channel Six started forward and then stopped like he had reached the end of a leash. Neither organization would dare use these pictures; the people of Selden Falls wouldn't stand for such an apparition staring at them from their television sets or their morning papers. It was just hideous, morbid curiosity that prompted the reporters to—

Jane Trott's left eye tracked slowly in its socket and looked at Simon.

Jesus God.

She was *looking* at him.

The glare of that one, glassy eye encased him in a block of ice; he couldn't move, he couldn't breathe, he was frozen in her accusing stare. *You did this to me*, the gaze said. *You set all this in motion. You. You.*

"You look pale, Mr. Jones," the cop said. "You need to sit down?"

It was all he could do to shake his head as the paramedics, looking sheepish, righted the stretcher and put the body back on it. Their latex gloves were smeared with blood. They got the sheet back in place and, moving more deliberately this time, successfully navigated the stretcher to the back of the ambulance.

"She's cut up pretty badly," Grady observed. Simon didn't argue. He was suddenly consumed with a desire to be the hell away from this place, this dank, dark, derelict clapboard heap, away from its rotten walls and its *psychic energy* and its *aura* and whatever the hell else Jane thought was here.

She couldn't have looked at him. She *couldn't* have. She was stone dead, nobody could survive with injuries like that. And anyway, it wasn't his fault. *She* was the one who gone all nuts over this place, had handcuffed herself to the altar. If she had just let him knock the place down like he wanted, none of this would've happened.

Her fault. Not his.

"I guess that about does it," Grady said. "I'll be in touch." He headed for the ambulance. Simon glanced at his car, but before he even took a step toward it the reporters descended on him like scavengers moving in on an abandoned carcass. Noah Thompson from the paper, unencumbered by a cameraman, got to him first, although Channel Six was right behind him. Noah was armed with a little notebook and half a dozen pens and the first thing out of his mouth was, "Mayor Jones, how does this latest incident affect the timetable for Quentin Farmer's project?"

"Well, I don't think it does," Simon said, edging toward his vehicle. Channel Six, with an adroit assessment of his trajectory, cut him off; the cameraman began setting up a tripod right in front of the driver's side door of his car. "The project will go ahead regardless of delays in the demolition. Mr. Farmer isn't going to hold up a million-dollar development over something like this."

"Mayor Jones." It was Fred Humble, a senior Channel Six reporter, stepping on Noah's journalistic toes. "How do you answer charges that your administration has been coddling Mr. Farmer?"

"Yes, how do you respond to that, Mayor Jones?" Noah said, shooting Fred a poisonous look.

"I hardly think *coddling* is the proper term for my efforts to obtain business, development, and employment opportunities for the people of the Selden Falls area," Simon said. Yeah, that sounded good. He was definitely performing better this time than when they had surprised him the other day. Maybe it was because of his rampant desire to get out of here. "It's what I was elected to do."

"Mayor Jones, I'd like you to listen to something," Fred said. He produced a small tape recorder from his jacket pocket.

"So would I, Mayor Jones," Noah said, pulling a considerably larger tape deck from the brown leather bag he had slung over his shoulder.

They were tag-teaming him like a couple of wrestlers, Simon thought. Next they'd pull out gaudy spandex costumes and start putting him in headlocks and half-nelsons. Before either of them could start playing their tapes, though, the ambulance siren whooped into life and it rolled away. Simon took advantage of the distraction to edge a little closer to his car.

After the siren had retreated into the distance, Fred hit a button on his miniature tape recorder and Noah hit a button on his larger one. In stereo, Simon heard a voice that he immediately recognized as Paul Shockton's, and he thought: Oh, shit.

Shockton was saying, "Look. Bottom line. Simon is leaning on me very heavily to make sure you don't cross paths with Quentin Farmer ever again. There are not many ways I can do that and make it stick. I can fire you. I can suspend you. I can—don't think I can't find grounds, because I can. Even if I have to manufacture them. But—"

As if they shared the same mind, the two reporters turned off their tape decks. They weren't even pretending not to be looking daggers at each other anymore. Quite clearly each had thought they had the only copy of that tape.

Simon said, "I have no comment."

Noah said: "Is it true you were leaning on Mr. Shockton?"

Fred said: "Has Mr. Farmer contributed to your re-election campaign?"

Noah glared at Fred, then said, "Have you accepted any money at all from Mr. Farmer for any purpose whatsoever?"

Fred, unruffled, said, "We're waiting, Mayor Jones."

Simon thought: To hell with this. "Excuse me," he said. He circled his car and got in through the passenger side and slid across to the driver's seat. Then he rolled down the window and said, "I categorically deny these outlandish charges. Tell you what, though. The two of you work out between yourselves the most ridiculous question you want to ask me, and send it to my office so I can issue an official *no comment*. Okay? Terrific. Bye."

And the reporters stared at him as he rolled up the window, threw the car into gear, and drove away.

When Calvin Trott had awakened to find Jane gone, the first thing he had done was open the gaudy box in which she kept her civil disobedience props. He immediately noted the absence of the handcuffs, and decided she had gone and attached herself to the old church. He wasn't surprised. There was no note; that didn't surprise him either. She always expected him to figure out what she was doing, and he usually did. Didn't need to be psychic for that.

She had left the key to the manacles behind this time; the last time she had tried something like this—when she wanted to stop the state from digging up some old graves to make way for a bypass—the cops had searched her, found the key, unlocked her cuffs, and carried her away. Not this time. He took the key and put it in his wallet, just in case he needed to let her out later.

He wished she had left this one alone, he really did; he didn't like that old place, not one bit. But as Jane had said, she was the psychic, and he was the skeptic. If she thought the place was safe and needed to be protected, well, nothing he could say or do would convince her otherwise. He might be able to forcibly drag her out, but he would never hear the end of it, ever.

So he had gone about his morning routine: shower and shave and eat and dress. Normal stuff, nothing dramatic or crusading about any of it. He had left for work—he taught shop at the high school—and hadn't given the matter of his wife's activism much more thought, beyond a vague notion that he would stop by the old church after he got out and see if she needed anything, like bail money.

But then the principal, Lance Dobbs, showed up in the middle of sixth period, while the kids were busy making lamps out of bits of sheet metal. Lance took Calvin into the corner, behind the drill press, and said: "The police just called."

Lance seemed fidgety, nervous. Calvin wondered if Jane had gotten herself arrested again. He said: "About?"

"About your wife."

Yep. Arrested. "She need me to come bail her out?" he asked.

"Well, no," Lance said, clearly wishing he were somewhere else. Yelling at a student maybe. "She's, ah … there's been an accident."

Calvin felt a chill in the small of his back. That place. That place had done something to her. "She all right?" he asked; knowing she wasn't.

"Well, ah, the thing is, she's …" Lance trailed off. Then he said: "I shouldn't be the one to tell you this."

"You're here," Calvin said. "Talk."

"Well, they found her in … in an old building by the canal. She's, ah … she's dead."

"Dead?"

"I'm afraid so."

Calvin stared at Lance. Lance fidgeted. "I'm sorry," he said. "They want you to identify the body. They've got her down at the coroner's office. They're going to do an autopsy."

"What happened to her?"

"I really can't—"

Lance broke off as Calvin grabbed the front of his shirt and twisted it in his fist. "What happened to her?" he said. His voice was flat and very, very calm.

After the briefest flicker of hesitation, Lance said: "They said something about crows—" Calvin let go of him and he stopped talking immediately, took a step back, out of easy grabbing reach. He smoothed his shirt and looked over Calvin's shoulder, toward the kids, worried about losing face in front of them. Calvin didn't care if they were watching. Calvin didn't care if they were dismembering each other with hacksaws.

"How do I get to the coroner's office?" Calvin asked.

Lance pulled a crumpled piece of paper out of his coat and handed it to him. It had directions scrawled on it in a sloppy hand. Lance usually had neat—punctiliously neat—handwriting. It must have rattled him, taking the call from the police about Jane. Calvin reached out to the principal, who shied away; Calvin patted him on the shoulder and said, "Sorry. Cover for me?"

"Sure, Calvin," Lance said. "Sure. I'll find somebody."

Calvin went out the back way, so he wouldn't have to go past his class.

Jasper Shoemaker Junior walked home from school every day, and every day he passed right by the firehouse. He had never noticed the sign on the door that said *Library* because he had never had a reason to go there before.

The glass door opened onto a narrow stairwell that smelled like paper. He climbed the steps and entered a dimly-lit realm of shelves and musty spines, racks of tattered paperbacks, sheafs of magazines and newspapers. A dusty old computer whirred noisily in the corner. Right next to the door was an old L-shaped desk, behind which a vaguely familiar kid from school—Eddie the Geek, Jasper thought, as distant memories of elementary-school taunts surfaced in response to the guy's face—sat reading a book with a picture of spaceships on the cover. He glanced up uninterestedly as Jasper entered, went back to the book, looked up again. "What're *you* doing here?" he said.

"What, I can't use the library?"

Eddie put the book face-down on the counter, cover spread. "Do you know *how* to use a library?" he asked.

It occurred to Jasper that he did not, in fact, know what resources were available at the library. He vaguely recalled them talking about it at school, but he hadn't exactly paid close attention; he remembered wondering why he had to waste so many hours a day learning useless things, like how to use a library. But Eddie was smirking at him, so he said: "Of course I fucking know." Then he turned his back on the counter and marched to the magazines.

Pretty shabby collection, just like a dozen or so, and only one copy of each, too. Still, there were several that seemed to be about business. He took a couple of them down and started looking at the contents sections for anything about Quentin Farmer.

From behind him, Eddie said: "Lift up the shelves, there's more magazines underneath."

"I was just starting with the new ones," Jasper said after a moment.

"Uh-huh." There was a pause, and then Jasper heard Eddie's book swish across the counter as he picked it up again. So he was startled when Eddie materialized next to him and said, "What're you after?"

Jasper looked up. "Huh?"

"What're you looking for?"

"Oh … uh, stuff about Quentin Farmer."

"The businessman? You doing a report on him?"

That would do. "Yeah," Jasper said.

"Okay. Come with me." Eddie led him to the computer in the corner and told him to sit down, which he did. The screen was dark, except for the words *press any key*, which were scooting around in changing shades of amber. Jasper looked at the monitor for a moment, then tapped the space bar. A menu popped up. "Select the articles CD," Eddie said.

Jasper complied, then said: "This thing doesn't have a CD."

"It's connected to a network," Eddie said. "Okay, search by subject."

Jasper tabbed to the recommended selection and pressed the enter key.

"Type the subject."

He typed in *Quentin Farmer*. Eddie the Geek reached over and punched a button, and a box popped up that said *working*. There was a pause, and then several article titles appeared on the screen. Eddie looked them over and, pointing with his finger for illustration, said: "We have that one, that one, and that one. The last two are on microfiche."

Jasper looked at Eddie and said: "Micro-what?"

So Eddie took him to the microfiche reader, showed him how to find the magazines and how to use the machine. He even supplied a couple of dimes so Jasper could print out the articles. By the time Eddie returned to his desk, Jasper had concluded that sometimes it was good to have a geek available.

Printouts in hand, he returned to the magazines and located the one with the article he wanted. Eddie's nose was buried in the book again, so Jasper surreptitiously folded up the magazine and tucked it into his jacket; but as he was heading out the door Eddie said, "You can check that out instead of stealing it."

"I can? I mean—uh, stealing what?"

"Just get a library card and the magazine is yours for two weeks."

"How do I get a library card?"

Eddie slid a form over. "Fill this out."

It wasn't a very big form. Just his name, address, phone number, and age. Jasper looked it over, then scribbled it in and handed it back to Eddie, who typed all the information into another computer. This one was hidden beneath the desk. A few seconds later a small printer attached to the computer spat out a label. Eddie fitted the label into a plastic sheath, slid the sheath into some kind of metal device, and pulled a lever; this transformed the label into a laminated card. It had a barcode on it, which Eddie scanned with a gun, like at the supermarket. Then he held out his hand.

"What?" Jasper said.

"Magazine."

"Oh." He took the magazine out of his jacket and handed it to Eddie. Eddie opened the back cover and scanned the barcode sticker on it, then handed it back along with the card.

"Two weeks," he said.

"Thanks." Jasper cocked his head. "You know a lot about computers?"

"Yep," Eddie said immodestly.

"Can you make other kinds of cards with that thing?"

"I'm not making you a fake driver's license, if that's where you're going," Eddie said. He had picked up the book again and didn't look up from it as he spoke.

He thought he was *so* smart, didn't he? "That's not what I was going to say," Jasper Junior lied. Then, in reckless irritation, he added: "I was going to invite you in on a deal that could make you a lot of money, but if that's your attitude, just forget it."

"Yeah," Eddie said absently, "sure. I want to rely on Jasper Shoemaker for my financial well-being. Let me guess, you're starting a chain letter, right?"

Geek.

Magazine articles in hand, Jasper stomped down the paper-scented stairs and went across the street. Oscar was behind the counter of the hardware store, as usual. Jasper confiscated the key to Oscar's apartment and went upstairs to study the articles in the laundry-scented comfort of the tiny living room. The laptop was sitting on the scuffed coffee table; he booted it up and left it running while he skimmed the stories about Quentin Farmer.

Before long, Jasper knew all sorts of useless information about Farmer: he was originally from Idaho; he wasn't married; he lived in a suburb of Buffalo in a house called Bluehill. He sounded like a real dork, Jasper thought; but now he had lots of possible passwords. He tried *Idaho, Buffalo,* and *Bluehill*. None of them worked.

Not disheartened, Jasper Junior plunged back into the articles. This time he actually read them. Any word or concept that seemed to be meaningful to Quentin Farmer went into the password field of the security program; all of them were rejected.

Son of a bitch. This always worked in the movies.

Of the three articles, the one in the magazine he had checked out seemed to go into the most personal detail. It was also the most recent one, so apparently Farmer was getting more well-known, or at least he had a better press agent than he used to. Jasper concentrated on that one; it was called "'Spud' Grows Up", apparently a reference to Farmer's childhood nickname back in Idaho, where he had been raised on, of all things, a potato farm. He read through it again, looking for something he may have missed, like Quentin Farmer saying, *Oh, yeah, and this is the password to my laptop.* Which, damn it all, he never did.

He ended up reading the article three times, giving himself a headache. He hadn't concentrated so hard since he'd found his father's stash of *Penthouse* magazines behind the water heater downstairs. Finally, though, he admitted defeat, and tossed the magazine in the trash; then he remembered it was from the library and debated whether or not to fish it out. He finally did, and that was when he noticed the little sidebar to the article about Farmer. It was right next to an ad for some Caribbean island; the ad featured a bronzed girl in a bikini made of clam shells, which had kind of distracted him from the teensy wedge of text.

Jasper read the sidebar. It didn't tell him anything he didn't already know; it was just a little one-on-one interview between a reporter and Farmer, a variety of softball questions. Stuff like *What's your favorite color?* and *What do you like to watch on television?* None of those answers were the correct password either.

The last question was, *What would you like to say to the kids who used to pick on you?* To which Farmer answered, *I'm not Spud anymore.*

Annoyed, Jasper threw the thing back in the trash. Who gave a shit what Farmer would say to a bunch of hayseeds out in the sticks?

The password prompt glared at him from the laptop's screen, demanding to know why it had been stolen from Spud. He wondered if anyone called Farmer *Spud* anymore. Probably not. Businessmen with lots of money didn't have nicknames like that.

He eyed the computer.

I'm not Spud anymore. Sounded like Farmer had never quite gotten over being picked on as a kid.

Jasper rubbed the tip of his nose, then typed *notspud*.

The laptop made a hollow chirping sound, and let him in.

7

Paige Fontana left the hospital shortly after three. She would have stayed longer, but a flock of orderlies and a nurse had arrived to bundle Henry off to radiology for his X-rays and his CAT scan and anything else the doctors thought might be necessary to keep themselves from getting sued should Henry drop dead in the next few days.

She had to go to Henry's parents' house to pick up Freddie. Along the way she stopped for a hamburger, so she could tell them she had already eaten when they asked her to stay for dinner. The gambit worked, although Florence gave her the usual evil looks and Joe leered at her when his wife wasn't looking and told her if she kept eating that junk food she would lose that cute figure. She had to resist a strong desire to tell him what *he* was on the verge of losing. If only kindergarten ran the whole day, she could send Freddie back to school and then she wouldn't have to deal with this nonsense.

She got home just before four o'clock. The neighborhood was quiet; the working people weren't home yet, the non-working people were about their afternoon business, the kids were doing homework or playing video games or whatever it was they did these days. A few of the older children were playing catch up the street. Henry had already purchased a baseball glove for Freddie, even though Freddie evinced no interest in the sport; Henry figured he would come around eventually.

She pulled into the driveway and looked at her house. The red spray paint was faintly bleeding through her hasty cover job; she would have to give it another coat, and maybe another one after that.

As for the windows, where fragments of graffiti appeared as meaningless crimson slashes, there would be nothing to do but scrape, scrape, scrape.

She and Frederick went into the silent house. Freddie plopped himself down in front of the television and fired up the video game. She thought about sending him into the backyard to play outside, like the big boys—it was one of those rare early March days when the sky was clear, the sun bright, the wind mild instead of vicious—but she decided not to. It was still kind of chilly; and, more importantly, someone might be watching, and decide to snatch him.

That reminded her: after the phone call from the hospital, she had forgotten to check the back of the house. She put the deadbolt on the front door and went into the kitchen and stopped dead right on the threshold, so the swinging door hit her in the backside as it closed.

The back door hung open, dangling crookedly from a broken hinge.

She quite clearly remembered setting the deadbolt; in fact, she could see that it had been ripped out of the wood. The frame was splintered where the post had been sunken into it, and the metal plate was on the floor, twisted all out of shape.

There was something in the sink, a dark, soggy, sinister lump, like a seagull covered in tar. She took a cautious step toward it.

It was a dead crow, looking up at her with glazed black eyes, its sharp beak pointed at her and partially open so she could see the rubbery tongue within. It looked like it had been run over by a car; its fat body was ruptured, stringy innards exploding out of it, wadded up in the basin.

She backed away, hands on her stomach. The hamburger she had eaten seemed to be trying to crawl back up her throat. She bumped into the door with her butt, kept going. Frederick was piloting his little suit-wearing bear through a maze of simple mathematical equations and didn't even look at her as she entered, which was good; she didn't want him to see the expression she felt on her face.

The guy might still be here. He might be hiding somewhere in the house.

They had to get out.

She picked up the portable phone, started dialing the cops. At the same time she edged over to Freddie and said, "We're going to play a little game. We're going to sit in the car."

Her son didn't look up. "That's not a game," he said, and he was an authority.

"It's a game I just made up," she said.

"It's not a game," he insisted.

A voice came on the line and asked her if she could hold. Before Paige could answer, there was a click and music started playing in her ear. With one hand, she reached down and shut off the television. The bear disappeared in mid-jump; he had a surprised expression on his furry face, which she assumed was coincidental. Then she dragged her son out of the house and into the car for another round of their new favorite game, *Waiting on Hold for the Police.*

Notspud. What a lame password. But hey, it got him in, and that was the important thing. Now he could cruise. Jasper dove into the computer head-first to see what he could see.

It didn't take too long for him to be thoroughly bored with the whole thing. No games, just business stuff. Spreadsheets and letters and memos. A database. An electronic card file, from which he got the number to Quentin Farmer's cellular phone. Whee. It all looked like very costly software, but it was colossally dull.

Oscar came in, looking tired. He stopped when he saw Jasper and said: "You still here? It's like eight o'clock, man. Your parents are gonna freak."

"No way." Jasper checked his watch. "Shit!"

"Don't tell them you were here, okay, man? I don't wanna get stopped by the cops again. Cost me two hundred dollars to repair the broken taillight and shit last time."

"Okay, sure," Jasper said. He switched off the laptop and slid it into his school bag.

"You, uh … you taking the computer?"

"Uh-huh."

"Why?"

"I cracked the password."

"Hacker! What is it?"

"Tell you later."

"Aw, come on, man, you said we would share!"

"We will," Jasper said. "We will, I just want to check it out a little more."

"He got anything good on there?"

"I didn't find anything yet. Just business stuff."

"None of them tittie pictures they got on the Internet?"

"The money he has, he gets all the tittie he wants," Jasper said.

"Oh." Oscar looked disappointed. "Well, if you find any, save them for me, okay?"

"Okay, sure. I'll talk to you tomorrow."

"Okay." Oscar stepped out of the way to let him by. It was just as well he was leaving; somebody was doing a massive load of laundry downstairs and they were using the most God-awful detergent he had ever smelled, like lemons soaked in Old Spice.

When he got home, there was a shiny white Channel Six van parked in the driveway. He circled the vehicle, peering through the windows; but he couldn't see into the back where, undoubtedly, the good stuff was. He tried the doors. They were all locked. Oh well. He climbed the stairs to the porch and went into the house and stopped dead and stared.

His father and mother were sitting on the couch, very close together, holding hands. His father was tricked out in a somber grey suit where the jacket and the pants actually matched and, beyond that, appeared to be made of the same fabric. Beneath the jacket he wore a white shirt and one of those Western string ties, the kind Jasper figured you shouldn't wear if you weren't in Houston or on a cattle drive. His mother was wearing a simple print dress and a small necklace and tiny stud earrings; usually her earrings were big enough to gag a cat, and her necklaces and bracelets could be used to tow railway cars. They both had strained, nervous, patently fake expressions, as they stared into the Channel Six camera being pointed right at their faces. The thing had a light on it so bright his parents would probably both be tanned by the time they were done.

Sitting in a chair opposite the sofa was a reporter, not the one his father had caught giving Quentin Farmer a blow job; this one was a brunette, though from what Jasper Junior could see she had a smashing body. As he entered, the reporter was saying, "And what are you going to do now, Mr. Shoemaker?"

A member of the film crew nudged over to Jasper and put his finger to his lips. Jasper was too shocked to make noise anyway.

"Well, I don't rightly know," Jasper Senior said. Jasper Junior had never heard such talk from him before. And when had he developed a southern accent? "I guess it depends on what my boss does. I mean, if he wants to make my life miserable because I do my job, what can I do about it? I can't quit. Being a peace officer is all that I know."

Jasper Junior thought: A *peace* officer?

Noreen gave Jasper Senior a reassuring squeeze on the elbow. Jasper Junior fought the urge to barf into his duffel bag.

"If you could say one thing to Quentin Farmer right now, what would it be?"

Jasper Senior visibly thought about the question. He looked searchingly into his wife's face. Jasper Junior felt himself shriveling up with embarrassment. At last, Jasper Senior looked straight into the camera and said, "The law applies to you too, Mr. Farmer."

The crew member near Jasper Junior said, out of the corner of his mouth, "Your father's a real ham, kid." Jasper just wanted to crawl inside his bag and pull the flap shut behind himself.

The cameraman shut off his scorching light and lowered his lens. The reporter stood up, and so did Jasper Junior's parents. "How'd I do?" Jasper Senior said. "I do a good job?"

"You did fine," the reporter said.

"This'll run tonight?"

"At eleven," the reporter said. "Again in the morning, probably. We need to edit it, of course."

"You think any of the national networks will pick up the story?" Noreen asked.

The reporter cocked her head. "Doubtful," she said. "He's not a national figure. Nobody in Idaho cares about Quentin Farmer."

She hadn't done her homework, Jasper thought; but he wasn't going to be the one to correct her.

"It's a human interest story," Noreen said. "Don't you think?"

The reporter said: "It doesn't matter what I think. I don't run the news departments at any of the networks. You're not going to retire off this incident, folks." She handed her microphone and the attendant equipment to one of her crewmen; the one who had spoken to Jasper had started breaking down the lighting fixtures.

As they cleared the junk away from the doorway leading into the hall, Jasper Junior brushed through, past his parents—who didn't even seem to register his presence—and on to his room at the back of the house. He closed the door, locked it, and took out the computer. He put it on his desk, between a terrarium full of dead plants and possibly a few hermit crabs and a McDonald's bag that still exuded the odor of fries after all these weeks. He opened the laptop and stared at the grey screen.

He couldn't *believe* his father was doing an interview on TV in full undertaker regalia. Jesus. He hoped nobody saw it. *The law applies to you too, Mr. Farmer.* Oh, that was terrific. Mr. Free Doughnuts preaches to businessman; film at eleven.

Humiliated. He was humiliated. He was going to hear about *this* tomorrow at school, he was.

At a knock on his door, Jasper quickly folded up the laptop and stuck it back in his bag. "Who is it?" he called.

"Lauren Wise." The brunette's voice, soft and smooth. "Your father told us how Quentin Farmer accused you of stealing his computer. We wanted to hear your side of the story."

And Jasper thought: Oh, shit.

Nick Garson found his way back to the Holiday Inn and, gun tucked into an inside pocket of his coat, went up to Quentin Farmer's room. He rapped on the door, hard. There was a pause, then the sound of a chain being undone. He couldn't believe it; Farmer was actually opening the door.

He reached into his jacket, touched the butt of the pistol; it was warm from being close to his body. He slithered his fingers over the grip, felt the diamond-etched pattern under his palm, rough and nubby. As the door began to swing inward, he whipped the weapon out and pointed it straight at where Quentin Farmer's head would be.

Except it wasn't Quentin Farmer opening the door. It was a tiny, elderly woman, and she was a good foot shorter than Quentin, so he was aiming well over the top of her puff of curly silver hair.

The old woman gaped at him. Nick dropped his arm and said, "Uh—"

She slammed the door in his face.

Nick stuffed the pistol back into his jacket and ran like mad for the stairwell. He rushed to the ground floor and out through the side door. His car was around front; he raced to it, jumped in, started it up, and roared out of the hotel parking lot in a cloud of dust and leftover winter gravel.

Some distance from the hotel, he pulled to the side of the road to think. Either Quentin Farmer's mother had come to visit, or he had gotten himself a different room, probably in a different hotel. He was always one step ahead, damn him.

Nick still had the phone book he had lifted from the gas station. He drove until he found a gas station with a pay phone, where he repeated the process of calling hotels looking for his former employer. This time, though, nobody would admit to having him there. He must have left instructions that his presence not be given out, Nick thought. The slick bastard was avoiding him. But Nick knew one place where Quentin was bound to turn up eventually: the future site of Canal Plaza.

Unfortunately, he had no idea how to get there from here.

He needed gas anyway, so he filled his tank and then went into the gas station's mini-mart. Figuring he would need food and drink while he camped out waiting for Farmer to show his face, he picked up a six-pack of beer, several bags of chips and pretzels, and a box of doughnuts for breakfast. He schlepped all this to the cash register. The kid behind the counter was wearing an ugly maroon vest and a paper hat that, inverted, would greatly resemble a French-fry boat. He had stringy orange hair and freckles all over, even on his ears, and his name tag said *Ivan*. When Nick arrived at the counter, Ivan looked up from a pilfered copy of one of the dirty magazines available from the rack behind him.

"Hi," Nick said. "Can you help me out?"

The kid looked at him and then, for some reason, punched a button on the cash register. The drawer popped open. "Dig in," he said.

After a moment it dawned on Nick that the clerk thought the store was being robbed. Obviously his concealed handgun was not as concealed as he thought. He said: "I'm not holding you up. I just want directions."

"You do?"

"Yeah."

"Oh." Ivan whacked the drawer with his palm and it banged shut. "Sorry, man. Didn't mean to offend you. Somebody comes in with a heavy-duty piece like that, you just assume, you know?"

"I understand," Nick said. "What I need is directions—"

"That a thirty-eight?"

"What?"

The kid gestured with a bony, freckled hand. "Your gun. A thirty-eight?"

"Yeah," Nick said. He knew this because he had been told it by the guy who had sold it to him.

"Man, a thirty-eight, now that's a *piece*, you know?" the kid said. Then he glanced at the door as it opened, jangling the old cow bell that hung on a piece of fishing line from the hydraulic arm. Nick very deliberately did not look that way. The fewer people who saw him, the better.

"Evening, officer," Ivan said.

Nick's head snapped around, but it wasn't a cop, it was just an old lady in a floor-length black coat and a plastic head wrap to keep the rain off her hairdo, shuffling back to the dairy section of the mini-mart. When Nick looked back, the clerk was giggling into the back of his hand. "Sorry, man. I had to do it."

"Ha ha. Are you going to give me directions or not?"

"Sure, man, sure. Where to?"

"River Road."

"River Road? Oh, that's easy. Just take a right from the lot, a left at the first light, go straight for a few miles, right at the yellow flasher, over the bridge, left just past it and you're on River Road."

The clerk said it all so fast Nick scarcely had time to write it down. He had gotten to the part about the flasher when the old lady arrived with a carton of milk. She paid for her purchase in quarters, then blew a couple of bills on one of the state's scratch-off lottery tickets, which she did not win. "Better luck next time, Granny," the clerk told her. She scowled at him and shuffled out the door.

"She comes in every night," Ivan said. "Some days two, three times. Buys one item and a lottery ticket. Got nothing better to do, I guess."

"Was that right or left at the flasher?"

"Right." The kid eyed him for a few seconds, then said: "So, you ever use it?"

"What?"

"The gun. You ever shoot anybody?"

"No. That was over the bridge, then—"

"You think you ever will?"

"No. Over—"

"Because if you pull a gun on somebody, man, you better be prepared to *use* it!" The kid made a pistol with his hand and blew away a display rack of Hostess cakes over near the coffee machine.

"That the way it works?" Nick said.

"Yep."

"Well, my gun isn't even loaded." Nick looked at his directions. "That's a left after the bridge?"

"It's not *loaded*?" Ivan was incredulous. "You're packing that kind of heat and it's not even *loaded*?"

The door jangled open. Nick inspected the hot dog machine to the right of the counter as the new customer paid for his gasoline. The weenie roaster supported the frankfurters on hot, greasy rollers that were in continuous motion, rotating the hot dogs clockwise as they turned. He idly wondered how far the dogs would have gone if they had actually been in motion instead of just rolling in place. There was some kind of metaphor there, he thought.

The customer left. Nick turned back to the clerk, and discovered that he was staring down the barrel of a handgun that was nearly as big as his own. "Jesus!" he said.

Ivan laughed and lowered the pistol. "See? Never turn your back."

"For God's sake, kid, are you trying to give me a heart attack?"

"I'm twenty-eight," the clerk said after a moment. "I'm not a kid."

Nick would have guessed seventeen. It was the freckles, he thought. "Sorry. It's the paper hat," he lied. "Makes you look younger."

"Yeah. I hate this thing." Ivan took the hat off, stared at it with evident hostility, and plopped it back onto his head. "Look, man, my point is that you can't be carrying that gun around if it's not loaded. I could've plugged you and you could've done jack to stop me."

"What would I do if it was loaded? Whip it out and shoot you first?"

"Sure. Standoff, man." The kid—whoops, Nick thought, the *twenty-eight-year-old gentleman*—looked around quickly, then reached below the counter. There was a sound like fingers rummaging through jelly beans, and then he produced a handful of dull silver bullets, which he plopped onto the counter in front of Nick. "Here. On the house."

Nick stared at the rounds. "You've got to be shitting me."

"Take them," the clerk said. "Really."

"I don't want them."

"Come on, man. Take them." The clerk looked at him with maniacally-focused blue eyes. "You worried about the video? It don't work, man. Hasn't worked in eight months." As if to demonstrate, the kid waved his gun in front of the goggling end of a camera lens sticking out from between a wall-mounted film display and a cigarette rack. Nick hadn't even noticed it before.

"Really, I don't want—"

Ivan turned and pointed his gun at Nick again. "Take them or I'll blow your fucking head off," he said.

Nick swept the bullets into his hand and dumped them into the side pocket of his jacket. They seemed very heavy against his side. The clerk lowered his weapon, then slid it under the counter. "See? A loaded gun is very persuasive."

"I see that." Lunatic, Nick thought.

"Guys like us, we got to stick together."

"Yeah," Nick said. "Well, uh, thanks." He headed for the door.

"Left," the clerk called.

"What?"

"After the bridge. It's a left."

"Oh." Nick had forgotten he had asked that question. "Thanks."

"Don't mention it," Ivan said.

"Just speak in your normal tone of voice," Lauren Wise said. She had a great voice, and she smelled like lilacs, and she had an impressive swell of chest under her demure reporter's jacket. Jasper Shoemaker Junior was half in love with her already.

They had dressed him up in a button-down shirt and a pair of dress pants he didn't remember owning. The pants didn't fit all that well. They weren't too small, like you would expect old clothes to be; they were too big. This led him to suspect that his parents had bought them very recently and planted them in his room.

He shifted uneasily on the sofa. The button-down shirt was stiff and scratchy. He kept trying to fold his legs, and Lauren kept unfolding them. He was doing this deliberately, because he liked it when she touched him. One good thing about the pants being too big: they hid his erection quite nicely.

"Just relax," Lauren said, touching his knee for the third time. "Don't fold your legs."

"Sorry," he said, unfolding them.

They hadn't bothered to set up all the lighting equipment again. In fact, they had bundled most of it away into the van. All that remained was Lauren with her microphone and her satchel, and the cameraman with his klieg light. At a gesture from Lauren he switched this device on, and Jasper Junior was blinded by a glare that seemed at least ten times brighter than the midday sun. He raised his arm in front of his face. Lauren reached out and lowered it. "Don't look into the light," she said. "Look at me."

He looked at her.

"Now, Jasper, when I talked to your father he told me that Quentin Farmer accused you of being involved in the theft of his laptop computer. How does that make you feel?"

"Uh, well, you know, I don't think, uh, that Mr. Farmer should go around making accusations he can't prove." Yeah, that sounded good. He glanced at his parents. They were standing near the cameraman, watching him. They weren't holding hands anymore, or even touching. That was more like what he was used to.

"You didn't take Mr. Farmer's laptop, Jasper?"

"Nope." The absolute truth. *Oscar* had taken the laptop.

Lauren Wise asked a few more loaded questions. By the time they wrapped up, Jasper Junior himself was almost convinced that he was really just an innocent bystander in this whole thing, unjustly accused by nasty rich Quentin Farmer. Then Lauren leaned forward and put her small, manicured hand on Jasper's shoulder and drowned him in the scent of lilacs. "Thanks a lot," she said. She smiled. Her teeth were all exactly the same size and white as fresh underwear.

"No problem," Jasper said. At least, that was what he *tried* to say; what actually came out was a choked squeak. Lauren laughed softly and stood up and began thanking Jasper Senior for his family's time. Jasper Junior, feeling a sudden need, hurried back to his room. He wanted to satisfy his urge before the image of Lauren Wise faded.

It only took him a few minutes to achieve his goal and then, feeling relaxed and rather contented, he sat down in front of the laptop. He turned it on and typed in Quentin's password and resumed his investigation of the system. This time, though, he opened up the icon for the hard drive and went through it folder by folder. What he found was mostly more of the same.

Except in a folder called *Downloads*. There he discovered a series of files with cryptic names, like *12YOB.GIF* and *13YOGX2.JPG*. He opened *13YOGX2.JPG*, and was launched into some kind of graphics application, with an hourglass in the middle of a blank screen. Momentarily, a picture appeared. It was quite high-resolution, good as a photograph; somebody had used a heavy-duty scanner to digitize it. Somebody, apparently, with an unhealthy interest in prepubescent girls.

Jasper Junior stared at the picture, uncertain whether to be appalled or aroused. Since he was feeling so relaxed, it didn't take long for him to decide he was appalled. He closed the picture. Figuring anything with a *YOB* in it would involve boys, he went through and checked all the *YOG*s. The girls involved in the pictures seemed to range in age from around ten up to maybe fifteen; at least, that was the implication of the filenames. The pictures mostly involved the girls dressed up as cheerleaders or businesswomen or construction workers or whatever, and they were generally quite disheveled and not really wearing the clothes they were wearing. Two or three involved either other girls, other boys, or adults.

Just to check, he opened one of the *YOB* files. Sure enough, it was the same deal, except with a boy. He decided he didn't need to look at any of the other *YOB*s.

He quit from the directory, and looked at the little black-shelled hunk of technology, and thought that what he had just discovered was potentially worth much more than the computer itself.

Somebody knocked on his door. Jasper quickly buried the laptop under papers and the McDonald's bag. "Just a minute," he called, sliding into an old pair of sweats that were lying in a heap under the desk. When he opened the door, his father was standing there, still in the undertaker's suit he'd worn for the interview. "You did a good job, son," he said. Still talking like there was a camera on him, Jasper Junior thought. "Your mother saved you some supper. Come on out and eat."

Jasper's efforts to demur met with no success, as did his suggestions that the elder Shoemaker just head back and he'd be along in a minute, so he finally accompanied his father out to the kitchen. His father walked with his arm around Jasper Junior's shoulders, which kind of freaked him out; physical contact usually amounted to a smack in the head, and he didn't know quite what to make of this sudden collegiality.

His mother was in the kitchen, sitting at the table; Jasper Senior plopped down next to her, and they both watched him eat and attempted to make small talk about school, about local events, about all kinds of stuff. Gradually the discussion—it wasn't really much of a conversation, Jasper Junior mostly just listened and nodded—turned to Jasper's tendency to land in the principal's office at least once or twice a month. His father explained that it would it be a really good idea if he kept his nose clean until school let out. It would be bad for their image if the son who had been so unjustly accused by Quentin Farmer acted like a juvenile delinquent in the classroom.

Jasper Junior, smelling a lawsuit in the air, agreed.

He was released back to his room after cleaning up his plate. He locked the door behind him and, hoping for no more interruptions, swept the coverings away from the laptop. The screen had gone dark. He pressed the space bar, but nothing happened. Then he noticed an amber LED flashing dimly above the thing's keyboard. It was right under a picture of a battery with an X through it.

And it finally occurred to Jasper that when Oscar had snatched the laptop, he had left its power cord sitting in Quentin Farmer's satchel.

Paige and Freddie spent the better part of an hour sitting in the car, doors all locked, engine running. Paige was tense and nervous, ready to put the car into reverse and roar backwards out of the driveway the instant the front door burst open and a maniac came charging out; Freddie was bored and fidgety and wanted to know why he couldn't go inside and play video games while *she* sat in the car. Finally, Paige told him that someone had left them a bird, and the police had to come and take it away. This engaged his interest, and he started speculating about why somebody might do such a thing. As she neglected to mention that the bird was dead, most of his explanations involved a friendly neighbor who thought they needed a pet.

At last, a black and white police car pulled onto the lawn. Paige got out, leaving Freddie in the car, as the officer came up the drive. He introduced himself as Alex Harrigan. Paige filled him in on what had happened; once she had gotten through the gruesome details, she freed Freddie from captivity, and the two of them followed Alex into the house.

The officer started his inspection in the kitchen. First he examined the back door, closing it and opening it several times. The broken hinge on top made it difficult to shut properly. Then he prodded the twisted deadbolt plate with his toe and said, "You might as well tape your door shut, Mrs. Fontana. Cheap metal plus cheap wood equals no protection at all."

"I kept telling Henry that," she said. "He never quite got around to putting in a better one." Eden Avenue was not exactly a high-crime neighborhood, so the issue had never been all that pressing; and since their new house in the hills was nearing completion, there hadn't seemed much point anymore. And now … well, close the barn door, she thought; the horse escaped!

"Maybe this'll motivate him," Alex said.

"Maybe," she said.

The policeman proceeded to the sink, inspecting the dead crow. He wrinkled up his face and said: "Yuck."

"I agree."

"What?" Freddie said.

"I'll explain later," she told him.

Alex said, "I hope you have some heavy-duty disinfectant."

"Tell me about it. Are you going to take the crow with you?"

"Yeah. I just have to get the rubber gloves and a bag out of my car. I'm sure as hell not touching that thing with my bare hands."

He went to the door in the corner, looked at Paige quizzically. "Basement," she said. He nodded, opened the door, and went into the cellar. Paige leaned against the counter and listened to the stairs creak as he descended, then listened to the silence.

Freddie said: "Mommy, why did somebody leave us a crow?"

"I don't know," she said.

"Why do we have to give it to the police? Can't we keep it?"

"No, honey, we can't keep it." He hadn't figured out that the crow was dead; he was too short to see into the sink, which helped keep him in the dark.

"Oh." Pause. "Can we get a bird?"

"Not right now," she said.

The cop came back upstairs. "You got an empty basement," he said.

"We're getting ready to move," she said. "My husband's building us a house up on Cool Road and we put most of our junk there already."

The cop whistled. "Tony," he said. Then he added: "You'd think he'd be able to get you better locks, then."

Paige thought: We found the horse; it's dead, let's beat it!

They went into the living room. Paige flopped onto the couch with Frederick and waited while Harrigan explored the rest of the house; this only consisted of two bedrooms and a bathroom, so it didn't take him very long. When he came back, he took Paige into the corner and told her nothing else seemed to be disturbed, no one seemed to be hiding anywhere. Apparently the intruder had only penetrated into the kitchen. "It's possible you interrupted him when you came home," Harrigan said. "Or leaving a crow in your kitchen sink might have been all he wanted to do."

"Why would someone want to do that?"

"I don't know, Mrs. Fontana. I assume you have no idea who this guy is?"

"No," she said. "No idea, I mean."

Harrigan nodded, and said: "I'll collect the crow and see if we can get anything off of it. Fibers, hairs, stuff like that." He paused, then said: "It's probably just neighborhood kids picking on you. This is typical young thug behavior."

"I hope that's all it is," she said.

Harrigan went out to his car and came back with a big, thick plastic pouch and a pair of dense rubber gloves. Paige accompanied him into the kitchen and watched as the crow went into the sack like a chicken being prepared for the freezer. Officer Harrigan spun the bag and closed up the neck with a twist-tie he bummed from Paige. Then he said, "Well, that's about all I can do for now. I'd get that door fixed pronto if I were you."

"Yeah," she said.

Harrigan left, gingerly carrying the sorry mass of soggy feathers.

Before he was even out of the driveway, Paige had closed the back door and wedged a chair beneath the knob. That done, she called a carpenter who sometimes did work for Henry. He promised he would get out tomorrow morning to fix it; but tomorrow morning wasn't soon enough, so she threw some clothes into a suitcase and took Freddie back out to the car.

Tonight, they would sleep in the hills.

Calvin Trott sat on the front steps of the police station and attempted to light a cigarette. It was difficult, though, because the wind kept blowing out the match flame, as if it knew he had quit years ago and was trying to prevent him from starting again.

The wind could go fuck itself; he needed a smoke.

It was a wild sky tonight: long narrow streamers of dark cloud stretched across the sky like so many strands of dirty pulled cotton, being strung all out of shape by a howling wind from the northeast, blowing out of Canada across the Great Lakes all those miles away, making the air smell like snow and ice.

He tried again to ignite his cigarette. Again the wind snatched the match flame and carried it away. When he tried to shield the match, his hand trembled so much he burned his palm. Finally giving up, he flicked the cancer stick into the gutter along the front of the station. Wasn't good for him anyway.

Simon Jones materialized out of the darkness, walking stiffly toward the front door. He stopped some distance away, stood there silently looking at him. After a moment Calvin said: "Got your wish, didn't you?"

"Believe me, Calvin, this was *not* my wish."

Calvin shrugged. Then he said: "You saw her."

"I *found* her."

"Yeah. They said." Calvin frowned. "Cuffed herself to the altar, they said."

"They had to use bolt cutters to get her loose."

"She was all … she was … I hardly recognized her, she was so messed up."

Simon said: "I know."

Calvin located another cigarette, stuck it between his teeth. This time he successfully lit it, ignoring the pain from his burned hand as he warded the overprotective wind from the flame. He'd probably get a blister, he thought. "So you'll go ahead and knock the church down now, right?"

Simon sighed. "When the police are done with it. Two or three days, they said. Maybe more."

"They wouldn't tell me what happened to her."

"I don't think they *know* what happened."

"Birds," Calvin said.

"Well, yeah, obviously birds. But birds don't just peck you to death. The paramedics thought maybe she had a heart attack or something, and the crows smelled it and went to work on her. Death scent, I guess you'd call it."

"Big hole right in her head," Calvin said. "How'd a crow do *that*?"

"I don't know. Maybe her skull had a weak spot. And they're powerful birds, from what I hear." Pause. "If there's anything I can do—"

Calvin waved a hand to show Simon it was okay. He didn't think the mayor could see him biting the end of the cigarette, mashing the paper between his teeth, tasting filter and tobacco on his tongue. He didn't dare open his mouth to say anything for fear of what would come out.

"I've got a meeting inside," Simon said.

Calvin nodded. Simon went in, patting him on the shoulder as he passed.

"Knock that building down, Simon," Calvin said. "Knock it down and bury it."

And the sky frothed, as if it could hear him.

8

WHEN SIMON GOT HOME THAT evening, Roland was sitting in the recliner watching television. He muted the program as Simon came in, but not before Simon figured out what was on: the local news. As Simon took his coat off and hung it in the front closet, Roland said, "You heard the reports?"

"No," Simon said. "I can imagine them, though."

"They've practically got you and Quentin Farmer sharing a cell at Midstate."

"You should have seen them today! Fred and Noah tag-teamed me at the old church. They were trying to outdo each other with pushy questions. It was like being stuck between *60 Minutes* and *Dateline*." Simon checked the answering machine. Six messages. "How many of these are from the press?"

"How many are there all together?"

"Six."

"Five," Roland said. "One's from that Nelson character."

Simon said: "Oh, marvelous. What did he want this time?"

"They moved to a different place. It's top secret information, where they are now. Only you and the police are supposed to know."

"What hotel?"

"Not a hotel, a bed and breakfast. The Farmhouse, it's called." Roland clicked the television off completely. "He didn't sound too happy—Nelson, I mean—about having to stick around. They were supposed to be leaving tomorrow, but apparently they've been instructed to stay in the general vicinity."

"I know, I know. I just spent two hours with Paul Shockton and three of Quentin Farmer's lawyers. If I hear the words *my client* one more time I'll scream." He hit the rewind button on the answering machine. He didn't feel like dealing with messages from the press.

"That's not going to make them go away," Roland said.

"I know." Simon rubbed the back of his neck. "Remind me why I wanted to be mayor again?"

"Because you wanted to revitalize the local economy and help our working families build a better life for themselves and their children."

"Oh, yeah. That was it."

"Sounds like a crock, doesn't it?"

Simon grimaced. "It seemed like a good platform at the time."

"So what's going on? Is Farmer pulling out?"

"No. His lawyers are just blowing smoke. I think." Simon went and sat on the floor in front of Roland's chair, hoping for a shoulder rub. He got one. "We've got to start making progress, though. As soon as the police give us the all clear, Karl Castle is taking the church down. Bang!" He clapped his hands together. "What a relief that'll be. That place gives me the creeps."

"You think they'll finally be able to do it?"

"Sure."

"You don't think Jane Trott might've been on to something?"

"What, that the church is defending itself? Don't you start with that supermarket tabloid crock nonsense." Simon had by now nearly convinced himself that Jane Trott hadn't really looked at him when they rolled her out, that the attack he'd suffered inside the church had been nothing more than stress or fumes or nerves or his imagination. He certainly didn't need Roland trying to drag him back to the Twilight Zone.

"Well," Roland said, "I can hardly wait to see what happens next."

The future Fontana residence had no furnishings except for a few lamps and some folding chairs. But it *did* have electricity, and phones, and water—cold only—and a functional furnace, and thick, sturdy doors with heavy-duty locks that worked. As she turned the deadbolt on the front entrance, Paige listened to the solid-sounding *clunk* of the steel post snapping into the steel plate inside the stout wooden frame. And then she slid the chain—links as big around as a pencil, attached to a brass plate secured to the frame with a half-dozen big screws and a large central bolt—into place, and stepped back, and thought: Nobody would be tearing *this* plate out of the door. Nobody human, anyway.

She took Freddie upstairs, to what would be the master bedroom, and spread out their sleeping bags on the floor. This room was at the back of the house, with wide, high windows overlooking the upward slope of the hill, thirty feet of grass and splotchy dark evergreens thickening into a forest at the far end. In the center of the back wall, near where the bed was going to go, a sliding glass door opened onto a balcony. There was no access directly from the ground, so she didn't need to worry about anyone coming in that way. And anyway, the entire house was alarmed, tied into the Security Blanket network, which would automatically dial the police if anyone broke in. This feature was operational; she had called the company and checked.

Freddie said: "Why can't we stay with Nanny and Poppy?"

"I told you, their house is too small." The real reason was that she couldn't take being around them for very long without Henry to run interference against Florence's evil eyes and Joe's wandering palms.

"There's no television," Freddie said.

"You can live without TV for one night."

"No I can't," Frederick said. He threw his arm across his forehead and collapsed onto his sleeping bag. "I'll die!"

Paige applauded dutifully.

"Thank you, thank you," Frederick murmured, in his best fading whisper.

Paige went to the glass door. The sky was positively evil tonight, moon high and bright, ringed in a ghostly corona of high-altitude diffusion. A witch's brew of clouds and stars and mist and darkness swirling overhead. She thought of *him*, whoever he was, inside her house; the image sent ghastly little wormy clenches up and down her spine. Some lunatic had smashed open her back door and walked right into her home and put a dead crow in her sink. The same person—presumably—had scrawled a curse across the front of her house in blood-colored spray paint, condemned her to hell on the telephone, told her she'd be eaten by vultures, or something.

Neighborhood kids? Dream on, she thought. This was serious insanity in progress.

Maybe he would go back there tonight, she thought. He would

come in through the kitchen door—he'd splinter the chair to pieces, probably—and he would go slowly through the house, looking for her. Maybe, when he didn't find her, he would do one of those weird psycho things. Maybe he would stab her mattress and pull out the stuffing. Maybe he would jack off onto her pillow. Maybe—

"Mommy?"

She looked at Freddie. He had gotten into his pajamas and had crawled into his sleeping bag. "Yes, honey?" she said.

"Can we go home tomorrow?"

"Uh-huh," she said. "Just as soon as we get the door fixed."

"Is Daddy gonna be home soon?"

"Yes," she said. "Just a few more days." Barring complications, she thought.

Frederick was quiet for a few minutes; then he said, "Mommy?"

"What?"

"Is Daddy going to give me my game back?"

"What game?"

"The one where you shoot the devils."

"I don't think so, honey," she said. Though she would've liked to shoot some devils right about now.

Frederick yawned hugely, and crawled into his sleeping bag. "It's not fair," he said. "Everybody else gets to play that game."

Paige turned and looked out the window. Despite the brilliance of the moon, it was very dark outside. She wondered if the creep was inside their house right now. Maybe he was writing all over her walls in candy-apple crayon. Maybe he was opening up her dresser drawers, rummaging in her underwear. Maybe was *putting on* her underwear.

Ugh. Made her want to jump in the shower for a year. But she kept visualizing it—some big hairy guy prancing around in her pastel lace panties—and finally, she couldn't help but start to giggle.

Calvin Trott switched off the television at 11:30, after the news, and then he sat awhile in his chair and stared at the screen. The top story, of course, was Jane. They had pictures of the church. They had pictures of Simon standing there watching the paramedics bring out a stretcher. They had pictures of the stretcher falling over, though they at least refrained from zooming in on Jane's shredded corpse as it spilled onto the mushy ground; instead they went back to Simon and his muddled expression of shock and fear and revulsion. They tied her death to Henry's accident, though to Calvin's mind you couldn't really equate running yourself over to getting pecked to death by crows. On the gruesome scale, there was really no comparison between the two.

They didn't air an interview with him. This was because he had punched out the reporter who'd kept pestering him for one.

From that story, they segued into the most God-awful burlesque he had ever seen Channel Six pull: an interview with Jasper and Noreen Shoemaker. Calvin knew the Shoemakers slightly, from several parent-teacher conferences they'd had regarding Jasper Junior; the people who had sat in his classroom screaming both at him and at each other bore no resemblance to the airbrushed, lacquered-up couple that manifested itself for the cameras. And then they trotted out the kid, scrubbed and fresh and looking like they had stopped him on his way to heaven, all purity and wounded innocence. Made him want to throw up.

There was going to be a delay in knocking down the church, a longer delay than there would have been if Jane hadn't died trying to keep the bulldozers away. They would have just snapped her handcuff chain with bolt-cutters and carried her off and then knocked the building down; but now, there had to be investigations and samples and photographs and committee meetings. Calvin thought of the crow that had been watching him, that time he was there, and wondered if it had already been hatching plans with its black-feathered cronies.

Crazy thought. But somehow, alone, late at night, on the day his wife had been killed on the altar of a ruined church, after several beers and not an inconsiderable volume of Jack Daniels, it didn't seem so crazy. It seemed, in fact, eminently reasonable. Crows were smart birds. And there were a lot of crows there. That many smart birds in one place were bound to come up with schemes.

Especially in *that* place. Because even though he wasn't psychic, even though he was just a regular, insensitive, *ordinary* guy, he knew that place was evil. Maybe that was something that you *had* to be normal to sense. Maybe whatever was there was slick enough to fool you, if you could perceive it well enough.

Anyway, they were going to leave the church alone for a while. Give the crows lots of time to plot their next move.

He couldn't let them do that.

He had a duty, as a human being, to make sure those crows didn't do anybody else like they'd done Jane.

He stood up, waited a moment for the room to stop whirling, then went to get his coat. He tripped over his boots and the floor came rushing up to meet him. He caught himself with his hands, so he didn't crack his skull upon impact; but the floor was just so comfortable, and he was just so tired, that he couldn't help but fall asleep right on the spot.

Henry Fontana stayed up late to watch the news.

The television was on, sound turned down low so as not to disturb the man on the other side of the curtain; because as soon as something woke him up, he started to sing. Show tunes, always show tunes; an aging performer on his last legs, maybe.

He felt pretty good, considering what he'd been through. They were even talking about sending him home by the end of the week. The drug they were giving him—they had him on codeine now, not the heavy-duty stuff they'd been giving him before—kept a lid on the pain, let him sleep comfortably at night without knocking him for a total loop. Normally it would have knocked him out by now, but he hadn't taken it yet. He'd overhead the nurses discussing something that had happened down at the old church—something other than his own accident, it seemed—and he had wanted to stay up and catch the news, see what was going on.

By eleven, his ribs were aching fairly badly; he hardly noticed, though, once the news came on and they started talking about what had happened to Jane Trott. Un-fucking-believable. Pecked to death by crows. Jesus, but he had gotten off easy.

Hadn't there been a crow on his car, just before it had jumped down the hill and run him over? Hadn't there been something up in the air?

An orderly came into the room, interrupting Henry's train of thought, and announced that it was time for his injection. Henry eyed the guy, then said: "What injection?"

"To help you sleep."

Henry said: "I don't need an injection to help me sleep." The orderly seemed vaguely familiar, though Henry couldn't recall ever actually having seen him before. Maybe they had met in the hallway or something. He was a very big guy, at least six feet tall, with round hairy arms and hair the color of dusty coal and a face like a rubber mask. Not somebody you were likely to forget, Henry thought.

"You're awake, aren't you?" the orderly said.

"I'm watching the news."

The orderly reached up and turned off the television. Having silenced the broadcast, he turned and said: "Okay, Mr. Fontana, just give me your arm."

"I don't want an injection. I've got my pill right here."

The orderly came around to the side of the bed and put a big hand on Henry's injured chest. "You don't have a choice," the orderly said. He already had the needle uncapped. Inside the plastic barrel, there was nothing but air.

"Hey, what're you doing?" Henry said.

Suddenly, the strains of *Yankee Doodle Dandy* burst from the other side of the curtain. The orderly looked up, startled. Henry grabbed the device for calling the nurse and pressed the button with his thumb. Then he swung his good arm around and punched the orderly in the nose. The man shook his head, made a faint squawking sound like an angry bird, and jammed the needle into Henry's arm.

Henry grabbed the syringe and twisted it, and the needle broke off.

The orderly backhanded him across the face. The man had big, rock-like hands, and the blow sent lights exploding across Henry's vision. The orderly hit him again, this time in his injured shoulder. A burst of agony exploded out from it in a red blossom snatched away his breath. Then the orderly grabbed the pillow from under Henry's head and pressed it hard against his face, muffling the sound of his roommate's singing. Henry thrashed and clawed at the pillow, heedless of the gigantic spears of pain his ribs and shoulder hurled at him. He reached up with his left hand and found the bed controls and began pushing them frantically. The elevated head section began to recline, forcing the orderly to stretch forward more to keep up the pressure on the pillow, allowing Henry a chance to snatch a breath before the orderly pushed the cushion down on him again.

Henry let himself go limp, hoping to fool the man into letting up early, but it didn't work, he just kept pushing, not letting any air get through; Henry started to get lightheaded, his lungs started to burn, his—

Suddenly the pressure was gone. Henry grabbed the pillow and threw it across the room and gulped huge mouthfuls of air. He couldn't see the night nurse, but he could hear her screaming hoarsely from the foot of his bed: "Security! *Call security!*" The orderly was at the window; he had opened it and, as Henry watched, he kicked away the screen, spread his arms, and dove out head-first.

From a sixth-story window.

His chest burned inside, his shoulder ached, there was a red pinpoint on his arm where the needle had gone in. The night nurse struggled to her feet, supporting herself on his bed frame, blood running from her mouth. She staggered to the open window and looked out wonderingly into the night.

Henry gasped: "He tried to kill me."

She looked at him like she'd forgotten he was there. "He jumped right out the window," she said.

Henry's roommate started to sing again, but stopped after only a few seconds.

The directions Nick Garson had gotten from the psycho-nut clerk proved to be accurate. He came to the construction site from the opposite direction as last time, so he had to make a left to enter it. The access road had been beefed up considerably; the earth was fairly dry and very bumpy. It sloped down to a broad flat area on the banks of the canal, where Quentin's construction equipment loomed between the mounds of earth and gravel and other stuff. All of it was in exactly the same position as before. He wondered when they were actually going to start working.

Nick drove his vehicle around behind one of the gravel heaps, out of sight of the road, and parked it there. The wind was blowing clouds rapidly across the vast dark sky. The moon was bright and full, sending a shimmer across the surface of the canal, illuminating the old church across the water, lighting it up in a ghostly corona. If he didn't know better he would've thought it was glowing itself, the walls and the tree decadently luminous, the high windows blazing. The illusion was so convincing that for a moment he thought someone had set fire to the place, that the interior was an inferno, that at any moment the flames would come shooting through the roof; but that didn't happen, and when the wind slipped a veil of clouds over the moon the lights went away and the place was just its old, dark, dead self.

He reached into the brown bag from the mini-mart and slipped a beer can free from its plastic noose. It was very cold, slick with condensation. He popped the can open and took a drink. It had been ages since he'd had beer. Seemed like all they kept in their house was ginger ale. He would scribble *beer* on the grocery list, but somehow Lois would never return from the store with it; then she would say if he wanted her to remember, he should come with her. It had never seemed worth the trouble.

It had been a fairly warm day, for an upstate March, but the night was crusting over with frost. He put up with the shivering for a little while, hoping the alcohol would keep him warm, which it didn't; then started the car and turned on the heat. He wondered how long it would idle before it ran out of gas.

He shifted around in his jacket, trying to fluff it up as much as he could. Something in his pocket clinked and clattered. Oh, yeah: the ammunition. He really did need to get rid of that.

Nick opened the door and climbed out. He left the car running so it would get good and warm before he shut if off for the night. The hum of his engine was the only sound he heard, and even that faded as he got around to the other side of the gravel pile. The ground sloped down to the canal at a very gentle angle. The water was placid and still, even though the trees were going crazy with wind. Funky. He stopped where the grass ended and the rocks began, an artificially steep bank of thick flat stones, as if the builders of the canal had thought it might otherwise chew too quickly into its sides and flow out over the surrounding land.

He reached into his jacket pocket. The bullets had warmed up some from his body heat. He curled his fingers around them and pulled them out and looked at them in the moonlight. The flat ends were shiny, the pointed ends dark. He wondered if they were some kind of special bullets, the sort that exploded or flattened out or turned into tiny shreds of shrapnel. He imagined loading them into his gun and shooting Quentin Farmer with them. Farmer would have such a shocked expression on his face as the slugs tore into him; unless Nick aimed for his head, in which case he wouldn't have much of a face left for any sort of expression whatsoever. Instead there would just be a ragged hunk of meat with blood and bone and brains flying away from it at a high rate of speed; and then Farmer would totter on his feet and then fall over and what was left of his brain would slosh out of his shattered skull and wibble-wobble on the ground like some esoteric gelatinous dessert.

Yeah … he could do that.

Nick looked at the bullets.

He looked at the canal.

He threw the bullets out over the water. They hung a moment in mid-air, and then they fell into the waterway like a handful of gravel. Little ripples appeared and grew, interlocked, faded.

He noticed a glow spreading across the water. The church, starting to light up again. He thought he could see shadows moving inside it, dancing across the windows. The limbs of the big tree shook in the icy wind. He could ear the old wood groaning and creaking; or was it something else he heard? Something *flapping?*

The crows he had seen before were still in their perches, still watching him. He could see them against the light that glowed from the hole in the roof of the church. He watched them back. The beer was getting to him already, he thought; he felt dizzy, lightheaded. Been too long since he'd had a drink. His tolerance was for shit.

What am I bid?

Nick shook his head at the faint, echoing whisper that drifted across the canal. He squinted at the old church, but he could hardly see it for its radiance. The glow seemed to ripple off of it in waves, waves of light that broke gently over him, each one touching him and passing over him like a cobweb caress. The feeling was soft, warm, gentle, lulling him into a stupor.

What am I bid for the life of the last Selden?

And then Nick found himself turned away from the church; he didn't recall having moved, and yet he was walking up the gentle slope, back to his car. The door was standing open, though he was sure he had closed it. The light kept breaking over him, shooing him along, like a mother prodding her reluctant child to bed. He climbed into his vehicle and locked the doors and shut the engine. He could still see the church, though by now it was white-hot and incandescent, all its actual details lost in the brilliance; it was like trying to trace the path of a filament in a lit-up light bulb.

Basking in the glow of the church, he closed his eyes and reclined his seat nearly all the way back, pulled his arms in from the sleeves of his jacket and hugged them to his body, letting the radiance keep him warm.

Some time later, he was drawn out of sleep by a persistent tapping on the driver's side window. He awoke feeling dizzy and disoriented, legs all tingling, arms weak as strands of rubber. Through the window he could see a broad dark thing, an amorphous silhouette, no details. Somehow the thing motioned for him to lower the window, even though it had no form; he foggily deliberated this notion, then—hardly even conscious of what he was doing—he managed to get one of his rubber arms to roll down the window. The dark thing outside moved, and Nick felt something falling into his lap, a rain of small, hard, heavy objects. Then the silhouette moved away and Nick rolled the window back up, cutting off the cold air that had come rushing in. He thought, vaguely, that he should find out what had just been dumped on him; but he drifted back to sleep before he could effectively convey this intention to his arms and hands.

Some time later, he was awakened again, this time by a chorus of shrill, discordant cries that seemed to jangle him into pieces. He looked around blearily; his head throbbed, his throat ached, his tongue felt slimy. The sky had lightened with the impending dawn, from black to medium blue. Across the canal the trees clawed at the heavens as if to rip it to shreds; and the highest, strongest claw was the one that rose from the roof of the church. It was festooned with crows, cawing in unison as if to frighten away the sun. Nick grumbled and shifted, provoking a tiny avalanche from his stomach to between his legs. Mystified, he slid his hand down to his crotch.

And there were the bullets, cold and round and hard as diamonds. He picked one up and held it in his fingers and squinted at it. He could've sworn he threw the ammunition into the canal. But here it all was, sitting in his lap.

Maybe he had just dreamed it.

The chorus of crows suddenly halted and somehow he knew, without having to look, that they were gone. An instant later he heard a very loud motor start up somewhere nearby; seconds later it changed pitch and was joined by a persistent beep, like the sound a dump truck made when it backed up.

As Nick tried to figure out where all this noise was coming from, he realized that his hands were doing something.

They were loading the bullets into his gun.

He couldn't for the life of him remember removing the weapon from his jacket, and he certainly didn't know how to load it; the proprietor of the shop had shown him, but he hadn't paid attention. Now he was stuffing bullets into the little cartridge thing like he was feeding it jelly beans. He watched his hands do their work, as if they were strange arachnoid creatures that had crawled into the car while he slept and attached themselves to his wrists. When they were done, they slammed the clip back into place and flipped a little switch or lever thing—the safety, he thought, though he wasn't sure—and then slipped the weapon back into his pocket.

Weird.

The beeping noises stopped, and the tone of the engine changed again. A few moments later a bulldozer trundled by in front of him. The guy driving it was wearing jeans and a red flannel shirt beneath a brown leather jacket. He didn't look like one of Quentin's men. Nick wondered where he was going with the bulldozer, and whether or not he should try to stop him. He decided against it. Maybe it was a local guy Quentin had hired. Besides, he really needed to take a leak.

He got out of the car and went down to the water, working out muscle kinks as he went; his bucket seat was not designed for extended slumber. He was in plain view of the road, but it wasn't busy and he figured he could finish his business before anybody came by. He unzipped his jeans and started to urinate into the canal, a good, long, high-arched stream. A very manly thing, urinating outdoors. Very back-to-nature.

He was almost finished when the bulldozer burst out of the trees across the canal and hung a sharp left, straight for the old church.

Calvin Trott had awakened, sore and sober, on his living room floor. The palliative effects of the alcohol had worn off, but its evaporation had left behind his drunken conviction that the old church had to go.

It was encrusted in his mind like the rime of salt that came from dried sweat. So he had gotten up and grabbed his coat and driven right out to the future site of Quentin Farmer's plaza.

Hot-wiring the bulldozer was easier than he had expected. So was driving it. It might have a new coat of shiny orange paint, but it wasn't much different from the heavy machinery he had operated during his stint in the army. It was kind of small, but since Karl Castle had removed his own equipment from the scene, it would have to do. And it certainly seemed to have enough power; it chewed through the woods, smashing down the saplings and the underbrush, the motor filling up the morning with its rumbling roar.

As he broke out of the woods, he saw a guy across the canal, pissing into the water and staring at him. He hadn't expected a witness, but he wasn't going to let that stop him. The bulldozer rumbled and bounced, rattled and clunked and clanked like a phalanx of medieval knights. The treads churned through the soggy earth, propelling him speedily forward. He angled it at the edge of the church; he would clip it in the corner, rip the left wall right out, and if that didn't work he'd swing around and do the right one too.

See, Simon? This wasn't so God damn hard.

Then he heard, over the noise of the motor, a metallic *clang*. He had no idea what it was. Then he heard another one, and felt a stinging sensation across the front of his head. An instant later blood poured into his eyes and he smelled burning skin. The blood blinded him, the odor sickened him. He wiped his face with his hand and his fingers came away sticky and red, and he still couldn't see anything.

Zing! Something whizzed through the air inches from his nose. He looked right, across the canal, blinking crimson from his vision. He couldn't see very well through the haze of blood, but it looked like his witness was pointing at him. Then he saw a tiny puff of smoke, and the wire mesh screen around his seat sparked and shook.

Christ! The guy was *shooting* at him!

Calvin ducked down low. He couldn't see a thing. Blood flowed around his nose, into his mouth, down his chin. The church was looming close now, nothing but a great black monolith through a haze of tears and blood. He thought he may have drifted somewhat off target and tried to steer the bulldozer left, back toward the corner. He didn't want to hit the place head on, or he'd be right in the middle of it when it collapsed.

Zing! Another bullet hit. This one tore through the wire and ricocheted off a metal support and winged him across the hand. He watched his skin open up in a black-lipped line. Blood rushed from the wound; he thought he could see ivory bone through the scored flesh. A second later the pain hit, and he shoved the hand into his armpit and squeezed it tight.

The bulldozer rumbled forward. The church was only a few yards away; he was heading straight for the front door. He lunged forward, grabbed the wheel, but it slipped through his bloody hands, he couldn't get it to turn.

And then, suddenly, the world groaned and tilted. Calvin fell forward, against the controls, as the bulldozer tipped front-end first into an inky pit scant feet from the front door of the old building. The blade hit stone with a crash, throwing Calvin forward through the opening in the front of the driver's compartment. He rolled along the hood of the bulldozer and fell through the gap between the blade and the body of the machine, landed on cold, damp rock, staring up at the opening of the pit he had fallen into. Above that was the front of the church, curving down over him.

Laughing at him.

The treads of the bulldozer were still running, only a few feet from his head. He shrank back from them, but even as he did the engine coughed a couple of times and died. The stench of diesel fuel sank down and enveloped him, overpowering the faint earthy odor of the pit. Calvin scuttled out from under the machine, crawling on his back like a crab. As he came out from under it he slid off the stone he was on, felt earth beneath his hands; he realized that he'd been sitting on the flagstone that had formed the front patio of the church. It had been a covering for some kind of subterranean hollow, and the bulldozer had been too heavy for it to hold.

God. Was he in some kind of crypt now? Stuck in a pit with century-old bones?

He stood. The bulldozer had fallen completely into the hole, but it was stuck at an angle. The blade had pierced the flagstone and was sunk deeply into the earth; the treads were jammed into the furrow they'd carved down the wall.

Blood still trickled into his eyes and he wiped them with his good hand. Who had that maniac been, shooting at him? Jesus, he could've been killed.

The cut in his forehead was bad, but the hand was worse; he had to do something to stop the bleeding. Before anything else, he had to do that. Calvin slipped out of his jacket. It was freezing in the hole, felt fifty degrees colder than it had aboveground. Gritting his teeth to keep them from chattering, he removed his old flannel shirt and ripped off the left sleeve. He wrapped this around his injured hand, pausing now and again to shake blood from his eyes. He managed to tie the makeshift bandage in place, then ripped off the other sleeve and tied it around his forehead. The wounds burned where the fabric touched them, but it was better than letting the blood just pour right out.

That done, he sagged back against the wall to catch his breath. He felt a little bit light-headed, from shock or loss of blood, he didn't know which. He wondered again what the hell this great big hole was supposed to be. The light coming in from above illuminated his end of the chamber, but it obviously stretched out beyond the reach of the rising sun, and in its depths was utter darkness. He thought again of old bones buried in the earthen walls, and shuddered to think what sort of people would have been interred in a place like this.

What was that?

He squinted, tried to fix on what he thought he saw, grey shapes twisting beyond the light; but when he wiped his eyes and looked again they were gone. Blood loss, he thought. Too much blood loss. The wall didn't seem quite solid behind him. It rippled kind of, like there was something inside it trying to get out. Felt weird, kind of grabby. Clutching, bony fingers. He stepped away from it, but then the floor started up, thrumming beneath his feet, pulsing, shivering. Like walking on a trampoline when somebody else was jumping on it.

He climbed up onto the bulldozer. It didn't shift under his weight, not an inch. He looked at its back end. Still five or six feet below the lip of the pit. He might be able to get hold of the edge, but it looked crumbly and unstable and would probably come apart under his hands, send him tumbling back into the hole. Even if he wasn't hurt and groggy and bleeding and half-blind, he wouldn't be able to climb his way out.

He crawled into the operator's cubby, with its walls of mesh and its dented metal roof. He wondered if the guy with the gun was going to come after him. He settled onto the tilted iron seat, and he saw the grey thing flitting around in the dark in front of him. He closed his eyes. It wasn't there. It couldn't be there. What could be moving around down here in this sealed-up hole?

He opened his eyes.

It was still there. It had moved closer.

It didn't have what he could positively call a *shape*. It was amorphous, sort of vague, like a large sheet of plastic wrap waving in a breeze. It would flicker and vanish and flicker again, somewhere else, in a different form. Calvin huddled down in the cab of the bulldozer and waited for it to go away, but it didn't, not this time. It kept coming closer, and closer, and closer, and it brought with it a chill, sharper and deeper than the air.

It stopped only a few yards short of the bulldozer, and he could see it now, see it in the ghostly light that wrapped around the edge of the pit and shone on it and through it. He saw vast wings, twenty feet tip to tip, brushing the earthen walls and knocking away clods of stone and mud. And a hump of a head, a suggestion of features, half-human, half-avian. And eyes, vast pits for eyes, full of intelligence and pent-up malice.

The thing spoke.

What am I bid, it said, *for the life of this pitiful thing before me?*

The two shimmering wings bent forward and wrapped themselves around the blade of the bulldozer, twisted around and around and around, snared it.

The bulldozer groaned.

It began to move.

It went forward slowly, tilting more and more toward the level, until its treads came free and it crashed down flat on the floor of the chamber. Something deep inside the machine rumbled in protest as it was pulled deeper into the lair of the thing, the bird-thing that lived under the church. And Calvin clung to his seat and trembled, and even though he was freezing cold inside his jacket, his body grew clammy with sweat.

But he couldn't move.

And the darkness closed over him.

And the wings enfolded him.

And when he tried to scream, he could only gasp instead.

9

Nick Garson had watched, with a sort of detached interest, as his hands had reached into his jacket pocket and pulled out his gun and started shooting at the man in the bulldozer. It was really fascinating, the way they worked: tiny little muscles under the skin would clench and relax, and his finger would squeeze the trigger or his aim would change or whatever. He wasn't sure if his hands ever managed to hit the guy—it was hard to see him through the mesh enclosure around the operator's seat—but they sure took a lot of shots at him.

It wasn't until the bulldozer crashed into the pit that Nick began to think that maybe this was something he could get in trouble for; and although he could argue that his hands were doing it on their own, the best he could hope for from that excuse was a trip to the psychiatric ward. So he tucked the gun back into his jacket and went back to his car, thinking that he would just be moving along back to Buffalo, leaving no one the wiser that he had ever been here.

There were still a lot of loose bullets on the driver's seat. He scooped them into his hand before he sat down, and then watched himself reload the gun. He wondered why they were doing that; maybe they were expecting to be called on to shoot someone else.

His two little friends were just sliding the clip back into place when he heard the sirens approaching. Somebody must have heard the shots and called the police. Bad hands, Nick thought. Bad, bad, bad! Loading the gun when they should have been helping him drive away! He got out of the car and ran around behind the gravel pile. He climbed the heap of loose stone, sliding and slipping, stopping just shy of the summit. Then he sprawled out on his stomach and waited.

The cop car came tearing in from the north, braked rapidly and stopped at an angle at the side of the road. Two policemen got out, looking around cautiously. They had their guns out; he could see the weapons in their hands. One of them pointed in Nick's general direction. They must have spotted the car, which evidently it wasn't as hidden as he had hoped, but he didn't think they could see him in his hiding place.

One cop reached into the cruiser and pulled out the radio mouthpiece and started talking into it, while the other kept his gaze flicking around the scene. They seemed quite wary. Reasonable, Nick thought, considering that there had been gunfire. Funny; he felt more like a witness than a perpetrator, as if he should run over to them with his palms in the air and say *I saw who did it, officers, it was these hands here!*

Of course, he wasn't about to do something crazy like that.

Nick turned onto his back and slid down the pile of gravel. Cars whizzed back and forth on the interstate, and he realized that he had been hiding in plain view of anybody going by on I-90; even his car must be visible from the highway, sitting there between the two mounds, for God's sake. Not exactly the low profile he'd had in mind. Well, too late now; couldn't change the past.

Staying bent over and keeping his head down, Nick scurried away from his vehicle. He tried to keep the gravel piles between him and the cops, so they wouldn't see him fleeing. He had to move fast; the place would probably be swarming with police in a few minutes. Then he thought of the old woman in the hotel and wondered if she had described him to the authorities. He might end up the object of a manhunt, and he hadn't even done anything! It was his hands.

He made it to the steep embankment at the edge of the interstate. Here the ground dipped into what looked like an old creek bed, half-full of freezing cold water, no current to speak of. It opened into the canal a few yards to the left. He got on his hands and knees and splashed along the icy channel, then darted right, under the I-90 bridge. He paused there and chanced a look toward the cops. They were still at their car, waiting, watching. No sign that they had seen him.

The bridge rumbled and shook as cars and trucks crossed it. Nick climbed to the base of the span, a wide concrete wall from which the girders arched over the gently rippling water. He climbed onto the wall, just beneath the girders, among the sand and small rocks. The bottom of the bridge was only a few inches from his head. Nick reached up and put the gun on the shelf created by the T in the girder above his head, then thought maybe he could fit up there himself. The ledge hadn't seemed very wide from the bank, but now that he was closer it looked like maybe he could balance on it.

He wiggled around beneath the beam. Angled support irons ran to it from the bottom of the roadway, giving him something to hold onto as he hauled himself up. The lip was maybe four inches wide, maybe less, covered with a dusting of grainy sand. The massive girder hummed under his feet and against his back, vibrated with the rumble of passing cars. The air smelled like dirt and pavement and metal.

Now he had to get across the canal.

Shuffling sideways with his back to the girder, continually losing his balance and catching it and losing it again, Nick moved out across the underside of the bridge. The canal was beneath him, dark in the shadow of the span; he thought he could make out a few pale shapes beneath the surface, tablets or something. They looked like tombstones, but they couldn't be; no one would build a canal right through a graveyard, right?

Additional angle braces came down to the girder at intervals, each one a barrier he had to traverse. He struggled with the first one for nearly five minutes, trying to force himself through the triangular opening without plummeting to the icy water some twenty feet below. He got wedged into the bottom vertex for a little while, and began to sink into a claustrophobic panic until he managed to wrench himself free; but that cost him his balance and he nearly fell, catching himself on the bracket at the last minute. His feet swung out over empty air, then back to the precarious safety of the I-beam ledge; he clung there for a while, eyes closed, trying to calm himself down enough to keep going. And in a way, his near-fall was a good thing; it revealed an easier way to get around the angle irons. At the next one, he just held onto the brace and swung around it and landed neatly on the other side.

Sure-footed as a crow coming to rest on a branch, he thought.

The bridge had a curve to it, and the underside of the far end wasn't facing the cops dead-on. When he finally reached it and slithered down to the abutment, ankles and knees aching, he just lay there for a little while, breathing. Then he rolled over, flattened himself onto his stomach, and crawled along the wall to where he could see the construction site.

His fear had been confirmed: more cops had arrived, and had fanned out over the locale. Two were checking out his car; others were walking across the distant River Road bridge, following the path of the bulldozer; still others were at the water's edge, where he had been standing not long ago. So many cops, and so many different angles, meant that somebody would spot him soon if he didn't find somewhere to hide, and fast.

Nick slid forward to the edge of the concrete, waited for the rumble of traffic, and—when it came—launched himself into the brush that grew along the edge of the highway. Thorns sliced him, creepers lashed him. The soil was rocky, battering and bruising him as he tumbled down the slope beneath the undergrowth. He finally came to a stop partway down the embankment, lying half-stunned under the knobby arms of a barren sumac. Through the dead, grey tendrils of the tree, he could see the cops poking around the bank of the canal, peering at the stones, kneeling and carefully collecting small, coppery things. Bullet casings, he realized. He hadn't even noticed them flying out of his gun, he was so intent on watching his hands.

He crawled away, sideways along the slope, into the forest. Though devoid of leaves, the profusion of slender trunks afforded him some cover. He cut left at an angle, away from the interstate. This took him toward the old church and the exploring cops, but being visible to the interstate left him too exposed to passing state police cars and truckers with CB radios, and as he recalled, the other side of the interstate looked too boggy to traverse, at least when viewed from the window of a speeding car.

Some distance into the woods, he stumbled over a ruined foundation, a low square of heaped stones and soggy masonry that marked the spot where a house-sized building had once stood. Now trees and brambles grew from its floor, creepers overran its tumble-down walls. Nick clambered into the interior of the thing, stumbled through it. The ground there was spongy beneath his feet, rotten floorboards buried under layer after layer of decaying leaves and spreading tendrils of vegetation. He came out the opposite side through a gap in the wall, an old doorway maybe, or just a spot where the stones had worn away. He passed something, an old iron valve sticking up out of the ground, prickly with rust. He ran his hand over it, wondering what it had been; it was attached to narrow corroded pipework than humped up from the humus like a snake, disappeared into the machinery of the wheel, and came out again from the other side and vanished back into the soil. Waterworks, he thought. He stepped away from it, but had only gone a few feet when the sound of his footsteps changed from soft *thuds* to hollow *thunks*; he hardly had time to realize he was standing on some sort of flat sheet of wood before it splintered under his weight and sent him falling, for what seemed like forever.

The chirping of his cellular phone roused Quentin Farmer from a deep and disturbing dream, in which he was taken before a court full of ember-eyed skeletons and convicted of indecent behavior for his dalliance in the car with Patty Chalmers. As punishment, the skeletons led him through the back door of the court room, which opened onto a high promontory jutting out from the edge of a massive black cliff that towered over a vast forest. The dark shapes of great carrion birds circled and swooped in the still, humid air. The skeletons had chained him to a post at the edge of the cliff, and before long the birds had started swooping down and snatching chunks of his flesh away with their claws and their beaks.

So when the phone woke him up, he was relieved to be out of that Promethean dream; but he was also confused, because his cellular phone *never* rang. Ever. No one knew the number. If someone needed to talk to him, they talked to Nelson first.

The phone trilled again. Quentin sat up, shook his head. God, what a nightmare. He could still feel the gigantic black birds ripping into him. When he thought about it, though, he could see where it came from. He *was* sort of like Prometheus, really; if he remembered correctly, Prometheus had been punished for bringing fire to the primitive, uncivilized humans, and he was being persecuted for bringing them jobs. Same thing, when you came down to it.

The phone chirped a third time. He had an awful hunch that he knew who it was. He retrieved the thing from the table, flipped it open, and said: "Hello?"

A voice he had never heard before said: "is this Quentin Farmer?"

"Yes," he said.

"Quentin Farmer, the businessman?"

"No, Quentin Farmer the circus acrobat," he said. "Who the hell is this?"

"I have your laptop."

Hunch confirmed. Funny; all of a sudden he wasn't sleepy anymore.

"Do you?" Quentin said. "That's interesting. And what was your name again?"

"Never mind that," the caller said. Sounded young, Quentin thought. A young voice with a transparently phony southern accent. "This is about you, not me."

"Okay," Quentin said, "you've got my laptop. So what?"

"I thought you might want it back."

"Keep it," Quentin said. "I already ordered a better one."

Pause. "Well, you know, I was reading a magazine and it said the data was the most important thing in a computer. Do you think that's true?"

"I have backups of all that information," he said.

"You do?"

"Yes."

"Even the pictures of little boys and little girls?"

Quentin didn't hesitate a beat. Couldn't show weakness. "What pictures of little boys and girls?" he said.

"You know what pictures."

"I'm sorry," Quentin said. "I'm afraid I don't." There was another pause, as if the caller hadn't expected him to deny the accusation, so he said: "Are we through? It's early and I have a meeting to go to this morning. I'd like to be fresh for it."

"Do you want me to give your computer to the cops?"

"Go ahead. Then I can cancel the order for a new one."

"What do you think they'll do when they get it?"

"They'll probably arrest you."

"No, they won't. They'll arrest *you*."

"I doubt that."

"No, they will. Let me tell you why. First, the dates on these pictures are from before you lost your computer. Second, I don't have a modem to download this stuff, but I bet you have one in your laptop case. Third, they already caught you getting your cock sucked in a car by the side of the road, so they've got you pegged as a pervert. Put all that together, and you have a problem."

Silence.

Quentin said: "You know what? I can't find those backups after all."

"That's what I figured."

"How much do you want to give me back my computer?"

"I'm thinking in the hundred-thousands."

Quentin said: "I didn't pay nearly that much for it when it was new."

"You're paying for *content*, man," the caller said. He had lost his southern accent somewhere. "Value added."

"When and how?" Quentin asked.

Pause. "We'll call you back with instructions."

Click.

Quentin sat a moment in bed, then jumped to his feet and padded to the window. From here he could see down into the valley, lying under a morning haze of mist. Frost patterns on the glass were softening in the sunlight.

Somewhere, out under that fog, someone had just hung up the phone. Somewhere, someone was laughing at him.

He saw a shape moving in the yard, crunching through the frosted grass. He wiped away the icy rime from his window for a better look, and saw that it was Tom Teller, one of their hosts. He was out without a coat in the morning chill—not too smart for someone his age, Quentin thought—and he was walking away from the house, staring at the sky. Looking for spaceships, maybe. Didn't people out in the country see spaceships all the time?

Someone knocked on the door. Quentin went and looked through the peephole and there was Nelson, fully dressed in shirt and tie, wearing those tiny round sunglasses that he never seemed to take off. Quentin opened the door and the sunglasses came inside, with Nelson right behind them. "I tried to call you but your phone was busy," he said.

"I had a call," Quentin said.

"You did?" Nelson said. "On the *cellular?*"

"I *do* have a regular telephone you could have used," Quentin said, pointing out the extension of the bed and breakfast phone system that sat on his table.

"Oh, yeah," Nelson said. "Didn't think of that."

Quentin rubbed his eyes. "So what's up?" he asked, just knowing it wasn't going to be anything good.

"Simon called a few minutes ago. There was a disturbance at the site this morning. One of your bulldozers was stolen. They found an abandoned car and freshly-fired bullet casings by the canal."

"What?" Quentin plopped down onto the bed. "What the hell *is* it with this place? Are we getting attacked by guerrillas now, Nelson?"

"Not that I know of, sir. Would you like to—"

"You go. I have a few calls to make, and you're already dressed anyway. You have full authority to do whatever needs to be done. Sign paperwork. Swear out warrants. Have people summarily executed. Whatever they need from me, you give them."

"Are you okay?" Nelson lowered his sunglasses and looked at Quentin over their round blue tops. "You look pale."

"I'm not sleeping very well. Can't imagine why." Quentin shook his head. "Maybe I need to rethink my policy about always being at the site when construction begins."

"Maybe," Nelson said. "So you don't want to come?"

Quentin nodded. "You handle it. I can't deal with this crap right now. I've got to make some more calls. I have a … a project that's threatening to blow up on me."

"Worse than this one?"

"You don't even want to know," Quentin said.

Nelson stood there a moment, then said: "Okay. I'll let you know what happens." He headed out the door.

When he had gone, Quentin looked at his cellular phone. Traitorous piece of plastic, taking calls from blackmailers. He had a project that was threatening to blow up in his face, all right.

This project, right here.

As Nelson drove up Marsh Road, he saw a police car parked lengthwise across the street, keeping traffic out. He pulled the Jaguar up to the barricade, powered down the passenger side window, and identified himself to the officer standing by the cruiser. The cop waved him on through, gesturing for him to park at the side of the road right in front of the entrance to the construction site. As he did so, he saw a red-faced man in an expensive-looking suit trudging up the access road to meet him. That would be Paul Shockton, he thought; Simon had said he would be there.

As he got out of the car, the red-faced man said: "You Nelson DeGrace?"

Nelson had never met Shockton before, though they had spoken on the phone; the voice was distinctive enough for Nelson to recognize the man in person. "That's me," he said.

They shook hands. "Paul Shockton," the red-faced man said.

"So what's going on?" Nelson said.

"The part that concerns you is the stolen bulldozer," Paul said. "As you can see, it was driven onto the road." He led Nelson along the thing's muddy tracks, up and over the canal bridge and down the other side. "He made a hard right here, into the vegetation." The narration was unnecessary: there was a gaping hole in the overgrowth on the side of the road, a sort of leafy tunnel leading straight to the old church. The structure was still intact, though the cops had cordoned off the front of it and were standing around looking at the ground there.

"Somebody hijacked the bulldozer and drove it to the old church?"

"That's right. There's a car parked up the road a ways. It's registered to Calvin Trott. That's Jane Trott's husband." After a moment Shockton added, "She's the one who was found pecked to death the other day."

"Right," Nelson said. He wondered if Shockton thought he had forgotten. Maybe he figured that sort of thing happened all the time in Buffalo, and so was nothing that Nelson found memorable.

"Come with me," Shockton said. Nelson followed the police chief along the newly-blazed trail through the overgrowth, staying in the right-hand track of crushed grass and weeds and brambles. Between the two lines of churned-up earth, the brush was already starting to spring back, though it seemed likely there would be a hole through the forest for years to come; snapped-off saplings and dismembered branches weren't as resilient as flattened weeds.

It was a short walk to the grassy area in which they had parked the first time they'd come here. There were several police officers wandering around, staring at the ground. They might as well have been hunched over squinting through magnifying glasses, Nelson thought; he wondered what they were looking for. The tracks of the bulldozer were obvious, two muddy ribbons running in a curved path to the front of the church, then being swallowed up by a gaping black hole in the ground.

Nelson did a double-take. Where had that come from?

"Yeah, how about that, huh?" Shockton said. "The front patio of the church was actually a lid on some sort of pit. We don't know what's in it yet. Other than your bulldozer, that is." One of the cops came over with a tiny paper bag. She handed it to Shockton, who unfolded the top and looked inside. "Good," he said, patting the cop on the back and sending her up the path through the woods.

"What'd she find?"

"Bullet. Flattened. Must've hit something hard."

"So somebody was shooting at our bulldozer. Is that what you're telling me?"

"That's what it looks like, yes. And before you ask why, I don't know. Come on." Shockton led him to within three feet of the pit. It was about fifteen feet square, with earthen sides and a crumbly, uneven lip. "Don't get too close," Paul advised, holding Nelson back from approaching any further. "The edges are unstable. We're looking into getting some timbers in to shore them up."

"I'll be careful," Nelson said, pushing forward. Shockton grunted as he went to the very edge of the hole, taking slow, tiny, measured steps. It yawned beneath him, black and vacant. Nelson slid his sunglasses to the end of his nose and looked into the abyss at his feet, and decided that *abyss* was probably too strong of a word. Now that he had his glasses off, he could see all the way to the bottom; it was only ten or fifteen feet deep. The flagstone which had formerly served as the lid of the pit was broken into pieces, with a big central split through the center and smaller fractures running from it, dividing the halves into fractions. The wall was deeply gouged where the bulldozer had gone down, and drying tracks of mud showed that it had rolled forward into the darkness—apparently the pit extended under the church—but it must have stopped now, because he couldn't hear its engine running.

He looked over his shoulder. Paul Shockton was a few feet away, arms folded. He didn't look particularly happy, but then again, Nelson had quickly pegged him as the sort of person who never did, even in, say, the throes of sexual delirium.

He said: "Any trace of the driver or the shooter?"

"No. We found a stack of spent casings, but no trace of who was firing them. We have Calvin Trott's car, but no Calvin. We have another car that we haven't identified just yet. Either or both of the drivers may be down there." Paul indicated the pit with a jerk of his thumb. "But like I said, it's unstable. Mayor Jones ordered me not to send anyone down there until we get the thing shored up and evaluated for stability. Apparently he thinks a cave-in on the police would make negative headlines."

"I tend to agree," Nelson said. He looked back into the hole. A loamy smell wafted out of it, tinged with diesel fuel and a touch of watery decay, like some animal had crawled into the hole and died.

Shockton said: "I'm going to have to let the press in here soon, so if you—"

He broke off as the ground under Nelson's feet suddenly crumbled away. The police chief lunged forward and Nelson reached toward him, but they weren't even close to catching each other. Nelson slid down the wall in an avalanche of dirt and mud and pebbles; he hit the broken stone with an ankle-jarring impact, fell onto his back, and found himself looking up into a square of steel-grey sky.

From down here, the top of the hole looked a lot farther than fifteen feet away.

He stood up and brushed mud off his coat, stamped it off his shoes. Nothing seemed seriously damaged, though his right foot hurt. Shockton's head appeared over the edge of the hole. "What'd I tell you?" the chief said. Nelson noted that his face was even redder than before, if that were possible. "You all right?"

"Yeah." Nelson looked around for his sunglasses. There they were. He picked them up and put them on.

"I'll have somebody bring a rope," Shockton said. The red face vanished.

A breath of wind stirred the hairs on the back of Nelson's neck. He turned and squinted into the darkness, and of course, his sunglasses turned everything to ink. He slid them down his nose and tipped his head to look over their rounded tops, but that didn't improve things much. He couldn't see anything beyond the column of light shining down from above.

He felt the faint wind again, whisking over his face. Like some large creature exhaling in the darkness. The concept was absurd, but unsettling nonetheless. So naturally, he needed to take a look, right?

Nelson tilted his head back and called, "Shockton!"

After a moment, the chief's head reappeared. "Yeah?"

"Bring a flashlight, too," Nelson said.

Quentin Farmer wasn't sure what to do; he had never been blackmailed before. He supposed he could just cough up the money, but then there was the classic problem: what if the blackmailing didn't stop? And if he just blew them off, well, they would go straight to the police, right? Probably wrap the laptop up in brown paper, like a porno magazine, and leave it on the cops' front door with a note explaining exactly how they could find their way to the nasty little pictures.

He got up and went to the window. The sky had clouded up as if in sympathy, and a few streaky spatters of rain were scattered across the glass. He visited all his projects when construction was about to begin, and usually got a sort of *hail the conquering hero* reception; here, he had become a target of thieves and blackmailers, deranged former employees, grouchy policemen.

He didn't know what the hell was wrong with these people.

He kicked the wainscoting in frustration. He couldn't believe he was being blackmailed by thieves. By *criminals*! Threatening to turn *him* in to the police if he didn't buy his laptop back from them for a hundred times its cost. He had been so stupid, downloading those pictures. He had just been curious, that's all. Curious about what he could find, if it was really as bad as he'd read and heard. It had actually turned out to be kind of hard to locate that sort of image, but he had persisted, and found them, and copied a few. It wasn't like he got any *pleasure* out of those pictures. No, they were sick. Warped. Perverted!

The phone trilled. He checked his watch. Nearly eight o'clock. Christ! He had a meeting with Simon in half an hour! He snatched up the phone and said: "Hello?"

"Is this Pedophiles Anonymous?"

A different voice this time. They were alternating on him. "Very funny," Quentin said. "What do you want?"

"Well, we've worked out a fee structure. We thought you might like to hear it."

"Just give me a figure," Quentin said, wondering what kind of jokers he was dealing with here.

"Okay. Our special this week is a laptop computer and all its contents, returned to you, for one million dollars."

Quentin shouted: "*What?*"

"One million dol—"

"I heard you! That's ridiculous! I can't raise that kind of cash here, now! Last time you said mid-hundred thousands!"

"Don't you think all our partners deserve a fair share?"

"Your *partners*? Who the hell are you, a consortium of proctologists? Two hundred thousand is as high as I'll go."

There was a pause, then the voice said: "Eight hundred thousand."

"Three hundred."

"Seven."

"Four. And that's my final offer!"

Suddenly he heard a struggle at the other end of the phone, and somebody said something he didn't catch; then a new voice came on —the one from the previous call—and said, "Sorry. He wasn't supposed to dicker. The charge is one million dollars, nonrefundable, non-negotiable. Leave the money in a briefcase behind the memorial at the park. Selden's Falls Park. We'll be checking for it every day. When we find it, we'll leave the laptop in its place. If the money isn't there by the end of the week, all rights to the laptop revert to the police."

Click.

Quentin Farmer threw the phone at the bed. It bounced on the mattress and plopped into the pillow. A million dollars! Who the hell did these people think he was, Nelson Rockefeller, for Christ's sake? The problem, he thought, was all the celebrity billionaires running around. Everyone figured if you had any money at all, you had at least a hundred million bucks.

But what was he going to do about it? He couldn't possibly give them what they were asking for. A million dollars would leave a hole in his assets much too huge to paper over with creative accounting. He supposed he could try scraping up as much as possible and hope it would satisfy them, but then they might just take the money and send the computer to the cops anyway. He didn't want to go to jail over some stupid pictures. He'd heard what happened to people like him in jails.

He wondered if what they had said about the files was true, if it could be proven that they were on there when the laptop was stolen. He supposed he could call his Information Systems department in Buffalo and ask them. If it was false, then he had no problem, right? He could just say they put the files on there after they stole the computer. Maybe he could just say that anyway.

He sat on the bed. There should be someone in IS by now. He was going to pick up the phone and call his people and get some answers.

It began to rain a little bit harder outside. He heard the drops peppering the glass, blown into bullets by the wind.

He didn't pick up the phone.

He didn't call his IS people.

If only he hadn't taken his laptop to the mall. If only he hadn't gotten busted in the car with that bimbo from the television news. Why'd she have to go and give him a blow job, anyway? Had he *asked* for one? No. He was just the victim of an overeager reporter's lust for a story. Well, she had a story *now*, didn't she?

He checked his watch. He had to leave, or he would be late for his meeting with Simon. He supposed he should be grateful the blackmailers hadn't told him to get the money by the end of the day. It gave him a little time to think, anyway, even if he didn't know what the hell he should be thinking about.

He got his coat from the closet and headed out of the bed and breakfast, into the rain.

While he waited for Shockton to return with the rope and the flashlight, Nelson took off his sunglasses, folded them up, and tucked them into his shirt pocket. The light was dimming rapidly in the pit, the result of a sudden and accelerating buildup of clouds overhead. Nelson didn't remember the forecast calling for rain, but as far as he was concerned meteorologists were only one step above shamans with chicken-feather totems anyway.

As the sun's illumination waned, the darkness beyond the edge of the pit seemed to lessen. He could make out, dimly, the outline of a large object fairly close to where he stood. The bulldozer, probably. He glanced up at the edge of the pit. Shockton still hadn't returned. All those cop cars, and none of them had a flashlight? Nelson started tapping his foot and, a few minutes later, began walking toward the shape in the darkness.

As he stepped out of the light, he became aware of a sour metallic tang in the air, like the odor of new plumbing or a tin bucket full of iron nails. Off the broken flagstone, the floor turned into a sort of dense mud, soft and yielding, slurping and sucking against his shoes. He was glad he was wearing one of the cheaper domestic pairs.

He reached the shape. He'd been right, it was the bulldozer; he could make out its shape, the caterpillar treads, the boxy operator's compartment, the wide blade in front. It was sitting there totally inert and abandoned. Take a crane to get the thing out of the hole, he thought.

He ran his hand along it; it was prickly with rust. Nelson frowned. Rust? On one of *Quentin's* bulldozers? Not likely. But when he rubbed his fingers more vigorously on the surface it crumbled beneath them, releasing a very strong metallic smell into air that was already sharp with the scent of iron. He slid his fingertips together and felt slightly abrasive dust dig into his skin.

Rust.

He glanced back at the mouth of the pit. Still no Shockton. Nelson moved farther into the darkness, sliding his hand along the bulldozer. Its condition didn't improve any, no matter where he touched it. When he drew even with the cab, he hauled himself up, clinging to the wire mesh, tried to look into the driver's seat. Too dark to see anything. Then the mesh broke and he fell off the bulldozer, landing on his back in the cold, sticky mud. He still had a section of iron wicker in his hands; it must have broken right out from the rest of it.

Nelson stood up. He didn't bother trying to brush off the mud, there was so much of it. As he looked at the hunk of mesh in his hand, he heard Shockton call: "Nelson! You down there?" As if maybe he had climbed out when they weren't looking.

Nelson walked back to the opening. The police chief's red face was silhouetted against a sky of churning clouds, and his thin hair was whipping around his head. He had a rope, but no flashlight. It was raining, Nelson realized; icy drops of water pelted his face, plinked into his hair and trickled along his scalp.

Shockton tossed down the rope. "Wrap this around your wrist," he said.

"Where's the flashlight?" Nelson said.

"It's starting to rain," Shockton said. "Walls might collapse. Besides, it's not your job to go poking around under abandoned buildings, is it?"

"I found the bulldozer." Nelson held up the section of frame. It was badly rusted, gone completely brownish-red, the once-smooth iron threads jagged and pitted. "It seems kind of the worse for wear."

"We'll come back after the rain stops," Shockton said. As he spoke, there was a low rumble from the distance, like an explosion on the other side of a hill. Paul looked up at the sky, his beady little eyes all squinty, like he was afraid of getting struck by lightning. "This weather is fucked up," he said, apparently to himself.

Nelson wanted to say, *Why should the weather be any different from anything else around here?* He didn't, though; wouldn't want the police chief to get offended and leave him down here in the dark. He tugged on the rope. It seemed secure. "What's this tied to, anyway?" he said.

"What? Oh, a police car. We'll pull you up. You won't get any traction on the walls, and we won't get any up here with our feet. Just loop it around your wrist and hold on."

Nelson didn't like the idea of putting something important like his hand in a noose, so instead he pulled his leather gloves out of his pockets, put them on, got a firm grip on the rope, and told Shockton to go ahead. Shockton signaled to someone, and a few seconds later the rope grew taut and slowly lifted Nelson off the ground.

Then he heard a sound like a backfire, and he was suddenly racing up the wall like some sort of vertical water skier. The rope burned through his hands, but he held on long enough to shoot out of the hole; then he let go and soared up in a gentle arc, right over Paul Shockton's very surprised-looking red face, landing face-down on the soft, yielding grass. The police car that had been pulling him smashed into the brush at the edge of the lot. It disappeared into the grey brambles with much snapping and crunching; and as Nelson pushed himself up off the ground, wondering if he had broken anything, he heard the sound of crumpling metal and breaking glass, and saw the boughs of one of the larger nearby trees shiver as if struck hard. Several of the cops were already running for the hole the car had made in the brush.

Nelson eased himself to his feet. His ankle throbbed from when he'd twisted it falling into the hole, but the soft ground had cushioned him from any further damage due to this incident. Paul came over and stood next to him, and they both stared into the overgrowth. Nelson could hear the cops crashing around in it, shouting and cursing.

Paul Shockton said: "Shit."

Nelson's palms stung like he had held them over a fire. He looked at them; the rope had scorched right through the gloves. In spots he could see his skin through the leather, red and raw. Friction burns. If he had looped the rope around his wrist as Shockton had suggested, he might have lost his hand.

The rain began to fall more heavily. Thunder rumbled, closer this time.

Behind them a crow cawed loudly, making Nelson jump. He turned to look, and saw a bird perched way up at the top of the steeple. A huge one, a full-blown raven. Looked like it could carry off a rabbit if it wanted to. Nelson thought he saw a tinge of white in its plumage, or ash-grey, standing out against the inky black feathers. It raised its wings and beat them against the air, as if to say: *I can fly!* And for an instant—only an instant—Nelson thought he saw something vast beyond the crow's own size, twenty-foot wings of smoke and soot, a bulbous head, eyes like rotten melons, hovering there over the old church like a wicked dark cloud. A smell swept over him, a stench like rotten cedar. Made him want to gag.

He shook his head, blinked.

The crows were gone. The little one, and the big one, too.

He glanced at Shockton, but he wasn't there anymore; he had headed to the spot where the police car had gone into the woods. Nelson was standing there alone.

Alone in the rain, with the church.

The old building groaned in the wind, a series of short, hiccupy creaks, as if it were laughing.

10

IT TOOK SOME TIME FOR Nick Garson to figure out he wasn't dead.

His first awareness was of sitting on something hard, uncomfortable, uneven; his left leg was completely numb below the thigh, his right burned with sharp, knife-edged pain. After a little while he managed to open his eyes, and he could make out a curving wall of old, rough, glistening stone right in front of him. Rain ran in rivulets down well-worn channels, and what didn't fall on him or the walls pattered into a dark pool of water a few feet below him. He had been saved from landing in the water by a thick and ancient metal grate; it had broken his fall and, apparently, one or both of his legs. The left one, which had somehow found its way between the bars, was quite stuck and totally unresponsive. The tight fit must have cut off the blood supply; the leg might even have gone and died on him, like an unfed pet. He shifted around on the grate but couldn't really move at all, because of the one leg that was trapped and the other that was shattered or something, felt like it was full of broken glass.

Lightning flashed overhead, momentarily illuminating the depths of his prison with white-hot incandescence. It didn't show him anything reassuring; he thought he saw scorch marks on the tired old stones, and a corroded iron pipe running down the opposite wall, branching out just above the grate, sending thin tendrils to three corroded iron spigots sticking out from the sides in a triangular pattern. And—a way out!—there was a rusty ladder to his left, just out of reach. He wiggled again but his leg wouldn't budge. He couldn't reach even the nearest rung.

God. He was trapped down here, unable to get free, unable to climb out. If the cops didn't find him he would die of starvation or gangrene or exposure, whatever worked fastest. No longer caring about being caught, he screamed, "Help!" His voice bounced back at him from all directions; it rose up the well like a rock thrown into the air, and like a rock it seemed to lose momentum as it climbed higher, finally stalling somewhere overhead, hanging there, then falling back down on him like a net spun from gossamer threads of doom. And as the net settled over him he began to thrash around, clawing at the stone walls with desperate fingers, leaving watery streaks along their aged surfaces. His leg twisted beneath him, just a little, as he screamed and writhed; but it didn't come loose.

When he had finally worn himself, out he stopped thrashing and sat there gasping for breath. The gulping sound came back to him like laughter. No one came to investigate. He wondered if the sounds of his struggle had risen even as far as his voice had.

Nick slumped against the cold wall of the well. He was very hungry; he hadn't really eaten anything since yesterday, except for a can of beer and some chips. And thirsty, too. Why was he so thirsty? He opened his mouth to catch the rain, but it was sour and dusty and made him want to gag. His head began to ache. It started out as a dull pain deep in his brain, and slowly turned into a sharp-edged throb pulsating between his eyes and the back of his head, like somebody was splitting his skull with a wedge. The air was cold and fetid and mossy. Every time he inhaled, the miasma of bitter rain and rusted iron and mildewed walls drove the wedge deeper.

He screamed again for help. This time, it seemed as if the sounds had barely escaped from his mouth before they turned to sand and fell back to cover his face in futility. He was going to die down here, he thought. He was going to die and disappear and no one would ever know what had happened to him. People would ask Lois what ever became of her husband and she would shrug and say—perhaps with a tear, or perhaps not—that he had just vanished, gone like a ghost.

He thought of the spigots. Did water come out of them? He had no idea why there would be water spigots in a well, but what else could they be? They surely didn't work anymore, but still, he reached out and pawed around the wall until he found one. The metal was like ice. He fumbled around, looking for a valve. There was a broad wing-like construction attached to the top of the spigot. He tried to turn it and it snapped off in his hand.

Shit.

He was getting very thirsty now; he was more desperate for something to drink than he had ever been in his life, as if the few droplets of rain he had swallowed had sucked all the moisture out of his throat as they went down into his stomach. He reached out with his other hand, found the other spigot that was within his reach. It sported the same type of knob. Gently, gently, he gave it a little twist; it resisted and he stopped, waited a heartbeat, tried again.

With a sharp little squeak, the wing turned.

Nothing.

Then the sound of the storm receded, faded away, plunging the well into an expectant hush. The rain fell, but silently; the lightning flashed, but there was no thunder. He still heard drops of liquid plinking into the water below him, but it wasn't coming out of the sky; he felt the calf of his dead left leg, and it was hot and wet and sticky. Blood. Blood was running down his leg, dripping from his foot down into the water.

From up above, he heard a metallic screech, like some ancient rusted machinery being forced into life. He thought of the valve he had seen just before falling into the well. Somebody was up there turning it, maybe. "Hey! Hey, help!" he cried. "I'm down here!"

No answer.

The creaking sound stopped; and when it did, he realized that the nozzle he had opened was hissing like a snake.

He smelled rotten eggs.

Gas! It was a gas jet!

He tried to turn it off. The valve snapped right at the stem.

God. God. God. The stink of sulfur grew stronger by the moment. The well was filling up with it. The pain in his head became a steady dull throb, as if it were being packed away in thickening layers of cotton.

The storm came back. The sound of rain drowned out the patter of his blood.

Darkness gathered at the bottom of the well.

He was going to black out soon, Nick thought; lack of oxygen, shock, maybe poisons circulating from his dying leg. He heard water rippling, splashing. Coming from below him, from the dark pool a few feet beneath him. He twisted around and tried to see what was going on, even though the movement filled his head with agony, like his skull was full of sharp, rusty nails and he was jostling them around.

A blackened hand slithered between the ancient bars, closed on one of them. He stared at it. Skin the color of schoolhouse chalk showed in patches between the charred flesh, the peeling, blistering, splitting burns that wept clear, glistening fluid along the fingers. Hallucinating. He was hallucinating. Shock, the gas; there were lots of reasons he could be seeing things.

A second hand found its way blindly through the mesh, got a grip next to the first. Nick heard a high-pitched whine; it was coming from himself, from the back of his throat, a terrified little warble.

The first hand fumbled to the left, toward his trapped leg. He thrashed wildly, energy surging up from some deep reserve, but his struggles only lasted a few seconds before the burst was exhausted. He hadn't budged at all.

The scorched, dead-looking hand touched him just above the knee.

A fragment of a voice said: *Burn.*

Pain shot up his leg. The pallid fingers were working into his flesh. They had ripped right through his pants. Blood flowed out over them, turning them crimson.

Oh, God.

He closed his eyes, desperately wishing for unconsciousness to come back, carry him away from this madness. None of it was real, none of it, lack of oxygen, that was all, that was why he was seeing these things, that was why his head throbbed and prickled like it had a cactus growing inside it.

A voice, a voice as faint and distant as smoke on the mountain, said: *What am I bid for the life of this pathetic thing I see below me?*

He opened his eyes.

He saw a girl lying on the iron grate with him, saw her in the golden sunlight that shone down into the well, directly overhead in a cerulean sky. The overarching trees, the clouds, the winter grey: gone, all gone. The three shiny spigots were intact and open and hissing.

Movement from the opening overhead. A dark shape up there, a man, looking down at them. He couldn't see any details, it was just a silhouette; but then the man held something out over the well, a blazing torch, and the fire lit up his face. It looked like a rubber mask, cruel and pallid features, a sharp hooked nose, eyes like shiny bits of charcoal.

He heard a voice float down from up there, the same voice as before; it said, *Goodbye, my angel.*

The man released the torch.

Nick watched the flaming brand fall toward them. It was falling right toward him, it was going to land right in his lap. The girl was sobbing, staring up at the torch, her eyes white with terror; but the gag on her mouth kept her from screaming, the rope around her wrists kept her from turning off the jets.

When the torch was still a few feet overhead, there was a flash of brilliance, of white heat. Nick heard the girl scream, joined his own cry with hers.

And then the roar of the flames carried both their voices away.

Paige parked in the side lot of the hospital. She and Freddie followed the usual route to Henry's room: in through the rear door, down a hallway that smelled of antiseptic and laundry, up the stairs to the sixth floor—her daily exercise, Paige thought, as she huffed along the steps; Freddie scrambled up them like a monkey—and down another corridor to room 616.

Except that this time, when she got there, the room was empty.

The bed on the left was primly made, but Henry's was a mess. His half of the room was cordoned off with yellow tape, and the window was open, no screen between them and a sixty-foot fall.

"Can I help you?"

The voice came from right behind her and made her jump. She turned and saw a guy standing there, a male nurse she didn't recognize. He looked rather on the stern side, like he'd be more comfortable in a cop's uniform than in hospital whites.

"What happened to the man who was in here?" Paige asked.

"I'm sorry," the nurse said. "Were you a relative?"

Paige stared at him.

"He died early this morning," the nurse explained. "Heart attack."

"*What?*"

"Daddy?" Frederick said.

"Mr. Keller was pronounced at three o'clock," the guy said.

Mr. Keller. Henry's roommate, not Henry. She wondered if she was a horrible person to be relieved that someone else had died. "I mean the other man in the room," she said. "Henry Fontana."

"Oh. I'm sorry. Didn't mean to scare you," the nurse said. God forbid he should ask her who she meant before telling her the person she came to visit was dead, Paige thought. Dope. "Mr. Fontana has been moved to a secure nursing unit," he continued. "Fourth floor."

"How do we get there?" Paige asked. The nurse compressed his lips and sighed, as if he couldn't believe she was so stupid that she didn't know where the secure nursing unit was. After he told her, she didn't bother to thank him.

The directions the guy had given led her to an unmarked and unremarkable door. As she pushed it open, she thought maybe he had sent her to the broom closet, just to be a rat; but no, the door let her into a fully-staffed nursing station, for all the world like any other in the hospital, except that all the nurses were male, and big.

The door clicked shut behind her, loud as a gunshot. The nurses turned to look at her, and a six-foot tall orderly materialized at her elbow. "Can I help you?" he asked, in a deep, rumbly voice.

"I'm here to see Henry Fontana," she said. The orderly stared at her. She felt like a kid caught in the hallway during Geometry class, as if she should produce a pass or something. Then she thought of something better than a pass, and said: "I'm his wife."

The orderly smiled. He had a lot of big teeth. "Sure, Mrs. Fontana. Your husband's doing fine. Just follow me." He led her down the hallway. The other nurses had gone back to their business, apparently no longer interested in her presence. "My name is Harlan Jovanovich. As Guido may have told you, this is a secure nursing station. It—"

"Guido?"

"Mr. Seminelli. Security on the sixth floor. Did you come from up there?"

"Yeah," she said. So the guy hadn't been a nurse after all. She had been so flustered, she hadn't thought to look for a name tag or asked him to identify himself.

"Anyway, as I was saying, this is a secure nursing wing. In addition to myself, there are two other orderlies stationed here around the clock, as well as an extra-large contingent of nurses, as you saw when you came in. We're all specially trained to work with this, ah, class of patients. The doors and windows are alarmed; they're all tied into the police substation up the street. We have video surveillance in the hallway at all times and are able to selectively monitor individual rooms."

He sounded like a tour guide, Paige thought. "Why all the security?" she asked. "I'm not complaining, if you're keeping Henry safe, I'm just curious." Harlan stopped walking, and was looking at her nervously. "What?" she said.

"Did, ah, did Guido explain how your husband came to be on this wing?" he asked.

"No."

Harlan sighed. "I don't suppose I should be the one telling you this, but ..." He leaned over and said, in a low voice, "Henry was attacked last night by one of our orderlies. He's fine, as I said," he added quickly, cutting her off before she could interrupt. "Henry managed to summon the night nurse, and the orderly fled—"

"Is he still on the loose?"

"He fled out the window," Harlan said. "A couple of nurses were outside having a smoke—they won't admit that's what they were doing, because it's a restricted zone, but we all know—and they saw him jump. According to them he had his arms out, flapping them, like he thought he could fly away. As you can imagine, this attempt was not successful. So to answer your question, no, he is not still on the loose."

They started walking again. "Anyway, regarding the secure wing: it's a special arrangement the hospital has with the prison. They outsourced some of their non-emergency infirmary operation to us because we can provide care more cost-effectively. Saves them hundreds of thousands of dollars a year, I'm told. Here we are." They stopped outside a room. It had a heavy wooden door, partially closed. Unlike Henry's previous door, this one had a deadbolt, with the knob on the outside.

"Well, thanks for the information," she said. "And thanks for keeping an eye on Henry."

"No problem," Harlan said. "Oh, by the way ... I'll be graduating from SFCC with a degree in business administration this May ... would you mind if I sent you an application?"

"Uh, sure, go ahead," Paige said.

"Great," he said, grinning widely. "That's *Jovanovitch* with two Vs." Harlan shook her hand and departed.

She stood for a moment and watched his hulking back recede, then went into Henry's room. He was sitting up in bed and looking her way expectantly. "I thought I heard a friendly voice," he said. Frederick broke free of Paige's hand and ran to Henry's bed. Henry hoisted him up and said, "Hey, kiddo."

"Are you okay?" Paige asked. His face was puffy, his nose swollen. She touched it gingerly and he winced.

"Got in a fight," Henry said.

"Did you win?" Frederick asked.

"I kicked his butt," Henry said. "Paige, did they tell you what happened?"

"Yeah," she said. "I have something to tell you, too, actually."

"What?"

So Paige had to call Harlan back to take Frederick, which he did, saying that they had a playroom up the hall. He slid the door closed behind him. When they were alone, Paige climbed onto Henry's bed and said: "We were being stalked."

Henry nodded, looked thoughtful, and said: "How come?"

"I wish I knew," she said. "The day after you had your accident somebody spray-painted *burn in hell* across our house."

"Jesus," Henry said.

"Probably not him." Henry laughed, then winced again. "Sorry," Paige said. She kissed his nose. "Anyway, when we got home after we visited you on Monday, the house had been broken into and I found a dead crow in the sink. We—"

"A crow?"

"Yeah."

"There was a crow on my car just before it ran me over," he said at length. "I threw Freddie's game at it to try to scare it off." He was silent a little longer, then said: "You know, that orderly looked familiar. I think he was one of the guys in the ambulance when they brought me here. I was sort of semi-conscious, you know?"

"Uh-huh," Paige said.

"And there was this ... uh, this *thing* ... out there in the marsh." He licked his lips. "This is going to sound crazy, but it was, like, a giant bird, and I could swear it was coming to get me—"

"Oh, honey, you probably dreamed that," she said. "After the car hit you."

"Yeah," he said. "Yeah, I guess that makes sense. But I *know* I saw a crow on my car." Pause. "I don't know why that would make somebody want to stalk us, though."

"That's because you're a normal person, hon," Paige said.

The door slid open and one of the nurses came in. He paused when he saw them in the bed together, and grinned. "Oh, stop," Paige said as she hopped off the bed.

"Nothing but innocent thoughts in my head," the guy said. He checked Henry's blood pressure and listened to his heart and then declared, "You're perfectly healthy. Why are you wasting our time?"

"Soon as the doctor says I can go, I'm gone," Henry said.

"Between you and me," the nurse said, "they're arguing about you. Dr. Sullivan and Dr. O'Shea want to send you home, but Dr. Clark wants to wait another couple days. I think they'll compromise on tomorrow."

"Can I get that in writing?"

"Sure," the nurse said. "Just as long as you don't want me to sign it."

After he had gone, Paige said: "I bet that was the guy, then. The same one who broke in and stuff."

"The cops'll fingerprint him," Henry said. "Then we'll know for sure."

"Poor Henry," Paige said. She kissed his nose again. "I would've told you sooner, but I didn't want you to sit here and worry about us. I didn't realize he would attack you."

"Well, you couldn't have known he worked for the hospital," Henry said. "Don't beat yourself up over it."

"Still," Paige said, kissing his chest lightly, just brushing her lips across his right nipple, "I wish there was some way I could make it up to you."

"Uh, Paige," he said thickly, as her lips moved lower.

"Mmm?"

"My door doesn't lock on this side, Paige."

She straightened up, looked at him for a moment; then she went to the door of his room and stuck her head out. She could see the nursing station at the end of the hallway. She called: "Guys?"

The nurses' heads swung around to look at her.

"Pretend there's a *do not disturb* sign on the door, okay?"

"Sure thing, Mrs. Fontana," one of them said.

"Thanks," she said, and she slid the door shut. She went back to the bed and started kissing Henry again, then remembered the video surveillance. She found a camera up in the corner, and draped one of Henry's pillowcases over the end.

From the hallway, she heard the nurses' cries of protest.

Grinning, she went back to her husband.

Thick, oily clouds squirmed in the sky and spat greasy dribbles of rain at the earth. Jasper Shoemaker Junior slouched through his classes and watched the rain fall and thought about how he was going to spend his half of the money. He didn't pay a whit of attention to anything anybody said all day long; this was normal behavior for him, so no one thought much of it.

At the end of the day, he went out one of the back doors, walked across the athletic field, and got into Oscar's van, which was parked at the side of the road that passed behind the high school. Oscar was sitting behind the wheel, the hard rock station cranked high. Jasper hated those dinosaur bands and turned off the radio as soon as he settled in.

"You're late," Oscar said. "I been sitting here for ten minutes. You know how the cops get when there's a van parked near the school."

"Chill out," Jasper said. "Nobody bothered you, right? You got to learn to *relax*, Oscar. That's half your problem. You're always so strung out, they think you're up to something even if you're not."

Oscar was silent a moment, then said: "I don't think the money is gonna be there yet. He can't raise that kind of cash this fast, he'll need to move assets around and stuff. Besides, he'll need some time to think it over."

"Well, we'll just go look," Jasper said. "Go to the park, walk around. You need to get out more anyway." Pause. "Come on, man, drive." Oscar started up the van. The engine sounded even worse than usual, like it had rocks in it or something. "First thing you do when we get the money," Jasper said, "you get a new car."

"Amen to that," Oscar said, as they headed for the park, and a possible rendezvous with financial independence.

The parking lot was empty as Oscar guided his van into a space near the entrance to the path that descended into the gardens. The pavement was still filthy from winter, covered in sand and branches and decaying leaves, sculpted into channels and deltas by the runoff of melting snow. Jasper scanned the debris, but there wasn't anything useful in it, just somebody's red knit mitten and what looked like the sole of a running shoe.

"I'll stay in the car," Oscar said. "Keep an eye on the laptop."

Jasper had dropped the computer off with Oscar on his way to school that morning, to get it out of the house, just in case Lauren Wise wanted to film in his bedroom or something. He said: "You brought it? Where is it?"

"Glove compartment," Oscar said. "I figured we can do the swap, if the money's there—which it won't be—and get this over with."

"Not getting nervous on me, are you, Oscar?"

"No," Oscar said. He was clearly lying, and lying badly. "But the sooner we get rid of the laptop, the sooner they got no more evidence against us, right?"

That sounded reasonable to Jasper, so he got out and walked down the soggy gravel path into Selden's Falls Park. The area had once been part of George Selden's extensive flower garden. George was the only grandson of John Selden, who had obtained some nine thousand acres of land in a grant back in the seventeenth century. John Selden had lived in a cruddy little cabin down near the creek, but by the time little George came along the family had gotten fat and rich and had built themselves a manor on a hill nearby. From their fancy house, they had a view of a splendid waterfall on the narrow stream known as Selden's Creek; and so the waterfall became Selden's Falls. The possessive was dropped from the name of the town, and the creek had since reverted to its original name in the language of the Oneida Indians; but on the waterfall, the name had stuck. Sadly, a rockslide in the early nineteenth century had reduced the falls to a series of rapids; the family line had followed the waterfall's example and come to an end when George Selden had died without any surviving children. All of George Selden's lands had passed into the hands of the town that bore his name, and they had maintained the flower garden ever since.

The only reason Jasper knew any of this was because it was printed on a very large plaque right next to the trailhead, which he stopped and read as he tried to gather up the nerve to go into the ravine and check for the money. He finally got moving when Oscar tooted the horn at him.

Beyond the plaque, the path sloped down a grassy incline toward the ravine, with smaller routes splitting off here and there to run along what would be banks of flowers come summertime, blooms in gaudy shades of yellow and red and blue. Wooden directional signs marked the intersections, giving information about what could be found down each divergent path; but right now they all had garbage bags tied over them, leftover protection against winter storms. Weather condoms, Jasper thought.

He stayed on the main path, following it into the gully, where it became a boardwalk elevated ten to fifteen feet above the stream floor. His footsteps on the walkway echoed like hollow blocks of wood clomping together. He zigzagged back and forth across the gulch before coming to the former waterfall at the head of the ravine. The rapids were somewhat less steep than a typical stairway; water poured over them, the creek was still swollen by the winter runoff. Come summer, it would just be a trickle.

On the hill that humped high above the rapids, he could see—barely—the building that had once been George Selden's mansion. Now it was a nursing home or something. The nursing home grounds were officially off-limits to park visitors, which made it a good place to take girls or have parties, up there among the thick pines that George Selden had planted all those years ago.

Where the boardwalk came back to solid ground there was a stone monolith six feet tall and four feet wide. On the face of the stone was a carving of an angel, wings spread, flying upward, arm outstretched and reaching for a hand that descended from above. Below the carving was an inscription: *For all the lost angels*. Jasper had no idea what the significance of the monolith was; the plaque at the entrance was not especially informative on the subject. All he knew was that it looked like it belonged in a cemetery.

Around the base of the monolith was a lip of stone maybe a foot wide. To get behind the marker, he had to sidle along this precarious ledge. He did so, clinging to the tablet with his fingers, and scooted around to the small promontory behind it.

And there, leaning up against the stone, was an imitation leather briefcase.

Holy shit. Farmer had actually coughed up the cash.

Jasper Junior scooped up the briefcase in his left hand and circled back to the front of the stone, where he dropped down and shook the briefcase. He could hear the wads of bills thudding around dully inside it. "See, Oscar?" he cried. "Money!"

Then he heard a booming voice from the hill where George Selden's house stood. "Drop the briefcase and don't move!"

And four uniformed cops came out from the thick trees. One of them had a camera; another one had a plastic cone attached to a tape recorder; the third had binoculars, the fourth a bullhorn. A fifth man was there too, a long-haired guy wearing sunglasses. Quentin Farmer's assistant.

Jasper stared at them. He thought he was going to pee his pants.

The cop on the end lifted up the megaphone and said, "Your father know what you've been doing after school, Jasper?"

Quentin Farmer was just glad he'd had the forethought to get a replacement hard drive overnighted to his hotel room.

The police moved in on the van after the kid went into the park. They bagged the freak behind the wheel easily enough; he saw a badge and turned into a blubbering wreck. He practically begged them to take the laptop out of his glove compartment; they obliged gladly. Quentin convinced Shockton to let him fire it up and see if his files were intact. It turned out, though, that the battery was dead. This didn't surprise him; they hadn't stolen the thing's power supply, so they had no way to recharge it.

He told Shockton he had to swap in a new battery, and Shockton told him to go ahead; he was too busy talking into a two-way radio to pay much attention to what Quentin was doing, which was fine with him. During the process of replacing the battery, he also popped out the removable hard drive and replaced it with the new, and gloriously blank, one he'd gotten from the manufacturer. The drained battery went into his laptop bag; the incriminating mass storage device went into his pocket.

"Damn it," he said after booting up the laptop. He hoped he

sounded truly annoyed. "They erased everything."

Shockton looked up from his walkie-talkie and said: "We've got him. It's Jasper Shoemaker's boy." Paul chuckled. "Channel Six and the paper are going to look pretty silly over this one."

Quentin handed the laptop over to Shockton, who spirited it away to one of the cop cars. A few minutes later the police who'd gone into the park emerged, Jasper Shoemaker Junior walking in their midst. Nelson trotted along behind them, his hair bedraggled with moisture, his coat filthy. Quentin wondered what had happened. "You fall into the ravine?" he asked, as Nelson passed.

"Long story," his assistant said. "I'll tell you about it later. You find the computer?"

"Yep."

"Data okay?"

"Erased," Quentin said.

"Oh. Too bad. Well, at least we have backups." Nelson shook some water out of his hair, then wandered over to the little informational gazebo at the mouth of the park. He seemed to be reading a smallish plaque that said something about lost angles. What the hell did that mean? He squinted at it. Oh, lost *angels*. That made more sense.

Quentin glanced at the police car into which they were loading the two would-be blackmailers. One of the cops was reading them their rights, but the kid kept interrupting, trying to tell them about the nasty pictures on the computer. Quentin could hear him saying, "Kiddie porn! Kiddie porn!" Yeah, keep talking, Quentin thought; incriminate yourself some more. He almost patted his jacket pocket, but caught himself.

The car containing the kid and the blob started up and pulled out of the parking lot. The other vehicles began to follow. Quentin called Nelson over to the Jaguar. "Let's get back to the Farmhouse," he said. "It's been a long day."

Simon Jones was in a better mood than he had been for quite some time.

The meeting with Quentin Farmer had gone well; it hadn't degenerated into a bitch session about the local police, media, or citizenry, and it hadn't involved threats to pull out of the project. In fact, Quentin had been downright tame; a pussycat. As it turned out, this was because he wanted help catching the people who had stolen his laptop and were trying to sell it back to him, but that was okay; they'd had a conference call with Shockton and a plan to recover Farmer's laptop had been developed. And to top it all off, he had finally beaten Kevin Kowalski at racquetball.

The only flaw in the diamond of today was Calvin Trott's disappearance and the incident at the church. Simon was afraid the discovery of a large subterranean chamber would attract archaeologists and historians more interested in unearthing the past than proceeding to the future.

Hm. That might make a good slogan. He scribbled it down on a piece of letterhead and put it in the filing cabinet under *Reelection*. The campaign would be underway soon; so far he had no opponent, but he didn't figure that would last much longer. Still, he could dream about running unopposed, couldn't he?

The phone rang. It was Paul Shockton. They had bagged the laptop thieves and recovered the computer; and one of the thieves was none other than Jasper Shoemaker Junior, who just last night—and again that morning—had appeared on Channel Six as a well-scrubbed, falsely-accused angel. Ha!

Then Paul said: "He claims the computer has kiddie porn on it."

Simon's internal confetti-throwing turned into a rain of broken glass. "Does it?"

"No, it's blank. We checked. The kid denies erasing it, says Farmer must've done it, but he didn't have the opportunity. I was watching him the whole time."

Back into confetti. "Terrific," Simon said. "Any news on the church incident?"

"Not really."

"How's Fanelli?"

"He's okay. Air bag protected him. If he was wearing his seat belt, he wouldn't even have broken his legs."

"Maybe you should make that a new policy."

Shockton made a verbal shrug noise. "They wouldn't go for it," he said.

"Shooter turn up yet?"

"No. But get this: the car we found is registered to a guy named Nick Garson. He was fired from Quentin Farmer's organization last

Friday. We found a couple of bullets on the floor under the driver's seat."

"How nice," Simon said. "Has Farmer been told?"

"Not yet," Shockton said.

"Did this Garson guy come here looking to kill his old boss?"

"Don't know. Maybe he was driving the bulldozer. Who can say?"

"Uh-huh," Simon said after a moment. "Is this good news, Paul?"

"Well, not really."

"Then tell me about it tomorrow."

"Sure, Simon. Whatever."

"Hey, Paul. How old is the Shoemaker kid?"

"Old enough that we can release his name."

Simon said: "Thank God for small favors."

"Or whoever," Shockton said.

Jasper Shoemaker Junior's mother was waiting for him when the police dropped him off at home. She was standing in the living room, wearing an apron smudged with chocolate, hair mussed and falling all around her face. All that was missing was the rolling pin. She looked like she wanted to strangle him, but all she said was: "Go to your room."

"Ma, I'm seventeen. You can't just—"

"Go to your room." She had a wicked gleam in her eyes, like she was hoping he'd give her an excuse to find that rolling pin and crush his skull with it.

He went to his room.

His parents had apparently gone through and removed everything from his room that could be used for entertainment. His telephone was gone, and his little stereo, and all his compact discs, and his small television set with the built-in DVD player—he'd bought that with his own money, too!—and all his tapes.

He went and flopped onto the bed. His head banged on the wall and he realized they had even confiscated his pillow. What the hell was this, some kind of boneheaded plot to show him what it was like in prison?

He dug an old flannel shirt out of the clothes pile and wadded it up under his neck. There, that was his pillow.

God, he was tired. He closed his eyes, but the fear in the pit of his stomach kept him from sleeping. He would just start to drift off and then it would jump up out of the darkness and hook its claws into him and whisper about what might happen to him. *You'll go to jail*, it would say. *You'll get slashed up in the shower. You'll sell your body for protection. By the time you get out, you'll be your father's age.*

Jesus, not that, he thought; anything but being his father's age.

There was only one thing to do: pin it all on Oscar and hope for youthful offender status.

The door opened and someone came in. From the way the floor creaked, it could only be his dad. He heard the old man settle into the desk chair, grunting around to get comfortable. There was a pause, and then Jasper Senior's voice said: "Well?"

Jasper didn't open his eyes. "Well what?"

"You *did* steal the computer."

"Maybe."

"Don't fuck around with me, Jasper. This is serious. The computer is worth over four thousand dollars. That's grand larceny. Plus I hear you were trying to sell it back to Farmer for fifty thousand dollars. They'll probably go for extortion on that one."

Jasper did open his eyes then. Fifty thousand dollars. Quentin Farmer was telling the cops they were hitting him up for fifty thousand dollars. That was smart. If he told them the actual amount, they'd naturally wonder what was on the computer that Jasper and Oscar thought he would pay that much for. Fifty grand was a much more reasonable amount for data. And what was Jasper going to do? Tell the cops no, they were blackmailing him for a *million?*

"Don't you have anything to say for yourself?" Jasper Senior said.

"I guess I fucked up."

"I guess you did." There was a pause, and then he said, "You got any idea how stupid this makes us look? You got any idea what this is going to do to our lawsuit? I just got a call from our lawyer. He saw the news and he's dropping our case. How are we gonna collect anything without a lawyer, Jasper? You tell me, you're so good at coming up with schemes."

"I guess we're not," Jasper said.

He heard his father grunt as he stood up. The chair creaked in relief. "I went to bat for you, son," Jasper Senior said, "and all the while you had his laptop hid right here. You made a fool out of me.

I'll remember that." The floorboards groaned as he walked out of the room. He slammed the door behind him.

Jasper got up and went to lock the door, only to discover that they'd removed that, too.

11

Nelson DeGrace finished combing his hair, verified that everything was in place, and slid on his sunglasses. It wasn't quite finished being dawn yet, but he could tell it was going to be one of those days where it was so bright that the sunlight felt like little bits of sand blowing into his eyes. He didn't like sunlight all that much; he often thought he would have made a snappy vampire.

He went to the window and opened the drapes and looked out at the slumbering world, at the frosted grounds of the Farmhouse bed and breakfast. It was on a street called Chicken Hill Road; couldn't get much more country-sounding than that, Nelson thought, which made it all the more amazing that Quentin had elected to move here. Just showed how desperate he'd been to hide from the media. They would never think to look for Quentin here; for one thing, the place wasn't even officially open until Memorial Day. They were paying double the normal rate for their rooms, but what the hell; it was Quentin's money.

He wasn't sure where the chickens were, but they were definitely on a hill; he could see Selden Falls down in the valley, a sad collection of grey and red and yellow buildings that all looked like they could use a thorough scrubbing. If he'd had a great big brush, Nelson thought, he would've done it for them. Scrub scrub scrub, lots of suds, and a shiny new city, just like that.

The canal was barely visible, glimmering in the morning light. With binoculars, maybe he would be able to see the activity at the old church: cops swarming around the hole, Channel Six trying to get footage, Quentin skulking around waiting to identify the bulldozer and anything else they might happen to find that belonged to him, like Nick Garson's body. Nelson was afraid he'd gone and shot himself. He felt kind of guilty about that whole situation, but he'd done what he could for the poor guy; it was just Nick's bad timing and Quentin's string of misfortunes that had led that particular chain of events to its unhappy conclusion.

Too bad Nick wasn't a little more patient, a little less anxious; today, Quentin was on cloud nine. He probably would've given Nick his job back, and a pay raise to cover his mental anguish.

In fact, Quentin seemed a little bit *too* thrilled to have his computer back. There wasn't that much data on there that wasn't backed up; just what he had entered while they were at the mall, as far as Nelson knew, and that was easy enough to re-enter, and the hard drive had been erased anyway.

So why was he so relieved?

Nelson absently stroked a strand of still-damp hair and stared into the morning. His sunglasses made everything look blue.

Was Quentin hiding something?

He turned and went into the hallway. Quentin's room was right next door. It was locked, but as always, Nelson had the key. He opened the door and went inside.

It didn't look like their hosts had tidied up yet. The bed was still unmade, a damp towel still hung from a bar in the bathroom. Nelson hooked the *Do Not Disturb* sign onto the door and closed it and wondered where to start. After a moment, he decided that the logical place would be Quentin's laptop case. He rifled it quickly and didn't find what he was looking for, just the extra battery and the power supply and some disks; the laptop itself was still in police custody.

Next he tried Quentin's suitcase. It was new, still smelled like leather. Quentin sure did go through luggage. Nelson often wondered what he did with his old bags. Maybe he gave them to retiring employees as tokens of appreciation. He went through the bag in a hurry, and didn't find anything out of the ordinary in there, either. He closed the suitcase and adjusted it to the same angle it had been at when he opened it. He thought a moment, then opened the door of the wardrobe. Quentin's long coat, the one he had been wearing yesterday, hung among his jackets and shirts. For his odyssey into the underworld—there was no way they were getting that bulldozer out of the hole, not until the ground firmed up a bit, so Quentin was going to have to get down and dirty—he had bought a cheap jacket from a local store. Nelson had had to take his picture while he was doing it; he was imagining a headline like *Developer Supports Local Economy* or something. Dream on, Quentin, Nelson thought.

He patted down the coat. There was something squarish and rather heavy in the inside pocket. He reached in, and pulled out the removable hard drive from Quentin's computer, and stood there holding it, staring at it, wondering what he'd be able to see if he could read the ones and zeroes.

After a moment, Nelson slid the hard drive back into the pocket. Then he went out into the hallway and back to his room, where he sat down in a chair near the window, just out of the sunlight. He told himself that finding a spare hard drive didn't really prove anything; it didn't mean, for instance, that Quentin had switched drives when the cops weren't looking. But you *did* have to wonder, didn't you, what that hard drive was doing hidden away in the pocket of the coat he had been wearing when they had recovered the computer?

Maybe he would ask Quentin when he got back.

Or maybe he would just pretend that the last twenty minutes had never happened.

Quentin stood right at the edge of the hole. The smell of earth and old metal wafted out of it, twisted together into a brittle, unpleasant odor that made him wrinkle up his nose; it was even stronger than the plastic smell emanating from the flimsy awning they had erected over the pit to keep out the rain. Not that it was actually raining today, but better late than never, right?

Behind him, he heard a tires crunching on gravel. He glanced over his shoulder and saw one of the police cars leaving, driving back to Marsh Road along the route the bulldozer had taken through the brush. This had become the *de facto* approach to the old church; they'd brought out a steamroller and flattened what was left of the vegetation, and then dumped crushed stone all over it to keep it down. Quentin had to admit it was a lot more direct and convenient than the muddy old access route from River Road. Coming in from the other direction, that first hill was just too steep, and the ground was too boggy. This new road was much better; it would make it a lot easier to demolish the old church when they were finally ready to proceed to that stage. For that, he supposed, he had to thank whoever had stolen his bulldozer. That lunatic Garson, probably.

Voices rose from the pit; somebody was saying, "One, two three!" A couple of guys from the contractor Simon had hired—Kastle Konstruction, a name Quentin found impossible to take seriously— had been down there all morning, banging away on buttresses that were supposed to reinforce the sides of the pit; the cops weren't letting anyone else into the hole until they were finished. They'd been working since before Quentin had arrived, and still weren't done. If he had known he was going to spend forty-five minutes cooling his heels out in the cold, damp air, he would've stayed in bed an extra hour or two.

As he pondered whether or not he should go back to the inn, or at least take a nap in his car, the top of a wooden ladder appeared over the edge of the pit. One of the topside members of Kastle Konstruction—or, as Quentin had begun to think of them, *Karl's Kommandos*—fitted it with two wooden hook things, L-shaped devices with rings on one end. Each post of the ladder was encircled with a ring, and then the Ls got hammered into the muddy earth to hold it in place. Quentin guessed this was some sort of a terminal stage in the shoring process; this was confirmed when, after a brief conversation with the Kommando, one of the cops on the scene—his name was Grady something, or something Grady—clapped Quentin on the shoulder and said: "Ready to go?"

"Sure," Quentin said.

"Okay. Here's a light." Grady handed him a heavy plastic flashlight, and then they both went down the ladder into the pit.

At the bottom, Quentin stepped off onto a flat slab of rock: the flagstone that had formed the cover of the hole. It was caked with dirt from the wide tracks of the bulldozer. To his right and left, the workers were testing out their shoring members, rapping them with hammers, kicking them, tugging on them. The sunlight filtering through the tent overhead made them all look kind of green. After a minute or two of this, they headed for the ladder and began climbing out; but one stopped in front of Quentin and proffered a hand. "Karl Castle," he said.

"Quentin Farmer."

"Welcome to the pit," Karl said as they shook.

"Remember," Grady said, once the amenities were out of the way, "don't touch anything. If you find something weird, call me. Okay?"

Quentin wondered what would be considered *weird* in the context, but said: "Okay." Grady nodded and flicked on his flashlight and aimed it into the darkness, playing it left and right at about eye level; the end of the beam plastered a circle against twisted poles of dark, rotten-looking wood, arm-sized tendrils all twined and wrapped around each other into a forest of knotty columns as big around as a man. They came through the underside of the church floor, filling up the last third of the pit.

Roots, Quentin realized; they were the roots of the big tree that grew from the floor overhead. What the hell kind of root structure was *that*? If Grady wanted weird, well, there it was, right in his face. He didn't appear overly interested in them, though; he didn't remark on them at all. Instead, he seemed to be concerned about the flashlight beam itself, which was made visible by tiny particles floating in the air, glimmering like flakes of mica.

"What's all that?" the cop said.

Karl Castle said: "Dust?"

"Awful shiny for dust." Quentin eyed the floating detritus; he didn't like the idea of breathing it in. Then he noticed that Karl had a surgical-type mask around his neck, so he bummed one off of him and put it on. That made him feel a little better. After a moment Grady did the same. Karl, apparently deciding that if they weren't going to breathe the dust then neither was he, slipped his own mask up over his mouth.

The three of them proceeded into the chamber, playing circles of light every which-way. Karl aimed his at the floor of the church. "I'm surprised this entire thing hasn't fallen in," Karl said. "Look at the dry rot."

It didn't look all that dry to Quentin; it looked slimy and filthy, thick crossbeams dark with age and decay supporting sagging two-by-fours. Even if the bulldozer had made it across the flagstone, he thought, it would have crashed right through the floor of the place. Its appearance of being built on a slab was strictly illusory. He said: "Must be the roots are holding it together."

"Yeah, is that something or what? Like somebody grew them that way on purpose. What's this?" They had come upon a pile of rusted metal, the remnants of some ancient machine. It wasn't very tall; Grady's light must have passed right over it. Karl and Quentin played their beams over it, and after a moment Quentin said: "That's my bulldozer. What the hell happened to it?"

Karl made a clucking sound, then said: "Guess you should've gotten it rustproofed." After a moment he moved away, farther into the pit, toward the root colonnades in the back; but Quentin stood and stared at the decrepit hulk. Rustproofing? To hell with that. This heap was so badly corroded, it would've had to be encased in a block of Lucite to protect it. No way should it have turned into junk so fast. And where the hell was the driver?

Quentin turned away from the bulldozer. The circle of light from his flashlight swept across the barren earth wall to his right, then fluttered over the root forest. There didn't seem to be anything down here, other than the wreck of his bulldozer. Just earth floor and earth walls and a stench of decay and a faint whiff of natural gas.

Huh?

He aimed his flashlight in the direction Karl and Grady had gone. He could see them through the columns at the far end of the pit; they seemed to be looking at something in the corner. Quentin headed that way, sniffing the air; the scent of gas remained steady. "You guys smell anything?" he asked as he approached.

"Ow!" Karl said suddenly. The circle of illumination coming from his flashlight jerked violently as he dropped it and stood up, clutching his wrist. "God *damn* it!"

"What?" Quentin said.

"Shit!" Karl took a step back, leaned up against one of the root-trees. Grady shined his light on the other man's wrist, on the bright red blood flowing from two long, shallow scratches in his forearm and a bite wound in his hand. "He stole my watch!"

"Who stole your watch?" Quentin said. "What the hell's going on? Somebody's down here?"

Grady glanced at him, then said: "See for yourself." He moved aside, revealing an ancient husk of a man curled up in a little ball in the corner. He was clutching a shiny gold watch in both hands, and shivering like a frightened rabbit.

"Who is it?" Quentin said.

"I have no fucking clue," Karl said. He kicked his flashlight away from the corner, sending light spinning crazily around the chamber. "But don't let him see your watch."

Nelson couldn't believe it; it was a *nice day* in Selden Falls. The sun was out, the sky was clear, the air was warm. Like a long-delayed guest, Spring was coming after all.

He decided to go for a walk. Get outside, do some thinking. He took his coat out of the closet, folded it over his arm, and headed to the stairs at the end of the hallway.

Instead of going down, though, for some reason he went up.

The first three flights of stairs were wide and carpeted, but the last one was narrow and made of bare, well-worn wood. They led to the cupola on the roof of the Farmhouse; apparently the little square chamber was popular with guests, because it was well-stocked with magazines and books. These resided in shelves underneath the faded green cushions of a window bench that completely encircled the room. A telescope was set up on a little tripod on the sill behind this bench; the lens aimed down into the valley below.

Sightseeing equipment, Nelson thought. He went and knelt on the cushion and peered into the telescope. Blurry. He found the focusing knob and got the scene to an acceptable level of clarity, and damned if he couldn't see the old church sticking up from the side of the canal. There was all kinds of activity going on down there; two or three police cars, a van that said *Kastle Konstruction*, and an ambulance.

Ambulance?

They seemed to be hoisting something out of the pit, although his view of that was blocked by a cheap-looking green plastic awning. God, he thought; not another casualty. Maybe they really *had* found Nick with a bullet in his head. It wasn't long before they got the victim, whoever it was, out of the pit; but then there were too many cops and paramedics swarming around, and he couldn't see who was on the stretcher.

He stood up. Well, whatever had happened, he'd find out soon enough. Wasn't anything good, that was for sure. He left the telescope where it was and wandered downstairs, into the kitchen. This was a wide, bright, airy room done up in white ceramic tile and various kinds of wood. The owners of the Farmhouse were engaged at the stove; the room smelled of sausage and maple syrup and melted butter. Nelson figured they were cooking for themselves, since the inn was technically not open yet.

The proprietors were an older couple, somewhere in the low seventies, Nelson thought. Tom and Raye Teller. He supposed garrulousness was a prerequisite of operating a bed and breakfast; if so, these two were eminently qualified to be innkeepers. They could discourse at length on any topic: the weather, sports, movies, you name it. The first night they'd been here, after he and Quentin had finally gotten away from the Tellers, Quentin had half-seriously suggested Nelson pay them to keep their mouths shut in the future.

Tom Teller glanced at him as he entered the kitchen. "Morning, Mr. Nelson," he said. "How'd you sleep? Storm keep you up?"

"Woke me up a couple of times," Nelson said, remembering the lightning, the thunder, the rain thrumming against the window, loud as a hail of gravel. Today's sapphire sky and glowing sun seemed like nature's sheepish apology for going berserk the night before.

"Me too," Tom said, "but they got it worse down in the valley. I sat up in the cupola and watched it for a spell."

"I was just up there," Nelson said. "Nice setup." Pause. "Were you looking at the old place by the canal?"

"I guess I might've," Tom said. "I try to keep an eye on things."

Raye said: "You going for a walk, Mr. Nelson?"

"Yeah," Nelson said. He had given up on trying to explain to them that Nelson was his first name.

"You want me to pack you a lunch?"

"I'm not planning to be out that long."

"Nonsense. Beautiful day, you won't want to come back inside. You just sit down at the table and I'll make you a sandwich. What do you want? You like turkey? And cheese? I'll make you a turkey sandwich." She elbowed Tom away from the refrigerator and began rummaging around inside it. Raye started to hum a little tune as she worked; it sounded like a lullaby.

Nelson sat at the breakfast table. It smelled of lemon cleanser, and its highly polished surface reflected a sunbeam right into his eyes. He pulled out his sunglasses and slipped them onto his face. Tom crossed the kitchen and fell into the chair opposite him and said: "So, that boss of yours got himself an early start today, didn't he?"

"He sure did," Nelson said.

"What's he doing down at the old barn, anyhow?"

"We're trying to get it demolished," he said, surprised. Nelson had figured everyone in the area knew about the misadventures of Quentin Farmer and the Church That Would Not Fall; on the other hand, there didn't seem to be any televisions in the Farmhouse, and he had never seen a paper cross the doorstep. It seemed that Tom and Raye hadn't been aware of Quentin's plans; they exchanged a glance that Nelson interpreted as dismay. "It's right across from the shopping center we're building," he added, in case they thought Quentin went around knocking down old buildings for fun.

"Shopping center?" Tom squinted at Nelson. "Don't recall him saying he was putting up a shopping center. Why there?"

"Well, it's not just a shopping center," Nelson said. He knew Quentin's presentation by heart, having delivered it—twice—to the Selden Falls zoning board, but he didn't feel like running through the whole thing for the Tellers. "It's a promenade."

"A what?" Tom said.

"A promenade," Nelson said. "In the summer we'll have music and puppet shows, canoe rentals, um, maybe an art gallery ..." He trailed off, because Tom was looking at him like he had two heads. "Um, anyway, to answer your question, we're building it there to take advantage of the canal."

"Plenty of space along the canal," Tom said. "Didn't have to put it there."

Wondering why Tom Teller gave a damn where Quentin built his plaza, Nelson said: "Well, see, this parcel belonged to the city, so we got it really cheaply. It ..." He trailed off again; this time Tom was giving him a dark look, like he'd just said that Quentin was bulldozing an orphanage to make way for the development.

Raye said: "Oh, Tom, stop glowering so. Makes you look old."

Tom Teller grunted, and said: "Well, Mr. Nelson, I wish you luck with your plaza. Hope nothing comes of it."

"Nothing comes of it?"

"Building there, I mean," Tom said. "Bad piece of land."

"I don't follow."

Tom sighed and stood. He was tall and gaunt and his face seemed flaccid and rubbery. "Been boggy down there, ever since they built the canal," he said. "Got to be careful or the land will just swallow you up."

"Oh," Nelson said. "Well, as far as that goes, we had surveyors and engineers and—" He broke off as Tom Teller exited through the swinging door to the interior of the house, leaving him speaking to no one.

Raye came over and gave him an overstuffed sandwich in a plastic zipper bag. "Don't mind Tom," she said. "He's always got something to say."

Guess so, Nelson thought. "Thanks for the sandwich," he said, standing and stuffing the plastic package into his jacket.

"You're quite welcome."

He went out into the backyard of the Farmhouse Inn, stood on the little porch to smell the air. It was chilly in the shade, but as he went down the stairs and out into the light he felt himself warming. The sun was good for something, anyway. He walked down the gently sloping yard, past a barren rock garden and an inert fountain, between burlap-covered shrubs and cut-back rose bushes, all the way to the edge of the forest. He got into the shadow of the trees and turned left and walked, alongside them, staying just out of the sun.

He had only been out for a few minutes when his phone trilled. He took it out of his pocket and said: "Quentin Farmer's office, Nelson speaking."

It was Michael Verdura, from the district attorney's office, calling to let him know that Quentin's lawyers had reached a plea bargain agreement in the Case of the Peroxide Blow-Job. Misdemeanor disorderly conduct, a small fine, and a tidy conclusion to the whole mess. Nelson thanked the attorney for the news, and the attorney said, "No problem, Mr. Nelson." He hung up before Nelson could correct him. As he put the phone away, Nelson wondered if one-named celebrities had this problem. He doubted it.

Well, things seemed to be resolving themselves quite neatly for Quentin. He would get off on the charge of public lewdness—no pun intended—and he had his laptop back, or would shortly, once the police were through with it; on a related topic, Jasper Shoemaker Junior was telling anyone who would listen the sad story about how his adult friend Oscar had enticed him into a life of theft and larceny. Nick Garson had dropped off the face of the earth. And within a couple of days, the derelict church should be history.

Nelson knew that, as Quentin's personal assistant, he should have a warm, satisfied feeling for the way things were turning out.

So why did he feel like they were dancing right on the edge of a disaster?

That morning, Paige and Freddie went to pick up Henry.

There had been a message on her machine when she had returned home from the hospital the afternoon before, a call from Dr. Clark asking her to please telephone him back as soon as possible. Paige had called back and been told the doctor was out on an emergency call, and had promptly freaked, thinking that something had happened to Henry in the brief interval between her leaving and arriving home; but the office manager had explained that no, Henry was fine, and in fact he was due to be discharged the next day and she should arrange to pick him up. The manager couldn't explain why Dr. Clark hadn't bothered to mention that in his urgent-sounding message; apparently, the staff at the hospital just enjoyed scaring people.

Paige had listened to the office manager recite a host of provisos and caveats to Henry's release, a laundry list of things he couldn't do, and things that should prompt them to rush back to the emergency room, and things that would require a visit but could wait until the doctors were done golfing, or whatever. She had scribbled it all down, but she was also going to pick up a written version when she got Henry. Sort of like an instruction manual: *A Guide to the Proper Maintenance of Your Husband.*

Paige parked in her usual lot, on the same side of the hospital as Henry's room; so they had to pass the spot where Henry's attacker had landed after he jumped out the window and tried to fly away. It was now official that the same man had been the one stalking her; she had checked with the police that morning, and they had informed her that his fingerprints had matched up to what they'd gotten from the cans and from Freddie's window. So both cases were closed, and they could get on with their lives without fear of further molestation.

The area around the impact site was cordoned off, but the tape was arranged to allow access through the entrance. Paige and Freddie walked slowly past the restricted area as they headed for the hospital door. "Don't look, Freddie," she said, covering his eyes, even though she was staring at the discolored pavement herself. The man had popped open like a rotten tomato, and had left the same kind of stain as one, too, reddish and pulpy. A crow, heedless of the barriers, was within the restricted area, hopping around the spot, eyeing it with interest. Probably liked the way it smelled, Paige thought; made her want to barf.

The side entrance admitted them to a whitewashed stairwell. The windows were open, letting in the smell of rain and wet grass and musty bark. As she reached the second-floor landing, a crow that was perched on the windowsill commenced a noisy show of flapping and coughing, startling her. She stood and watched it thrash spastically against the screen, as if it were desperate to get inside. She wondered if it was the same crow they had just seen, if it smelled more of that good stuff within the hospital walls.

Frederick said: "Mommy, what's that bird doing?"

"I don't know, honey," she said. "Maybe it's sick." She took her son's hand and they continued onward, upward, leaving the squawking bird behind.

But there was another one outside the window of the third floor landing. A bigger one, nearly the size of a chicken, she thought; it had flecks of white in with the black of its feathers. Not much, just a smattering, but she had never seen a crow that was anything but black. It didn't thrash around like the one downstairs; it just sat there, staring intently into the stairwell. The screen was poked full of small round holes.

Beak marks.

She could tell when the crow noticed her, even though its head scarcely moved; she suddenly became aware of its attention, sizing her up as a potential goody. Her, and Freddie too.

Nobody looked at Freddie that way. Not even a stupid bird. She let go of her son's hand and went to the window and whacked the screen with the back of her hand. "Get lost," she said.

The crow didn't flinch. It didn't even blink. She hit the screen again, and this time the crow—moving so fast its head was a blur, so precisely she didn't even feel the puncture at first—stabbed her with its long black beak. She pulled her hand away and left a few glistening drops of blood hanging in the sunlight, floating there for what seemed like seconds, shivering, shimmering globes of crimson. Then they fell, and hit the windowsill, and sounded like bowling balls dropped from a great height.

And the crow just stared at her with those steady midnight eyes.

Frederick said: "Mommy?"

She backed away from the window. There was a small, neat, hole right in the middle of the back of her right hand. The thing's beak had slid deftly between two of the bones, letting it drive deeply into her flesh. She wiggled her fingers. Everything seemed to work; the bird hadn't gotten any muscles or tendons or whatever other important stuff was there.

She looked at it. It looked back. Its little black tongue flicked out across its beak, like it was tasting the blood it had drawn from her; and it burbled softly, a happy little crow noise.

What the hell kind of bird was this?

The injury was beginning to sting. She thought of the sorts of things crows did with their beaks—pecking at roadkill leapt immediately to mind—and decided she needed to get the wound looked at quickly. "Come on," she said to Frederick. Keeping her wounded hand elevated, she led Freddie out of the stairwell and into the third floor hallway, just in time to nearly get run over by a stretcher being wheeled to a room. An old man lay on it, shivering under his blanket and moaning softly. He was connected to a gleaming bag of saline, and with his right hand he was clutching what looked like a gold wristwatch.

She flattened herself and Frederick against the wall and the cart rumbled by. They turned into a room on the right; and as they did the old man's head lolled to the side, facing her. His eyes opened. They were milky black, like frosted onyx, and deep as the night sky. For an instant their gazes were locked, and then they rolled him into the room and the contact was broken.

For some reason, the old man's face made her think of the placid eyes of the crow, the crow that had stabbed her. Paige realized she was shivering, too, just like the old man; she stayed flat against the wall and took several slow, deep breaths and got her twitching muscles under control. Freddie didn't seem to notice anything amiss; he was craning his neck, looking at the room where they had taken the old man. She pulled him around and they went up the hallway toward the nursing station, and an alternate set of stairs.

One of the nurses looked at Paige as she and Freddie passed, and said: "Are you all right, ma'am?"

Paige nodded, not trusting her voice, not wanting to stay on this floor; the old man had given her the creeps, and the crow was waiting outside. She hurried away before the nurse could ask any more questions. She pushed into the stairwell and went up the last flight to the fourth floor, then down the hallway to the secure wing. She knocked; an orderly—not Harlan—let her in. Then he got in front of her and said: "You're bleeding."

"I'm aware of that," Paige said.

"What happened?"

"I got pecked by a bird. Got any antiseptic?"

A smile flickered across the orderly's face, and he said: "I think we can scare some up." He sent her over to the nursing station, where they clucked over her and cleaned her hand and smeared it with antibiotic and bandaged her up. The antiseptic felt funny under the gauze, kind of bubbly and tingly, like it had started fizzing against her skin. Well, that must be what it was supposed to do, she thought; maybe it had hydrogen peroxide in it or something.

One of the nurses asked her when her last tetanus shot had been, and she told them about how, last summer, she had stepped on one of Freddie's bayonet-carrying toy soldiers while walking barefoot in the back yard. This elicited a sympathetic collective wince, and much patting of the shoulders and other carrying-on. Paige wondered why they were fawning over her so much, until she caught two of the nurses checking out her legs as she sat on a stool getting her hand dressed. Since the weather was so nice and Henry was coming home, she had put on one of her shorter skirts. It was nice to know she could still attract the attention of things other than birds.

She could see the video monitors from her perch, a bank of six of them; she thought about the other day, when she'd gone down on Henry in his hospital bed. Made her neck get a little warm, thinking about what a bad girl she'd been. Then she noticed that two of the monitors were showing the same room from different angles; it occurred to her that this meant there were two different cameras in at least one room. Had there been another one in Henry's room that she hadn't seen?

Her neck got very warm. Maybe she was more of a bad girl than she'd thought.

Suddenly she heard Henry say, "What'd you do to yourself?" She looked in the direction of the voice, and Harlan had Henry in a wheelchair right next to the nursing station.

"A crow bit her," Frederick said.

"And when did you become a paraplegic?" she asked.

Harlan said: "Nobody ever *walks* out of a hospital. The only way out is to get pushed."

"Or jump," one of the nurses said. There was a momentary silence, and then he added: "Don't all laugh at once."

Paige stood up and thanked everyone for patching her up; then Harlan swung Henry around and they started squeaking toward the exit. She and Frederick followed. Her injured hand felt weird, kind of numb and tingly, like the pins-and-needles sensation of a body part that had fallen asleep. The antiseptic had stopped fizzing, and now was just warm. But by the time they reached the discharge desk, all those sensations had stopped and it was back to normal. Just stung a bit, that was all.

Harlan let go of the wheelchair and said: "End of the ride, Mr. Fontana."

"Thanks, Harlan." Henry stood up stiffly, then shook the orderly's hand. "I'll expect to see that résumé soon."

"You sure will, Mr. Fontana. Thank you." Harlan turned the wheelchair around and trundled it back into the depths of the hospital, as the woman behind the desk started hunting for Henry's paperwork.

A few minutes later, the three of them went out the side door of the hospital, into the warmth of the sun. Felt like spring today, Paige thought. A good day for Henry to be coming home. As if reading her thoughts, Henry gave her hand a squeeze and said: "Great day to get paroled, isn't it?"

She squeezed him back, but said nothing; they were passing the spot where the orderly had hit; she was looking at it, and remembering. Paige noticed Henry eyeing the cordoned-off area too. His face was blank, but she could imagine what he was thinking; after all, the guy had nearly killed him.

When they had gotten some distance from the hospital Paige

stopped and looked back at the building. At first she didn't see the big crow, and was relieved that it had gone; but then she spotted it on the ledge outside a third-floor window. For some reason, she thought it was the room the old man had been taken to, though she couldn't tell from out here, of course.

Henry noticed her standing there, and said: "What're you looking at?"

"The crow." She pointed at it. "That's the one that got me."

"You dirty rat," Henry called.

Freddie picked up a stone, and had his arm cocked to throw before Paige noticed what he was up to. A sudden irrational panic flooded her, filled up her throat like cotton; a fear that he would somehow actually hit the bird, and it would come after them some night, it and its friends, blotting out the stars above her house as they settled onto the roof. She wanted to grab Freddie's hand, to stop him, but it was too late; he had already flung the rock in the instant it took her to realize what he had in mind. She watched the projectile fly, the jagged grey shape standing out against the weathered brown brick of the hospital. Please, God, she thought, don't let it hit the bird.

Henry said: "Frederick, civilized people don't throw rocks at hospitals."

The rock hit the bricks between the second and third floors, yards beneath the crow but otherwise dead-on. Paige began to breathe again. She was being ridiculous, anyway; it was only a bird, it didn't

—

The crow's head flicked down to the impact point, then around to look at them, its cold black eyes like rifle sights. Somehow, even at this distance, she could feel their gaze.

Her hand twinged sharply, like the beak was piercing her flesh again. She made a little squeak and hugged the injured member to her body.

Henry said: "Paige? What's wrong?"

The crow's head swiveled around, once more to stare at itself in the darkened window of the old man's room. And just like that, the pain went away.

Coincidence, she thought; just coincidence. She turned to Henry and said: "Nothing. I'm just being silly. Come on, let's get you home."

The three of them walked through the shade of the poplars, into the sun.

PART TWO: PROMENADE

12

AUGUST CAME, AND SOME THINGS had changed in Selden Falls; from Nelson's point of view, the most notable of these was the state of Canal Plaza, which would be opening the next day. Quentin and Nelson had arrived earlier that morning for one last tour of the place; Quentin's long-standing policy of visiting his projects just before construction began and again just before they went into operation remained unaltered, despite the events of last March. In fact, since he had managed to come through that mess unscathed, he had become even more cocky than usual, and he still wasn't quite back to his normal level of self-satisfaction.

Some things hadn't changed in the five months since they'd last been in Selden Falls. Simon was as nervous and accommodating as ever; maybe even more nervous, because of the election looming in November. Their hosts at the Farmhouse—Quentin had wanted to stay at the old place again, much to Nelson's amazement—had apparently forgiven Quentin the transgression of bulldozing the old church and were as talkative as ever. Downtown Selden Falls was dead as it had been last time; Canal Plaza wasn't likely to help that situation any, despite Quentin's claims of its potential to attract day-trippers from other areas.

The most distressing thing that hadn't changed, though, was the fact that this weekend promised to be as nondescript and boring as every other opening ceremony Quentin had dragged him to. Nelson wondered if he could beg off next time; there was never anything to do except trail along after Quentin as he flitted from one store to the next like a bee on a mission of pollination. Never time to check out the local culture, such as it was. Never time to have fun.

Ha. Nelson stay home while Quentin went off to an opening? Then who would fetch his slippers and newspaper in the morning?

Nelson sat down on the side of the low, wide flower bed opposite the stores and waited for Quentin to finish up his inspection of the second level. Saturday—the day of the grand opening—couldn't arrive soon enough. There would be fireworks, free canoe rides, a band. Prizes. Hullabaloo. Quentin was going to throw a grand old party for Selden Falls, but first he had to check out the merchandise, visit the kitchens, inhale the scents of fresh carpeting and new wallpaper and chrome racks full of clothes, the hot aura of electronics, the aroma of exotic foods packaged in boxes that could nearly be considered art.

Nelson sat in the midst of the place that Quentin's money had built, and tried to imagine what it would look like from the air. It wasn't unattractive, for a strip mall; the former grassy, reedy, soggy lot had been transformed into a multitiered stucco-and-concrete terrace, whitewashed to a brilliant ivory, dotted with trees and shrubs in big cement pots and painted with broad, streaky banks of flowers. The slope of the bank hadn't been particularly sharp when they had started, but the importation of tons and tons of earth and stone had taken care of that; Quentin had wanted a terraced plaza, and by God, that was what he got.

Still, Nelson couldn't shake the feeling that it might have been more sensible to just work with the land the way it was, and save the terrace for someplace with a real hill. He wondered if that meant it was getting to be time to look for a new job.

The second level—Nelson's current location—was the most densely packed with stores, thirteen of them in all, their signs fresh and inviting, front windows so clear you might walk into them if you weren't paying attention. Steps that were white as a movie star's teeth and steep as a movie star's salary led to the canal promenade below, with small shops and bistros and the canoe house, and to the top tier above, with a large Indian restaurant, a coffeehouse, a couple of smallish stores that sold things such as terra-cotta wall hangings shaped like animal heads, and the plaza offices.

The stairs up and down were on opposite ends of the plaza. This was supposedly one of the brilliant things about the design; Quentin called it brilliant, anyway, and that made it so, although Nelson figured the shoppers would just find it annoying that they had to do so much unnecessary walking, especially come January. You had to pass every single store to travel from the top to the bottom. Window-shopping, strictly enforced. Ramps ran beside the steps, maintaining a fairly reasonable grade via switchbacks, but the place was handicapped-accessible only in the loosest sense of the term. Nelson wouldn't have wanted to try navigating a wheelchair up or down those paths.

He looked up at the higher level of the plaza; he could only see the very top of the facade, high pinnacles of steel slathered with concrete, triangles alternating with ovoid crests, a clock tower smack in the middle. It was a new design they had copied from some outlet mall Quentin had been to the year before. The snow was going to pile right up behind that facade in winter, Nelson had said, but who was he? Just Quentin Farmer's assistant. Not anyone whose opinion needed to be taken seriously.

Well, when the roof started to sag from the weight of all the snow, they'd be sorry they hadn't listened to him. So there.

Quentin came out of a store near the end—sporting goods place, guns and knives and fishing poles; Nelson wondered how it had made the upscale cut—and announced: "Canal-side." He vanished down the stairs. Nelson sighed, stood, and went after him. The stairwell was hemmed in by high concrete walls; the farther down he went, the higher they got, until they were at least seven inches above his head. They bounced every little sound back at him, from the whisper of his breath to the squeak of his new and not entirely broken-in shoes to the jingle of the Jaguar keys in his pocket.

The steps let him off at the left end of the promenade, to the right of the canoe house. He wandered across the concrete. The brass railing between him and the water seemed to glow in the warming light of the sun, and the brilliant white cement was alive with illumination. To the right, at the far end of the promenade, the terrace narrowed into a sort of causeway, a paved walking path along the side of the canal. It followed the gentle curve of the water down to the I-90 bridge, where it widened into a small, sheltered amphitheatre. Nelson wasn't too sure about that amphitheatre; it was an afterthought, an addition somebody in marketing had come up with, and he figured it was too close to the interstate to be useful for anything other than heavy metal concerts. But the designer had insisted that its accordion-like timber walls would block the noise of passing cars; and of course, Quentin had bit. Oh well; it hadn't added that much to the cost. He just hoped nobody drove a truck off the interstate and smashed into the orchestra shell. God knew the lawsuits something like that would generate.

The concrete walkway emerged from the other end of the amphitheatre, passed under the interstate bridge, and continued along the bank of the canal through what could almost be called wilderness. It ended a mile or so away, forming a little cul-de-sac where a wooden observation tower allowed you to climb up and observe nature from a safely elevated position. Nelson wasn't exactly clear on what nature was actually observable from there; apparently it was a wetland preserve or something. Ducks and herons and stuff. There was a little plaque on it that said something about appreciating the wonders of the world; more likely, he thought, it would end up as a place for local teenagers to appreciate the wonders of illicit sex. But maybe he was being ungenerous.

Quentin was in the canoe house to Nelson's left, where a dozen red fiberglass watercraft swayed gently in their moorings. Beyond that were several small docks for the imaginary boats that the plaza would attract; there were also iron mushrooms along the promenade in case any of them cared to tie up on their travels along this disused stretch of canal. Nelson watched his boss test the structure of the dock by jumping up and down on it. Like a kid, he thought; a kid checking out his new treehouse. He plopped down on one of the mushrooms and rubbed the back of his neck, thinking it was time for a haircut.

Across the water was the spot where the old church had stood.

The decrepit, derelict building had been replaced by a little rock garden, a high embankment of brown earth and wispy grass, like an adolescent beard on a fresh grave. There were supposed to be flowers, scads and scads of flowers, but hardly any of them had bloomed; the grass wasn't doing too well, either, coming up yellow and stunted. Bad soil, Nelson thought. Bad *something*.

He remembered what Tom Teller had said, back in March: the ground down here would swallow them up. But the only thing the ground had swallowed up had been the old church, under the onslaught of Karl Castle's machines. Nelson remembered the crows rising up from the big tree as its branches shook and quivered, emerging from the tangle of limbs like black water from a squeezed sponge. A cloud of them, spiraling into the air, squawking and coughing, circling in ebon spirals and then scattering, vanishing, as the aged structure collapsed into its own basement. There'd been a bloom of splinters and dust, rising from the pit like brimstone vapors. The big tree had toppled over and dashed itself to pieces against the muddy earth.

All the traces of the place were gone now, hauled away or smothered under imported soil; but as he stared at the dry brown earth with its stunted growth, Nelson found himself wondering what was going on beneath it, if burial had been the end of it.

Quentin appeared next to him, arms folded, scowling across the water. "I told them I wanted *wooden* canoes," he said.

"Fiberglass is cheaper," Nelson said.

Quentin cocked his head at him.

"It'll last longer, too," he added.

"It doesn't fit the aura I'm trying to create," Quentin said.

"I don't think anyone will notice any aura problems," Nelson said. Quentin only grunted. After a moment Nelson said: "I wonder why none of the flowers are growing."

"What?" Quentin said.

Nelson indicated the former site of the church with a nod of his head. "The flowers aren't growing. The grass looks like shit. I wonder why."

"Knuckleheads probably never watered it," Quentin said.

"It hasn't been *that* dry this summer," Nelson said.

For a moment, Quentin didn't say anything. Then he said: "Maybe it's cursed ground." Nelson looked up at him, and their gazes met; Quentin started to chuckle, and walked away, up the promenade toward the amphitheatre.

Nelson looked back across the water, and couldn't find it amusing.

Paige Fontana hated the Pine Ridge Nursing Home.

It wasn't that there was anything wrong with the building itself; it was actually quite a pleasant structure, down a long curved driveway on acres of rolling land sparsely forested with—truth in advertising here—pine trees. It was adjacent to a golf course and, Paige suspected, was owned by the same people; residents who were able to handle the rigors of golf were allowed to use the course, weekdays only, at cut-rate fees. Blacktop paths curled throughout the grounds, passing under copses of trees, along the little stream before it plunged into the ravine, over a pond via an arched footbridge. It was all very idyllic and Waldenesque, until you parked in the gravel visitors lot and went into the nursing home itself, which smelled of liniment and old laundry and windows that were rarely opened.

Take today, for instance. As she and Henry got out of the car, she scanned the face of the building for a window that was open to the summer air, but she saw nothing but a complement of reflected suns. She heard, faintly, the hum of the building's massive air conditioning units; she had never figured out where they were.

As they walked up the sidewalk, someone in the distance shouted, "Fore!" Henry made as if to duck. Paige attempted to giggle, but couldn't manage it.

They went up the steps of the front porch. The broad verandah was generously appointed with places to sit: wicker settees, gliders, stiff Adirondack chairs, settles. None of them ever seemed to be occupied, though, and Paige wondered if it was because of the apparition who haunted the swing on the extreme left of the porch. It was one of those wooden built-for-two swings, thick boards suspended by heavy silver chains from an even thicker strut in the roof. Built for two, but always holding one: the old man she had encountered in the hospital, just after the crow had stabbed her hand.

She knew from the television news and the papers that he had never been positively identified. When they had found him in the pit beneath the old church—the place Henry had been going to knock down, before his accident—his clothes had been ragged tatters, his shoes scraps of slimy leather. There was a wallet in his pocket, but it was ancient and decrepit and its contents were moldered beyond recognition, and he didn't have any teeth in his mouth to compare to dental records, and his fingerprints weren't on file anywhere. He had old, healed scars—what looked like flesh wounds across his forehead and the back of his hand—that had proven to be no help at all in identifying him. Eventually he had been classified a malnourished transient, a ward of the state. Quentin Farmer, in a successful bid to portray himself as a compassionate philanthropic type, was paying for the man's residence at Pine Ridge.

The old man didn't sit like a normal person; he squatted. His feet were flat on the seat of the swing, his legs were bent, and his arms were folded at his sides. Like he was perching or something. He never said a word, he just looked around with those deep black eyes that reminded Paige of the night sky, tiny chips of the universe embedded in his sunken pallid face. As always, he watched them pass, stared right at her and made her shiver. At first, Paige had responded to this by saying hello to him, which had prompted him to cock his head at her as if trying to understand a strange and unfamiliar sound; now she just hurried by and tried not to look at him, though she usually couldn't help but sneak glances. Henry just ignored him.

Then they went inside, and she had to brace herself for Florence.

Florence had been doing fine after Joe's sudden heart attack; she remained fully self-sufficient, taking care of the house and the yard, planting flowers in the beds in front of the house, shipping Paige and Henry vast amounts of food that they promptly threw away. But then she'd fallen in the shower, hit her head and broken her hip, and that was pretty much the end of her independence. She needed constant care now, and hated it, and took it out on them. A visit couldn't go by without invective or icily hostile stares from the bed where Florence spent most of her time. That was why they never brought Frederick anymore; they left him home with a sitter instead. Which became something else for Florence to vent about. Why did they never bring her grandson? Did they want him to forget about her? And so on, and so on, blah, blah, blah.

They passed through the lobby, in the part of the building that had once been George Selden's home; Henry signed in at the front desk and they went into the old living room, which was a waiting room now, with magazines and seats and a few antiques, relics of the place's previous incarnation. Swinging doors in the back wall gave admittance to the long, white, antiseptic corridor that was the north wing of the mansion, where Florence lived; they took the stairs to the second floor and stopped on the landing. Henry looked at Paige and said: "Ready?"

Paige made as if checking her armor. "Ready," she said.

They went into the hallway and entered Florence's room. Henry said loudly, "Hi, mom!"

She wasn't there.

Henry looked around blankly. Paige suffered a flashback to the time he had vanished from his hospital room and she'd been told he was dead, except this didn't scare her nearly as much.

A nurse came in. "Are you looking for your mother, Henry?" she asked. So few people visited the residents of the home that the staff quickly learned the names of those who did. Paige wished she could return the favor, but the nurses all seemed alike in their little white outfits. As soon as she spoke, though, Paige remembered that she was the one they referred to as English Nurse.

"Yeah," Henry said. "You know where she is?"

"She's having a walk about the grounds," the nurse said, with a trace of a smile.

Henry and Paige goggled at her. Florence's walker was standing in the corner in a shaft of sunlight, all gleaming chrome except for where her hands had worn it away; even when she was using it, the best she could manage was an inch-an-hour shuffle.

Henry said: "You're kidding."

"She's made quite a dramatic turnaround," English Nurse said. "Earlier in the week she started taking small steps. Then she started walking up and down the halls. Now she can even manage the stairs." Her smile broadened. "It's become quite difficult to keep tabs on her."

"Why didn't anyone call us?" Henry said.

English Nurse said: "I expect she wanted to surprise you. And we've, ah, we've had a bit of an epidemic lately. Three residents died this week within hours of each other, and two others coded. It's kept us rather busy." She checked her big black watch. "Speaking of which, I'm late for an inservice. Excuse me." And she was gone, her white tennis shoes soundless on the oatmeal-colored floor.

"Was she serious?" Henry said.

"Couldn't have been," Paige said. "The doctors said Florence would never—"

Then Florence appeared in the doorway, looking flushed and slightly winded. She stood without clutching the door frame or leaning on the wall, and fixed them with a critical gaze, and said: "What are you two doing inside on such a beautiful day?"

* * *

The opening of the plaza had drawn a fair number of people; not the sort of throng you would get in a more densely populated area, but certainly not bad, considering the location. There were even a couple of small yachts tied up at the promenade, though Nelson suspected they had been hired by Quentin to make it look as if Canal Plaza really was going to draw in recreational boaters.

As far as speeches went, the ones today weren't that bad, meaning that they were all fairly brief. Simon Jones went first and gave a short spiel about how good this would be for the economy, how many people it employed—he said a hundred, even though it was only ninety at the moment—and then introduced Quentin, whose statement was even shorter. He thanked the locals for their support and steered well clear of anything that might dredge up memories about his misadventures back in March. Then, with much pomp and circumstance, Kevin Kowalski cut the ribbon, and the throng moved in like ants invading a picnic. Nelson fought his way out of the advancing column, hopping up to sit on the pebbly edge of one of the flower beds, and watched them spread out. Down on the promenade, the band began to play. He didn't recognize the tune, but it had a nice summery air to it.

He watched Simon and Quentin and Kevin engage in a round of handshaking and backslapping. They were mouthing congratulations, though of course he couldn't hear any of them over the babble of the crowd and the honking of some obnoxious brass instrument, which seemed to be positioned directly below him even though it was really way down next to the canal. Funny acoustics.

God, it was hot. He ought to hook up with an outfit that made enclosed malls, he thought. Get to sit in air-conditioned comfort instead of right out underneath the sun. He squinted up at it through his thick blue sunglasses, and thought: Go away.

Something on the roof moved quickly, catching his attention. He thought it was a person—it had looked like a person, anyway, someone dressed all in black—going from one of the crests to another; just a flash though the gap between them. A photographer maybe? Somebody from the local paper trying to get a shot from a different angle? A ninja coming to kill Quentin? He squinted at the facade, but the person didn't reappear.

"Mr. Nelson, isn't it?" a voice right next to him said. He looked, and the voice belonged to the cop whose son couldn't possibly have stolen Quentin's laptop. Then he recalled that this was actually a *former* cop; he remembered Quentin telling him, with badly-concealed satisfaction, that the man had quit the force not long after their departure from Selden Falls. Just a step ahead of getting fired, Quentin had said.

"Nelson's my first name." Why these clowns could never remember that was beyond him. "Nelson DeGrace."

The cop—*ex*-cop—offered a hand, which Nelson shook. His grip was hot and flabby. "Nice layout you got here," he said. "I pass it every day on my way to my other job."

Nelson, wondering where this conversation was going, said: "Oh?"

"Yep, I sell cars now. At the Wilson Chevy, up the road." He trailed off, gaze straying over the shoppers milling around, then up to Quentin and Simon and Kevin on their little platform. The three of them were joking around like old friends at a college reunion.

"Was there something you wanted?" Nelson asked.

"Well, ah, no," Jasper said. He shifted around in what Nelson took to be discomfort; then he realized that the big man was actually attempting to show off his uniform. A patch over the left breast pocket said, in tiny gold letters, *PLAZA SECURITY*. And on the pocket itself was Quentin's logo, the Q with a globe inside it.

Nelson said: "You work for *us*?"

Jasper beamed. "Yep. Part-time security, that's me."

Nelson said: "How the hell did *that* happen?"

The beam crumpled and collapsed. "Well, you know, I needed more money coming in … selling cars don't pay as well as you might think."

Especially when you're a local celebrity for making a fool of yourself on television, Nelson thought, remembering the man's appearance on the news with his wife and son.

"And besides, you know, I had law enforcement experience," Jasper said, looking worried. "I just wanted to let you know I'm on *your* side now."

"Well, just lie low until Quentin's gone, okay? I don't think he'd react to this with my equanimity."

"Beg pardon?"

"He'd pop a gasket," Nelson said.

"Oh, uh, sure. Okay." Jasper Senior scratched his head. "I just wanted to say, you know, if there's anything I can do for you, just let me know."

Nelson nodded, then said: "Actually, there *is* something you can do for me."

"What?"

"I think I saw somebody on the roof. Can you go check it out?"

Somebody on the roof. Jasper Shoemaker Senior wondered if Nelson knew that to get onto the roof you had to climb up a spindly little ladder and then push your way through a stupidly narrow trapdoor. Jasper stood at the base of said ladder and scowled at the underside of said hatch, fifteen feet above, and thought: Of *course* Nelson knew. He seemed like the type who knew everything. The long-haired rat-bastard was having some fun with him, that was all.

Somebody on the roof. Like shit.

Jasper started to climb. His belly scraped against the rungs as he ascended. He remembered during the interview, they'd tentatively raised the question of his ability to run and climb and engage in strenuous physical activity, and he'd raised the question of weight discrimination, and the issue had never resurfaced. He hadn't expected to be asked to climb around like a monkey on his first day, for God's sake. He was going to start going to the gym when he got the time, but no, he couldn't even get a chance to do that before they started making all kinds of demands on him.

He reached the underside of the hatch and clung there like a barnacle. After resting for a few seconds, he swung the lever around to unlock the door, pushed the hatch open, and proceeded the rest of the way up the ladder onto the hot, pebbly roof. It felt like it was about a million degrees up there, the sun beating straight down on the black tar and the crushed stone until they overflowed with heat and radiated it back. He was getting cooked from two sides as he stood there and looked around for Nelson's intruder.

He moved away from the hatch, toward the front of the building, where the facades formed an uneven waist-high wall. The band was playing something that sounded Mexican, even though they were a bunch of pale Caucasians in cheap red suits. He stopped and leaned against the facade, nearly burning his elbows and forearms; he stood back with a yelp and didn't touch the blazing hot concrete again. He backed up a pace and looked out over the terrace. People were moving along it in both directions, pointing, eating, shopping. The smell of hot dogs made his stomach rumble eagerly; there was a vendor down on the promenade handing them out in paper boats for free, and the vapors from his grill were drifting Jasper's way. He hoped the guy didn't run out before he made it down there. The canal was a mass of reflected sun, broken up by a smattering of canoes paddling up and down.

He saw, just for a second, a flicker of green light from beneath the clock tower. Like the other embellishments to the plaza, the tower was a bare network of metal struts and beams at its bottom; it was only solid from the point where it became visible above the facade. Jasper wandered that way, squinting in the light; the sun was right in his face, and he couldn't see a thing underneath the spire. Grumbling, he headed toward it, just so he could say he had.

He stopped right next to the tower. The cavity underneath it was empty, but someone might have climbed the narrow ladder to get at the workings of the clock. He wasn't about to do that himself—he didn't even know if he would fit up there—but he figured he could take a look inside, at least. He bent over and forced himself through the gap in the supports. There was a heavy-duty light switch against the wall of the facade; he fumbled for it with his left hand as he turned his face toward the stifling blackness above.

And saw two greenish disks looking down at him. Eyes, big as oranges, reflecting what little light made it into the upper reaches of the tower.

Jasper forgot all about the light switch. He started to squeal, tried to fling himself backwards, through the supports; but before he could shove himself between them, a chunk of the darkness dropped onto him. Stiff feathers scraped his face and cheeks; talons the size of arrowheads dug into his chest, right through his ribs. The squeal died in his throat as air farted out of his punctured lungs.

Down below, the band started a crescendo.

Night. The fireworks would be popping off soon. A new band had taken over in the amphitheatre, playing evening music, slow and melodic. As he stood in the back row, leaning against the railing with the canal to his back, munching on his dinner—a hot dog, supposedly vegetarian, though it was impossible to tell beneath the smothering layers of ketchup and a shredded substance that may have been sauerkraut—Nelson had to admit that the accordion walls of the orchestra shell did indeed muffle the traffic noises. Trucks would rumble on by and he wouldn't hear them until they were already past, crossing the bridge over the canal. So that was all right.

A couple of teenagers rushed by, giggling. They didn't stick around to listen to the music. The girl was wearing these absurdly short shorts, blue and white striped. A little higher and tighter and he'd be able to see her underwear, assuming she was wearing any. He watched them run on up the walkway, lighting up as they passed one of the electric lamps, vanishing into darkness, lighting up again, getting farther and farther away. Looked like he'd been right about the nature tower.

He found himself wondering how long, exactly, it had been since he'd had a date. Seemed like around the time Quentin had bootstrapped him out of the clerical pool. Coincidence?

The music stopped and he looked at the stage. Kevin Kowalksi, all red in the face—Nelson had seen him making many trips to the bar in the temporary VIP lounge on the top terrace—walked to the microphone, which until then had been standing quite alone and forlorn-looking in the middle of the stage while the band played instrumental selections from the elevator songbook. He started to talk, but Nelson could hardly hear him. Clutching the mike with one hand as if it were keeping him erect, which it probably was, Kevin fumbled with the cables and then tried again. This time his voice boomed out of the speakers hidden in the folds of the accordion walls. "Let's have a big hand for the Fluorescents," he said, and there was a dutiful smattering of applause. When it died down Kevin said, "The fireworks will be starting shortly, so if everyone would please look to the—"

The rest of his statement was drowned out by the concussive explosion of an aerial bomb that rattled the ice in Nelson's Coke.

After the opening salvo, a flurry of streamers and blossoms and flaming stars burst into life over the canal, reflected in the dark water, lighting up the trees that grew thickly along the other side. Quentin materialized next to Nelson and leaned against the railing, eyes on the sky. He was still clutching the same plastic cup full of mysterious amber liquid that he'd been carrying all evening. He did this so people wouldn't continuously offer him drinks, although Nelson had seen Kevin escorting him to the watering hole several times that evening.

"Good turnout," Quentin said.

Boom!

"Seems like it," Nelson said. Then he added: "Hope they stick around after the free hot dogs are gone."

"They will," Quentin said. "This is *culture*, Nelson. Something Selden Falls sadly lacked before we came along." His voice was a little bit slurred, Nelson thought; maybe his policy of not drinking at his own events had lapsed.

A red flower bloomed overhead. The petals turned blue, and then white, and then vanished. How all-American, Nelson thought.

Quentin said: "Did I tell you I saw that fat slob cop whose kid tried to blackmail me? He was wearing this stupid uniform. Looks like a janitor. Ha!"

Nelson refrained from telling him that Jasper Shoemaker was now one of his employees. Then it occurred to him that he hadn't seen the big man since sending him to check if anyone was on the roof; maybe the guy had had a heart attack up there or something. He didn't look like he was quite up to heavy physical exertion. "You saw him?" Nelson said. "When?"

"Oh, I don't know. It was a while ago."

A while ago. That was helpful, Nelson thought. Well, what could have happened to Jasper on the roof of a shopping plaza in broad daylight? He watched screamers zip around the sky, then said: "Did you say his kid tried to *blackmail* you?"

"Did I?"

"Yeah, you did."

"Oh." Quentin gave his cup a shake. "What the hell am I drinking?"

"I'm sure I don't know," Nelson said. "Back in March, you told me he wanted to sell you back the data. You didn't say anything about blackmail."

Quentin tossed his drink into the canal just as a brilliant

chrysanthemum erupted overhead, making the ice and alcohol sparkle on its way to becoming a seriously watered-down beverage.

"What'd he try to blackmail you about?" Nelson asked.

Quentin slapped him on the shoulder. "Don't be so *serious* all the time," he said. "Is that all you think about, work work work? Lighten up. Have a drink. Have two. It's on me." Quentin headed back toward the plaza, toddling unsteadily along the walkway, hanging onto the railing with one hand.

Nelson wondered, for the first time in months, what had been on that hard drive he had found in Quentin's coat. Too late now to do anything about it; it was probably all thoroughly erased. Maybe he was an accessory to something, he thought.

A starburst of color just above the treetops drew his attention back to the fireworks. He didn't think pyrotechnics were supposed to go off that close to the ground. He could see fiery streamers falling through the trees like will-o'-the-wisps and wondered if anything would ignite. But only a few of the embers reached the ground, and they all winked out, one by one.

Nelson took a sip of Coke. It was getting quite flat.

Then there was an explosion that shook the ground he stood on, and a column of flame shot straight up out of the forest like a beacon, rumbling with the dull roar of a bonfire. He gawked at it; the plastic cup slipped from his fingers, hit the ground. Coke splashed his ankles. Behind him, he heard a smattering of applause. He couldn't believe it; what kind of a moron would think this was part of the show?

The fire shrunk and winked out, evaporated like steam from a geyser. But there was something falling out of the sky, a flaming ember plummeting toward the amphitheatre. Nelson watched it come, a burning meteor shaped like an X. He took a few steps away from the rail, but unnecessarily; the projectile fell short, splashing into the canal a few yards from shore. Whatever it was, it continued to burn for an instant after it hit, until the water came rushing back and closed over it and smothered the fire.

The waves from the impact slapped gently against the cement wall of the promenade. Nelson grasped the brass railing and looked down into the black water. In the pale glow of the moon and the sporadic light of the fireworks, he could see the dark, ill-defined shape floating in the canal.

A body. It was a body.

Somebody thought to turn on the promenade lamps, flooding the night with pink illumination, dazzling his eyes.

Somebody cried, "It's a dead guy!"

He blinked, chasing away the spots of light in front of his eyes, and he saw it in the good light, the charred, pathetic corpse that had crashed Quentin's party. It was floating face-down and spread-eagled, and it appeared to be missing at least part of a leg.

Overhead, the fireworks popped away, reflected in the still, dark surface of the canal.

13

When Jasper Shoemaker Senior let himself into his house late that night, he was tired and sweaty and his arm itched like crazy where he had cut it. He had a long, deep, mostly-healed gash all the way from his elbow to the back of his hand, and he couldn't remember where the hell it had come from. His chest itched, too, and it hurt a little bit to breathe; a sharp, spiny feeling in his lungs, like he'd accidentally inhaled a handful of ground-up glass. Not pleasant. He hoped it wasn't his heart; he'd been meaning to start exercising, really he had, and he didn't think it would be quite fair for his heart to seize up on him before he'd had a chance to make up for all those years of pork rinds and spare ribs.

No one else was awake, except maybe Jasper Junior, watching the little television in his room; but he wouldn't come out until tomorrow afternoon, probably, what with there being no school to get up for. That was good; he felt like shit, and probably looked like shit, and didn't want to run into his son or his wife and have to explain to them that no, he wasn't drunk again, he was *sick*, damn it.

So he stood in the living room for a moment and listened and, hearing nothing, proceeded into the hallway. He stumbled into the bath and shut the door, locked it, turned on the lights and looked at himself in the mirror. A pale and haggard face looked back at him, greenish almost, dark circles like the missing portion of a crescent moon under his eyes.

See? He was *sick*.

The front of his uniform had a big tear in it, diagonally up the chest. He couldn't remember ripping it on anything; on the other hand, he couldn't really remember much of anything, once he had climbed up onto the roof looking for that imaginary prowler. Maybe he'd suffered heatstroke. Could he get worker's compensation for that?

He struggled out of the uniform. It was pretty much destroyed, but Noreen ought to be able to put it back together. He'd tell her he got it caught on some machinery in the boiler room or something. He wasn't wearing his undershirt; he didn't know what had become of it. Or maybe he hadn't put one on that morning, it had been so hot. He really couldn't remember. He pulled off his sweat-soaked pants, and stood there looking at himself.

What was that?

He had three long, thin scars in his chest that he couldn't recall ever noticing before. He touched them and they were hard and itchy. He shaped his fingers into claws and positioned them over the welts, and they lined up pretty well. The gaps were a little bit wider than his own chubby digits could manage, but not by much.

Huh. Maybe he *was* drunk after all, and had had himself a good old time, and just couldn't remember it. After all, there had been quite a few hot teenagers scampering around the plaza in skimpy summer outfits. Wouldn't that be a kicker? Fuck some young babe, and forget about it? Why, that would be like it had never happened.

His underwear had slipped down and he gave it a little tug, covering up the wispy curls of pubic hair just above his member; then he slid his hand inside and adjusted things and tried to remember when the last time his wife's hand, or any other part of her body, had been in that general vicinity. It was around about the time of their television appearance, he guessed. Yeah, that was it: March.

Holy God, how had he survived since March?

Oh, look; he'd inadvertently gotten his best buddy all awake. It was starting to poke through the top of his underwear, pressing against the bottom of his belly. He double-checked to make sure the door was locked, and then he stepped out of his shorts and sat on the edge of the tub and gave his friend some sorely-needed attention. There was lubrication from something—sweat, he guessed—so he didn't need to borrow any of Noreen's Avon cream. Just as well; she'd found a curly little hair in the jar one time and given him a look of such curdled suspicion he'd had to immediately defend himself against an accusation that hadn't even been leveled—not officially, anyway—which had only made her more suspicious.

He realized that this line of thinking was putting his buddy to sleep, and thought about something else: one of the girls he'd seen at the plaza. She'd been wearing shorts that were practically up the crack of her ass. They'd never have worn stuff like that when he was a kid. When he was a kid, people had a sense of decency, of morality.

He grunted. Oh, yeah … looking good in those shorts …

He managed to keep himself quiet while his best buddy spat up all over him. When it was finished, he cleaned himself off with a baby wipe, then pitched it into the toilet; but before he flushed he noticed something and knelt down for a closer look at the napkin. He leaned over, peering into the bowl. Just being in this position made his stomach do flip-flops, like it figured that if his face was this close to the can he was supposed to be throwing up.

Closer inspection confirmed what he had thought: where the threads and smears of his semen ran across the napkin, it was turning brown, like the stuff was eating through it or something. What the hell did *that* mean?

He didn't want to know. He flushed the toilet, and collapsed onto the side of the tub and sat there, staring up at the mirror. It reflected the wall above his head. His arm and his chest itched like crazy. Scratching them only made it worse.

After a couple of minutes, he realized that his best buddy had started to throb. He couldn't see it beyond the curve of his belly, so he reached down and touched it and found it hard as a rock and pointed straight at the ceiling. How'd it wake up again so fast? He gave it an experimental stroke, and it was smooth as silk and sensitive as a tripwire. He took his fingers away, but it was too late; it spat up again, coating his jostling belly with sticky goo.

He stood up, looked at himself in the mirror. His sallow, waxy complexion and shadowed eyes made him look like some sort of creature from out of a zombie movie. He ran a hand through his thinning hair. The wounds along his arm and chest seemed to be turning a sickly shade of purplish-green.

He wished he could remember how all that had happened.

His stomach felt sticky and unpleasant. His head was thick and heavy, as if someone had popped the top open and stuffed it with gravel. Jasper turned on the shower and jumped in and stayed beneath the stream, washing himself all over, until the scalding water turned cold. Then he climbed out and toweled off and looked at himself again. The hot water and the vigorous scrubbing had turned him bright pink, had lightened the bags under his eyes to the color of weak tea.

That was more like it.

He switched off the fluorescents and the nightlight flickered to life, casting weird shadows up his face, making him look like a man in a rubber mask.

Jasper grunted and headed for bed.

Outside a crow was coughing, the sound like laughter.

By the morning, they had pieced it all together: an ember had fallen into an old well across the canal, and the well, somehow, was full of natural gas. The resulting explosion had blown the contents of the well sky-high—including the body, which had already been identified from dental records as Nick Garson—and then the well had collapsed on itself, smothering the fire. Simple as one-two-three.

Quentin folded up the newspaper as Raye Teller slid a plate of pancakes in front of his face, and reminded himself that nothing was ever simple in this town.

"He used to work for you, didn't he?" Raye said, indicating the newspaper article with a nod of her head.

"Yes."

"They said they found exploded bullets in his pocket. They think he's the one who was out there shooting back in March."

"I hadn't gotten that far."

"Yep, the power company, they're gonna dig up those old gas pipes and rip them right out of the ground, they are. Claim they didn't even know the pipes were there." She shook her head. "All that money we pay them and they don't even know where their pipes are. We probably paid for that gas leak for years, we did."

"It must be very frustrating for you," Quentin said. Then he picked up the paper again and used it as a shield between him and Raye.

"You sure do get up early, Mr. Farmer," she said. The paper did almost nothing to screen out her voice. "That's a good thing, though. The early bird—"

"The early bird catches the worm, a rolling stone gathers no moss, a stitch in time saves nine," Quentin said. Inside the paper they had a picture of Nick Garson falling out of the sky. He looked like a flaming plus sign. Quentin wondered who had had the presence of mind to snap a picture.

He shook his head. He couldn't remember much of what happened that evening; his tactic of clutching a drink all night to get out of making trips to the bar hadn't worked very well. That Kevin Kowalski guy had followed him around making toasts to this and toasts to that, and he suspected he had gotten quite thoroughly blotto. Well, at least he didn't have a hangover.

"We couldn't make it to the grand opening," Raye said. "Tom was a little bit under the weather. We'll have to go there some time, see how the old place has changed."

"Make sure you buy something when you go," Quentin said. "Support the local economy."

Nelson squeaked into the kitchen. Quentin wondered when those new shoes of his would be broken in. He looked at his assistant over the top of the paper as Nelson slid into the chair opposite his; distorted images of himself peered back at him from the round blue lenses of Nelson's sunglasses. "Did you hear the latest?" Nelson asked.

"What latest?" Quentin and Raye said simultaneously.

"The power company already started digging for the gas pipes," he said. Raye slipped a few extra pancakes in front of him. "Thanks," he said, digging in.

Quentin stared at him. "Well?" he said after a moment.

Nelson looked up from his plate. His eyes were invisible.

"They found bodies," he said.

From the promenade, Jasper Shoemaker Senior couldn't see his former colleagues on the police force tearing up the ground in the forest across the canal; but he could hear the rumble of the machinery, the shouted commands, the earth sighing as they ripped it apart. A few months ago he would've been there with them, investigating what appeared to be century-old murders; instead he was a car salesman and weekend rent-a-cop, making sure nobody tried to steal a plastic Buddha from the trinket store. It was truly appalling, how his investigative abilities were being disused.

"Shoemaker."

And how come every place he worked, people called him by his last name? Lack of respect, that was why. He turned around and saw the manager of the plaza, Monroe Parker, standing with folded arms over by the canoe house. "What?" Jasper said.

"We've got a canoe rental that never came back. Some kids." Monroe held up a piece of paper. "I want you to … what happened to your uniform?"

Noreen had refused to sew his shirt, so he had done it himself. Unfortunately, threading the needle was about the extent of his expertise in fabric repair, so the job was not as unobtrusive as he would've liked. "I tore it yesterday in the clock tower. Nelson thought he saw someone up there and I was checking it out."

"You look like somebody stitched you together out of corpses. For God's sake, Shoemaker, just *ask* for another shirt. We'll supply it." He shook his head. "Anyway, I want you to call this kid's parents and find out if he's home."

"Now?"

Monroe raised an eyebrow. "Yes, now."

"It's not even eight yet."

"What's your point?"

"They're probably asleep."

Monroe said: "Well, then you'll be waking them up, won't you?" He held out the paper, but Jasper didn't take it; after a moment Monroe tossed it at him and it fluttered to the ground like a wounded bird. Jasper knelt and snatched it up and stood, resisting an inexplicable urge to stuff it into his mouth.

"I hired you in spite of your history, because I believe in giving people second chances," Monroe said. "Shape up, okay, Shoemaker? Don't make me look like an ass." He turned and walked up the stairs. Jasper watched him go, his hand trembling.

When Monroe was out of sight, Jasper crammed the folded-up paper into his mouth and began to chew it. Munching away on the note, he went into the canoe shed, all the way to the back, around behind a vertical sheet of plywood that concealed the circuit breakers for the promenade lighting. He fished the sopping, mangled wad out of his mouth, looked around, and pressed it into the crook of a roof support. Then he stepped back and looked at it and wondered why he'd done that. He took the note down and unfolded it. The writing was smudgy and blurred from his saliva, but still readable. He took it up to the offices in the top tier of the plaza to make the call. By the time he got there the paper had turned all brown and brittle, like he had soaked it in coffee and then dried it out; but that was okay, he remembered the number.

As it turned out, the parents—Robinson was the family's name—were not asleep. They were awake, and nearly frantic. Their son, who had signed out the canoe, hadn't come home last night. He had gone to the grand opening with his girlfriend, and she hadn't returned either. Jasper, trying to reassure them, suggested that maybe the two kids had rowed up the canal a ways, beached, gone off into the woods for a quick screw, and just fallen asleep. The stony silence which greeted this idea told him it didn't make the Robinsons feel much better. They must be Catholics, he thought.

He knew he was right, though. They would see.

After he got off the phone with the parents, Jasper went and reported to Monroe Parker, who found his theory about the disappearance of the kids plausible and sent him up the walkway to see if he could find them. Jasper almost protested that his feet wouldn't take that much walking but thought better of it, and went.

The haze in the sky was burning off quickly as the sun climbed higher, heated things up. Jasper traipsed up the blacktop path, squinting through the light, looking for the red hull of the canoe on either bank of the waterway. It seemed as if he could feel the temperature increasing little by little, each additional degree prickling against his skin; the heat had started out stifling, and was now proceeding to intolerable.

He entered the shadow of the I-90 bridge and stayed there a little while, out of the sun, cooling off. Trucks and cars whizzed back and forth across the overpass. He wiped the sweat from his forehead, ran a hand through his hair. Felt thicker in the heat, stiff with crusted sweat. The placid water reflected blue sky and the last glowing wisps of high, thin clouds. He panted and stared at the canal and found himself very much inclined to jump in.

Then he thought of Monroe, and losing another job, and started walking again.

Past the bridge the trees crowded in from the right, young ones mostly, tangled with creepers and sumac and brambles that reached to the edge of the pavement before ending sharply, like severed tentacles. Birds twittered and chirped from within the foliage, though he couldn't see them. He wished the trees would give him some shade, but the sun was in the wrong place for that. He squinted up at it in the sky and thought: Wouldn't it be nice if the sun just went away?

At last, he reached the end of the walk. His feet felt like they were splitting into pieces inside his shoes. The path curled in a gentle loop, back on itself. There was a little wooden observation post in the middle of the loop. He climbed up it, grunting, just so he could say he had done so when Monroe asked. From this perch he scanned the vicinity for a trace of red.

And he found it, the canoe, pulled up onto a narrow strip of muddy beach where a tiny stream let into the canal. Footprints in the mud led up the bank, over the lip of earth and into the trees on the other side. It was on the opposite side, and some distance back in the direction he had come; he had walked right by it without seeing it. The brilliance of the sun must have blinded him. He shifted around, getting comfortable on the bench on top of the observation deck, and watched the forest wall near the canoe, and waited.

Before too long, there was movement across the water. He watched as a teenage boy came out of the woods, followed by a girl. They were covered in leaves and twigs and were looking at the sky as if wondering where it had come from.

Ha! He'd been right. Felt good to be right, for a change.

The two kids piled into the canoe, pushed off, and started awkwardly paddling back toward the plaza. They didn't appear to see him crouching on the observation post; they didn't even look in his direction, actually.

Once they had gone, he started climbing down the stairs. As he neared the ground, one of the steps snapped with a resounding *crack* and he tumbled the rest of the way to the blacktop. There was a sudden flurry of activity from the surrounding brush, like small animals scurrying away. As he picked himself up, Jasper noticed a sneaker, mostly hidden by leaves and vines, right at the edge of the path. He crept forward slowly, until he was on his hands and knees right in front of the shoe; then he separated the foliage with his hands. Disturbing the vegetation released a miasmic stench into the air, rot jockeying with excrement for control of Jasper's nasal passages. Thorns scraped his skin but didn't pierce it; leaves came loose, fluttered down to land on the corpse he had just discovered.

The sneaker was attached to a foot.

Which was attached to a leg.

Which was attached to a kid with his eyes ripped out.

Jasper stayed there a moment, then two, smelling decay, watching centipedes and beetles scurry off the body, out of the light.

The odor was oddly, gruesomely, appealing.

There were a couple things he could do. He could give into the urge rumbling up from his belly—which would, he somehow knew, mean giving in to some other thing, some force, something begging for admission. Or he could stand up, walk back to the plaza, tell Monroe what he had found.

But … the smell just made his mouth water.

Because he couldn't help himself, he bent over and took a bite out of the kid's left calf.

He spit it out almost immediately, horrified at himself. The dead flesh left a sour taste in his mouth, raw and bloody and rotten. He stood, his stomach churning like it was going to leap right out of his throat, the rush of his own blood thrumming in his ears like the sound of wings; he stumbled away, to the edge of the canal, and then he vomited into the water.

But what came out was not his breakfast.

It wasn't even his stomach.

It was a torrent of viscous, salty, glistening slime.

The flood of mucous hit the water, where it hung together like a jellyfish. It floated there, shivering and quivering; and then it began to ripple, began to move, like it was going to ambulate away. Unnerved, Jasper wrenched a large stone from the bank and slammed it down through the wad of phlegm. The impact broke it into pieces, which melted and sank into the cool, dark water.

What the hell was happening to him?

Yesterday's sky-diving corpse and the bodies found across the water had naturally put a damper on the second day of grand opening festivities, but they were going ahead anyway. Quentin couldn't attend—he had been called away to an urgent meeting in Utica, thirty miles or so to the east, where another of his projects was threatening to tank in a sea of local opposition—and Nelson found himself pressed into service as a substitute. He quickly concluded that he had been set up: the task which Quentin had sloughed off on him involved handing out cheap coffee mugs with the Canal Plaza logo on them, answering questions about the place, acting like he really loved being in Selden Falls. Not the sort of thing the boss enjoyed. Nelson didn't enjoy it either, but unlike Quentin, he had no one to foist the duty off on.

The job of answering questions was especially burdensome, because reporters from the local paper and from Channel Six, disguised as regular people, kept coming to his booth for mugs and then asking him stuff he couldn't or wouldn't answer. Their first topic of interest was the dead kid who had been found up at the end of the walkway; the subjects didn't improve much from there. Did he think they should have provided security along the walkway? Did he think this death was related to the death of Jane Trott? Did he think people could feel safe shopping at Canal Plaza? And so on and so on, all kinds of leading questions that they knew full well he wasn't going to answer. He no-commented most of them, and when he finally ran out of mugs, he was convinced he'd given at least half of them away to employees of local media organizations.

He started packing up the empty boxes when someone knocked on the side door of his little booth, which was actually the marionette stage for Quentin's theoretical puppet shows for the kiddies. Nelson sighed and said, "I'm out of mugs and I have no comment."

There was a pause, and then another knock.

Nelson said: "Who is it?"

"Jasper Shoemaker."

Great, Nelson thought; plaza security. Now he felt safe. He nudged the wooden latch apparatus with his foot, turning it to free the door, and then gave it a kick. It swung open and Jasper was standing there, a stout silhouette against the blaze of the sun. "What's up?" Nelson said.

"I didn't get a chance to tell you last night, I didn't find anybody up on the roof."

"Huh. I could've sworn I saw somebody up there. Well, thanks for looking."

"No problem."

Nelson continued to gather up his boxes. When he had them in a manageable pile, he hefted them and stood and noticed that Shoemaker was still there, and looked like he hadn't moved at all in the last five minutes.

"Was there something else?" Nelson asked.

"No, I guess not," Jasper said. But he still didn't move. He just stood there, looking at Nelson with beady, dark, gleaming eyes.

"Can I get out of here, then?" Nelson said, with elaborate patience.

"I guess." Jasper backed up a few paces and Nelson squeezed by with his armload of boxes, though he had to jostle the big man to do it. As he walked away, Nelson felt Jasper's gaze boring into his back and wondered what the hell had gotten into him. Maybe he thought Nelson had sent him on a wild goose chase to the roof. Maybe he was just mentally unstable.

As he walked away, he heard Monroe Parker's deep voice say: "Shoemaker, I want to talk to you." Yeah, that was a good idea, Nelson thought; take him away and run a psychological profile on him.

He took the boxes to the Dumpsters behind the top tier of the plaza, where he deposited them on a growing mountain of other cardboard containers. It was already getting filthy in the euphemistically-titled waste management area, which consisted of a strip of pavement maybe fifteen feet wide, separated from the parking lot by a high wooden fence designed to block customers' view of the trash. The back doors of the restaurants were all open, and the mix of aromas wafting from the kitchens combined with the stale smell of yesterday's garbage produced a truly appalling odor.

Several fat crows were hopping around, spearing scattered leftovers with their sharp black beaks. They ignored him completely.

He tried to remember where in his job description it said he had to staff cheesy souvenir stands and dispose of refuse, but couldn't. He looked at his watch: three o'clock. Quentin was due back tonight, and tomorrow they would head back to Buffalo, leaving Selden Falls for what, in Quentin's case, would be the last time in a long time; and in

Nelson's case, perhaps, for the last time ever.

He could hardly wait.

Paige said: "Your mother *what?*"

Henry, looking sheepish, rubbed the back of his head and said it again: "She wants to move in with us."

They were sitting on the balcony outside the master bedroom of their home on Cool Road—several months old now, but still new—in a swing very much like the one that the strange man at Pine Ridge always sat in, except that this one didn't squeak and wasn't turning black with age. Frederick was playing in the yard below, chasing his Golden Labrador puppy around and around in circles in the grass. The sun had sunk low toward the trees, but retained enough energy to keep them all sweating. Warmth, especially the warmth of the summer sun, tended to lull Paige to sleep; but at the moment, an entire bottle of Valium wouldn't have been enough to knock her out.

"She has a perfectly good house," Paige said.

"She says she doesn't need a big house all to herself anymore."

"Well, *I* need a big house all to *myself*. She'll follow me around giving me the evil eye. She'll second-guess everything I do. She'll interfere with raising Frederick. She'll—"

"She promised not to do anything like that."

She stared at him. "Yeah, right," she said.

"She did!"

"Oh, I believe she promised it. But if you believe she'll *keep* that promise, I have a nice bridge to sell you."

"Will you at least think about it?"

"All right." Paige turned and stared straight ahead with her brows knitted. Then she turned back to him and said: "No."

"Okay," Henry said.

"You heard the doctor. She's made an incredible recovery. She's in better health than she has been in years. She doesn't *need* to move in with us."

"I said *okay*. Calm down. I don't want her to move in, either." Which Paige knew, of course; he'd just felt obligated to make the effort. The dutiful son. Unfortunately, that put her in the position of villain: *Sorry, Mom, Paige says no.*

Oh well. It wasn't like that was going to change Florence's opinion of her any.

Henry got up and went in through the sliding door. Paige rocked a while by herself and watched Frederick wear himself and the puppy out; both collapsed in a heap in the grass, panting. After a few seconds the dog began to slobber at Frederick's face and, giggling, he hid it beneath his arms.

She checked her watch. Pushing eight o'clock. "Frederick," she called, "time to come in and get washed up."

Freddie rolled over and stood, his clothes a mass of dirt and grass stains, and started running up the gentle slope of the yard toward the house. The puppy bounded along after him. As they ran, she watched the forest. The leaves were an impenetrable wall encapsulating the house, with only glimpses of darkness beyond them. Before they had actually moved in, she had never noticed the woods were so dark; visiting in the daytime, they always looked pleasantly sylvan. Toward evening, though, they started to get sinister, furtive. Toward evening, they concealed monsters.

She heard the kitchen door beneath the balcony open and close as Freddie entered the house. She turned her back on the woods and went inside and closed the sliding screen door behind her. Henry was just hanging up the telephone; he looked at her, shrugged, and grinned kind of stupidly.

She said: "Did you just call your mother?"

"Maybe," Henry said.

"Did you tell her she wouldn't be moving in with us?"

"I may have mentioned it."

"And what did she say?"

"She took it pretty well. I was surprised." He rubbed the back of his head. "She said we would change our minds."

"Oh," Paige said. "Well, I guess that proves it. She's getting senile."

Quentin Farmer did not really have an emergency meeting in Utica. He went there, all right, and he paid a visit to the mayor, and he checked on the future site of his development—no derelict churches or other eyesores nearby, thank God—and then he proceeded to the local art gallery and a couple of nearby historical sites. He managed to kill most of the day in such a fashion, starting the drive back to Selden Falls at around eight o'clock in the evening, thus avoiding the duty of handing out coffee mugs, which was really more of a lackey function anyway.

At eight-twenty, he heard a news report about the corpse that had been found on the Canal Plaza nature trail, and nearly drove into a bridge abutment. He managed to recover before having to test out the Jaguar's supplemental restraint system, and settled in to listen to the story. The corpse had been identified by dental records as Gordon Gentile, a local teenager. Sixteen. The coroner was unable to explain why the body was in such a state of decay, since by all accounts Gordon had been alive the previous day; he had attended the grand opening of Canal Plaza with his girlfriend, whose name had not been released yet. The girl had never come home after the festivities; police were searching the woods, posters were going up, the whole missing-person machinery was grinding into action.

Management of Canal Plaza, the reporter said, had no comment.

At eight-thirty, as Quentin got off I-90 at Selden Falls, he was talking to Nelson on his cellular phone. "For Christ's sake, can't *one day* go by without dead people turning up at the plaza?"

"Things were pretty quiet until we came back," Nelson said, his voice crackly. "Maybe we're bad luck."

"We're the best luck this crummy town has had in twenty years," Quentin said. "Did you talk to the press?"

"I no-commented them."

"Who found it?"

"Who found what?"

"The body, for God's sake."

"Oh. Plaza security."

"Give me a *name*, Nelson," Quentin said. After a moment Quentin heard Nelson say something, but it was obscured by a burst of static. "What?" he said. "What was that?"

"Jasper Shoemaker," Nelson said.

Shoemaker? Where did he know that name from? Then it clicked, and he snapped: "*What?* That fat clown is working for me?"

"Yes."

"Have him fired." Quentin clicked off the phone. Jesus, he couldn't believe it. After all the trouble that jerk had put him through, he'd had the gall to apply for a job at the plaza? And, worse, he'd *gotten* one?

Quentin decided to stop by the shopping center and see how much damage the cops had done, crashing around looking for dead bodies. The lot was deserted when he pulled in, except for Monroe Parker's car over near the wide cement mouth of the terrace and a beat-up old Chevy in the corner; it was a Sunday evening, so the stores had closed a couple of hours earlier. He parked the Jaguar in a handicapped spot near the entrance and got out, stepping into an arena hemmed in by sodium lights. It wasn't completely dark yet, but the sky had lost enough of the day to trigger the lamps. Kind of a waste of electricity, he thought. He'd have to talk to Monroe about getting their sensitivity lowered.

He walked around to the mall offices. The door was locked with one of those electronic keypunch pads; he tried to remember the combination, realized that he had never actually known it in the first place, and pushed the bell instead. He heard a faint *ding-dong* sound from inside the building, but nobody buzzed him in; after a few minutes he rang the bell again, with identical results.

He whacked the door with his fist. "Hey!" he shouted. "Anybody in there?"

As his voice died away, it seemed to take all the other noises with it, sucking the sounds out of the air and leaving it a silent, expectant void. Quentin sensed the hush behind him and around him and suddenly had the oddest feeling, a nervous tightness in his chest and bowels, like he'd jumped up and started laughing at a funeral and now everyone was silently staring at him. He turned around slowly, looked out over the plaza and the canal and the darkness that encompassed it all. The terrace was mostly dark; only a few of the lights were illuminated, every third or fourth one. Along the promenade, the lamps were a string of pinpoint pearls, sending glowing reflections across the surface of the canal. The scene was quietly deserted, police investigators and customers and staff all gone, no one present except for him and, somewhere, Monroe Parker.

So why did he feel like he was the center of hostile attention?

He saw movement, or thought he did, a shadow stealing across the water like a spreading oil slick. He looked at the sky, gloomy with onrushing night; nothing there, nothing coming. He took a step toward the flower bed, with some vague idea that he would jump up onto it and then be able to see more, but he had only taken a couple of paces when he heard the door click open behind him. He turned, and Monroe Parker was standing there looking at him, his eyes and mouth hidden in shadow, the light playing tricks with his face, making his nose seem sharp and beak-like and cruel. He was sweating, his face glistening, even though Quentin could feel cold air pouring out of the open doorway.

"Monroe," Quentin said. "You all right?" The manager made no response, except to cock his head and stare at him with a shadowed gaze. "How're, ah, how're things going?" His voice was faltering; he wondered why.

Still, Monroe said nothing.

Then he looked up at the sky.

Quentin heard a rush of air just before something bowled him over, sending him sprawling across the still-warm concrete. He felt a sharp tearing pain in his back, felt his spine go suddenly hot and wet with blood. He rolled onto his side, kicking at the thing that had torn into him. Monroe still stood in the doorway looking at him, his face a blank and gleaming mask.

The attack stopped as suddenly as it had started. Footsteps moved away from him. He saw a bulbous form join Monroe at the door, and after a moment he realized it was Jasper Shoemaker. Where had he come from?

"Why are you just *standing* there?" Quentin said. "Help me, for God's sake."

Silence.

"Christ." He reached around, felt his back. "I'm bleeding. I'm *bleeding*. Call an ambulance."

They didn't move.

He fumbled his cellular phone out of his pocket, flipped it open. He started punching numbers, his fingers leaving bloody smears on the lighted buttons. Jasper Shoemaker came over and plucked the phone out of his hand. He carefully shut it off and folded it up. Quentin stared up at him, then at Monroe, who had come over to stand beside him.

Shoemaker made a rumbly, sticky sound in his throat. Quentin couldn't see what was happening, but it sounded like the man was about to throw up all over him. Seconds later the big guy doubled over and stuff poured out of his mouth; but it wasn't a warm rush of vomit that splattered over Quentin, it was something else, something thick and sticky and icy cold, and it sunk into the slashes in his back, putting out the fire that rushed up and down from the wounds.

But what replaced the pain was something worse, something itchy and crawly and probing, penetrating, corrupting. The feeling of numbing, arctic chill crept up his spine, up the back of his neck. It spread into his skull, where it turned his brain to brittle crystal and shattered it and gobbled up the pieces.

"Shoemaker," he mumbled, through lips that were going numb, using a tongue that was turning to rubber in his mouth, "you're fired."

14

"WHAT THE HELL'S GOING ON, Paul?" Simon said into the phone. "All of a sudden we've got Jonestown here?"

"Three old bodies wrapped in tar paper is hardly Jonestown, Simon," Paul Shockton said, his voice crackling and popping over the cellular link. Simon had reached him in his car; he was on his way back from the coroner's office. "These guys have been dead for eighty years. They can't pin this one on you."

"What about this kid they found on the nature trail?" Simon said. "What's up with that?"

"Looks like he's been there awhile. He's in an advanced state of decomposition. That's really all I know right now. I mean, sure, we identified him from dental records, but we don't know how he got there or why he rotted so quickly."

"Jesus, Paul, don't talk about him like he's a piece of fruit. Someone could be monitoring."

"Sure, Simon. Whatever."

"Sorry, didn't mean to snap. Keep me informed, okay?"

Shockton sighed. "You know I will. And, Simon?"

"Yeah?"

"I know it's an election year, but try to relax."

Simon hung up. Try to relax, Shockton said. Sure, he would relax, just as soon as dead people stopped appearing on a daily basis. He wanted to be known for bringing jobs into the area, and instead, his people kept turning up corpses. He thought about calling the coroner and getting more details, but decided not to. Shockton had said he would keep Simon informed, so that's what he would do.

Christ, but he needed a game of racquetball. He told his secretary he was going out, and headed to the courts. He ended up staying at the gym for three hours, not even playing against anyone, just whacking rubber balls around and pretending they were members of the press.

Driving home that evening, Simon spotted the first political advertisement of the season: a sign in somebody's yard. The thing was nearly as large as a billboard and, unfortunately, was for his opponent, Karl Castle. It sported a big picture of his smug face, a rising sun behind it, a cityscape beneath it—like he was God or something, hovering above the town—and Karl's catch phrase, *Building a new future for Selden Falls*. Simon thought: Ha ha, very clever.

The fact that he had no similar phrase was beginning to worry him.

It was common knowledge that Karl's campaign—or would that be *kampaign?*—was running short of money, but that hadn't stopped the man from appearing on local talk radio, and distributing leaflets, and driving around town on a bulldozer with a recording blaring from loudspeakers. He was running the sort of shoestring guerrilla campaign that had gotten Simon into office last election; meanwhile, Simon's own reelection effort had yet to get off the ground. He would fire his campaign manager, if that didn't mean firing himself.

In addition to the usual infuriating personal attacks—especially veiled references to sexual preferences—Karl had begun using Quentin Farmer against Simon in a three-pronged attack: accusing him of coddling Farmer's indiscretions; implying that he had received kickbacks in exchange for bending various rules and ordinances; and suggesting that he didn't *really* care about local businesses, because he'd allowed Farmer to use his own people in constructing the place instead of local contractors.

Simon couldn't decide which thrust irritated him the most, but all of them seemed to be effective with various sectors of the public. He had people working on rebuttals, and he had issued official denials of the more serious charges; but responding was always harder than attacking, especially because there was a grain of truth in some of Karl's statements. Maybe he *had* coddled Farmer a bit. Maybe he *should* have fought harder for local companies to be involved in construction. And he hadn't taken any money, of course, but he *had* bent the rules on Farmer's behalf. He'd thought his constituents—people like the guy who had a sign for Karl in his front yard—would thank him for his efforts. Instead they were being used to club him over the head.

It all made him rather wistful for his days as an accountant.

He was still thinking about the whole election thing when he passed Henry Fontana's house fifteen minutes later. He and the Fontanas were practically neighbors now, only four or five miles apart. He would have to call them up and invite them over; smooth out any hard feelings, get them on his side, get them involved in his reelection effort. Because, to be perfectly honest, Karl's campaign was not the only one that could use an infusion of cash from well-heeled contributors. And besides, it had been ages since they'd seen each other; the last time had been not long after Henry had come home from the hospital. Simon had dropped by to visit for a while, long enough to ascertain—in what he had thought had been a subtle fashion—whether or not Henry was going to sue the city. He still remembered what Paige had told him in the driveway: *Thanks for coming by, and next time you can just call and ask if we've talked to an attorney.*

Thinking about Henry's accident inevitably led him to think about Jane, and Calvin, and the old church, and the hallucinatory attack he had suffered when he had gone inside, when the crows had chanted *Selden* and the tree had turned into putrid flesh and he'd seen a shadow hovering above the rooftop. Thank God that place was gone now. He knew there had to be some physical explanation for his delusion—maybe spores from all the mildew growing on the walls and ceiling—but he felt better knowing the building had been destroyed.

Now he had people turning up dead under mysterious, gruesome circumstances; and he had a teenage girl who had disappeared; and again, it was all going on down at the canal, near where the old church had stood, as if the place were still exerting some malign influence. Which was absurd, of course; it was just a *building*, for God's sake. He was starting to think like Jane Trott. No, there was a human agent behind what was happening; a psychopath, a serial killer.

Was it just coincidence that the deaths started up again when Quentin Farmer came back to town? Could he be the target, somehow? Could he be the perpetrator?

Well, that was for Shockton to find out; he was making discreet inquiries along those lines. Such speculation wasn't Simon's forte. He couldn't spend all his time digging up the past; he needed to focus on the future. Specifically, the future of his career.

Hm. *Focus on the future.*

Was that a potential slogan?

Nelson was watching the eleven o'clock news when he heard someone go tromping by his room, and since there was no one else on the third floor of the Farmhouse bed and breakfast, he figured it had to be Quentin. The footsteps went right past his door, surprising him; he'd expected a knock and a *good night*, at least. Instead, nothing.

He gave Quentin a few minutes to settle in, then called him on the cell phone. It rang and rang, and when the voice came on informing him the cellular customer wasn't answering, as if he couldn't figure that out himself, he shut the thing off and went into the hallway. Quentin's door had a *Do Not Disturb* sign hanging off the knob, still swinging slightly; Nelson hoped he hadn't picked up another trollop. He rapped on the door. After a moment, Quentin's voice came from inside: "Yes?"

"It's Nelson. You all right?"

"I'm fine."

"Nobody answered the phone at the plaza. I'll have to talk to the personnel department tomorrow about the Shoemaker situation—"

"I changed my mind. If I fire him now, I'll get all kinds of bad publicity. It'll look like I'm canning him because he found the body."

"Okay," Nelson said. "Okay, that makes sense." Pause. "Are we still on track to go home tomorrow?"

"We're not leaving," Quentin said.

"We're not?"

"I want to stick around a few more days. Until things are under control."

Things were never going to be under control, Nelson thought. "But —"

"Is that a problem?"

The edge in his voice told Nelson it wasn't permitted to be a problem. "No, sir," he said.

"Good. Nelson, can you read?"

"Yes, sir."

"Can you read the sign on my door?"

"Yes, sir."

"All right. Just checking."

Chastened, Nelson returned to his room.

Paige awoke with a start from a disturbing dream, a dream where she'd been walking through a desolate, stunted forest, and the branches were full of dark birds with wicked black beaks and eyes that gleamed like oily coals, and they all kept nattering at her in the voice of Henry's mother.

She got out of bed. Her body was damp from the heat and the stress of the dream; she and Florence had never been more than formally cordial with each other, and since the old woman had gone to the nursing home their relationship had deteriorated to the point where Florence referred to Paige only as *her* or *that woman* or, when she thought Paige couldn't hear her, *that bitch*. It wasn't senility, it wasn't Alzheimer's; it was just the old nastiness that Florence no longer thought she had to keep under wraps.

And now she wanted to *move in with them*? Yeah, sure; her, and Jack the Ripper too.

The sheen of perspiration on her skin made the air feel icy. She slipped into the light negligee that was puddled on the floor like a pool of milk, let it settle around her bare thighs. Kept her a little bit warmer. She went to the sliding door, pulled aside the sheers, looked into the sky.

It was raining. The sky was blotched with clouds, the drops plinking softly against the outer screen panel. A light summer rain, taking the humidity down a notch. She put her hand on the door; the glass was very warm to the touch, and when she removed her palm it left a misty, fading image of itself behind, a sad, evaporating ghost.

Nights were dark up here, much darker than nights in the village. The forest was charcoal-black, the yard a lake of ink held in by tufted walls. She was trying to talk Henry into security lights in back, but he would just look at her and say, *security from what?* Because there was zero crime on Cool Road, and they had the Security Blanket alarm if anyone tried to break in, and—despite what had happened to them a few months ago—he still seemed to think that bad things happened only to other families.

Suddenly a plane of yellow light swept out across the grass. A few seconds later Freddie's still-nameless puppy bounded into view, dragging its nose across the ground as it searched for a place to do its business. As it drew away from the house the dog slowed, then stopped, looked around, sniffed the air; and then it began to yap, like one of those battery-operated mutts at the novelty store with the *shuffle-wag-woof* repertoire. The puppy didn't appear to know what it was barking at, but it was doing so with enthusiasm and vigor. After a few seconds it seemed to decide that barking wasn't a good idea, and settled into a throaty little whine. It flattened itself against the ground, and its spiky hackles went up, and it fixated on a spot at the edge of the forest, near the wooden shed.

Paige opened the sliding door and crept out onto the balcony and looked where the dog was looking, but couldn't see anything. The light didn't reach that far; the shed was nothing but a black blob against the darker wall of the trees.

Wait.

What was that?

There was something behind the shed after all, she thought; part of the shadow had shifted, as if trying to conceal itself from the yapping little monster. It was probably just a large, skittish animal, she told herself; a deer, a wild turkey.

A humongous crow, with white in its feathers.

Frederick toddled into the splash of light, coming out to get the dog. The shadow shifted again, more noticeably this time. Whatever it was, it saw him.

It saw him.

Paige flattened herself against the railing of the balcony and shouted, "Frederick, get back inside this instant!"

He looked up at her and waved. "Hi, Mommy!"

"Get back inside!"

"Okay! Just let me get Herman!"

Paige turned around and raced out of the bedroom, down the hallway, new shag carpet burning her bare feet. She stormed down the stairs, bounded into the kitchen, where the cold linoleum jabbed shocks up her ankles. Frederick had left the back door open. He was already coming toward the house, carrying the puppy, which was growling in its throat and looking up at the house, toward the balcony off the master bedroom, she thought. "Hurry up, Freddie!" she said. "Hurry up!"

He came up the three concrete steps and put the dog down. Its nails skittered on the linoleum as it started chasing its tail. Paige slammed the door, locked it, chained it. Frederick said, "What's wrong, Mommy?"

What *was* wrong, anyway? Just Paige, cracking up again. "Nothing," she said, after a moment. "I just didn't want you outside in the rain."

"It's warm rain," Frederick said. His pajamas were spattered with dark spots. She ruffled his damp hair. The dog squatted in the corner, lifted its tail, and began depositing tiny brown sausages on the floor.

As she often did when under stress, Paige started to giggle.

"Bad Herman!" Frederick said, in his most authoritarian voice, which wasn't particularly authoritarian at all. The dog looked at him and wagged its tail and continued its business.

"When did you name him Herman?" Paige said.

"Just now," Freddie said. He added, proudly, "I thought of it all by myself."

Herman finished making a mess and then rocketed out of the kitchen. Paige heard his little feet bounding up the stairs. Frederick went after it. Still giggling, Paige cleaned up the droppings, then shut the light and went upstairs herself. She entered the bedroom, closed the door behind her. She circled to her side of the bed, and noticed that the sliding doors were still open. She shut both of them, then sat down on the bed and gave Henry's shoulder a little push. He grumbled and looked at her with one baleful eye.

"We have *got* to get security lights," she said.

"Don't need them," he mumbled.

"Yes we do."

He said something incoherent, then got up and staggered off to the bathroom. The door closed; a line of light appeared beneath it. And Paige noticed a dark blotch on the bed where he'd been lying, a stain maybe as big as her hand. She switched on the light. The blot was crimson, and fresh.

Blood.

"Henry?" she said, crossing to the bathroom door and rapping on it. "Come out here." She heard the toilet flush and then the door opened, and Henry was standing there, naked, looking cross.

"What?" he said, as she examined the front of his body, looking for injuries.

"Let me see the other side," she said. He grunted and turned a little bit, and she found the wound: three fresh cuts between his shoulder blades, ragged narrow slices oozing drops of red blood. They seemed to be puffing up, forming welts. "Do you feel these?" she said, tracing one with her finger without actually touching it.

"These what?"

"Your back is cut," she said.

He craned his neck, trying and failing to look at the injuries. "It itches a little bit, now you mention it," he said. "Feels kind of tingly. Doesn't hurt."

"Come on," she said, giving him a shove back into the bathroom. "Let's get you cleaned up." Paige sat him on the edge of the tub. With a fresh washcloth she wiped down the cuts—the welts had pretty much pinched off the blood flow already—and then dug the antiseptic out of the medicine chest. She squeezed some onto her fingers and rubbed it on the wounds. After a few seconds the cream began to fizz and bubble. She lifted her hand away and watched the white lotion turned a curdled yellow-brown as it soaked into Henry's flesh.

Déjà vu. That had happened when they dressed her wound at the hospital, the day the crow had stabbed her. The stuff they had put on her hand had fizzed beneath the bandage.

"Henry?" she said.

"Yeah?"

"I think we should get you to a doctor," Paige said.

Henry laughed. "Don't be silly," he said. "Just a couple of cuts. I probably had an itch and scratched too hard." He reached his left arm behind his back, demonstrated his itch-abatement technique; and it did look as if his fingers could reach the area that was injured.

"I guess that's possible," she said.

"What else could it be?" he said. "You think something flew onto the balcony, came into the bedroom, rolled me over, scratched up my back, and flew away again? I think I would've woke up for that." The antiseptic was all gone now, fully absorbed into the wounds. The welts seemed to be going down already; the blood seepage had completely stopped. Henry stood up, patted her on the head, then headed out of the bathroom.

Then he stopped, and looked back at her. "I'd like to meet the thing that could do all that," he said.

As Paige turned out the light, she muttered: "That makes one of us."

Quentin called Nelson into his room early that morning, when the rising sun was still just hinting at its presence with a pinkish fringe above the hills to the east. When Nelson entered, Quentin was standing by his window looking out at the dawn, at the valley that swept out below them, at the threads of lividity creeping across the sky.

"Close the door," Quentin said, without turning around.

Nelson closed the door.

"I've been thinking about your position," Quentin said.

"Oh?"

"Yes." Quentin put his left hand on the window frame. His knuckles were white, like he was clenching his fingers on the dark wood. "You haven't seemed yourself lately. You've been distracted. You've been edgy. I wonder if you're happy with your job."

"Well, I—"

"Unfortunately I don't have another position for you. I don't know what you'd be qualified for anyway. What was it you were doing before you became my assistant?"

"Clerical pool," Nelson said after a moment. He couldn't take his gaze off Quentin's hands. The fingers of the left one were tightening and loosening, tightening and loosening on the frame; the fingers of the right one were doing the same thing to the sill. His fingernails were made little scraping, scratching noises.

"You see? I can't send you back to the clerical pool, and I can't promote you to upper management."

"Why not?" Nelson said; although he would never take such a position anyway. Too much more hassle, for not enough more money.

"I just can't," Quentin said. "I never realized it before, but this is a dead-end position. I think it's time you moved on to other fields of endeavor."

Nelson said: "Could you at least look at me while you're firing me?"

"No," Quentin said. "I can't."

"Okay, well ..." Nelson trailed off. Losing the job didn't bother him so much; losing the money was another thing altogether. But what was he going to do? Grovel, like Nick Garson? He said: "Effective when?"

"Immediately. There's a check for a month's severance on the dresser. Talk to personnel, they'll give you a recommendation for whatever job you apply for."

Nelson saw the slip of blue paper on the dresser and picked it up; it was a check made out to Nelson DeGrace, a five and four zeroes in the box—which would be more like a year's severance—even though *five thousand* was scrawled across the amount line. The writing was shaky, as if Quentin's hand had been trembling as he held the pen. Quentin had punctiliously neat handwriting, usually; and he *never* made mistakes like this, not when money was involved.

"Take the Jaguar back to Buffalo, *now*," Quentin said. His voice was tight, like he just barely had it under control. "Leave it at corporate. I'll take a flight back out of Syracuse."

"A *flight*?" Nelson said. "You don't fly. You hate planes." Quentin did not respond, and after a moment Nelson said, "Okay, well ... whatever. I guess that's all then. I'll clean out my stuff when I get back to the office." He went back to the door, opened it, hesitated.

Quentin was still by the window, staring at the sky. It was getting brighter out there, the sun peeking over the tips of the hills. Nelson slid his sunglasses onto his face; the polarized lenses filtered out the glare, and he caught a glimpse of something approaching the house, a wispy, gauzy, indistinct blob. It was like a dark cloud, except it appeared to be propelling itself with a flapping motion; and the instant he saw it, it disappeared, dissolved with one stroke of a sunbeam.

What did his former employer see, looking out into the morning?

Nelson said: "What's *really* going on, Quentin?"

Quentin shook his head, waved him away.

After a moment, Nelson went into the hallway and closed the door behind him, went to his own room next to Quentin's, and began to pack.

He was just finishing up when he heard a sudden, thumping, chaotic crashing from Quentin's room, like someone was picking up furniture and flinging it around. Porcelain or glass shattered musically; and he heard a wailing cry, trailing off into silence, like the call of a gigantic bird.

Then, silence. It was all over in the space of three seconds.

Oh, shit.

Nelson went to Quentin's door, tried the knob. Locked.

But Quentin hadn't asked for his key back.

Nelson unlocked the door and pushed it open, and goggled at the mess. The table near the window had been bowled over, shattering its marble top and the porcelain washbasin that had rested on it; its pieces lay scattered among the dark streaks of water across the carpet. The sheets were partially off the bed, heaping over the edge of the mattress nearest the window, which was raised, letting in the cool, moist air of early morning. A breeze rustled the sheers that hung not inside the room but outside of it, dangling through the window, fluttering at the dawn; the curtain rod was torn from one of its support and sat at an angle with one of its panels missing.

Quentin was nowhere to be seen.

Nelson went to the window. Where Quentin had had the wood in a death grip earlier, the varnish was scraped down to the lighter surface beneath, a series of deep scratches, as if he'd been worrying at the frame with a knife. Nelson leaned over, put his head out the window. No sign of Quentin; no sign at all.

Then he saw a flash of purple and gold from the lawn. The missing curtain panel, fallen into a rose bush a dozen yards from the house, the gilded thread picking up the light of the rising sun. How the hell had that gotten way out there?

He raced out of the room and down the wide, soft stairway. Tom Teller was on his way up, dressed in what looked like one of his wife's robes. It only came down to his knees, showing lengths of knobby, white-haired leg. When he saw Nelson rushing down at him, Tom flattened himself against the wall and said, "What was all that noise?"

"Accident in Mr. Farmer's room," Nelson said. "We'll pay for it." He swept by the innkeeper, flew out through the kitchen. Raye Teller had her back to him, frying something on the stove. He hardly even smelled it, he went through so fast, carrying little curls of the aroma out into the fresh air of the morning.

There was a light breeze, rippling the grass, rustling the trees. The spidery limbs of the rose bush waggled in the wind. The curtain panel lay just at the edge of the shrub, pushed into a sad little wad of fabric up against the plant. Nelson prodded it with his foot and, when it didn't bite him, picked it up. Something fell out of it and fluttered to the grass. He took a step back and looked at the thing, lying like a tiny sliver of night.

A single long, black, grey-tinged feather.

He knelt and took it, and it felt hot and alive in his fingers, seemed to vibrate in his grasp.

Nelson was still standing there holding the curtain and the feather when the back door opened and Tom Teller came out. "Mr. Farmer's not in his room," he said as he approached. "Looks like there was a fight in there or something."

"I know," Nelson said.

"What you got there?"

"Part of the drapes from Quentin's room."

Tom Teller said: "What's it doing out here?"

"I don't know," Nelson said. The sun was coming up over the hills, red and swollen, and he raised an arm in front of his eyes.

"What's with the crow feather?"

"Is that what it is? Crow?"

"Yep."

"It was inside the curtain," Nelson said.

He held it out to Tom, but Tom didn't take it. "I think you ought to put it down," he said. For some reason, Nelson thought that sounded like a good idea. He dropped the feather, but before it hit the ground, the breeze gusted into a wind, snatched the bit of plumage, and swept it off across the hillside. It danced and bobbed like a thing alive. Tom nodded, and said: "Dirty birds. Never know what they been into."

Nelson said nothing. He watched the feather vanish into the woods.

The wind dwindled and was gone.

"Come on back inside, Mr. Nelson," Tom Teller said. "Get yourself some breakfast and call the police." The old man turned and walked stiffly back toward the inn. After a moment, Nelson followed him.

As he entered the kitchen, he suddenly remembered the big, mottled crow he had seen at the old church, back in March, just after they'd dragged him out of the pit. Black, tinged with grey. Just like the feather that had just fluttered away.

He had also seen a bigger shadow over the place, an image of a bird as big as an airplane. The same thing—he had to admit this, even though it raised a very disturbing question—he had seen in the air that morning, winging its way toward the Farmhouse.

The thing Quentin had been staring at, he thought, when he had been frozen at the window as he'd fired Nelson that morning.

Quentin had had the creature's home demolished—if *creature* was the right way to describe this phantasm—and now that he had returned, it had come and taken him. Maybe he had known what was going to happen; maybe he had sensed his impending doom, the way Nelson had sensed, back in March, that they were on the verge of something disastrous. Maybe by sending him away, Quentin was hoping to save him from sharing his fate.

"Mr. Nelson?" Tom said. "You want to use the phone?"

"What?" Nelson said. Then: "Oh. Yeah. Yeah, thanks."

Tom Teller escorted him to the telephone in the den. Nelson punched buttons, hardly paying attention to the number he was dialing, because he was wondering: What had they set free?

The shrilling phone jarred Simon Jones awake. He fumbled around on the nightstand for it, knocking over some magazines and a partially-full glass of water, but he didn't find the phone. After a moment he realized this was because he had somehow ended up on Roland's side of the bed, and Roland had taken over his. Simon clambered over Roland—he stirred and muttered, but didn't wake up—and grabbed the handset. "Simon Jones," he said. He never just said *Hello?* anymore.

"Simon? It's Nelson. Nelson DeGrace."

"Who?"

"Quentin Farmer's assistant," the voice said.

"Oh, right." Simon glanced at the digital clock. As he watched, it changed to five-thirty. He tried to remember why he enjoyed being mayor. "What, uh, what can I do for you?"

"Quentin's disappeared."

Simon waited for him to elaborate, but he didn't. "All right," he said at length. "You suspect foul play?"

"I suspect *something*," Nelson said. "I just don't know what. He disappeared from a third story room at the Farmhouse. I found one of his curtains out in the yard with a black feather inside it."

Simon rubbed his eyes with the back of his hand. The alarm clock would be going off in fifteen minutes. He hated being awake when the alarm clock went off. "Why are you telling *me* this? If you think he was kidnapped, call the cops. Call Shockton. They get paid to do this kind of stuff."

Nelson didn't say anything. Simon heard him breathing, breathing, breathing; and then he said, "There's something wrong, Simon. With this town. With that old church we knocked down. There's something wrong."

"Okay, I hear what you're saying." Simon wondered if Quentin's assistant was on medication. "I don't think there's anything more, ah, more *wrong* with Selden Falls than with any other community. We've had our share of problems, but—"

"What problems? What happened in Selden Falls a hundred years ago? Where did those bodies come from? What was that old church *used* for? Where are all the records, Simon?"

"Look, Nelson, I hardly think it's appropriate to call me at six in the morning and start asking me—"

"*Nobody knows*, Simon. When we were here in March, at the park, I saw a monument that said *for all the lost angels*. What does that mean? The library couldn't tell me, they didn't have any records. Said something about a fire. You don't even *have* a historical society, for God's sake. Nobody knew what the deal was with the old church, either. That councilwoman who tried to find out—"

"Jane Trott."

"Look what happened to her, pecked to death by crows, for God's sake. And her husband, what happened to him? Where'd he go?"

"He must've left town."

"Then who was the old man they found under the church?"

Simon said nothing, because he had nothing to say. Who was the old man under the church? He didn't know. What had the building been used for? He didn't know. Why would Calvin Trott leave town without even sticking around long enough to bury his wife? He didn't know.

And what had happened to him, Simon, when he was inside the church?

Panic attack, that's what.

He'd been able to believe that for a long time now, through all the quiet months of spring and summer when nothing happened that couldn't be explained by politics, by nature, by chance. None of this weird stuff that Nelson was trying to push onto him. It wasn't possible. It was, in fact, ludicrous.

"Mayor Jones?" Nelson said.

"Look, Nelson, you're asking me all kinds of questions I can't answer and you're telling me all kinds of things I already know. You're getting yourself all worked up and it's not going to do anyone any good: not me, not you, not the missing girls. My advice to you is, call the police and explain to them what happened to Quentin, or what you think happened, and let them worry about finding him. I don't know what you want from me."

There was a pause, and then Nelson said: "Simon?"

"Yeah?"

"What do you mean, *missing girls?*"

Simon flopped onto his back, stretching the phone cord across Roland's face, who grumbled and swatted at it like he thought he was being buzzed by a fly. "Look, Nelson, do we have to talk about this now?"

"You have another girl who disappeared? Is that what you're telling me?"

"Yeah, that's what I'm telling you. We have a nineteen-year-old girl who vanished outside a convenience store. She went in to buy cigarettes and the guy wouldn't sell them to her and she left in a huff; then the clerk heard her scream and went outside. The girl's car was there, the door was open, the dome light was on, the driver was gone."

"So that's two," Nelson said. "Two missing girls, a dead boy, and now Quentin. Last time there was Jane, Calvin, and Nick Garson. How many are there going to be *this time*, Simon?"

God, but this was not what Simon wanted to hear at five-thirty in the morning. "Look, Nelson, I'm having enough trouble with this situation without you starting serial killer rumors."

Nelson said: "I wish a serial killer were *all* I was worried about."

Well, that was it; Nelson had successfully creeped Simon out. He did *not* need to deal with this crap before breakfast. "I'm hanging up now," Simon said. "Call me back when you have something besides conjecture and scary stories."

He reached across Roland and dropped the phone into its cradle.

Five seconds later, the clock radio went off.

15

Nelson didn't call the police.

After getting nowhere with Simon, he left the den and went into the front hallway. He could hear Tom and Raye talking quietly in the kitchen, probably about the damage to Quentin's room and how much to charge for it. Well, that was the company's lookout, not his.

He went through the front door, stopped on the porch. The Jaguar was at the far end of the small parking lot, under the spreading, drooping boughs of a willow tree. This, in itself, was unusual; Quentin never left the Jaguar under a tree if he could avoid it, because doing so invited birds to shit all over it. He must have been in a hurry to park it, get out, get into the Farmhouse. Maybe he thought he'd be safe from whatever was coming for him, once he was inside.

Wrong.

Nelson went to the car. Dew clung darkly to his shoes. The air was cool and humid, with a hint of fog hovering over the valley. Already, though, the ascendant sun was heating things up. Insects in the trees thrummed to each other with a sound like New Year's noisemakers. It was going to be a hot one, he thought.

As he unlocked the door of the Jaguar, he noticed something on the backrest of the driver's seat, a black stain on the tan leather. He opened the door, then took out a handkerchief and rubbed the stain lightly. Color came off on the white fabric, a ruddy brownish smear.

Blood.

Carefully, not touching the stain itself, Nelson folded up the handkerchief and dropped it on the passenger seat. He returned to the house and got a towel from the linen closet, draped it over the back of the driver's seat, climbed in, and drove to the police station, where he managed to convince a cop to come out and look at the blood on the seat of the car. The cop examined the stain, shook out the towel and peered at it intently, then said: "You have any trouble with this?"

"Excuse you?" Nelson said.

"The Jag. I hear they break down a lot."

"It's not any worse than my Chevy," Nelson said. "What about the blood?"

"Me, I only buy Japanese. Never have a lick of trouble with a Japanese car."

"That's very patriotic. What about the blood?"

"Well, there's not really very much of it, and it's obviously not fresh. If it wasn't so damn humid it'd probably be all dried up by now." The cop produced a rubber glove and pulled it on, then drew his finger along the back of the seat. He showed the brownish smear on his fingertip to Nelson. "See?"

"Saw it already, thanks," Nelson said. "Don't you think this implies some kind of foul play?"

The cop shrugged. "Could be a lot of things. You said you saw him this morning. Did he seem okay?"

"He didn't seem *injured*, but he was acting weird."

"I've seen your boss guy on television," the cop said. "Looked like he always acts weird."

Oh, goody, Nelson thought; an armchair psychologist. "So what you're saying is, you're not going to look for him."

"Can't. He hasn't been gone long enough. Look, for one thing, nobody could just swoop through the window and steal him. Besides, you said you didn't search the room; for all you know, he threw his stuff out the window and hid under the bed." The cop grinned. "He's probably out getting blown by a reporter right now, as we speak. If he doesn't turn up in a couple of days, then give us a call."

"Thanks a bunch," Nelson said.

"No problem."

The cop snapped off the glove and proffered the stained towel to Nelson. "Keep it," Nelson said, as he climbed into the car. "You might need it for evidence later."

On break that morning, Jasper Shoemaker wandered away from the plaza and, without any real idea where he was going, crossed the bridge over the canal and crunched up the gravel path to the site of the old church. The area had been converted into a park, so it was, in theory, open to the public; but he had never seen the public take advantage of it, and now, of course, it was cordoned off by police tape and haunted by earth-moving equipment, big shapes lurking not far off, hulking shadows visible through the trees.

The access road opened up into what had been the ragged field surrounding the place; now it was a gravel parking lot. The curving side of the wall of flowers loomed in front of him like a bulwark; a shiny brown sedan was parked in its shadow. The car looked familiar, Jasper thought; he went to it and looked it over and found it to be unoccupied.

That was okay. He could wait.

He walked up to the terraced garden. It was designed to mimic— on a smaller scale, of course—the layout of Quentin's plaza, almost directly opposite it across the water. A narrow ribbon of concrete wound through the levels to the top, where benches of wood and iron gave a view of the shopping center. You could sit and contemplate it for hours, if you wanted to. There might as well have been a sign on it, to the effect of *Let us all gaze upon the glory of Canal Plaza.*

Jasper walked around behind the earthen wedge, running his hand along the hot brown bricks. There was still energy coming from the site; he could feel it flowing into his palm, his hand tingled as he soaked it up. The sound of wings filled up his head. He closed his eyes and listened to them.

"Shoemaker!"

Jasper's head snapped left at the commanding voice: a reflex, since he no longer worked for Paul Shockton, who was now approaching from the excavation off to the left.

"What the hell are you doing here?" Shockton demanded. "This is a restricted area, and as I recall, we canned your ass in April."

"As *I* recall, I resigned," Jasper said evenly.

"Same difference. You're trespassing in an active investigation. That's a no-no for private citizens like you, Shoemaker."

Jasper stared at him, and after a moment said: "I quit my job at the dealership."

Paul's face turned incrementally redder. "And I give a shit because … ?"

"I'm full time security at the plaza now."

"Marvelous. This is not the plaza. Quentin Farmer does not own this patch of land. And even if he did, it's still the site of an investigation. So mosey on back to your beat, or I'll arrest you."

Jasper didn't move. He stood there with his palm flat on the stone, soaking up the energy, letting him fill it up, listening to the wings. Shockton turned redder and redder, as if he were quickly ripening.

At last he said, "Do I have to eject you myself?"

"I guess you do," Jasper said.

Shockton growled. He stepped up and grabbed Jasper's arm.

Jasper let the power from the stone flow through his own body and into Paul Shockton's. The chief's teeth clenched, his eyes widened and bulged and seemed ready to burst out of his skull. Then all the red drained out of his face, and his irises rolled up into his head.

Jasper lifted his hand from the stone, cut off the flow. Paul Shockton crumpled to the ground, twitching, as if he'd just gotten a massive electric shock. Jasper knelt beside him, extended the index finger of his right hand; his ragged, unevenly-trimmed nail stretched out into a coal-black talon, curved, wickedly sharp. He drew it in a line across the back of Shockton's neck, a neat little incision, deep into the thick, flabby meat. Blood welled out of the cut.

Jasper coughed, from deep into his lungs. Coughed again. He felt the stuff rising in his throat, bubbly and viscous. It rose into his mouth, stinging his tongue with its salty tang. He pushed it to the inside of his lips, opened them, and dribbled the sticky phlegm into the wound in Paul Shockton's neck. It flowed into Shockton's body, even where Jasper had missed; it had its own method of getting around, an oozing, slurping, undulating motion. The stuff knew where it had to go, and went there.

Jasper stood up, wiped his shiny, sticky lips. Shockton lay still; but he would be getting up again soon enough. Already the lips of the wound were knitting themselves back together, sealing the stuff up inside, where it would be protected.

He checked his watch. Break had been over for ten minutes. Well, he didn't think he had to worry that Monroe would yell at him.

After all, *he* was the one running things now, wasn't he?

Nelson parked behind the plaza and climbed out of the car. He went to the front entrance of the offices, a glass door sealed with an electronic lock, and punched in the code.

Nothing happened.

Huh. Maybe he had dialed it wrong. He punched the combination again, but the tiny LED stayed red instead of turning green. Nelson stepped back and eyed the door. They must have changed the code. Nelson stewed about this for a moment, then rang the bell.

And waited.

And waited.

And then the venetian blinds behind the glass twitched, and the door creaked open with the bulky form of Jasper Shoemaker behind it. He was wearing his brown security guard outfit, hair slicked into a crest, eyes sharp and darting; he looked kind of like a cockatiel. His gaze at Nelson was almost one of incomprehension, as if he couldn't quite figure out what manner of creature Nelson might be.

"Hi," Nelson said.

Jasper stared at him.

"Has Quentin been here?" Nelson asked.

Jasper continued to stare at him.

"I'm looking for Quentin," Nelson said, slowly, in case the big man was having trouble hearing or something. "Have you seen him?"

The security guard's ponderous head slowly shook.

"He hasn't been here?"

This time Jasper shrugged.

"Look, I'd like answers in English, please," Nelson said. "Has Quentin been here, or hasn't he?"

No response at all this time, just a stare.

Nelson pushed his way forward, into the hallway. Jasper gave ground without complaint, moving backwards and flattening himself against the wall on the right as best he could manage. His nervous gaze never left Nelson's face as he entered the building.

Behind him, the glass door clicked shut; and then they were standing there in the deserted hallway. The only sounds were the faint rattle of the air conditioner blowing frigid air from vents in the ceiling and the fluorescent lights buzzing slightly in their ceiling fixtures. Shoemaker maneuvered around in front of him, keeping him from coming in any farther. He said nothing; he just stood there and stared.

"What's gotten into you?" Nelson said, looking Jasper up and down. "A couple days ago I couldn't shut you up. You run out of things to say?"

"I guess," Jasper said.

There was a moment of silence, and then Nelson said: "Awfully quiet this morning. Where *is* everybody?"

"Meeting."

"Oh, is that why it took you so long to get to the door? I interrupted a meeting?"

Jasper nodded.

"What's it about?" Nelson asked.

Jasper Shoemaker grinned. "Future plans," he said.

"Oh? That doesn't sound like a meeting that *everyone* would have to go to."

"They're all being kept informed."

"They are? Now, see, I *know* that's not the way Quentin does business. Is he aware of what you're doing?"

"We have full authority to proceed."

"You do?"

"Yep."

"Well, would you mind if I sat in on the meeting for a while?"

Still smiling, Jasper said: "You don't work for Quentin anymore."

Nelson hadn't expected him to know that. After a moment he said, "Says who?"

"Quentin. Last night. He stopped here."

"He did?"

"Yep."

"Then do you know why there's blood in his car? Or why he disappeared from his room this morning?"

Jasper said nothing.

"What the hell is going on here?" Nelson said. "Is Quentin behind this? Did he tell you to get rid of me?" The big man shrugged slightly, smiled mysteriously, said nothing. "If that's it, you tell him to come out and say it to my face. You hear me? I deserve better than this and that stupid stunt he pulled back at the room—you probably know all about that, too, don't you? You probably all had a good laugh."

"It wasn't that good of a laugh," Jasper said mildly.

"I woke up the *mayor*, for God's sake, and ranted all this unbelievable crap at him. I went to the police. So if Quentin is here, you tell him I want to talk to him. Now."

Jasper's face split into a wide, easy, shit-eating grin. "Come with me," he said, lumbering up the hallway. Nelson followed. They stopped at an electronically-keyed metal door on the left, where Jasper punched some numbers. He disappeared through the opening, gesturing for Nelson to follow. Nelson stepped through the doorway and into a landing. A steel ladder was bolted to the wall on the left, running up to a sort of hatch in the ceiling; on the other side, stairs descended into the basement. A pale light shone from down there, cheap bulbs with cheaper enclosures. No need for appearances in this part of the plaza. There was a low, rhythmic noise, like well-oiled machinery, coming from downstairs.

Jasper, starting down the steps, looked over his shoulder and said: "Wait here."

Nelson caught the door with his foot and held it, just in case. "Okay," he said.

The big man pointed at the door with a thick finger and said: "Close it."

"I want to leave it open," Nelson said.

"Close the door," Jasper said.

Go to hell, Nelson thought. "Okay, okay." He swung the door wide, pulled his foot out of the way, let it start to close. "What's the big deal, anyway?"

Shoemaker grunted, turned his back, and started down the steps again.

Nelson grabbed the handle just before the door shut, opened it a crack, and stuck his foot in it again; this time, Jasper didn't turn around.

Something was going on, that was for sure, Nelson thought; but what? Was it really some dark and sinister force spat up from the wreckage of the old church? Or was it just Quentin, jerking him around? He'd seen it plenty of times; once Quentin crossed someone off his list, his behavior toward that unfortunate person could range from the indifferent to the reprehensible to the bizarre.

This definitely qualified as bizarre, he thought.

He stood there with his foot in the door, listening to the sound of the machines humming downstairs; there wasn't an actual moment when he suddenly knew that they were *voices*, not machines, it was more of a gradual realization, him paying closer and closer attention, stretching out farther and farther so he could hear them better.

Voices; they were definitely voices, murmuring some incomprehensible nonsense. It wasn't just aimless noise, though; it had a pattern, it had a structure. Like they were worshipping something, chanting to it. He couldn't pick Jasper's voice out of the general babble; and even if he could, he found himself doubting that he would be able to understand what he was saying.

He crept still farther from the entrance, his left leg stretched back so his foot would hold the door open. He made it to the railing and peeked over the edge. Nothing down there but stairs, and an open door where they ended; the voices emanated from there. He craned his neck and listened, his hair dangling down into the stairwell, but he still couldn't make out any words. Not ones he could identify, anyway.

Then the door slipped away from his foot and clicked shut.

Seconds later he heard a sound, a great thrumming of wings, as if some massive bird were preparing to take flight in that chamber at the bottom of the stairs. And a shadow fell across the light that shined from the opening, a big, creeping, amorphous shadow; it slid forward, touched the foot of the stairs, began oozing up them, almost like a physical thing.

The chanting stopped, all at once. The sound of beating wings grew louder.

Nelson decided it was time to leave.

When he turned around, he saw that they had installed an electronic lock on this side of the door, too, as if they not only wanted to keep people out, but also keep them in. *That* was why Jasper wanted him to close the door; to trap him, for easier disposal. He closed his eyes, tried to remember the buttons Jasper had pushed; but it was impossible, the man's fingers had moved too fast, and he didn't have time to guess at the combination right now. He needed to get out, and he needed to get out fast.

He looked to his left, at the steel ladder running up the wall to the hatch in the roof. He didn't see any lock on that. Either an oversight, or they didn't think they had to worry about anyone using it.

Nelson jumped onto the ladder and started climbing. He could *hear* the shadow moving up the stairs, sounded like sucking mud, like rustling paper. It was coming up; coming after him.

He reached the underside of the hatch, shoved the lever around and pushed the trapdoor open. His head was assaulted with drops of water.

Raining. When had it started raining?

He hauled himself out onto the pebbly roof and let the hatch close. He heard the locking lever snap back into place. He rolled away from it and stood up, damp stones and bits of tar clinging to his clothes.

Hoping the heap of cardboard was still there, he ran for the rear of the plaza.

Paige and Frederick returned from grocery shopping a little before noon. She backed into the driveway, punching the wide white button on the remote control clipped to her visor. The garage door obligingly rumbled open; she pulled into the garage and shut off the engine and sent the door back down again.

She and Freddie got out of the car. She unlocked the trunk, then handed her son the keys and sent him to unlock the door to the kitchen and disarm the Security Blanket. It had been a while since they had gone to the supermarket, so the trunk of her little car was quite stuffed with plastic bags, as if she had dismembered several bodies and neatly packaged up the parts. She gathered up several bags in each hand and then, once she got properly balanced, staggered up the five concrete steps to the kitchen door. Freddie had apparently closed it behind him. She struggled to get a grip on the knob through the bag handles and failed, so she set them down on the landing and tried the knob.

Locked.

Freddie wasn't following routine today. He was supposed to leave the kitchen door open for her; he certainly wasn't supposed to lock it. She knocked on the door, then stood there and waited. The door didn't open. After a minute, she gave it a couple of good, swift, loud kicks.

Still no answer.

Getting nervous, she pounded on the door with her fist and shouted, "Freddie! Let mommy in!"

After a second, the doorknob rattled. Paige backed away so it wouldn't hit her when it swung out; which it did, with great force. Would have knocked her right off the step if she hadn't gotten out of the way.

Behind the door was Henry's mother. The bitch had tried to smash her with the kitchen door. Freddie stood next to her; her bony left hand was locked on his shoulder. "There's no need to make such a fuss," Florence said after a moment. "I was just saying hello to my grandson."

Paige managed to paste a phony smile across her face as she said, "Hello, Florence, it's good to see you. What are you doing here?"

"Mommy, Grandma is moving in with us," Frederick said.

The phony smile got stretched paper-thin. "No, honey, that's just something your father and I are discussing," Paige said.

"You won't even know I'm here," Florence said. "I'm staying on a cot in the laundry room for now." A nasty little mysterious smile spread across her bloodless lips. "Until a room upstairs becomes available, anyway."

Paige found herself staring at Florence. Until a room became available? Where did the old lady think she was, a motel?

"It didn't take long to move; I don't have much," Florence added. "I don't need a lot of fancy things, like some people, but I do still have a few belongings in storage. They can be brought over once I'm settled in."

Paige said, "Now wait a—"

"What's in my house can be sold," Florence said. "Since I'll be living with you, I won't need all that furniture."

Paige took advantage of Florence's interruption to count quickly to ten, so as not to say something sharp and cutting and wholly inappropriate for Freddie's ears. "I'm sorry, Florence," she said. "I think we're having a communication problem. You're moving back into your own house, remember? Look at you, you're fit as you ever were. You don't need to—"

"Oh, I know I may *seem* just fine," Florence said. "To a common person, anyway. But the doctor says I still need special care so I don't hurt myself again. He says I have very brittle bones." After a moment the enigmatic little smile came back and she added, "I'm not as young as I used to be."

Actually, Florence looked better than she had in a long time, Paige thought; but that was apparently the observation of an ignorant common person. "How did you get in, anyway?" Paige asked. She was having trouble maintaining a polite tone of voice. "How'd you get around the alarm?"

"Henry dropped off a key for me at the home this morning and told me I could start moving in. He gave me the code for your button thing, and somebody from the home drove me out."

Henry had done that? Paige didn't believe it. She said: "Well, I guess I'll, uh, have a talk with Henry, then."

"Do that," Florence said. She turned Frederick around and said, "Come on, Freddie. You can help Grandma clean up Mommy's kitchen."

And Paige stood there on the top of the steps and counted to one hundred, while a pint of ice cream and some frozen vegetables slowly defrosted in the bags.

Quentin followed Jasper Shoemaker and Monroe Parker up the stairs from the basement conference room. It wasn't being used precisely according to its purpose; even though most of the people who worked in the plaza's administrative office were down there, Quentin wouldn't have exactly referred to what was going on as a *conference*. And although he was part of it, he still wasn't entirely sure what it was all about.

He could hear the wings, of course; he could always hear the wings. They followed him wherever he went, the thrush of their beating filling up his head. Sometimes—as when they had carried him away from his room at the bed and breakfast—they were so loud they drowned out everything else, so loud they were deafening; other times they retreated to a background murmur, almost gone but not quite, occasionally coming out with a burst of noise to remind him that they were there. And he didn't even want to *think* about how they had sounded in his dreams last night.

Right now, the wings were very loud, very near. They were accompanying him and the others as they went upstairs to kill Nelson.

They came to the landing. Jasper paused, looked around.

"Where is he?" Quentin said.

"He must've got out," Jasper said. "Rat-bastard caught the door again, I bet." He opened the door and went out, first left, then right, stalking up and down the hallway; then he came back in and said, "Long-haired freak's gone."

"I guess he decided not to wait," Quentin said, glad his assistant had gotten away.

"We'll find him," Jasper said. "He can't have gotten very far."

"Why do we have to bother with him?" Quentin said, as they walked back to the stairs. "I told him to go back to Buffalo. He'll probably head out of town as fast as he can——"

Before he even finished speaking, Jasper Shoemaker Senior belted him across the face with the back of his hand. Quentin went sprawling across the concrete, his skull clanging against the ladder to the roof. The big man gave him a disgusted look, and said: "Because I don't like him."

Quentin's mouth tasted like blood. He stared up at Jasper, said nothing. The security guard's hands were balled up into fists; he looked ready to fall on him and keep on pummeling. Monroe stood, impassive, in the corner. "I don't like *you*, either," Jasper said, "but I have a use for you. I got no use for that little fuckhead."

He lay there under the hatch, felt moisture seeping through his clothes from the floor. He looked up at the trapdoor with sudden comprehension.

Quentin saw, quite clearly, two paths before him. One involved betraying Nelson, wholeheartedly embracing the flock, merging and submerging himself in their power. The other involved holding his tongue, letting Nelson escape, and in that way retaining—as much as he could—a drop of humanity, deep in the morass they'd made of his mind. Maybe enough to pull himself out of here, someday.

He stirred, started to rise. Jasper took a step forward and kicked him in the side. The air whooshed out of him and he sagged back to the floor. The big man loomed over him, made as if to kick him again. Quentin scrambled away from him, against the ladder, and said: "Wait! The floor's wet!"

"Who gives a shit?" Jasper said; but he stopped, eyed Quentin, waited.

Quentin pointed at the hatch. "Rain," he said. "Get it?" Then, after a moment, one last hesitation on the brink of the abyss: "Nelson went up the ladder. He's on the roof!"

There was a pause.

The wings thrummed in Quentin's ears.

"I'll go get him," Jasper said.

As Paige brought the last of the bags into the kitchen, Florence was busily wiping up the stove with a rag. Paige and Henry had cleaned the kitchen just a few days ago, but it was apparently still dirty by Florence's standards. Frederick sat on a stool at the breakfast counter, watching his grandmother work.

As Paige began putting the groceries away, Florence made a tsking sound and said, in a stage whisper, "Your mother cooks on this filthy stove, Frederick?"

"Uh-huh," he said.

Paige muttered: "One, two, three, four ..."

"So unsanitary," Florence said.

"... five, six, seven, eight ..."

"I'll make you and your father something nice tonight," Florence said, "after I'm done cleaning."

"Sorry, Florence, we're going out tonight," Paige said.

"Going out?" The old woman's dark little eyes glittered at her. "Henry didn't say we were going out."

Paige shoved a carton of milk into the refrigerator so hard that it knocked over a half-dozen bottles of condiments, which she then had to straighten up again. "Well, that makes us even, since he didn't tell me you were moving in. And *we* doesn't include you."

"It must be nice," Florence said. "To have so much money, I mean, that you can go out whenever you don't feel like cooking. But Henry always was a hard worker."

Meaning that she was a leech, of course. "We're not going to a restaurant," Paige said. "We're going to someone's house."

"Whose?"

"The mayor's."

Florence made a dismissive gesture. "That pervert."

"He's not a pervert."

"You shouldn't take my grandson to such people's houses. They can't be trusted."

Great. A whole new plateau of arguments stretched out before her. "I'm not interested in your opinion on the subject," Paige said.

"Run and get cleaned up," Florence said, giving Frederick a little tap on the shoulder. He jumped off the stool and headed out of the kitchen.

Paige shut the refrigerator and opened the door to the pantry. It looked like someone had rearranged the food into different groupings; gosh, who could have done that? She glanced at Florence over her shoulder, and was startled to see that the old woman had crept up behind her, nearly close enough to touch her, and was in fact reaching toward her with her long, thin fingers and her painted nails.

"Jesus, Florence, don't sneak up on me like that!" Paige said.

Florence drew her hand back. She had a thin, flat smile on her face, just a hair shy of a grimace. "We'll come to get along," she said. "Just as soon as you learn to see things from my point of view."

"You mean never?" Paige said.

The telephone rang. "I'll get it," Florence said, turning and bustling to where the phone hung on the wall. "It's probably Henry."

"If it is, I want to talk to him," Paige said. She had tried to call him at work after finding Florence in her kitchen, but he had been out of the office. She watched the old woman pick up the phone and start talking quietly into it, hiding her mouth with her hand. She couldn't hear what was being said, so she put down the can of soup she was holding and went into the living room and picked up the extension.

"… you disappeared," Henry was saying. "What are you doing at the house? How'd you get there? You scared the hell out of me, Ma."

Ha! Henry *hadn't* let her in. She'd snuck over under her own power somehow, the sneaky old liar. But how'd she get past the alarm?

"I know that little bitch was the only reason you wouldn't let me move in with you," Florence said. "Well, now I'm here and she'll just have to accept it."

Paige noticed movement at the periphery of her vision, and turned toward the door to the kitchen. Florence had come into the dining area and was standing next to the table, watching Paige, a sly grin on her face. The phone cable was stretched out behind the old woman like an umbilical cord.

"Don't talk about her like that, Ma," Henry said.

"I can talk about my son's whore any way I want to," Florence said, looking straight at Paige, still grinning, like the two of them were sharing a joke at Henry's expense.

After a moment of stunned silence, Henry said, "I hear one more thing like that out of you, and I'm on the phone with Pine Ridge—which is where I'm taking you when I get there, because believe it or not, I don't want you in my house either—and I'm setting up a mental evaluation for you. Understood?"

The grin on Florence's face faltered at last, as if she had expected Henry to say, *Yeah, you're right, she's a whore, let's get rid of her.* It occurred to Paige that maybe Henry was on to something; maybe his mother *was* mentally ill, getting Alzheimer's or dementia or one of those other nasty ailments that ate your brain up like it was so much Jell-O.

Why couldn't there be a disease that made you get *nicer*?

"Am I making myself clear, ma?" Henry said. "You're going to stay out of Paige's way, and I'm going to come home, and then we're going to go back to the nursing home. Do you hear me?"

"I hear you," Florence said. The grin had been replaced by a sour, crafty look, as if some promising plan of hers had been dashed but she was already working on another one. It was a look that made Paige want to lock the old woman in the trunk of her car, drive her to some remote wilderness, and leave her there.

Henry said: "Put Paige on."

"She's out in the yard," Florence said. "I'll tell her you called."

"Ma, go get—"

She pushed the hang-up button on the phone with her thumb.

Henry muttered, "Jesus Christ." Then the line went dead.

Paige slowly returned the telephone to its cradle. She could have jumped in at the end, but didn't know what she would have said. Besides, it was hard to contemplate having a conversation with Henry while his mother stared at her with those blank eyes, that rubbery face.

"Children," Florence said. "They grow up, and they just don't want to mind anymore."

While Nelson had been in the offices, the plaza had opened for business; he could see over the high wooden fence that separated the rear of the building from the parking lot. Customers' cars were already scattered around the blacktop. As he crunched across the gravel roof—walking carefully, not running, because he didn't want them to hear him in the offices below—he saw a knot of teen-age girls walking from a beat-up station wagon, walking toward the entrance of the terrace, walking into … into what?

He didn't know. There was *something* here, something that had come out of that old church across the canal. It had adopted Canal Plaza as its residence now, it was lurking in that room beneath the offices, sucking people in and *changing* them. Like Shoemaker—the Shoemaker he knew was nervous, fawning, toadyish; nothing like the smugly taciturn man he had just encountered. And Quentin; what had they done to Quentin?

He reached the back end of the roof. The pile of cardboard boxes was still there, was higher than he remembered, in fact, though the rain was making it soggy. Hoping there was nothing sharp in the heap, he held his breath and jumped. The boxes crumpled beneath his feet, crushed and collapsed with a sound like popping bones. He fell deeply into the pile, and ended up buried inside it. As he started to thrash his way free, he heard the steel door of the office bang open.

Nelson froze, and waited, and hoped the pile didn't shift and give him away.

Heavy footsteps crunched on the blacktop. They seemed to be receding. Nelson waited, scarcely breathing, listening and waiting and listening some more; and when the crunching was gone he slowly, slowly, began pushing the boxes, trying to get a look out without making too much of a ruckus. Every time he got one box out of his way, though, two or three more fell to take its place, and he finally gave up and started squirming his way out of the pile. In a few seconds he tumbled out onto the damp, malodorous pavement. The reek of the Dumpsters seemed to have settled into the blacktop, to be slowly released, like some sort of huge area re-odorizer.

He rolled over and stood up, and Jasper Shoemaker was just coming around the corner of the building.

Nelson kicked the boxes into the big man's path, and ran. The heavy, crunching footsteps started up behind him, faster than before. Cardboard thumped and crumpled as Shoemaker plowed through the boxes. Nelson glanced back and saw the security guard coming full-steam, his beer gut bouncing beneath his uniform, his face a porcelain mask with onyx chips for eyes and fluffs of black cotton for hair.

Nelson speeded up as he neared the end of the plaza building, putting all his energy into a panicked sprint. He reached the corner, where there was a narrow gutter between the building and the wooden wall; once through there he would be in full view of the shoppers and the store employees, right out in the open. They wouldn't try anything there. He hoped.

As he rounded the corner, he looked back at his pursuer. Jasper had fallen behind, his face turning shades of crimson; he might be under some malign influence, but he was also out of shape. Nelson returned his gaze to the direction he was running, just in time to smack face-first into a wall of chain link that hadn't been there yesterday. It caught him like a net, gave beneath his momentum slightly and then snapped back, sending him sprawling on his back on the warm pavement. He staggered to his feet. The wall was actually a gate, closed with a chain and a padlock on this side, sealing off the alley. Beyond it was an eight-foot corridor leading onto the terrace.

Okay, he remembered it now; it had been open last time he came through, carrying those stupid boxes. Wasn't open anymore, was it?

He jumped, caught the chain link with his fingers and toes, and began to climb. As he neared the top, the footsteps came around the corner. He vaulted the rest of the way, swept in an arc over the top of the gate, landed hard on the other side. He spared a look back as he ran toward the concourse. Jasper stood on the other side of the gate, his face flat and expressionless, watching him.

Nelson looked away, kept running.

Behind him, he heard a great thrum of wings, but he didn't look back again; and when he reached the end of the corridor, he cut hard to the left, racing along the terrace. He felt a rush of wind just behind him, felt a hard gust against the back of his neck; but whatever it was, it didn't touch him, it didn't slow him down.

There were a few customers on this level, mostly clustered around a little café near the entrance, where white iron chairs and tables had been set up beneath sheltering umbrellas that sparkled in the sun shower. He slowed to a fast walk, and surreptitiously looked behind him. No sign of Jasper. He didn't know what had blown out of the alley at his heels, but it had missed him and didn't seem to be chasing him now.

His feet chafed from running in shoes that were meant only for padding slowly along carpeted halls. He felt intolerably warm inside his dress shirt and tie. He loosened his collar as he passed the breakfast-eating patrons. A few of the diners—the ones who had seen him come tearing out of the alley, he imagined—gave him odd looks, which he had to ignore. He wondered if they were in danger, if the strange cabal he had heard in the cellar beneath the office was somehow contriving to bring them into its membership.

Nothing he could do about it. Yet.

He reached the entrance to the plaza, the archway of concrete and polished bronze and glass lettering. To get through it, he had to pass the front door of the office. Menace lurked behind the gauzy white curtain and the venetian blinds that hung beyond the yellow lettering on the door. As he passed it the sheers fluttered slightly, and he saw one dark eye looking out at him; but the door didn't open; and then he was through the arch and into the parking lot. Away from the maniacs.

He went to the Jaguar, got in, and turned the key.

Nothing happened.

He tried it again.

Nothing happened.

"Son of a bitch," he said. They must have done something to the car, disabled it somehow. Not a chance in hell that he could figure out what it was and fix it. He sat there a moment, then took out his cellular phone and switched it on. He would call a tow truck, get the car taken to a garage and repaired.

At about the same time that he realized that he didn't know the numbers of any local garages, he noticed that the phone was flashing *no signal* at him. Which was absurd, because he had used the phone around here many times.

Unless Quentin had canceled his service. After all, it was a corporate phone.

He thought for a second, then pulled out his wallet and flipped through his credit cards. He had three of them, all corporate. He had a card of his own, of course, but he had left it in Buffalo. He never carried his own plastic on a business trip.

He had the most awfully plausible suspicion that none of his corporate cards would work anymore.

He got out of the car. No point in even trying to figure out what they'd done to it; what he knew about cars could be written on his thumbnail with room to spare.

He left the phone on the dashboard, but he took the credit cards, just in case.

Florence advanced into the living room. Paige held the phone in front of her like a knife and said, "Stay away from me, or I swear to God you'll eat this telephone."

"Be careful what you swear on," Florence said, a nastily prim little smile on her face. She continued to advance. Paige fell back, watching her mother-in-law walk. She moved easily, fluidly, as if she had never broken her hip, as if she hadn't been virtually bedridden just a week ago.

She moved like a woman half her age.

The crafty look was all over Florence's face. "Henry's had lots of women, you know," she said. "Especially while you were big and fat with Frederick. I met a few of them. Trash, but what can you expect? He only wanted them for one thing."

"You're full of shit," Paige said. She bumped into the wall. Couldn't retreat any farther. Florence came up to her, just a few feet away. She had a vague, dry, dusty smell about her.

"Ask him and see what he says."

"All I'm going to ask him is how he came out of a thing like you," Paige said. The cord to the telephone receiver was stretched taut across the living room. She could whip it around the old woman's neck, pull it tight. It was almost scary, how tempting that was.

Florence leaned over and whispered, directly into her ear, "I've almost got this family where I want it. All I need to do is get rid of you."

"I feel the same way about you," Paige whispered back.

Florence smiled again. Paige couldn't see it, but it seemed she could hear the old dry skin slide like paper across the old woman's gleaming false teeth. "Well," she said, "then we understand each other. Let's see who wins."

Paige pushed her away. "I can already tell you that," she said.

"Me."

"You're too confident," Florence said.

"I want you out of here today. If you don't go with Henry, and go quietly, I'll call someone to come and remove you. Is that clear?"

Florence shrugged.

"I'm not kidding," Paige said. "I swear to God, I'll throw you out of here myself."

"There you go," Florence said, "swearing over your head again."

Chuckling, the old woman went up the hallway to the room she had appropriated. Paige watched her go; and when the phone suddenly started honking in her hand, protesting that it had been off the hook too long, she nearly had a heart attack. She pushed the button down with her thumb to shut the thing up. Then she started dialing Henry's number at work, to see if he was there, find out what the hell was going on. Before it connected, though, she hung it up with her thumb. She couldn't talk to Henry now; she wasn't sure she could control her voice.

She stood there for a moment, then put the phone in its cradle and crept up the hallway. She heard faint ripping noises coming from the laundry room. Peering around the edge of the door, she saw Florence sorting clothes. She took out one of Henry's shirts, shook it out, and dropped it in the washer. Next came a pair of his jeans; these also went into the tub. Then she pulled out one of Paige's blouses. The old woman scowled at it, and ripped it in half, and dropped the pieces of fabric onto a small pile of other torn-up garments.

The old bitch was shredding her wardrobe.

Paige stepped into the doorway and said, "What the hell are you doing?"

"I'm doing the laundry," Florence said, not looking up. "The proper way."

"Well, have fun," Paige said. She stepped back, closed the door, and locked it. As she walked away, she heard Florence try the knob, then start to pound on the door.

Freddie was just coming back downstairs. "Where's Grandma?" he said.

Paige tousled his hair. "She's doing the wash," she said. "The proper way."

* * *

As he walked away from the plaza, Nelson was acutely conscious of how close the cars were as they zoomed by on his right. It wouldn't take much effort at all for someone to push him out into the road, right in front of one. So he walked with one eye on traffic and the other eye on the tall grass to his left, and he wondered where the next shot was going to come from.

A half-mile or so from the plaza, Marsh Road passed under I-90 and then crossed a major local thoroughfare. There were two gas stations and a small strip of stores—which Quentin was hoping to put out of business, then buy on the cheap—at the intersection. One of those places had to have a pay phone, he thought. He could make a few calls, assuming his phone card still worked, and he could find out if his credit cards had really been canceled. Both of which he could've done back at Canal Plaza, except that would have meant walking right back into the middle of whatever was going on, which he didn't feel up to just yet.

He was nearing the I-90 bridge. Vehicles whizzed back and forth across it. Construction was still going on: shoring up the span, or stripping the rust, or painting over the graffiti, or something. The metal underside of the bridge was obscured by a network of scaffolding and ladders and walls of thick, corrugated plastic. There didn't seem to be anyone working on it at the moment; in fact, he couldn't recall ever having seen anyone at the site doing anything other than standing around with an orange flag, holding up traffic and collecting seventeen bucks an hour to do it.

The construction left no room to walk along the shoulder under the bridge; it was blocked by a tangle of equipment and parts and nylon fencing. Nelson drifted right, into the traffic lane, as he approached. The scaffolding seemed very low; it had a warning sign posted on it with the maximum clearance, but a section of milky plastic—a window of sorts, he supposed—had come loose and was draped down over it, obscuring most of the writing. Through the opening formed by the dislodged sheet, he could see into the sheltered area beneath the bridge, where thin wooden struts and more plastic formed a sort of hanging chamber.

As he passed under the catwalk, he heard the wood creak over his head. He stopped and looked up at the warren of planks and tubes and plastic walls, but he couldn't see anything or anyone up there.

Maybe it was just the wind.

A car went by a few feet from him and blared its horn as it passed. Nelson jumped and swore at the driver, who just kept going. He started walking again. Now he kept one eye on the spidery network overhead, and another on the road; but traffic seemed to be nonexistent all of a sudden, as if all the drivers had had a meeting and decided they were going to start avoiding Marsh Road, effective immediately.

He came to the other side of the bridge. The nearest gas station was a dozen yards away. The pay phone clung to its side.

Nelson heard a faint noise overhead, a gentle ripping sound, almost inaudible.

He started to look up.

The top half of Paul Shockton, Selden Falls chief of police, swung down, seized him under the armpits, and yanked him up into the plastic tunnel before he had even finished turning his head.

Another car came along.

After it had passed, Paul Shockton swooped down again and picked up Nelson's sunglasses, which had fallen off his head.

Part Three: A Murder of Crows

16

SIMON JONES HADN'T BEEN ABLE to get hold of Paul Shockton all day; no one at the police department knew where he was or what he was doing. The last time anyone had heard from him had been that morning, when he had radioed in that he was at the former site of the old church—now known as Trott Memorial Gardens, God help them all—and was just going to take a quick look around.

Simon had ordered a police car out to the park to see if Paul's vehicle was still there; it wasn't. The fact that Paul had vanished from that spot, of all places, made Simon a bit uneasy. Not that there was anything *unnatural* there—panic attack, Simon thought, that was all he'd had, a panic attack, and Nelson was full of shit, probably on drugs too—but hey, Paul might have fallen into one of the holes or something.

Yeah, and then his car had driven itself away.

What Simon wanted from Shockton was a progress report on the bodies; he finally called the coroner directly to get one. The coroner explained that he believed the skeletal remains belonged to two men and a woman, all of whom had been dead for decades. Each skull had a neat round hole in the exact same place, right in the middle of the forehead; although there were no exit wounds, none of the skulls contained a bullet, leading the coroner to believe that the injuries had been inflicted with a sharp instrument rather than a gun.

After listening to a report on people who'd been dead for eighty years, Simon moved onto someone who had only been dead for one day. "What about the boy they found at the plaza? Why was he in such bad shape?"

"That's a problem. From the state of the body, he'd been dead at least three weeks. But from the insect population, he had probably been there for under a day."

"Insect population?"

"You don't want to know," the coroner said.

"So how did the body decompose so fast?"

"Well, that's the thousand-dollar question."

"What's the thousand-dollar answer?"

"I don't know yet," the coroner said. "I was working on it when you interrupted me."

"Oh. Okay, well, just keep me informed," Simon said.

"You'll be the first to know," the coroner said frostily.

Simon hung up. He'd like to replace old Dr. Death with somebody less obnoxious, but coroner was an elected position, damn it all, and no one was running against the guy this year.

His speakerphone beeped. He pushed the button and said, "Yeah?"

"Kevin Kowalski is holding on line three," his secretary said.

He pushed line three, picked up the phone, and said, "Give me some good news, Kevin."

"I'm calling from the hospital," he said. "A tractor trailer ran into the scaffolding beneath the I-90 bridge on Marsh Road a little while ago."

"So?"

Kevin said: "One of the things that got knocked out of the scaffolding was Quentin Farmer's assistant. He's dead."

Silence.

"Simon?" Kevin said.

"I said *good* news, Kevin," Simon said.

Paige was sitting on the front step when Henry came home. He pulled into the driveway and got quickly out of his car and said: "Are you okay?" And then: "What're you doing out here?"

Paige stood up, brushed herself off. "I got sick of hearing Florence pounding on the door," she said.

"Huh?"

"You heard me." She went into the house; she could hear Henry hurrying along behind her. "Paige, where's my mother?" he asked.

"I think I may have accidentally locked her in the laundry room while she was washing your shirts the proper way. Not the way I do it. I don't put the detergent in correctly, or something. She told me so."

"You locked my mother in the laundry room?"

"Yes," she said. "Since we don't have a place in the attic for your crazy relatives."

"Oh, Lord," Henry said.

"You told her it was *me* who wouldn't let her move in with us, didn't you?" she said. "You said, *I'd love to have you, Ma, but Paige won't let me.* Didn't you?"

He flopped onto the couch, rubbing the bridge of his nose. "I may have made the situation sound like that," he said after a moment.

"Well, she took that as her cue to move in and start threatening me. Hope you're happy."

He said: "Where's Freddie?"

"In the backyard with the puppy. He won't hear you groveling for forgiveness, which you're going to do starting now, right?"

Henry grimaced at her. "I know, I shouldn't have made it sound like that. I'm sorry. She probably didn't tell you I called here and talked to her, but I did, and I told her I didn't want her here either."

"I know. I was on the extension when you called."

He looked at her, obviously surprised. "You were? Why didn't you say something?"

"I was too pissed off to speak coherently," Paige said. "Listen. When I got home from shopping she was in the kitchen. She claimed you gave her a key and the code to the burglar alarm. You didn't, did you?"

"Of course not," Henry said.

"But she got in. The alarm didn't go off. How'd that happen?"

"I don't know, Paige, but I swear to God I didn't give her the combination *or* a key. You think *I* want her here? I don't."

"That makes two of us."

"But we can't leave her locked in the laundry room forever."

"Sure we can," Paige said. "We'll plaster up the entrance, put on a new room, buy a new washer and dryer—"

"I'll take her back to the Pine Ridge," Henry said. "I already told her that's what I was going to do, and I meant it."

"You'll take her now?"

"I'll take her now. I don't know how much longer she'll stay there; she'll be ready to move back to her old house soon." Pause. "You'll still try to be nice to her when she visits, even though she said all those things about you, won't you?"

"I'll be nice when she visits," Paige said. "I won't be nice when she moves in. I won't be nice when she calls me your little whore. I sure as hell won't be nice when she threatens me. Next time, old lady or no, I'll kick her ass."

"Calm down, for God's sake," Henry said. "You will not kick her ass. I'm not going to spend the next five years visiting you in prison."

She tried to glare at him, but it dissolved into a giggle and she collapsed onto the sofa next to him.

"This isn't funny," he said.

"I know," Paige said; but she couldn't stop giggling.

"I'll go upstairs and get changed, and then I'll let her out and take her back to the nursing home. Okay?"

"Okay," Paige said. She sat there and watched him go slowly up the stairs, moving like a man with a migraine. Then she flopped over sideways, and listened. Florence had stopped pounding on the laundry room door. Paige wondered what the old woman was doing in there now. Maybe she was putting all of Paige's whites and coloreds together in one load; assuming she hadn't torn them all to shreds, of course.

She heard Henry's voice float down the stairs. "Paige! Come up here!"

She went up to their bedroom. Henry was in his shorts and undershirt, and he was over by the screen door. He said: "Did you leave the glass door open when you went out?"

"Yeah," she said, "but the screen door was locked."

He stepped out of the way, and then she could see that the plastic mesh had been shredded in the center. It hung in fluttery tatters, as if someone had taken a pitchfork and ripped through it, leaving a gaping hole big enough to walk through.

"Holy shit," Paige said.

"She might be old," Henry said, half-appreciatively, "but she can still climb like a son-of-a-bitch." He looked back at her over his shoulder. "Still want to try and kick her ass?"

* * *

Kevin Kowalski met Simon at the side entrance of the hospital and led him down to the morgue in the basement, where the attendant slapped open one of the metal doors and slid out a tray bearing a big zippered bag of black plastic. Like a laundry sack, Simon thought; except when the attendant opened it, there weren't dirty clothes inside, there was the pale, battered body of Nelson DeGrace. After his initial shock, Simon realized that, for some reason, the corpse was still wearing sunglasses. He glanced at the morgue guy and said: "I don't think he needs his shades anymore."

"They're sort of stuck," the attendant said. "I can't get them off without damaging the body or the glasses. The coroner will have to remove them when he does the autopsy."

Simon looked away from the corpse. It smelled pretty rank. "What happened?" he asked.

Kevin said, "He was dead when the truck hit the scaffolding, but we don't know what from."

"What'd the truck driver have to say?"

"You'll have to ask the cops. From what I gather, the clearance sign was covered up by some plastic. The trucker had been under that bridge lots of times and thought he could make it again. Turns out he had a new rig that was just a couple inches taller than his old one."

"Has Farmer been notified?"

"We can't seem to get hold of him. That's why I called you. We did notify his corporate headquarters, and they told us Nelson had been let go that morning."

"What about family?"

"None that we know of," Kevin said. "Their HR department has no records on that subject."

Simon nodded. He wondered if he should mention the phone call he had gotten from Nelson that morning, and decided not to. After all, just because Nelson was lying in a drawer in the basement of the hospital, it didn't mean Simon had been wrong not to take his wild suppositions seriously.

But where was Paul Shockton these days?

Then he noticed something about the corpse, and said: "Where are his hands?"

"They're gone," Kevin said, unnecessarily; Simon could see that they were gone. Then Kevin added: "So are his feet."

"He doesn't have hands *or* feet?"

"No."

"Why?"

"The coroner will have to figure that out," Kevin said. "It looks to me that they rotted away, but I'm not the authority on such matters."

"Jesus." Simon turned away. This was entirely too similar to the dead kid they'd found at the end of Farmer's nature trail, all rotted to pieces in a single day.

Kevin told the attendant to close it up. Simon heard the zipper click and the steel drawer rattle back into place, heard the heavy door clank shut. Then Kevin asked the attendant to please excuse them, and the guy headed out of the locker room.

After the swinging door stopped swaying, Kevin said: "Do you know where Mr. Farmer is, Simon?"

"I haven't talked to him in a couple of days," Simon said. "He doesn't keep me advised of his itinerary."

"Your hands and feet don't just fall off in the space of an afternoon," Kevin said. "Somebody did this to him. I talked to the police and they said Nelson had gone there to report that his boss was missing. They didn't say it, but I got the impression he was blown off."

"Not again," Simon said.

"Yep." Kevin grinned briefly. He looked much calmer than Simon felt; but then, he always did. Simon figured it came from having worked in the emergency department for seven years before moving into administration. "Our tax dollars at work. Okay, Simon, here's the thing: Karl Castle is going to get wind of this, and he's going to use it. How many murders have we had this year? Mysterious deaths? Disappearances? Something's got to be done, Simon. I'm telling you this both as a council member and as a friend. People have *got* to see that you're doing something about it. A cause has *got* to be found."

"You think I don't know that? What do you want me to do, frame somebody? For God's sake, Kevin, the cops are working on it."

"That's not good enough. Have Shockton appoint a task force. Appoint a task force yourself. In case you haven't noticed, Karl is trashing you on the radio on a daily basis. He's practically taken over WSKY's talk show. And have you seen the polls?"

"I don't read that crap," Simon lied.

"Yeah, sure. Show me a politician who doesn't read polls, and I'll show you somebody standing in line at the unemployment agency." Kevin slapped the door to Nelson's drawer with his open palm; it rang hollowly. "This is where your career is going to end up if you don't do something quickly. And there's room in here for both of us."

"Don't say stuff like that," Simon said. "Bad luck."

To make sure that there weren't any unwanted surprises or changes of plan during Florence's journey back to the nursing home, Paige and Frederick rode in the back seat. The trip was silent; after a few miles Henry turned on the radio, but they were talking about a dead body that had been found hidden beneath a bridge and he turned it off again. Paige wondered who it was this time.

When they reached the home, instead of parking in the regular lot, Henry took the car up the extended circular driveway to the front steps. He helped Florence out of the car and up the steps—she had suddenly acquired difficulty walking, perhaps after having injured herself climbing up to their balcony and ripping down their screen door—which left Paige and Frederick without much to do except mill around on the porch and wait for him to come back. They did this under the watchful eye of the mute resident who was, as usual, perched on the swing at the end of the verandah. Paige couldn't help but steal glances at him, and every time she did he was staring at her.

A nurse with a tired face came out and bustled past Paige. She was carrying a tiny paper cup and a glass of water on a tray and wearing a rubber glove on her right hand. She went to the old man on the swing and said, "Time for your medicine." Paige watched her take a small pill from the cup and put it on his tongue; she followed it up with the glass of water, which she tipped down his throat. The old man's wattled throat wiggled as he swallowed.

"There you go," she said. "I'll be back later, okay?"

The old man didn't say whether it was okay or not, but the nurse started to leave anyway; Paige stopped her by saying: "Excuse me?"

"Can I help you?" the nurse said.

Paige nodded toward the old man and said, "How come he never talks?"

The nurse looked over her shoulder at her patient; he was still staring at Paige. "We don't know," she said. "Trauma, maybe. There's nothing physically wrong with him, except high blood pressure; he's actually strong as an ox."

"He stares at me every time I come here."

The nurse pointed at Paige's chest and said, "Do you always wear that necklace?"

"This?" Paige lifted it up, her shiny silver locket, heart-shaped, containing a picture of Henry on one side and Frederick on the other. "Yes. It was my grandmother's. Why?"

"He likes shiny things," she said. "Tin foil, silverware, jewelry, marbles. Be careful. If you get too close, he might try to take it, and it'll be a struggle to get it back."

"He takes shiny things?"

"Oh, yeah. He keeps them in a drawer in his room. He also likes bits of thread, yarn, string, that sort of thing. We actually have to keep his door locked from the outside or he wanders around at night stealing light bulbs and extension cords. We keep expecting him to build a nest." A smile flickered across her face; then the tiny black beeper on her belt started to chirp, and the tired look came back, and she said: "Excuse me."

The nurse went back into the building, leaving Paige and Frederick and the elderly resident alone on the porch. Paige looked at the old man. His eyes were so dark, it was almost impossible to tell where his gaze was focused; but she knew it was on her.

She moved her locket inside her shirt. He kept watching her for a little while, then looked away.

How about that. He liked shiny things, just like the birds at the pet store.

That's what he was. He was a Bird Man.

Henry came out of the nursing home and said: "Ready to go?"

The three of them went down the stairs, got into the car. Henry drove the remaining dozen yards to where the driveway widened in front of the nursing home's garage; he executed a three-point turn there, and they drove past the front porch of the home again. Paige looked out Henry's window at the swing where the Bird Man always sat, but he was gone now; the old dark glider swayed gently in the afternoon breeze.

Henry glanced at her and said, "Looking for someone?"

"Yeah," Paige said, "but I guess he flew away."

* * *

Quentin sat quietly in a corner of the basement conference room—the lair—and watched his nominal employee, Jasper Shoemaker, have a telephone conversation with Paul Shockton, the chief of police. Jasper was chewing Paul a new asshole, and seemed to be savoring it more than was strictly necessary.

"The *first* thing I ask you to do," Jasper said, "and you fuck it up. You left the body right up there in the scaffolding! What's *wrong* with you, Shockton? What did you think would happen when the workers came back?" Pause. "I know it wasn't the workers who found him, but they would have if that truck hadn't come along!"

They were talking about Nelson, Quentin thought. He hadn't been allowed out of the offices since they brought him here, but there was a radio in the break room upstairs, from which he had gleaned that his assistant had been murdered and the body stashed under a bridge. They had caught up with him after all. Oh well; better Nelson than him. He wondered what it was that Jasper needed him for; so far, all he'd done was write a check—a big check—to something called the *Committee To Build The Future*. Whatever the hell that was.

"I know it was broad daylight," Jasper said into the phone. "You've got a brain, right? You could've figured something out. At the least, you could've hidden him over on the side on top of the concrete. Then the truck wouldn't have knocked him out. Jesus, Shockton, use your—what? Okay, take it, but call me back." Jasper hung up, looked at Quentin, and said: "He has the mayor on the other line."

Quentin nodded.

"I'm going upstairs," Jasper said. "Watch them, would you?" He stood up, his ponderous belly shivering beneath his uniform; and he trundled out of the room, leaving Quentin alone in the basement.

Alone with the girls.

He glanced to his right, where the two teenagers lay bundled up on the floor, wrapped in a blanket and tied up with nylon cord. They weren't squirming much anymore, though they had been earlier in the day, when he had first been brought here; he wondered if they had fallen asleep. He didn't know why they were there; *meat*, Jasper called them, as if they were going to cook them up and eat them.

And then there was the bird.

It was a crow, a great big crow, the color of ashes in a fireplace, black dusted with grey and white. It hopped and fluttered from place to place in the conference room, looking at this and that, peering at things—the big multi-line telephone, the computer that sat silently in the corner—as if wondering what they were. Occasionally it perched on top of the girls and pecked at them halfheartedly through the blanket. Maybe that was what Jasper meant?

Mostly, though, it just sat on top of the hanging fixtures, or on top of the rolled-up projector screen, or on some other perch, observing the activities going on below it.

They hadn't told him what that big bird was doing there; but he knew, in an instinctual sort of way. It was doing what he was supposed to be doing; it was keeping an eye on things. Overseeing the operation. Somehow, the big crow was higher up on the pecking order than any of them, even Jasper. Kind of weird, being subordinate to a bird.

The telephone chirped. Quentin looked at it. It chirped again, and again. He looked at the ceiling and wondered if he was supposed to answer it. The crow was nearby, staring at him; he thought he saw it nod and, taking that as permission, he flipped the phone into his hand and said, "Hello?"

After a moment, a gruff voice said: "Who's this?"

"Quentin Farmer."

"It's Paul Shockton. Where's Shoemaker?"

"He stepped out."

"I have news."

"I can pass it along," Quentin said.

"The mayor is calling up a task force to investigate the recent disappearances and deaths. He wants me to head it up. I'll be hand-picking the members of the team. When I've got a list of names I'll fax it to Shoemaker so he can make the necessary arrangements. Got that?"

"Yes," Quentin said.

"Good." There was a pause, then Shockton said: "We'll deflect attention elsewhere. Away from us. Tell Shoemaker that, too."

"Okay," Quentin said.

"Make sure he gets the message," Shockton said, and he hung up.

Quentin went upstairs to deliver the news. He found the big man in the break room, eating someone else's lunch; Quentin could tell because the food was coming out of a brown bag labeled *Renee*. Shoemaker listened to the information, nodded a couple of times, and sent Quentin back down to the lair.

As he descended the stairs, Quentin became aware of a rank stench, like rotting garbage, rising from the conference room. Had it always smelled like that and he just hadn't noticed? He supposed it must have; he had gotten used to it was all. He entered the room and flicked on the ventilation system. Hidden fans overhead began to whir, sucking up the air, sucking out the smell. The big crow was perched on the girls again, pecking away at a bit of hand that it had managed to uncover. The owner of the hand didn't flinch as the sharp, dark beak repeatedly pierced the flesh, tore away tiny bits, and swallowed them. Quentin wandered over to see why there was no reaction from the girl, and realized that the odor was particularly strong in that corner of the room.

He knelt down. The crow stopped pecking and looked at him with dark, gleaming eyes. It had stripped quite a bit of meat from the hand, leaving numerous ragged wounds in the yellowing flesh. Bone glistened from the holes. Quentin felt the blanket with his hand; it was moist and yielding, as if it were filled with something soft and kind of gelatinous. He untied the rope and partially unwound it from the bundle. The crow hopped off as Quentin undid the bonds, fluttered off and perched on the desk immediately to the right. It watched him as he lifted one flap of the blanket, then another, unwrapping the two girls.

A stench bloomed from the bundle as he opened it, gaggingly powerful, the oppressive aroma of decay billowing up with mushroom-cloud ferocity; he licked saliva off his lips, swallowed it. The bodies were naked and were in very bad shape, covered with pustules and blisters ranging from nascent to burst and oozing. Despite its distended condition, their blotchy skin seemed loose and wrinkly, as if he could pinch it between his fingers and tear it right off them.

He looked at the crow. It seemed to have lost interest in him, and was instead looking at the corpses he had unwrapped from their shroud. It fluttered down and landed on the one on the right and began walking around on the yielding flesh, its little claws leaving small tick marks that did not disappear. It walked all the way up her body, hopped up to her chin, and tore off her left eyelid. The little flap of skin came away easily, and the crow swallowed it in a gulp.

Quentin shooed the bird away. It squawked and fluttered across the room, landing on the rolled-up screen for the overhead projector, where it stared angrily down at him. He looked away from the bird, back to the dead girl on the right. Despite the decrepit state of the rest of her body, the eye beneath the decaying lid was still bright and clear as polished glass. The iris was bluish-green, and if she had been alive, she would have been looking right at him.

He stayed crouched there for some time, looking, wondering, shifting position to get a better view of the art of decay playing out on the canvas of their naked flesh. He found himself getting hard, getting aroused in the same kind of in-spite-of-himself way he had when he'd taken those pictures off the Internet; but he resisted the urge to reach out and touch them. Necrophilia was one barrier he was not ready to cross.

Until he noticed that the one exposed eye was tracking his movements, following him as he changed his position. The girl was alive. Trapped in a shell of putrid skin and rotten flesh, shredded by the attentions of the gigantic crow, the girl was alive.

Well, that changed everything, didn't it? She was alive; she might even enjoy herself.

Quentin Farmer stood up, and slowly began to unbutton his shirt.

Simon was watching Roland put the finishing touches on dinner when the doorbell rang. "That'll be them," he said. "What are you making again?"

"Pork chops with corn bread stuffing, vegetables, and Bananas Foster for dessert," Roland said.

The doorbell rang again. Simon said: "What kind of vegetables?"

"I already told you twice," Roland said. "Go get the door."

So Simon went and got the door. It was, indeed, the Fontana family, Paige and Henry. He opened the screen door and they came in, and he noticed that they had brought Frederick. Paige must've caught his expression, because she said: "We would've gotten a sitter, but somebody didn't give us much notice."

"I, uh, I don't know if he's going to like what we're having."

"I ate at McDonald's!" Frederick exclaimed.

"Well, super," Simon said. "Come on in."

He led them into the living room. Frederick looked at the television, then at him, and then said: "Do you have Nintendo?"

"Nope."

"Playstation?"

"No."

"Do you have a computer?"

"Yes," Simon said.

"Do you have any games?"

"No. Sorry."

Frederick gave an exasperated little sigh, as if he just couldn't believe how lame Simon was. Simon stood there for a moment wallowing in his lameness, then said, "Well, follow me." He led them up the hallway and into the dining room, which connected to the kitchen on the right and the living room on the left. As he got them settled, the swinging door to the kitchen bumped open and Roland stuck his head in. "Dinner's almost ready," he said, before vanishing back inside.

"In case you don't know, Roland is a chef at LaFountain's," Simon said. "Tonight he's making one of his specialties, stuffed corn bread —"

Roland's head reappeared. "It's pork chops stuffed with corn bread," he announced. "Don't listen to anything he tells you." Then he vanished again.

"Is that your roommate?" Frederick said.

"Roommate? Uh, sure, whatever," Simon said.

"Nice place you got here," Henry said. Simon could see him inspecting the joints between the walls and the ceiling and the woodwork around the windows. Showed how long it had been since he'd had the Fontanas over; the last time—before the previous election—he had been living in an apartment complex in the city. "Built to your specifications?"

"I picked it out of a book."

"Who was the builder?"

Simon said, into the back of his hand, "Karl Castle."

"What?"

"Karl built it. My architect set it up, I didn't have anything to do with it." Pause. "By the time I found out there were already contracts and stuff." Pause. "You know I'd rather have had you do the construction—"

"Uh-huh," Henry said.

Paige stood up and gave Simon a quizzical look. He said: "Through that door and down the hallway, first room on the right."

"Thanks," she said, heading through the living room door.

"So," Henry said, "Paige tells me you're hoping for an endorsement."

"Your wife," Simon said, "is entirely too clever sometimes."

Paige meandered through the living room. She couldn't quite figure out the decorating scheme. Modern-brutal, maybe: a television stand that didn't look much different from a pile of orange crates, for instance, and a coffee table that seemed like a slab of wood attached to legs made of pieces of metal that someone had found lying by the side of the highway. She suspected that such intentional crudity did not come cheaply.

The hallway opened from the opposite end of the living room and ran the length of the house. It was narrow and tall, with skylights. Maybe they made the corridor seem a little less oppressive during the day. But now, at night, as she walked along beneath them with the walls close on either side, she had this prickly feeling down the back of her neck like they were exposing her to some sort of scrutiny.

Silly girl, she thought, passing through the first door on the right.

The decor in the bathroom was not noticeably dissimilar to that of the living room, except that it involved a bit of wicker, which took the edge off the harshness of the wrought and cast iron. A big window next to the vanity showed her Simon's backyard; he had a couple of security lights—maybe *he* could convince Henry to get some for their house, she thought, since she couldn't seem to do it—and they spread a grey, washed-out illumination across his yard.

Then she turned on the light, and the view through the window was transformed into a translucent image of herself. She closed the window blind; it was irrational, since there were no other houses nearby, nobody to peer in at her, but she just couldn't use the toilet with it open like that.

When she went to wash her hands afterwards, she noticed that the pump soap dispenser was encased in what looked like black iron, though she suspected it was plastic. She pinged it with her finger, and it rang hollowly under her nail. It really *was* metal.

She wondered if whoever had picked out the furnishings for this place had liked to paint light bulbs black as a teenager.

She finished washing up, then squinted at herself in the mirror. Was that a grey hair in her front curl, or just a blonde one? She got it between her fingers and stretched it out and looked at it minutely. Grey. She gritted her teeth and yanked it out, and it didn't even hurt all that much. Score one small victory against the years. She dropped the hair into the sink and flooded it away with water, then turned the wooden stick to open the blinds.

As the slats turned, in the instant between the time she could see through them and the time they were open far enough for the window to become reflective, she got another glimpse of Simon's backyard; and in that instant, she saw a large, dark shape dart into the woods near the far end of the yard. Moved sort of like a person, she thought, but it seemed fuzzy. Maybe it was a bear.

Yeah, a bear. That was it: there were bears in the woods up this way. She would tell Henry about it, and then he'd *have* to get lights. Otherwise, maybe someday they'd let their dog out, and it wouldn't come back. She thought of the shape she had seen in their own yard, the thing that had been watching Freddie. Maybe her reaction hadn't been so irrational after all.

After a moment she went and turned off the light, then returned to the window, hoping for another look at the creature. However, there was no activity in the yard now; it was dark and quiet. She scanned the woods for some sign of it, but saw nothing.

Wait. What was that?

Not far from where the thing had gone into the woods, there were two large, pale-green disks, staring back at her.

Eyes.

Did bears have eyes that big?

As she watched, the orbs pulled back, vanished into the brush. The thing, the creature, whatever it was—not a bear, and she knew it— was on the move. She reached up and, with a trembling hand, turned the wooden stick to close the blinds again.

A knock on the bathroom door made her jump. "Paige?" Henry's voice. "You okay in there? Why's the light off?"

"I was looking at something," she said, straightening up, going to the door. She opened it, letting the hallway light spill in.

"Looking at what?"

"Nothing," she said. "Some kind of animal outside. It's gone now."

Henry went to the window and split the slats with his fingers and looked out at the night. She pulled him away from it. If there *was* something out there, something with eyes like radioactive baseballs, she didn't want it to see them. "Is dinner ready?"

"Been ready," he said. He took her arm and escorted her back to the dining room, which smelled like a restaurant.

After pork chops and Bananas Foster, both of which were excellent, they retired to the living room. Frederick promptly fell asleep on the couch; Paige managed to act interested in politics for a while, though she ended up nodding off once or twice herself. Roland seemed just as bored as she was, and eventually wandered back into the safety of the kitchen. Simon and Henry, however, were quite animated, discussing the implications of a victory by Karl Castle in the elections coming up in the fall. They were both just blowing smoke, she thought. Simon wanted to hang onto his job, and Henry didn't want a business rival running the town.

She finally started yawning pointedly enough to convey to Henry that it was time for them to leave; ten minutes later they were in the car, trundling along the rough, narrow, unlit road, sweating in the humid warmth that held everything in its grip like a hot and clammy hand. Bands of cloud arched overhead, dribbles of darkness blotting out the stars, taking on a smoky glow as they passed near the moon.

"I think that went pretty well," Henry said.

Paige said nothing; she didn't know what they had talked about that could have gone any way, well or otherwise. All they'd done was complain.

From the back seat, Freddie's sleepy voice said, "I'm hot."

She turned up the air conditioner. The resulting blast of icy wind seemed to stiffen her damp blouse right on her. But after a few seconds the wind stopped, and the fan made an odd grinding sound, like it was clogged with something. She felt the car jerk, and jerk again; then it sputtered to a halt. Various lights illuminated on the dashboard. Henry looked at them and said: "Holy shit."

"What?"

"All these things can't possibly have gone wrong at once." He tapped on the plastic shield over the lights, as if that were going to help; but the only thing that happened was that all the power locks engaged. This was probably not related to the tapping, Paige thought, but you never knew, what with all the computers and gadgets in cars these days.

She heard a faint, whispery sound coming from the dashboard, like something was in there, moving around. She said: "Henry?"

He was pressing the unlock button—which didn't seem to be working—and muttering, so he didn't see the thing, the viscous, bubbly thing, start to ooze out of the vent on her side of the car. It turned upward and began climbing up to the top of the dashboard. Paige stared at it, aghast. She pulled her feet up underneath her and said, in a slightly more urgent voice, "Henry!"

"What?" Then he saw it, and said: "What the hell is *that?*"

"Get out of the car," Paige said. She pulled on her lock, but it was stuck. "Henry, turn off the car so we can open the doors."

He shut off the car; the dashboard stayed lit up like a Christmas tree, and the lock still wouldn't budge.

The wad of gunk had reached the windshield and was now motoring up it, gathering speed, heading for the roof. It left a thin, gleaming trail behind it, like some gruesome mutant snail.

Frederick yawned and sat up on the back seat. "Are we home yet?" he said.

Henry pulled the key out of the ignition; it had no effect on the situation. Paige edged to the middle of the front seat and began to bang against the electric sunroof, never taking her eyes off the gunk, which had by now reached the fabric on the inside of the roof. The spongy material soaked it up and it vanished into the padding; the only sign of it now was a progressive moistening of the upholstery.

It was turning to the right, towards her and Henry.

She felt the sunroof buckle, and said: "Get ready to climb out, Frederick!"

Another hit, and the rectangle of metal popped out, clattered across the roof and clanged to the ground. She quickly pulled herself out of the car. Henry hauled Frederick out of the back seat and lifted him toward her. She reached down to help him out, felt his fingers brush hers.

Then she heard a rush of wind and the shaggy flutter of massive wings. She started to turn, and saw something coming out of the darkness, a face, gaunt and pinched and leering.

Henry's mother.

What on earth—

Florence crashed into her, and picked her up, and flung her out over the road.

The pavement went by beneath her, came rushing up toward her.

She hit it head-first with a jarring, scraping impact; and then everything faded to black.

17

The pain in her head clawed its way through her brain, up to the thin, brittle bones behind her ocular sockets, forcing Paige Fontana to open her eyes.

She was lying on her side in the middle of the street, on the hot, dry pavement; a warm little puddle of drool had collected under her cheek. Her head throbbed like it had been whacked with a hammer. The arm beneath her body was numb from being bent at the wrong angle, squashed and deprived of blood. She rolled onto her back. The sky was prickly with stars.

What the hell was she doing in the road?

She heard a sound, rolled her head left to look. A car, headlights glaring, was coming around the curve of the road. She was wearing a black dress; the driver probably wouldn't see her in time, would probably run right over her. She tried to push herself erect but couldn't, her arm was tingling like crazy and wouldn't support her weight, her legs felt like sausages.

The car came rushing toward her.

She rolled out of its way, onto the shoulder; the car roared by only a few feet from her head. One of its tires ran over her trailing hair, catching a handful in its treads and yanking it out of her skull. She swore at it, using all sorts of salty language she'd been storing up ever since her encounter with Florence earlier in the day. It didn't help any, but it made her feel a little better.

Florence. Paige rubbed her forehead with the back of her hand. Hadn't she seen the old woman come flying out of the darkness like a vengeful harpy, just a little while ago? Hadn't it been her who had thrown Paige off the roof of the car, into the road?

It was impossible, but that was what she remembered.

She sat up. Vertigo swirled around inside her head like water draining, and she steadied herself with her conscious arm. After a few minutes she felt sturdy enough to stand; a few minutes more, and she managed to totter across the road toward the dark shape of Henry's car. It was parked on the opposite shoulder, totally dark and inert. The pavement felt rough under her feet, and she had trouble walking; she realized she had lost one of her pumps. She didn't bother looking for it; she just kicked off the other one as well, and kept going.

She stopped a cautious distance from the car, just in case anything came out of it; she looked it over, and wondered if she had made a mistake, or if it was the moonlight that was making her husband's new vehicle—the replacement for his drowned little subcompact— look like it had been left out in a swamp for at least a decade. She limped around in front of it; three of the four interlocking rings were still on the grille, but one had fallen off and was lying on the pavement next to the remains of the license plate.

She stood there and stared at the empty car and she could *hear* it getting older, falling apart, with a sound like tinfoil being slowly crumpled. As she watched, the front bumper pulled loose without warning and crashed to the pavement right at her feet, making her jump and curse. Rust cascaded after it, whisking like falling sand.

She stood there and listened to the car groan in the silence of the night.

Where was her husband? Where was her son?

What had that old bitch done with them?

The leaves rustled in the woods, but Paige didn't feel a breeze; something was in there, moving around. She thought of the dark thing she had seen in Simon's backyard, and in her own. Something following her around? Something stalking her, the way that crazy intern had, all those months ago?

The sounds of furtive movement in the trees was coming closer to the edge of the road. She backed away from the forest, and said: "Who's there?"

Immediately, the noises stopped.

Somewhere in the forest, a crow began to caw. But it didn't sound quite right; it sounded too big, it sounded too throaty. If it *was* a crow, it was a crow with a megaphone.

She turned away and started walking quickly, back toward Simon's house. The crow stopped cawing and the movement sounds started up again, stealthy little noises, something trying to move silently and not quite succeeding. It was behind her and to her left, creeping through the forest, shadowing her movements.

It was just a phobia, she told herself. Crows were harmless. Just a phobia.

Yeah. Tell Jane Trott crows were harmless, see what sort of response you got.

A car whizzed by on her right, honking as it passed; the driver didn't stop to ask if she needed help, didn't even slow down. She watched the red taillights vanish around a curve. As she rounded the bend herself, she came into view of some homes; they were all on the left, the same side as the quiet little leaf-sounds. Yellow squares of light glowed from their walls, inviting her to come and knock on their doors for sanctuary. She hesitated, then headed for the nearest one, a split-level set well back from the road, its manicured lawn illuminated by a black iron lamp that stood beside a chalk-white sidewalk. A large window was partially open, soft music drifting from it, classical piano, strings, woodwinds.

As she reached the edge of the grass, a blob of shadow darted from the trees, stole across the lawn, and disappeared into the bushes near the front door of the house. She stopped dead at the shoulder, watched, waited. The bushes rustled slightly, then stopped, then rustled again.

Not very adept at stealth, whatever it was. She hurried away from the house, watching the shrubs out of the corner of her eye; just before they passed from her sight the shadow slunk out of them, back into the woods, still following her.

She wondered if it could possibly be Florence, if the old woman had stuck around to finish the job that had been botched by Paige's awakening before she was run over. Maybe that was why she had been so smug when they brought her back to Pine Ridge; she was already planning to come back and take her son and her grandson, take them and spirit them away using some mysterious power she had somehow acquired.

She was starting to sound crazy, Paige thought. Strange powers? A seventy-year-old woman somehow getting onto a second-story balcony and ripping down a screen door with her bare hands, then flying around in the night twenty miles from her nursing home? A seventy-year-old woman who would never walk again, but had made a miraculous recovery.

Paige wondered if *miraculous* was the right word, or if there was some other, less heavenly, description that should be applied to what had happened to Florence.

She passed the rest of the houses on the left, homes nestled into their little pockets of yard in the midst of the trees. On the right, forest had given way to meadow: pasture, maybe, or fallow farmland. Whatever it was, there weren't any homes there.

At each house she passed, she saw movement in the darker places of the yards; at least, she *thought* she did. At this point she wasn't sure she could trust anything she thought she saw.

At last, she started seeing houses on the right; Simon's was the fourth one. *On the right,* the opposite side from whatever it was that was shadowing her. But it was quick, she had to get there before it could cut her off. She took a sidelong glance to her left: nothing there, just a house and a yard.

Behind her, she heard sudden movement. Someone coming at her fast. She didn't hesitate, didn't look back; she bolted for Simon's house.

The pavement was rough and warm. She felt her nylons split open on the sole of her right foot when she stepped on a sharp pebble. It bit painfully into her heel but she clenched her teeth and kept going, because it didn't matter that her foot was bleeding. It didn't matter that her head was pounding. All that mattered was that the night was silent, and something was chasing her.

Simon would help her. He *had* to help her. He was the mayor, for Christ's sake.

Up the steps. Her palm slammed into the doorbell; it rang loudly. She yanked open the screen door and pounded with the knocker. "Simon!" she screamed. "Simon!"

Then the wind whistled in her ears, and iron bands folded around her waist and neck. Hands fumbled across her body. She kept her grip on the knocker, but the handle twisted and snapped like cheap plastic as the thing behind her dragged her off the porch and into the bushes.

The foliage closed over her, like the sea over a drowning sailor.

That night, Quentin returned to his room at the inn.

Jasper Shoemaker had fixed what he had done to the Jaguar—it was simple enough, something to do with disconnecting a wire, though Quentin would have been as helpless as Nelson at figuring it out—and Quentin drove back to the bed and breakfast and parked in his accustomed space near the front door. It was late; the inn was dark and silent. The entrance was unlocked, as usual; he went in and crept up to his room, where he found a message pinned to his pillow. It was written in Tom Teller's shaky hand, relaying that the police wanted Quentin to call them if and when he returned.

He picked up the phone and dialed the cops. They wanted to ask him about Nelson, of course; he had told them Quentin had been abducted from the inn. Nonsense, he said; Monroe Parker had picked him up and driven him to the plaza for a meeting. Who else had been there? Well, Jasper Shoemaker, their head of security; and Paul Shockton, the chief of police; and other plaza staff members. He really hadn't the faintest idea what Nelson could have been thinking. Maybe was trying to stir up trouble; after all, he had just been dismissed. Quentin lowered his voice to a whisper and confided to the officer that he thought Nelson may have been using drugs.

After he hung up, he thought: Well, that was easy. He felt sort of bad about doing that to Nelson, but it couldn't be helped; and anyway, he had tried to warn him off. It wasn't his fault if Nelson hadn't listened.

He got out of his clothes, stuffing them into the bottom drawer of his dresser. They were beyond any hope of cleansing, soiled with dirt and blood and the putrid excretions of the rotten girls in the basement at the plaza. The best fate they could hope for, other than burning, was burial.

His hosts had replaced the basin his rapid departure had smashed. He rinsed his face in the lukewarm water, then decided that it was too stuffy and hot in his room and opened the flue wide. The central air unit pushed a cool breeze through it, soothing his burning face.

He went into the bathroom. Chrome and porcelain gleamed at

him, distorted reflections of himself moving across them as he went to the mirror and inspected himself. He was looking fine, he thought; his new condition agreed with him. His paunch had shrunken, his muscle tone had come back. Even the threads of grey in his hair had gone; it seemed to be darkening, though, streaks of ebon dust spreading through the blonde. He looked five—no, ten—years younger. Felt it, too. He remembered feeling his vitality come back as he had violated the girls; apparently sex with semi-corpses was good for his health.

He made a muscle, looked at it, smiled. He did ten quick jumping jacks. He didn't jiggle or wiggle or flop around, his feet were sure, he didn't end up winded or anything. He felt better than he had in years. Full of energy. Ready to take over the world. But before he did any conquering, he needed a shower; he was still kind of sticky from what he'd done to the captives, and he couldn't sleep in the bed in such a condition. His hosts would certainly notice the stains when they did the laundry.

And then, of course, he would have to kill them.

The sudden bong of the doorbell shattered Simon's concentration and he came before he wanted to, spurting all over Roland's face. Roland made a coughing sound as some of it shot up his nose. "Sorry," Simon said, rolling off of him. Roland got onto his side and fumbled for a tissue. As Simon stood, he heard Roland blowing his nose.

Pounding echoed through the house, and a woman's hysterical voice shouted Simon's name. "You've got women beating down your door," Roland said, still coughing.

Simon pulled on his robe and headed out of the room. As he went through the house, the pounding stopped abruptly; this worried him and he sped up into a run. As he neared the front door, he thought he heard the sounds of a struggle. He flicked on the porch light and flung open the door, and there was nobody there, no one at all; but he heard someone thrashing around in the dogwood tree next to the step. The thing was monstrously large, desperately in need of a trim; you could hide half an army within its spreading branches. Right now those branches were shaking madly, as if there were indeed an army inside and it was engaged in a battle.

He reached into the front closet and took out an umbrella, then returned to the porch. Holding the umbrella like a sword, he said: "Who's there?"

The thrashing stopped.

Then it started again, much more gently; and he thought he heard soft footsteps, fleeing into the night.

A filthy, pallid hand reached up and grasped the edge of the porch. It was followed by another. Simon edged away from them, pointed the umbrella tip at where the head would come up, and waited. Moments later an auburn mane rose from the foliage that pressed close against the porch, framing a pale, smudged, tear-streaked face.

Simon said: "Paige?"

"Help me," she said, reaching up to him.

He took her small hand and hauled her onto the landing. Her hair was matted with leaves and small branches; she looked like she had rolled down a hill in a barrel of dirt. Her black dress was torn at the chest, revealing the lace brassiere beneath. Simon said: "Jesus Christ, Paige, what happened? Are you okay?"

She nodded. She was breathing hard, like she had just climbed a mountain.

"Are you okay?" he repeated. "Did someone … I mean, were you ___"

"Let's go inside," she said.

They did. Roland was just coming up the hallway, face freshly scrubbed. He looked at Paige, did a double-take, and said: "What happened to you?"

"She was attacked," Simon said. He brought her into the living room, where she collapsed onto a chair.

"Are you all right?" Roland asked.

"I'm okay," she said. "He didn't hurt me. He just stole my necklace."

"Did you see him?" Simon said.

She nodded. "It was the Bird Man."

"Who?"

She shook her head and held up her hand, gulped air, and said: "Henry and Frederick are gone."

"What?"

"Something attacked us in our car. I don't know what it was. There was this … this thing, and the car stopped working, and this *thing* came out of the dashboard and it was coming toward us and we couldn't open the doors and—"

"Slow down," Simon said. "What thing?"

"I don't know. It was like slime or something. Came out of the dashboard." She fell silent, shoulders shaking. Then she said: "And we couldn't get out, so I bashed through the sunroof, and I climbed out, and I was trying to help Frederick out when something hit me and knocked me out. I woke up in the street. I almost got run over."

"Was it this … uh … this Bird Man character?"

She shook her head. "No," she said. "He just grabbed my locket and ran away. This *thing* attacked me and left me in the road, like it wanted me to get hit by a car. I need to go to the bathroom."

It took Simon a moment to realize that this was a request, rather than part of her story; then he said, "Go ahead."

Paige got up and hurried down the hallway. Shortly, the sound of vomiting echoed up the hallway.

"Slime? Bird Man?" Roland said. "How much did she have to drink?"

Simon shook his head, then shrugged.

"Should we call the police?"

"Not yet," he said. "We need a better story than this."

Paige returned a few minutes later. She looked a little calmer, a little less frantic. "It's okay," she said. "I'm all right now. Can I borrow an old shirt?"

Roland went to fetch her one. Simon waited until he was out of earshot and said: "Paige, you should tell the police what happened."

She shook her head.

"Why not?"

"It's too crazy."

"What's too crazy?"

"I think the thing that attacked me on the roof of my car was Florence. My mother-in-law."

Thunderous silence.

"Told you it was crazy," she said.

Roland returned and handed her one of his old flannel shirts. "Thanks," she said, slipping it on and buttoning it up. It made her look like she was half lumberjack, half socialite.

Simon said: "You think your *mother-in-law* came out of the woods and attacked you and kidnapped your family?"

She nodded.

After a moment Roland said: "I've heard of pushy in-laws, but—"

Simon silenced him with a glance, then said: "Your mother-in-law has to be, what, seventy?" he said.

Paige said, "I know what it sounds like, I really do. But if you'll come with me, I can show you something. Something that'll change your mind."

He and Roland exchanged another glance. "I'm game if you are," Roland said.

"No, one of you has to stay here," she said. "Just in case something happens to us."

Simon agreed to drive her back to her car; Roland watched as they walked down the driveway to Simon's vehicle. She glanced back at him, a shadow behind the screen door, and suppressed a shiver. Too many shadows, tonight.

Inside the car, before he started the engine, Simon said: "Look, Paige, you've obviously been through a lot tonight—"

"I haven't been through so much that I can't remember what happened, if that's where you're going," she said. "I know it all sounds crazy, but it's the God's honest truth."

He shrugged and started the car, and they rolled out of the driveway. "All right, well, you should at least get checked out by a doctor," Simon said. "You blacked out. That's not something to fool around with."

"I'm all right," Paige said. "Just a headache."

"I don't see how—"

"I'm all right," she said again. "There's nothing wrong with me that kicking Florence's ass won't cure."

A few moments later, the ragged remnants of her vehicle came into view. Funny how much longer the distance seemed on foot, being chased; but they'd actually gotten scarcely a half-mile before being attacked. She said, "There it is. Pull over."

He eased up behind it, his headlights glaring against its rusted backside. It had deteriorated since she had left it: the trunk had fallen in; and the rear axle must have broken, judging from the way it was sagging to the left; and the back bumper and one taillight had come loose, the bumper on the ground in a festering heap of chrome dust, the taillight dangling from its socket like a popped eye.

After a moment Simon said: "This is *your* car?"

"The same one Henry took you out to see three hours ago."

Simon got out and went over to the rusting husk. He looked at the tires—flat, every one of them—and ran his hand along the slope of the trunk, up to the roof. He circled around it, stopped at the shoulder and picked something up, an oblong piece of metal, like a shield. He held it so she could see it in the glow of the headlights; it was the sunroof, gleaming, perfectly intact. He leaned it up against the car, and bent over to look through the hole where the passenger-side window had once been.

He reached inside, perhaps to pick something up.

Paige saw movement in the back seat of the car.

"Simon!" she shrieked. "Look out!"

He jumped back just as a dark shape lashed out; she heard him grunt, saw him fall back from the car, clutching his hand. The shadow clambered over the rotting remains of the front seat, slithered to the window, poured through the opening. She couldn't think of anything else to do, so she reached over and leaned on the horn. The thing looked at her, a fuzzy, sinuous dribble of darkness, of dusted ebony. The headlights lit up its eyes, pallid green rings in what passed for its head.

Jesus. That was it: the thing she had seen in Simon's backyard. Not Florence, not the Bird Man. *This.*

How many fucking monsters were there?

Simon scrambled away from the thing. He snatched up the sunroof and held it in front of him as the creature slurped across the ground, slashing with appendages so dark and so fast Paige could hardly see them even in the glow of the headlights; but Simon somehow managed to block the blows with the sunroof, every time. With each impact she heard the clang of claws on metal, saw his arms shudder as they held the sunroof.

Paige opened her door for Simon and climbed over the center console, into the driver's seat. Simon, retreating before the creature, darted into the car and slammed the door shut. He was still holding the sunroof. Paige threw the vehicle into reverse and they roared backwards up the shoulder.

The shadow coiled into itself like a snake, then shot into the air.

Paige bootlegged the car, tires screeching, wheel jerking in her hand. Then they were racing up the road, back toward Simon's house, away from the thing.

"It got my hand," Simon said.

She said nothing.

"It got my hand," he said, louder this time. She glanced at it. Blood was running from two swelling gashes near the left side of his left hand. From there, her gaze flicked to the sunroof. It was shredded, the paint and outer layer of metal ripped away in a crosshatch pattern of three-line scores. Where the metal was exposed, it was beginning to rust.

"How'd you do that?" Paige said. "How'd you block it?"

"Racquetball," Simon said. He picked up his car phone, punched a button, and after a moment said: "It's me. Lock all the doors and windows. Watch for my car." Pause. "Just do it!" He hung up.

A minute later they pulled into his driveway. Paige honked the horn and after a moment Roland appeared at the front door, gawking at them. "Let's go," Paige said. The two of them bolted out of the car, up the steps, into the house.

"What's going on?" Roland said, as Simon and Paige rushed past him. She heard him blundering along behind them as they ran to the bathroom. Once they got there, Simon perched on the edge of the bathtub, clutching the wrist of his injured hand and rocking back and forth while Paige rummaged through the medicine chest.

"How's it feel?" she asked.

"Numb."

Roland came into the doorway and said, "What the hell is going on?"

"Do you have any antibiotic? Antiseptic? Anything?" Paige asked.

"If we do it's in there," Simon said.

She shoved bottles and tubes and little plastic jars out of the way. "I can't find any!" she said. "Damn it, Simon—"

"It's not my goddamn fault we don't have kids who need patching up all the time!" Simon said.

"Hello! What's going on?" Roland said.

She finally found a tube of antibiotic ointment way at the back, but there was hardly enough in it to put on a splinter and it had expired nearly three years earlier. She cursed and threw it in the garbage. Simon watched her, a sick expression on his face; his skin was pale, his face glistening and clammy-looking. She didn't know if it was fear or some effect of the thing's claws digging into him.

"Would somebody *please* tell me what's going on?" Roland said.

"Simon was attacked," Paige said. Then, to Simon: "What if we —"

She broke off at a splintering crash from the living room.

Paige looked up sharply and said: "Did you close the front door?"

"Yes."

"Jesus," Simon said. "Is that thing in the house?"

In the momentary silence that followed, Paige heard a faint ripping sound, like a cat sharpening its claws on upholstery; but this sound was louder, and it was harsher, and it was advancing up the hallway. Roland's head swung right, toward the living room; his eyes practically bugged out of his head, and he said: "What's *that?*"

Paige grabbed Roland's hand, pulled him inside, shut the door and locked it.

"It's hollow," Simon said, standing up. "It won't keep that thing out." He scrabbled at the latch on the window, slid it up. Simon popped open the screen, pushed it. It fell away into the night. "Out," he said. "It's about eight feet to the ground."

A long, lazy scratching sound rasped from the closed door, as of a single, sharp nail being dragged across the wood. Paige imagined that *thing* outside the room, separated from them only by a few layers of veneer. Those claws had sliced through sheet metal; wood wouldn't even slow them down.

"Paige," Simon said, "*go!*"

She clambered head-first out the window, clinging to the sill with her fingers as she swung her feet around and dropped to the sloping lawn. A few seconds later Simon landed with a soft *thud*, rolled, stood unsteadily.

The crunch of shattering wood crackled through the open window. Roland came flying out head-first, as if he were diving into a pool; he curved downward, hit the ground in a crumpled heap, and didn't get up again.

"Roland?" Simon said.

A shadow rose in the lighted window, a green-eyed silhouette.

"Simon, come *on*!" Paige cried.

"Pick him up!" Simon said. "Help me—"

Roland stirred, groaned. The thing slurped out of the window, oozed down the face of the house. Paige lunged across and grabbed Simon's uninjured hand and half-dragged him away as the shadow pounced on Roland's prostrate body. Simon howled when he saw that, broke away from her and ran back toward the bubbling shade. Paige cursed and took a step after him.

Then she thought about Henry and Frederick, and stopped.

If she let this thing get her, they were gone forever.

She ran.

She ran to the front of the house, where they had left Simon's car. It was still running, the engine humming softly, vapors drifting from the tailpipe. She got inside, threw it into reverse, backed up the driveway and stopped at the edge of the road.

Where was she going to go?

Who was going to help her now?

The passenger door opened and Simon slid in next to her.

"Get us out of here," he said hoarsely.

Henry wasn't sure where he was, but it smelled foul and decrepit, like an old, musty, abandoned house with a leaky roof. He couldn't see anything; there was no light, not even a sliver of illumination creeping around the sides of a door or through the gaps in a blind. He didn't know if Paige and Frederick were here; and he couldn't call to them, because there was a gag in his mouth. It wasn't very tight, but it was sufficient to keep him from making any noticeable noises.

He was tied to something; he thought it was an old beam, damp and spongy but firmly anchored and not going anywhere. The ropes were taut enough to hold him, but not enough to hurt. Circulation was not cut off anywhere. Somebody had been very careful to make sure he was comfortably restrained.

He heard something: a door creaking open, then footsteps. Stairs groaning. After a moment a voice came out of the darkness: "Henry."

He looked around. "Ma?" he said.

"Yes." The footsteps swished toward him across protesting floorboards.

"Jesus Christ, Ma, where are we? What's going on? Are you okay?"

"I'm fine, Henry." The footsteps stopped nearby. He could hear her breathing softly, each breath a subtle whiskery sound.

"What the hell happened?" he said. "We were in the car and—"

"I know," she said. "It's all right."

"It's not all right, Ma, for Christ's sake. I'm—"

"Hush," Florence said. "She had some business to take care of to make sure we weren't disturbed, but now Mother's here." She moved —he heard the rustle of her clothes, or maybe it was her skin—and one of the ropes fell away, freeing his right hand. She took it. Her touch was warm and paper-dry, almost scaly.

He felt something sharp and sticky just prick his palm.

"Ma, what're you doing?"

"I'm taking back my son," she said; and a blade sliced into his hand. He cried out, and she said: "It'll only hurt for a second." And indeed, the instant of pain was followed swiftly by numbness, as if the weapon were so cold it dulled the nerves in the skin it cut through.

No; it wasn't the knife, it was something else. Something in his hand, some kind of viscous, slimy, frigid glop, soaking into the cut and deadening it, dribbling through his fingers, pattering to the floor.

"I don't know how that bitch spoiled this," Florence said, "but she isn't here now, and this time it will work."

"Ma. For God's sake, what—"

"Hush," she said.

"Where's Frederick?"

"He's here," she said.

"Did you hurt Paige?"

"No," Florence said. "Didn't I promise you I wouldn't hurt her?" Pause. "I left her in the road. She may have been hit by a car, but that's hardly *my* fault."

"*What?* Have you lost your mind?"

"No," Florence said. "I'm taking back what's mine, that's all."

"I'm not yours to take back, Ma," Henry said.

She chuckled softly, and said: "We'll see about that, Henry."

They were miles from Simon's house, driving down into the city, into the well-lit streets of Selden Falls. Simon stared out the windshield, stared into the night, and kept seeing it over and over in his mind, the creature dropping from the window, falling upon Roland; and the claws—

He realized Paige was saying his name, looked at her. She was staring straight ahead too, gripping the wheel very tightly. "What?" he said.

"I asked what happened to Roland."

"Oh," he said. He thought a moment. He should be able to answer this; he'd been replaying it in his mind just a second ago, but when he had stopped thinking about it for an instant it turned into a blur. It took him a little while to get it all back into focus, and then he said: "Claws. I just saw claws. They were as long as my finger. Up and down and up and down. They were black but I swear they turned red."

Paige said nothing.

"This is it," Simon said. "This is the thing that's been killing people. I bet it killed Nelson and chopped off his hands and feet. I bet it killed those girls." He held up his hand so she could see it. The two cuts had formed welts, tall and hard and puffy, and they weren't bleeding anymore. "What's going to happen to me, Paige?"

"I don't know," she said.

He poked one angry red ridge with his finger. The touch sent a burning sensation shooting up his arm and he stopped. "Did you see what happened to the sunroof where it cut it?"

"I saw it."

"Is that going to happen to my hand?"

"I don't know, Simon." Paige pulled into the parking lot of a supermarket and got out of the car. She leaned back in and said, "Wait here. It might be too late for this, but I'm going to pick up something for your hand." Then she slammed the door and hurried into the store.

Simon looked around. The amber lights seemed to emit a sparkling vapor that drifted around the lot. Beyond those, the night hung dark and deep and deadly. Simon closed his eyes and he could see the shadow thing working on Roland, the claws ripping and rending, each descending talon whipping through the cloud of blood raised by the one that was on its way out.

Jesus. If Karl Castle ever got hold of this, he'd have one hell of a campaign issue.

The driver's side door opened and Paige dropped into the seat. She held a tube of antiseptic, already opened. She squirted it onto the back of his hand, over the welts. Nothing happened, though the cool cream had a soothing feel to it.

"I hope it's not too late," she said. "Rub it in."

He began working the ointment with his fingers. "*You* hope it's not too late?" he said.

"I don't have too many friends at the moment," she said. Then: "What was that about somebody getting their hands and feet chopped off?"

"A guy named Nelson. He was Quentin Farmer's assistant. I got a call from him this morning; he said Quentin had disappeared from his room, he suspected foul play. He was talking all kinds of wild stuff. Said the church Karl bulldozed was cursed, said Selden Falls had no past, nonsense like that." Pause. "I mean, it sounded like nonsense."

"What'd you say to him?"

"I hung up on him, actually."

"Can we talk to him?"

Simon raised an eyebrow. "They chopped his hands and feet off. He's dead."

There was a moment of silence.

Then Simon said: "We need the cops. Let's go talk to Paul Shockton."

Paige hadn't been to the Shockton homestead in years; it had expanded since she'd last visited. The main house—white stucco with a red clay roof, like it had been picked up by a tornado in Santa Fe and been deposited here—had always been large, but now it had grown into a mansion at the end of its long driveway, like a fetus swelling at the end of an umbilical cord. The old attached garage had been covered over with swirled concrete, supplanted by a combination garage and in-law apartment separated from the house by the wide spot where the driveway curved back on itself to form a circle. The entire place was hidden from the road by maples and bushy pines; it made Paige think of some feudal plantation, broad and self-sufficient and kept running by the efforts of an army of serfs.

A spur branched off the driveway to the right, where it curved under a big carport on the side of the house; this was where Simon had been told to park when he had called Paul from the car phone. Paige pulled underneath the terra cotta roof and stopped the car.

"Do we go knock?" Paige said.

"No, he said he'd meet us out here." Simon eyed their surroundings with obvious surprise; clearly he had never been out here before. "I must pay Shockton too much," he said.

Paige shook her head. "His wife owns the newspaper."

"I know," Simon said. "I try to forget about that, or I start getting this urge to tell Shockton to make her reporters lay off me."

"You could try it, but you wouldn't get anywhere." She drummed her fingers on the wheel and looked around the shadowed enclosure. The carport was supported by slender, tapered columns that ended in what looked like carved heads, though that was probably just a trick of the light; they were probably that old pretentious standby, pineapples. Symbols of hospitality. The driveway continued out the other side and looped grandly around a stand of ash; behind the trees, a tall barn-like building flanked by lower wings was visible. Looked like a stable.

"Where *is* he?" Simon said.

"Don't ask me," Paige said. "You're his boss, you set this whole thing up."

She heard a horse whinny faintly, confirming the stable theory. When had Paul gotten interested in horses? They must belong to his wife, she thought.

A side door of the house opened and a shadow slunk out. It didn't move much differently from the shadow in Simon's backyard, and she had to fight down an irrational burst of panic. It was only Paul, she thought; it wasn't one of those *things*.

"There he is," Simon said, unnecessarily.

Paul stopped in front of the car, into the glow of the high beams. He was wearing a suit, black and expensive-looking. Paige examined him warily; his face looked weird, she thought. Rubbery, fake, like he was wearing a mask. It was probably just the way the headlights lit him up, but still, there seemed a cruel edge to his profile that she didn't remember. Maybe it came from four years as chief of police.

Oh, hell. Might as well be honest with herself: she wasn't comfortable around any of her old boyfriends, especially this one. She wondered if he had told his wife she was coming; probably not, or the woman would be out here with him, armed with kitchen utensils.

Paige glanced at Simon—who was already getting out—and said, "I don't feel good about this."

The mayor stopped halfway out of the car, looked at her, and said: "You can stay in the car if you want to." Then he stood up and closed the door. She watched him go around in front and decline to shake Paul Shockton's hand, pointing out his injury. They talked for a few seconds and then Paul's head turned and looked at her, sitting there behind the wheel. He waved her out of the vehicle. Paige slowly turned off the lights, shut the engine, and got out of the car.

Simon started to make introductions, but Paige forestalled him. "We know each other," she said.

"You do?" Simon said, sounding surprised.

"Been a while, Mrs. Fontana," Paul said. "I like your outfit."

"Just call me Paige, for God's sake," she said. "Can we go inside?"

"I'm sorry," Paul said. "My wife is entertaining some people from Gannett; I don't put on this monkey outfit for just anyone." He gestured at his suit, which she now realized was a tuxedo. "I thought we would use the stable."

He turned and walked up the driveway. As Paige and Simon followed, Simon whispered, "Is something going on between you two?"

"Not anymore," she said. "Ancient history."

The far side of the loop was illuminated by a lamp on a tall post. The angle of the light made the stable seem impossibly tall, turned its high windows into leering eyes. The narrow car path curved around in front of the two doors, one human-sized and one for the horses; a split-rail fence snaked in from the wide field beyond the stable to run alongside the driveway, ending at the wall of the building.

Paul slid the horse door open and they all went inside. The central corridor of the stable ran the length of the building. The door in the end opposite them was open, a square of night set into the wall, though there was a chest-high gate across it. The big central chamber was lined with stalls, four on each side, but only a few seemed to be occupied. She could hear the horses shifting around, crunching straw beneath their feet, occasionally snorting.

"Newspaper business must be pretty good these days," Paige said.

"It's not Hearst Castle, but it's home," Shockton said. He sat on a stack of hay bales near the entrance. "So what's this big news that couldn't wait until morning, Simon?"

"I was attacked tonight," Simon said. That was what they'd decided to say, on their way up here; they would make it sound as if Simon were the target, skip the rest of it: The Bird Man, Florence, the car crumbling to dust. They wanted Shockton to help them, not have them committed.

"By who?" Paul said.

Paige wandered off to look at the horses. The stall nearest where Paul was sitting housed a grey horse dappled with white. It was pressed up against the right-hand wall of the stable, ears flattened, whites showing at the edges of its eyes. It looked just like she felt, she thought.

Paul said, "Mind they don't bite you, Paige. They've been upset ever since a dog got in here earlier today."

At the sound of his voice, the horse's ears flattened still farther, and it bobbed its head and snorted. "Hey, calm down," Paige said softly.

Simon said, "I don't know what it was—"

"It. What do you mean *it*?" Paul asked.

"I'm sorry, I meant *him*," Simon said. "None of us got a good look at him. He was all dressed in black and he was carrying some kind of hook—"

"A hook? You mean like a curved knife?"

"Yeah," Simon said. "A short, curved knife. One in each hand."

"A two-hook assassin, huh?" Paul said. "You must be getting important."

"He killed Roland. Shredded him right in front of me." Paige shot the mayor a look; that wasn't in the script. He didn't seem to be paying any attention to her, though. He had an angry, distant look on his face; probably replaying the scene in his mind. "I got away with just the cuts I showed you."

Paige turned away. The horse had stepped closer to her; she cooed at it and it seemed to relax a bit which, in turn, calmed her own jangled nerves.

"Just a couple of scratches," Paul said. Which was true: Simon's injuries *were* just a couple of scratches now. If she hadn't seen them herself, the deep, ragged-edged wounds going all the way to the bone, she wouldn't take them seriously either. It looked like he had maybe picked up a cat that wanted to be left alone, but it didn't look like he had just escaped evisceration.

"He just nicked me," Simon said. "But this guy—he wrecked my house. He smashed through my front door. Look what he did to Paige's dress, he nearly sliced her open. I want a cop up there, now."

"Why didn't you just call one?" Paul said.

"With that guy hanging around? Not on your life."

She began to pet the horse's ears. They were soft and fuzzy, like bits of felt. It lowered its big head so she could scratch it better. She turned and rubbed her cheek against its broad, flat face, just in time to see a man-sized shadow pull back from the open door at the opposite end of the barn. A shadow, and a flash of green where the eyes would have been.

She straightened up, ready to tell Shockton that it wasn't a dog making his animals nervous; but then he said, "Okay, let me get this straight. Some guy breaks into your house while you're having, what, a dinner party? He's got two curved knives and he's slashing them here and slashing them there, and he kills your, ah, friend, and you and Paige here run out the front door and drive straight down to my place without calling anyone first. Is that what I'm hearing?"

The hair prickled along the back of Paige's neck. What was Shockton getting at?

Simon said, "Uh, well ..." Not wanting to look foolish in front of his subordinate. But was that the only danger here? Because it sounded to her like Paul Shockton was trying to make sure no one else knew they were coming to his house, and why would he care about *that*, unless—

Oh, shit.

As Simon hemmed and hawed, Paige said: "My husband." It was all she could think of, and as soon as she said it she realized that if Paul knew that Henry had been abducted, it wouldn't work. Because after all, if Florence was one of them, and if Paul Shockton was one of them, then wouldn't it be logical that they would all be working together?

Paul's voice drifted around the corner of the stall: "Your husband what?"

"He was there," Paige said. Simon was looking at her, but at least he wasn't overtly gawking, thank God. All they needed was for him to say *What the hell are you talking about?* and they were dead, or something.

Shockton stepped out from behind the stalls so he could see her. "Why didn't he come with you?"

"He took our son home," Paige said. "Freddie's pretty hysterical right now."

The chief's dark gaze bored into her, through her, right through her head. "Where is he?" he asked, and his eyes seemed to be trying to pull the truth out of her before she could even answer. He didn't quite believe her, but he didn't quite *not* believe her, either; and she could tell, somehow, that it wouldn't really trouble him to let them go, that he they could be dealt with later rather than sooner, if necessary.

She opened her mouth, with no idea what was going to come out, the truth or more bull; but Simon must have seen or sensed her predicament, because he put a hand on Paul's shoulder and turned the chief around to face him instead. "Are you going to send a police car to my house or not?" he said.

Thank God. Paige slumped against the stall. She wanted to think that, whatever Paul had been doing to her, she could have resisted it; but she wasn't sure, not sure at all. The horse whickered and bobbed its head as if in sympathy.

"Tell you what," Paul said. "Why don't we all drive up there together, and I'll take a look around?"

Simon shook his head. "You have to get back to your guests," he said. "You don't want to give Gannett the brush-off and waste your monkey outfit, right? Besides, I can't put the chief of police in that kind of position. You might get hurt."

Shockton said: "I don't think there's much danger of that."

"Better safe than sorry."

Paul stood there a moment, just looking at Simon, maybe trying to do that thing to him that he'd done to Paige; if so, it didn't seem to work. Then he looked back at her, but she was ready for it this time, and when she felt that little flicker start up in her mind she blew it out, just like a candle flame.

The corner of Shockton's mouth twitched up in a smile. His eyes were cold, and his eyes were dead, and his eyes said: *You think you're tough, but I'm not really trying, that's all. I don't believe any of this shit, but I'll pretend I do just in case you're telling the truth, because I can always take care of you later.*

What he said with his voice was: "All right, I'll make some phone calls, get some people up there. We'll find your assassin, if he's still around." It was crap, and he knew that she knew it was crap; he was smiling that flat, shit-eating grin she remembered him using when he thought he was managing a situation. "Do you want to wait here?"

He knew the answer to that. "No," Paige said. "We'll go back and check on Freddie."

Paul opened the horse doors and they exited the stable and followed him back to the car. Simon took the driver's seat this time. Shockton gestured for him to roll down the window, which he did; then the chief leaned over and said, "Where can I reach you?"

His breath smelled like old cedar, Paige thought. Old, mildewed cedar, if there was such a thing.

"Try the car phone," Simon said.

"Okay," Paul said. "We'll be in touch."

Simon rolled the window up and they backed out of the carport. Paul stood there, a shadow in the dark, watching them. Simon executed a three-point turn and they were driving away, gravel crunching under the tires. When they reached the street, Simon turned left and then said, "They got to Shockton, didn't they?"

"Sure looks like it," Paige said.

"How'd you know he didn't know about Henry?"

Paige said: "I didn't."

Simon took a few turns, apparently at random.

"Why are they trying to kill us?" he said at length.

"You think *I* know? I mean, I know what Florence was after, and the Bird Man just wanted my necklace. Shockton is another story. He doesn't just want to kill us, or we'd already be dead."

"You think he would've just done that? Just killed us?"

"He runs the police department," Paige said. "Who would stop him?" She stared out the window a little while, then said: "Where are we going, anyway?"

"You tell me." Simon pulled into a little shopping center at the bottom of the hill and parked under one of the lights. "I wonder if he'll really send anyone to my house," he said, looking at the sky.

"He might," Paige said. "Will it matter?"

"Probably not, I guess." Simon ran his injured hand through his hair. "I don't know how to handle this," he said. "I can't make a deal with it, I don't even know what these … these *people* want, and I don't think they'll tell me. I can't take it to the council, I can't take it to the press, I can't take it to the voters. I don't know what to do."

"Look, Simon—"

"I can't believe this is happening." He was starting to sound hysterical, like he was on the verge of panic. "It's like some nightmare —"

"Shut up," Paige said. She kept her voice from rising to a shriek, but only with an effort. He closed his mouth and stared at her; probably no one had told him to shut up since he'd become mayor. "If you go down that road, you might not be able to get back. That thing killed Roland, and he's dead, and we can't change that; but Henry and Frederick are still out there somewhere, and we need to figure out what that bitch did with them. We can't trust the police. We can't trust anyone. So don't you dare go off the deep end on me, or I'll kick you in the butt."

After a moment he said, "I'm sorry, I just—"

She held up a hand to silence him, and he shut up again.

Where would Florence have taken Henry and Frederick? Not back to their house on Cool Road; that was Paige's territory, she knew it too well. Not back to Florence's house, either; Paige had had five years to get to know the ins and outs of that place almost as well as her own.

That left one obvious place. She should have thought of it ages ago.

"Pine Ridge," Paige said. "Take us to Pine Ridge."

"Where?"

"Pine Ridge. It's a nursing home." Pause. They didn't move. "Go, go, go."

"I don't know where it is."

"Then get out and let me drive," Paige said.

Henry could tell when his mother was coming back by the creaking of the floorboards. She came up to him and stopped a few yards away and said, "How's your hand?"

"Okay," he said. The numb feeling had traveled up his arm and down his chest, but it seemed to be going away, and his hand felt perfectly normal again. Itched a little, that was all.

"I'm going to untie you now," she said. "All right?"

"All right."

He heard a faint *snick* and the ropes fell away. He stepped away from the beam, rubbing his arms, his wrists. They were stiff from being immobile for so long in the cold, damp air.

"I brought Frederick," Florence said. "He wanted to see his father."

"See me? It's too dark here to see anything."

"I found a lamp." She struck a match; the dim, red, flickering light made her face look weird, an eager ruddy visage, shadowed and strange. Not his mother's face at all; it belonged to a stranger hiding behind a sharp nose and hard glittery eyes and ruffled hair dark as coal. She lowered the match to an old oil lamp, lit it, fumbled the globe back into place. Her hands were trembling; not from nervousness or palsy, Henry thought, but from excitement. As she turned the tiny metal wheel, a circle of illumination grew up around them, beyond which strange tall shadows lurked: boxes and clothes and broken furniture, the skeletons of things life had used up and stashed away for possible future reference.

They were in an attic, Henry realized. An old, dank, cluttered attic.

Then he took a closer look at his mother, and said: "Ma, did you dye your hair?"

"No," she said.

"Then where's the grey?"

She straightened up, smiling. "It's wonderful," she said. "It gives you back the years. All you have to do—" She reached out with an open palm, then curled her fingers together. "Is take them."

"Huh?"

"Daddy?"

It wasn't Frederick's voice he heard, it was a stranger's; and when Florence, smiling a wide and secret smile, stepped out of the way, it wasn't Frederick he saw, it was a teenager—no, older than that: it was a man scarcely younger than himself.

He looked at Florence. "What the hell is going on?" he said. "Who's this?"

"Well, I could hardly take so many years from *you*," she said. "Twenty-five years means less to a child than to a man. And I knew you wouldn't believe what I could do, unless I showed you."

"Are you telling me this is Freddie? What kind of a stupid trick is this? Jesus Christ, Ma, how dumb do you think I am?"

"It's not a trick," Florence said. "It's immortality."

"You're out of your mind. This guy could be my brother."

"Why doesn't Daddy recognize me, Grandma?" the guy said.

"Say something to him so he knows it's you."

"Okay, um …" The guy she was trying to pass off as Frederick looked thoughtful, then brightened and said: "Oh, yeah! Remember how you took my game away because I kept swearing at it? The one that came with my video game?"

Henry stared at him, aghast. "Jesus," he whispered.

"Hey, I *forgot* about that game," the guy said, accusingly now. "When are you gonna give it back?"

Henry looked at his mother. She ruffled the hair on the man's head, sent him off to sit on an old trunk in front of a gigantic black wardrobe near the edge of the lamplight.

"What the hell did you do, Ma?" Henry said. He couldn't accept that this was really Freddie—although, God, the guy certainly resembled Paige, could've been her fraternal twin almost—but he would play along and find out what craziness his mother was up to.

She smiled. "It's simple. It's the breath. You just take the breath."

"What the hell does that mean?"

"It's wonderful, it really is. When I took the first few years from the other residents, I knew—I *knew* I would have to take more. They don't have much to give, poor things, and what they have is weak, and I wasn't sure how to do it at first, I didn't have good control, and I took too much sometimes; but I learned, I got better, and the more I took the younger I felt—"

"You're telling me this is how you were walking around?" Henry said. "This is how your hip healed?"

"Yes," she said. "The years came back and made me better."

"This is why those residents died?"

"I didn't do it on purpose," she said. She didn't sound particularly contrite about the mishaps. "I took too much. But none of them had a lot of time left anyway."

He stared at her, her smiling face, the thick black mane surrounding it. Her skin was smooth but yellowed, stretched tight over the bones beneath; and her eyes were like chips of obsidian. Maybe the years had come back, but they hadn't made her young again; they might have juiced her up, rejuvenated her, but it was just a fresh coat of paint on an aging structure. It might be immortality, but it wasn't eternal youth.

Youth, and age, and stolen years … and something clicked. "The guy they found in the basement of the church," he said. "The one who always sits on the swing. He really *is* Calvin Trott, isn't he?"

"I wouldn't know," she said. "He doesn't talk."

"He's Calvin Trott. Something happened to him under the church and he got old, like Freddie. Is he the one who made you like this? Did he do it, Ma?"

"He didn't do it on purpose. I don't think he does *anything* on purpose. He tried to take my brooch—you know, the nice one, the orchid with the diamonds?"

"I keep telling you, Ma, they're rhinestones."

"No, they're diamonds."

"Whatever. So he took it?"

"He took it," she said, "and I grabbed it back, and he bit my hand. Just a little bite. It took a long time for the little bite to finish working; but when it did, I knew—I knew, and I figured out what I could do. Just look at me now! And immortality isn't all, Henry. No, it isn't even close to all. I can do such things—"

"I don't want to know what the hell else you can do. I really don't."

Her little smile thinned out. "But, Henry, I made you like me—"

"I'm not like you," he said. "Look at you. You're a freak. You're a monster. You killed those people, you tried to kill Paige, and you talk about it like it's nothing!"

What was left of the smile vanished altogether. "I cut you free too soon," she said. "You're not ready yet. I see that now."

"I'm not ever going to be ready, Ma. Whatever you're trying to do to me—"

"Oh, you'll thank me," she said. "Count on that."

Silence.

After a moment she tilted her head to one side, then darted across the room, right past Freddie, taking the lamp with her. Henry watched as she stopped at an ancient window, the glass covered up by boards nailed at odd angles. She scrabbled at them with her left hand, ripped one right out of the wood, nails and all.

Tearing down the walls one-handed. Jesus, Henry thought, she had the strength of a maniac.

She made a sound, a little frustrated screech, like the cry of a bird denied some treasured prey. "What's the matter, Ma?" Henry said.

She looked at him, her mouth twisted up in a snarl.

"Someone's coming up the driveway," she said.

18

"WHAT DO YOU EXPECT TO find here?" Simon asked, as Paige parked his car in the deserted visitor's lot of the Pine Ridge Nursing Home.

"I don't know," she said. "Maybe nothing. Maybe my husband and my son. Maybe some answers, at least."

As she opened the door, Simon said: "Wait."

"What?"

"There's a light in the attic." He was pointing up at the eaves of the old building, the part that had once been George Selden's mansion. A yellow light flickered from between the boards on the inside of the window, striated illumination glowing into the darkness. "Someone's watching us."

"Could be," Paige said.

The light went away. Simon said, "I'm not feeling too good about this all of a sudden."

"Stay here, then." She walked away from the car, toward the front porch, but after a moment she realized he really *was* staying behind, and she looked back over her shoulder and said: "Oh, come on. Unless you want to stay out here, alone."

Shamed or frightened into movement, Simon stole along after her.

Up the front stairs. There was the swing where the Bird Man liked to sit; it was vacant now, rocking gently in the light breeze, as if he had just abandoned it and it hadn't stopped swaying. The joints creaked as it moved.

She stopped at the front entrance, touched the handle. Simon caught up with her, eyed the door. "It's probably locked," he said, half hopefully.

The button went down under her thumb and the door popped open. She pushed it inward. It swung silently across the shiny hardwood floor.

"Or maybe not," Simon said.

They went into the lobby. To the left of the door was the front desk. Every other time she had visited—during regular hours, of course—Paige had been greeted here by a nurse in a starched white outfit, given a book to sign, and directed to the appropriate room. Every time, as if she couldn't remember the room number on her own. But now the desk was vacant, the chair gone; but it looked as if the station had been occupied until quite recently. A green-shaded lamp was switched on, pouring light on a thick magazine open to the first page of an article called *Sex And Vegetables*. She wasn't sure if it was about improving your diet, or having fun with cucumbers.

Simon said, "Somebody got up in a hurry. The chair is knocked over."

Paige circled around behind the desk, knelt down and examined the overturned chair. There weren't any marks on it; no scratches, no blood. She reached out to right it, but Simon said, "You probably shouldn't do that."

Yeah, probably not. She stood up and looked around. The old place was silent as a mausoleum, except for the steady creaking of the swing out on the porch. Stairs opened onto the lobby across from the desk, darkly polished wood gleaming in the light from the green-shaded lamp. Florence had been in the newer part of the building, so Paige had never climbed those steps to the upper levels of George Selden's former home; she didn't know the layout up there. Florence —if it was Florence who'd been up in the attic with the flickery lamp —apparently did. Which was why she'd brought Henry and Frederick to this place, even though she hated it. Home court advantage.

She walked slowly to the foot of the stairs. Simon crept along behind her. They both stood at the bottom, looking up. The steps clung to the wall, leaving an open chimney straight to the top of the house. Three stories; thirty feet of open space, ending in a paneled ceiling.

"It's so quiet," Simon said.

"If you say *too quiet*, I'll be forced to kill you," Paige said.

"Threats, threats, threats."

A threadbare green runner flowed down the center of the staircase, a ribbon of carpet just wide enough for a single person to walk on. Paige stepped up onto the runner; the stair groaned beneath her. Probably wouldn't seem loud during the day, but it sounded like a fire alarm right now. She moved closer to the wall, and took the next step. It groaned too, but not as noticeably. She looked over her shoulder; Simon was still on the first floor. "Stay close to the wall. It's quieter." He nodded, and started after her. Together they ascended through the house, which was silent now, except for the protestations of the stairs. She couldn't hear the swing creaking anymore; either the wind had died down or they were getting too far away. For some reason the loss of that sound made her more uneasy, as if now there were nothing outside the nursing home to go back to.

They stopped at the second floor. A plastic sign on the wall said *Administrative Offices* and a smallish reception desk stood in the hallway, but this area was clearly not staffed at night. The light was off, the computer on the desk shut down and sleeping under a thick plastic cover. Up here, the only illumination came from a single fluorescent tube in a panel above the desk. The stairs started up again a few yards to the right.

At the opposite end of the landing, up a short run of shabby hallway, a door sagged open; it was labeled *SECURITY*. Paige approached it cautiously, nudged it with her shoulder to send it swinging inward, revealing a small, dim, cluttered office. No one was present, though there was an empty chair and a half-eaten sandwich on the desk. A small videocassette recorder perched on a shelf to the right of the workstation, but it was smashed and its guts were hanging down over the edge. A bank of miniature television screens was mounted above the desk; these had also suffered evisceration. The screens were all shattered, the chassis splintered by powerful blades; one picture tube had been completely dislodged and lay in pieces on the desk in a puddle of spilled soda.

As Simon stopped beside her, she heard a sound from downstairs, a faint click, like a deadbolt turning.

She looked at him and said, "Did you hear that?"

"Yeah."

"Somebody locked the door."

"I heard it," he said.

She left the demolished security office and went to the railing and looked down the throat of the stairs. Nothing: no noise, no movement. She glanced at Simon. He was right next to her, staring downward; and suddenly he pointed and hissed, "Look." She did, and watched as a shadow moved through the spread of greenish light from the desk lamp. Silently and steadily as a canoe splitting the placid waters of a lake on a windless day, it crossed in front of the lamp.

A few seconds later, the light went out.

"It's her," Paige whispered. "It's Florence."

They waited at the railing a little longer, like emigrants reluctant to leave the deck of their ship as it pulled away from the dock. The stairwell dropped into darkness now; the first floor was visible, but only barely, a grey rumor at the bottom of the steps. No sound, no movement, no hostile creatures came up at them. "If it *is* her," Simon said, "what's she doing?"

Paige looked at him. "Waiting. We're just giving her time to outflank us." She started up the next flight of stairs, which ended at the third floor. This level of the old house seemed to be completely disused; dust had settled on the railing and the floor, the carpet was threadbare and quite possibly original, the walls were devoid of pictures or plaques or signs. The landing faced nothing but doors, the heavy old wood dry and cracked, not polished and smooth like the surfaces downstairs; they were all the same size, massive things with carved lintels, and they were all closed except for a slender one to the immediate left of the stairs. That one was plain and unadorned, and it was ajar. It had a deadbolt on it, but the wood was splintered where the post had once gone in; reminded her of the back door to her kitchen, back in March, after that lunatic had broken in and left her a crow.

She got her fingers behind it and gave it a tug and it creaked outward, revealing narrow, dusty stairs leading up into inky blackness. Paige looked at Simon. In the dim light that reached them from below, his face was pale as milk.

"You want to keep going?" she whispered. Her voice echoed in the stillness.

"It's awfully dark up there," he said. "Maybe we should come back in the morning."

"Morning might be too late," Paige said. "I'm going up." She stepped into the stairwell. It smelled like mildew and old wood. She noticed a switch on her right, and flipped it; after a moment a feeble, ghostly light came timorously to life: dusty, long-disused fluorescent bulbs. They flickered and convulsed, like she was trying to raise them from the dead. Still, they were sufficient to illuminate the vast, chaotic attic into which she was climbing, a vault full of broken furniture, boxes, racks of clothes, a catalogue of the disused and the discarded. She wondered if any of the stuff dated to when the Seldens had lived in the house.

"Henry?" she called softly.

No answer.

The attic was sweltering and oppressive; it felt like it was a hundred degrees up there. She started sweating inside Roland's flannel shirt. At the top of the steps she emerged onto bare floorboards and looked around the cavernous chamber. The roof peaked fifteen feet or so overhead, though it was barely five feet at the walls. The structure was supported by thick columns of old, dark, rough-hewn wood, spaced unevenly around the attic. The column nearest her had a length of hospital strap puddled up at its base. She knelt down and examined it more closely. It had been knotted at the back, but seemed to have been severed with a sharp blade.

Somehow, she didn't think that cutting edge had belonged to a knife.

Holding the strap, she stood up and turned to Simon—he had followed her up, as she had known he would—and said, "She had someone tied up here."

Simon nodded, then started snooping through the boxes against the wall on the right. Apparently something there had caught his interest. She started to ask him what he had found, but then the floor creaked behind her and she turned.

Stopped.

Said: "Henry."

He was standing there, looking at her.

From the stairwell she heard a rush of air, a flutter of wings. She snapped her head to look that way, making herself dizzy. A dark shape was roaring into the attic, and for an instant she thought it was a bird, a crow the size of a person; but it wasn't, it was Florence, it was Henry's mother, all dressed in mourning black, with her arms spread wide and fingernails black as soot, curved and bladed.

She felt Henry's hand on her shoulder; he spun her around to face him. From the corner of his mouth he said something; it sounded like *drop*, but in the beating of the wings and the swirling of the wind, she couldn't tell for sure.

Then his fist was coming right at her face.

Simon heard the wings coming and, turning, saw an old woman come soaring out of the stairwell. Had to be the elusive Florence, he thought; and damned if she didn't seem to be flying, she was moving so fast, her legs pumping, shooting her up the steps. Her arms were spread, fingers splayed, each ending in a slice of razor an inch long. She wore a black dress that clung to her gaunt body, the dark color offsetting her sallow, wrinkled skin and the cruel avian mask that was her face.

The apparition swept out of the stairwell and landed on the floor and turned, arms spread like tree limbs, nails chipped and dirty, like a banshee come howling out of a swamp or a ghoul fresh from digging corpses. Simon started to shout a warning, but it froze in his throat as he realized that Henry Fontana was there, and that he was in the process of punching out his wife.

The old woman shrieked, a triumphant caw, and then whirled and lunged at Simon. He stumbled backwards into the pile of boxes he'd been examining. They crashed down around him; papers and books and old newspapers fluttered and tumbled and clattered to the floor. An old pair of tiny leather shoes bounced off his head. What looked like an antique wooden coat rack toppled over and broke into pieces at the divisions. A withered yellow arm shot through the whirl of faded manuscripts and moldering tomes and seized Simon's shirt and dragged him out of it.

"Got you!" Florence said, her voice a cackle, as she lifted him up. He dangled, squirming, in her grip. His shirt dug into his armpits, slid up his back. The old woman drew back her free hand, claws clicking against each other, curvingly wicked, just like the claws that had ripped Roland to pieces.

Henry Fontana shouted: "Ma, stop!"

She looked back at her son, snarling. Simon could see her teeth. They were the color of tea, tiny gravestones protruding from the grey flesh of her gums. "Why?" she said.

"You can't kill the mayor, for God's sake," Henry said.

"*I* didn't vote for him," the old woman said.

"Use your head, Ma," Henry said. "What'll happen when the cops find him? You think Paige didn't tell them what happened on the road? His friend Roland isn't here—you think he'll let you get away with this?"

Roland, Simon thought. They didn't know he was dead. Paige had been right: whatever had been at the house hadn't been Florence. Maybe that would be enough to keep them alive, for a little while at least. They'd bluffed Shockton with Henry; now they could bluff Henry with Roland.

The old woman hesitated. "So I'll kill this Roland person, too," she said. "Whoever he is."

"Okay. What about the police? Will you kill all the police, too?"

She made a frustrated sound, but the claws slipped back into her fingers. Retractable, like a cat's. What the hell *were* these things? "What do we do with him, then?" she said, giving him a little shake.

Simon looked at Henry. He seemed to be considering the question. "Put him down for now," he said at length.

The old woman shook her head. "I can hold him."

"Ma, would you drop him? I can't think with him dangling there."

Florence began to lower her arm, but then Simon's shirt tore and he fell anyway, landing hard on the floorboards. He scuttled away from her, into the toppled heap of boxes, and lay there watching her. Henry watched her too, never taking his gaze from her as he backed up to a nearby wardrobe and rapped on it with his knuckles. "Come on out, Freddie," he said.

After a moment the wardrobe opened; but Frederick Fontana didn't come out of it, a man did, a full-grown man Simon had never seen before, though he *did* look a lot like Paige.

Simon wondered what the deal was with this guy, and decided he probably didn't want to know.

The man from the wardrobe looked at the floor and said: "Mommy!" He dropped to his knees next to Paige and shook her. "Mommy! Wake up!"

"She's all right," Henry said. Simon heard Florence mutter something, but he couldn't tell what. It didn't sound friendly. Henry looked at his mother and said, "I didn't quite catch that, Ma."

She smiled at Henry, gruesomely; the jaundiced skin of her face pulled up in a grimace, shifting pallid stretches of parchment-colored flesh, letting all her discolored biters glisten in the sickly light. "All I said, dear, was that you should let me kill the bitch."

"Enough of that, Ma. Jesus."

Simon's right hand stole through the papers, toward the broken coat rack.

She cocked her head at Henry, evaluating him. It made Simon think of a bird eyeing a worm. "You've got to choose, Henry. Me or her."

The head of the coat rack, that was what Simon wanted, with its curving, pointed ribs of wood. It had snapped a couple feet down from it. He got his hand on the wood, slid along it past the break, gripped it tightly. Like one of those medieval weapons he'd seen at the Renaissance Fair up north, the kind they used to use for bashing people's heads in.

"Ma, would you stop?"

He was losing his cool, Simon thought; she seemed to be goading him deliberately. Then he realized what was happening: she was *testing* him. Finding out if he was really on her side. And Henry didn't realize it, he wasn't playing along, he was going to set her off.

"What do you want her for, anyway?" Florence said. "Just for something to fuck?"

"Ma! For Christ's sake, shut up."

She turned to her son and said: "You ungrateful child. After all I've done for you."

Test over, Simon thought; failing grade for Henry. He tensed, tightened his grip, got ready to move.

"What you've *done* for me?" Henry said. "What you've *done* for me is attack my family, try to kill my wife, kidnap me and my son—"

Florence screeched and leapt at him. And Simon, too, would be jumping to his feet any second now, armed with the top of a coat rack, rushing to help his good friend Henry.

Any second.

The old woman knocked Frederick aside. He stumbled backwards into the wardrobe, knocked it over with a crash. Henry tried to catch her wrists, managed to do it but went down under her charge. She was changing; the claws were out, fully extended, ready for action; ripples were chasing each other up and down her skin, dark pulses and twitches passing just below the surface.

And any second, Simon would get up and race around the mouth of the stairwell, right up behind the old woman. He would sweep the barbed tip of the coat rack at her head, and it would thud into her skull with a thick, hollow, splintery sound, and she would go down in a heap on the spongy attic floor.

He would be doing that. Any moment now.

Then Paige sat up, holding something that looked like an old radio. She raised it up and brought it down two-handed on the back of Florence's head. The radio split open, disgorging a torrent of tubes and wires that cascaded down her shoulders. The old woman made a sound, a frustrated little caw that dragged into a sigh. Paige probably didn't need to, but she whacked Henry's mother again with the broken pieces of the radio; and Florence sagged off to the side, and collapsed.

Henry looked at the broken radio in his wife's hands. "Jesus," he said.

"Are you all right?" Paige said.

"I don't … I'm not sure." he said. He held up his left hand. A livid scar went up the middle, like someone had tried to chop his palm in half. "She *cut* me. She said it would make me like her."

Simon stood up, walked around to them. He was still holding the coat rack. Henry looked at it, then at him. "Were you planning to ever use that?" he said.

"Sorry." He tossed the ersatz weapon aside. He wondered if he was physically shrinking, or if it was strictly mental. "Froze."

Silence. In the quiet, Simon heard someone crying: the guy who was supposedly Frederick Fontana, clambering out of the broken wardrobe, sobbing like a little kid.

"Who's that guy who called me *mommy*?" Paige said.

"Freddie," Henry said.

"*What?*"

"My mother … did something to him," Henry said. He sounded exhausted, Simon thought. "She aged him so she could get younger, or some shit like that. To prove to me that she could do it."

She goggled at him.

"God, I'm tired," Henry said.

Paige went to the wardrobe and helped her son—who now seemed to be older than she was—out of it. He looked a bit banged-up, but didn't seem to be hurt.

"You didn't really punch her," Simon said. It sounded like an accusation as it came out, and he supposed it was, in a way; Henry had scared the hell out of him. Maybe if he hadn't done that, Simon would've been able to act instead of just lying there.

"Stage punch," Henry said. "I told her to drop and she did, thank God."

Simon nudged Florence with his foot. "What are we going to do with her?"

"I don't know," he said.

"Simon," Paige said.

He looked at her. Frederick stood next to her, snuffling. Paige was kneeling beside the smashed wardrobe, reaching inside of it; then she stood up, holding a yellowed newspaper so he could see the front-page headline. It said, *George Selden dedicates Lost Angels Memorial*, and below it was a picture of the stone tablet in the park at the foot of the Pine Ridge Nursing Home.

"I found our past," Paige said.

Paige followed the others as they carried Florence out of the nursing home. Simon held her feet, Henry her hands; she stayed unconscious the whole time, though she twitched and made little noises as they bumped and creaked down the steps. Paige trundled along behind them, holding Freddie's hand and leading him along. He moved with a drunkenly unsteady gait, unused to his long legs and tall body; he was still trying to walk like a five-year-old, but his center of gravity was way off from what it had been a few hours earlier.

They all went out into the warm dimness of the night. In the distance, water splashed through Selden's Falls Park, past the Lost Angels Memorial, on down to the canal where the old church had stood. Henry and Simon carried Florence to the back of the car, while Paige tucked Freddie into the back seat and belted him in.

"Mommy?" Freddie said.

"What, honey?"

"When am I going to be small again?"

"I don't know," Paige said. "We'll figure something out. You stay here, okay?"

"Okay," he said.

She shut the door and went to the others. They had the trunk open; Henry was using long, thick, elastic cords with hooks on the end to truss up his mother, who was lying on the pavement. She watched them for a moment, and then Simon looked at her and said, "They're for holding the trunk shut when there's something big in it."

She knew what they were for. Simon was just babbling. She looked up at the attic and said: "I'm going back in."

"Why?" Henry said.

"To get some of those old newspapers," she said. "See if there's anything that can help us." And, after a moment: "You *know* whatever's going on didn't just start when they knocked down the church. It's got roots. Nelson guessed as much, didn't he, Simon?"

"Yeah," Simon said. "Yeah, he did."

Henry tested the cables. They all looked pretty secure to Paige, but better to take no chances with the thing that used to be her mother-in-law. "Be careful," he said, not looking at her.

"I don't think there are any more like her here," Paige said.

"Probably not," Henry said, "unless you count me."

"You're not like her," Paige said. "You proved that just now. You must get immune to it after the first time. Remember? When you had those cuts on your back?"

Henry only grunted. Simon gave her a worried look, as if to say *Are you sure you're not leaving me with a monster?* She shrugged slightly, then turned and walked back to the nursing home, up the front steps. She paused at the door and looked at the parking lot. In the whitewash of the security lights, she could see Henry and Simon picking up Florence, one at each end, guiding her into the trunk.

How many people ever had to do *that* to their mother?

She went inside, heading for the stairway; but then she stopped, and thought about the Bird Man. He was on the same floor as Florence; she'd seen him at the window on rainy days, staring out into the sky like … like a caged bird.

She knew—*everyone* knew—that he'd been found under the old

church. What had he seen down there? What had happened to him?

And before she could change her mind, she was going into the residential wing of the Pine Ridge Nursing Home, to visit the Bird Man.

The hallways were as still and silent as the administrative offices had been. Florence must have done something to the staff, Paige thought; there should be *someone* around. She didn't know much about the workings of a nursing home, but she didn't think they would leave it so empty. Not unless they had been interfered with.

She came to the room she thought was the Bird Man's. The doorknob had a push-button lock that popped out when she turned it. Paige took a breath and held it, then opened the door and went inside.

The room was dark, but in the moonlight she saw that the window was open. She could hear crickets outside and, faintly, the splashing of the stream through the park. She went into the room. The sheets were rumpled but the bed was empty; the occupant of the room was not currently in evidence. Maybe he was still out there, haunting someone else's night.

The Bird Man's window faced the parking lot. She poked her head out, looked around. Simon was standing near the trunk of the car, arms folded, looking watchful; she couldn't see Henry. The windowsill, six inches or so of rough white concrete, ran the length of the building.

She turned away from the window, went to the dresser, opened the top drawer. It was full of junk, but it was all neatly organized: on the left, string, yarn, twine, a couple extension cords, two light bulbs, a belt; in the middle, wads of tin foil, squashed aluminum cans, bottle caps, silver keys; on the right, jewelry, ranging from the outrageously cosmetic to the tastefully subdued. She scuffed around the accessories and found her locket, which meant the Bird Man had definitely been back since she had encountered him on the hill; he had just gone out again.

She picked up her necklace and slipped it into her pocket and went back to the door, but stopped and then turned as she heard a scraping noise from behind her.

The Bird Man was coming home to roost.

He slid in through the open window, then shut it and went to his dresser. She pressed herself flat against the door and watched as he clicked on the wall lamp, flooding the room with light. He didn't appear to notice her. He just opened the top drawer and began pawing through his baubles and shinies and widgets.

Paige took a deep breath and, trying hard to control her voice, said: "Calvin Trott?"

The Bird Man's head snapped around. His black, nervous eyes looked at her.

"That's who you are, isn't it? Calvin Trott?"

He cocked his head at her, as if wondering who she was talking to.

"I need to know," she said. "Please? Can you talk to me?"

He squawked at her, a quiet little sound, incomprehensible, uncomprehending.

"Remember your wife?" she said. "Remember what happened to her at the old church? Remember the crows?"

The dark eyes narrowed. He remembered. Or maybe he didn't understand a word of it, and he was just tired of hearing her talk at him.

"*Think*, Calvin. Remember?"

After a moment he said: "Jane."

His voice was shrill and rusty; it didn't sound human so much as it sounded like an uneducated parrot learning to speak. But she felt a little thrill shiver through her. *Jane*. As in Jane Trott.

He *was* Calvin.

Then he started coming toward her, his fingers shaped into hooks.

"Jane," he said again.

Uh-oh.

"I'm not Jane, Calvin," she said.

"Jane. Jane." His fingers dug into his shirt, began pulling it open. Buttons popped off and hit the floor and rolled across the tile. His chest was old and sagging and hollow and covered in wispy white hairs, feathery, like down.

"*No*, Calvin. I'm not Jane."

His fingers fumbled with his pants.

Oh, God. He thought she was his dead wife and he wanted to make love to her.

Her hand closed on the doorknob, gave it a twist.

He came at her in a sudden rush. She flung the door open and fell into the hallway and slammed the door in his face. Before he could open it again, she slapped the button with her open hand, locking him in. She lay on the floor, staring at the door, vindicated in her belief that he was Calvin Trott but none the wiser for it. She heard him trying the knob, *click-clack*, *click-clack*, and she realized that he might not be able to get out through the door, but he could always use the window.

Henry's voice startled her: "What are you doing on the floor?"

He was coming up the hallway toward her. She said, "What're you doing here?"

"I was going to help you with the boxes, but you weren't in the attic. I thought you might've gone to Florence's room." He looked at the door as Calvin began beating on it with his fists. "Who's that?"

"Him Tarzan," she said, pulling herself upright. "Me not Jane."

19

THE MORNING SUN, FILTERED TO a bluish orange by the living room curtains, woke Simon up. He sat up on the couch, yawned, stretched. He felt exhausted and sore, as if he'd spent the night dreaming about getting pummeled. He got up and padded to the glowing curtains, pulled them slightly open and looked out; but it wasn't the sun he had been seeing, just a reflection of it, glowing off the windows of the house across the street.

How about that. Even the sun wasn't what it appeared.

He returned to the sofa, sagged into it. After a moment he looked at the shabby heap of cardboard to the left of the coffee table: cartons full of old newspapers and letters and other junk from the attic of the nursing home. None of them had been in any shape to go through the boxes last night, so the old paper that Paige had come up with was still on top of the nearest crate. He picked up the aged piece of newsprint and looked at it closely for the first time. It was dated August 19, 1910; the yellowed photo had George Selden, stern and stiff in a suit and tie and mustache, surrounded by equally stern and stiff men with mustaches and one man in a police officer's uniform, standing in front of a rugged stone tablet inscribed with the words *For All The Lost Angels*.

He hadn't known that George Selden had dedicated the memorial that sat at the bottom of the park, or that it had been carved from what had been intended as the front of his slot in the family crypt; but he *did* know that George Selden had died only a few days after this picture was taken. The date to the right of the dash on his bier was August 22, 1910. That was one of the things he remembered from his visit to the mausoleum, halfway up the hill at St. Peter's cemetery.

Simon wondered if George Selden had known when this picture was taken that he was dying; if the thing that killed him had been slow and lingering, like cancer, or quick and unexpected, like a heart attack. It would make a good story, he thought, if Selden had given up his massive headstone knowing he would be dead soon. It imparted a sort of nobility to the gesture, something not normally associated with the Selden name. Might be worthwhile to give the story to the municipal publicists, turn the park and memorial into a bit more of an attraction than it currently was.

He turned the paper over and read the rest of the article, which explained the history of the Lost Angels Memorial. It seemed that in the late winter, spring, and early summer of 1910, a dozen young women had vanished from the Selden Falls area. Each missing girl was named, along with the date she was last seen; the final disappearance was July 10. A month later, with none of them found, the memorial went up.

The last girl to disappear was Catherine Selden, age seventeen.

Not so noble after all, then. If one of the missing girls hadn't been his daughter, George Selden would probably be resting quite comfortably behind that great big stone, and the only thing in the ravine at the park would be water.

He looked at the boxes again. They were totally out of place in the brightness of the living room; they were relics, they belonged back in the attic from which they'd been taken. But if what was happening now really was somehow rooted in what had happened decades and decades before, this was their only chance to figure out the link, these moldering, fragile, often unreadable documents.

He looked at the article a bit longer, then carefully laid the brittle newspaper on top of the box of clippings and went around past the stairs, down the hall to the bathroom. It was right across from the laundry room, where they had put Florence, which meant that he had to pass within a few yards of the old woman. He imagined he could *feel* her, just beyond the wall, radiating a hostile, destructive aura. Like she was trying to bring the house down on them. Nonsense, probably, but he figured he could be forgiven for it, considering what had happened last night.

When he came out of the bathroom again, he thought maybe he would look in on her and see how she was doing. He touched the shiny doorknob, hesitated, then went to the kitchen and got a big knife from the rack and went back to the door.

He turned the knob.

It came off in his hand; the door fell inward and clattered to the floor and broke into a dozen rotten pieces.

He looked around in shock. This room, this one room, seemed to have aged two hundred years overnight. The wallpaper was peeling, the washer and dryer rusted and brittle-looking. The cot on which they had laid Florence was a mass of sagging, broken aluminum tubes, decrepit stuffing, rotted fiber. Everything was coated with a thin, glistening sheen of slime. The old woman lay in the wreckage, still bound with the bungee cords Henry had put on her last night.

Thank God for the agelessness of nylon, Simon thought.

Florence wasn't looking too good. Her skin had shriveled on her body like shrink-wrap, tightening around every joint, every bone, sallow and sunken and dry as old leaves. Her dress had moldered away, leaving her naked; tufts of black hair littered the mattress beneath her barren head, which was turned to him with an imploring look, a knobby protrusion at the end of a matchstick neck. Only her eyes remained unchanged, black chips hewn from glassy rock. Henry had told them what she'd said, about taking the years; but she seemed to have spent most of her stolen energy destroying the room around her.

His perception about her aura hadn't been so far off after all, apparently.

Her mouth opened and closed rapidly, like a fish gulping for air; except, he thought, she was gulping for *him*, trying to suck his time away, too, like she'd done to Frederick. He backed away, not daring to turn his back on her; and he returned to the living room, where Paige was looking at the paper from 1910. The morning paper—the current one, from today—was on the coffee table; Paige must've gotten it out of the door.

"Your mother-in-law is in bad shape," Simon said, wondering if his voice was as trembly as the rest of him.

She looked over her shoulder at him, then at the picture of George Selden, then back at Simon again. She said: "You look just like him."

He was wondering when she would notice that; Paige noticed everything. "George Selden was my great-grandfather," Simon said. "What are we going to do about—"

"*What?*"

"Don't go getting all goofy over it," he said.

"The great George Selden left an heir?"

"Hardly," Simon said. "He left an illegitimate daughter, who had another daughter, who had me. The first daughter's family moved away when she was six, and the second daughter's family moved back when she was twenty." He shrugged. "If I were an heir I would have gotten some of his money, which I didn't."

"Holy shit," Paige said, smirking; but there wasn't any mirth in it. "I'm in a room with royalty."

"Cut it out," Simon said. "Listen, what are we going to do about Florence?"

"How is she?" Paige said.

"She's not good," Simon said. "I don't know what's going on, if she's trying to tear down your house or what, but she looks like she's about a thousand years old now and the room's all covered with gunk." Pause. "Is Henry awake?"

"No, he's sleeping."

"How's Freddie?"

"Also sleeping. Jesus, Simon, he's older than me and he's got the brain of a five-year-old. What am I going to do about that?"

"I don't know." The mayor sat down on the sofa, glanced at the morning paper; the bottom half was facing up. "Hey, look at this," he said, taking it. There was an article about the Pine Ridge Nursing Home, where the entire night staff had been found locked in the kitchen freezer by the morning shift. He read the high points to Paige.

"Do they know it was Florence who attacked them?" she asked.

"Doesn't say," Simon said. "Nothing about the attic, either, or about Florence being missing. Just that they're being treated for hypothermia, and police are investigating." He lowered the paper. "Wonder why she didn't kill them. She sure was ready to kill me."

Paige shrugged, then said: "Um, Simon, there's a headline you might want to know about."

"There is? What's it say?"

"Mayor's homosexual lover murdered," Paige said.

"*What?*" He flipped the paper around and started reading the article that went with the headline. God, but it was a hatchet job, and full of inaccuracies to boot. For starters, they had Roland killed in his bed, not in the backyard; and they had his throat cut, supposedly with a straight knife; and someone had apparently planted bondage equipment and a book of snuff pictures in the room, or else the paper was simply lying about the police finding such things.

"Shockton," Simon said. "That bastard. He's setting me up."

"Let me *out!*" Florence wailed, her voice thin and shrill from the laundry room.

Paige closed her eyes; Simon kept reading. "I'm wanted for questioning."

"Surprise."

"I wonder why they haven't come here yet. Shockton knows we're together."

"They're waiting," she said. "They can't just show up, they need a reason. Maybe they'll pretend they got an anonymous phone call or something."

Simon slammed the paper down on the coffee table. "I'm amazed they don't have a commentary from Karl Castle about my moral turpitude. That would just be the icing on the cake."

"Maybe tomorrow," she said. "He needs time to write it."

"God damn Shockton," Simon said. "I might as well start packing up my office at city hall right now."

"This is not about the election, Simon," Paige said. "This is about kids dying. It's about Freddie, and Henry, and—"

"Don't lecture me," Simon said. "I swear to God, the last thing I need right now is a lecture, Paige."

"Okay … Simon?"

"What?"

"Why are you carrying a knife?"

"Oh." He'd forgotten he still had it, and put it on top of the paper on the table. "I wanted to be armed when I checked on Florence. Speaking of Florence—"

"Don't," Paige said. "Not yet, okay?"

"She's not going to go away."

"You think I don't know that? Just wait for Henry. Okay?"

"Okay, Paige." Pause. "Want to take a look at the stuff we brought back?"

"Yeah," she said. Then, after a moment: "Yeah, I wanted to show you something." She reached into the sagging crate near her, and pulled out a drawing in a frame made of old, dark wood, with glass across the front. The frame hadn't kept the paper from becoming rippled with moisture, and it was stained across the bottom, but it was mostly legible. Simon recognized what it was immediately: an old map of the city. A date in the lower left-hand corner had fallen victim to the water stain, but it looked like it said 1908.

He took it, held it in his lap so Paige could see it too. "Here's the Selden mansion," Simon said, pointing to a square in the upper left-hand corner. The stream wound nearby, the falls illustrated with great curls of plummeting water and clouds of vapor. Talk about hyperbole. If they had a falls like that, maybe they would have more tourists. Simon traced the river with his finger, tapped the glass front of the map, and said: "Here's where it goes into the canal now." The canal itself did not appear on the map, but there was a faint double line cutting the map into two sections, and tiny writing that may have said *proposed waterway*. George Selden, he knew, had been instrumental in getting that canal built, though his role had largely been behind the scenes. He'd wanted to be able to float merchandise from his fabric mill down to the main canal, and then to the Great Lakes or down to New York City.

River Street ran alongside the stream for several miles, then curved away and up toward the mansion. He scrutinized the area around River Street; a large section of land was marked off with a dashed line, and at the edge of that quadrangle a tiny scratch of a road snaked around to the front of the field, ending at several buildings. They were labeled: *House*; *Barn*; *Stable*.

Paige said, "It must've been nice to live when buildings on a map were individually labeled."

"Yeah," Simon said absently. "And when there were no antibiotics and everyone had seventeen kids and most of them died before they were eight." Simon put his finger on the quadrangle. "This is it. This is where the old church was. Quentin's development is right across the way from here."

"Are you sure?"

"Yeah." He touched the bounded area. "This is mostly swamp

now. It's where Henry's car went in. See how this little stream used to go through it? The canal changed the water dynamics. Turned it into a wetland."

"That all used to be a farm?"

"Looks like it." Simon squinted at the map, held it up to the light. "Yeah. Look, it says so. It's a farm."

"Does it say who owned it?"

"Not sure," he said. "What's this say? Haller?"

"No, I don't think so. Looks like Teller, maybe?"

"Yeah." He lowered the map. "Teller, Teller … I know that name."

"From where?"

"Let me think," he said. He looked at the map again. He looked, and looked, and saw a tiny thread of road leading up into the hills on the opposite side of the map from the mansion. Chicken Hill Road. It ran right past the farm, but now that stretch of it was called Marsh Road instead, because of the bog.

Chicken Hill Road. That rang a bell, too.

He saw movement out of the corner of his eye: Henry coming down the stairs, he thought, fixated on trying to remember. Teller, Chicken Hill Road … they were related somehow, weren't they?

Weren't they?

The Farmhouse. That was it.

"Quentin is staying at a bed and breakfast run by people named Teller," Simon said. "It's called the Farmhouse and it's on Chicken Hill Road. That can't be a coincidence, can it?"

Paige shrugged, and said: "Do you think they're involved?"

"I don't know." Simon glanced at the stairs, expecting to see Henry, and said: "Henry, do you think—"

The words got tangled up in his throat, and choked him.

It wasn't Henry.

It was Florence.

She was leaning up against the banister at the bottom of the stairway, her yellow, black-nailed fingers clutching the wood. Her back was heaving with labored breath. She pushed herself away from the banister after a moment, staggered into the breakfast nook in the alcove between the stairs and the swinging door to the kitchen. She steadied herself against the table there, bony hands clutching the wood, talons digging into the veneer. She was stark naked, a hairless, jaundiced stick figure, hollow chest expanding and contracting, thick spit dribbling from the corner of her mouth, coal-black eyes staring at them with undisguised hunger.

"Oh my God," Paige said.

Simon went for the knife.

Florence lunged at him.

He wouldn't have thought she had it in her to strike that quickly, from her performance getting to the breakfast nook; but it must have been just that, a performance, because she moved like lightning, fell on Simon with a little shriek, an urgent need written on her face. She dove over the couch at him, knocked him to the floor and upended the coffee table, rolled with him across the carpet. He hadn't even gotten close to the knife.

Simon fought her, but she had uncanny strength and speed, born of desperation or whatever ungodly power it was that kept her alive. It was only a matter of seconds before her nails would score, and then—

And then Paige appeared beside them, and she had the knife, and she slammed it right into the old woman's back. Her body was so narrow that the blade ran her through, the point popping out from between her shriveled breasts. Florence made a sort of gurgling sound, backed off a hair; Simon shoved her and she went stumbling backwards, reeling off-balance, right into the table in the breakfast nook. It hit her in the small of her back.

With a sound like branches snapping, she broke nearly in half.

Paige pulled Simon to his feet, but he didn't look at her; he stared, aghast, at what had happened to the old woman. The top part of Florence's body was flat on the tabletop, but her legs and lower torso were still standing erect. Her arms waved frantically through the air, scrabbling at nothing.

Simon's side itched terribly. She had gotten with her claws. Paige wasn't looking at him, but at the old woman, so he tucked his shirt back in—it was black, it wouldn't show the blood—and said nothing. If it turned him into something like the old woman, so be it. Maybe it would be for the better. Give him more of a fighting chance against these things.

"Jesus Christ!"

He and Paige both looked at the stairs, where Henry stood, staring at the creature that had been his mother. The old woman heard his voice and craned her head, lolling on her crinkled neck, to see him. "Henry?" she rasped. "Henry?"

"I'm here, Ma," he said. His voice was shaky.

"I can't move, Henry," she said. "Help me."

Paige said, "She attacked Simon. He pushed her into the table and I guess … I guess her spine broke." Her voice sounded just as unsteady as Henry's.

Henry stood there a moment, then picked up one of the pillows Simon had slept on and brought it to the table. Florence's thrashing arms stilled at his approach, and she said, "There's my baby. There's my—"

He pressed the pillow down on her face.

She didn't struggle; maybe she didn't have the strength, or maybe she welcomed the release he was giving her. Henry stayed there for a very long time, pressing on the cushion; and when he finally let go of it he left it on her face and stepped away from the table, trembling all over.

"Rest in peace, Ma," he said.

Quentin Farmer went down to breakfast, just like things were normal.

Tom and Raye Teller seemed startled to see him; he had expected that, of course, and he was ready for their questions, answering with the story that Paul Shockton and Jasper Shoemaker had cooked up. He explained to them about Nelson's drug problem, at which they nodded their heads and clucked their tongues and said yes, they read about it in the paper. What a shame, he seemed like a nice man; and Quentin said he was, before he started snorting his paycheck.

He noticed the morning paper on the table, and started reading it while he waited for his scrambled eggs. The headline about Simon grabbed and held his attention. It certainly looked like the mayor was in trouble; this wasn't going to go over too well with the voters. The big, splashy story about the violent murder of Simon's lover had even pushed the article about Nelson onto an inside page and had shrunk it to the size of a postage stamp.

After finishing the article about Simon, he read the one about Nelson: how he had been found under the bridge, how tests had indicated the presence of cocaine metabolites in his system. As the story developed, it was going to reveal that he was being investigated in connection with the murders; at least, that had been the plan. Maybe there had been another decision, one Quentin wasn't aware of.

"Here's your eggs, Mr. Farmer," Tom said, sliding a plate in front of him. Quentin put down the paper and picked up his fork. Tom continued to lurk near the table, although Raye had disappeared to somewhere; after a moment he said, "Shame about Mr. Nelson."

"Mr. DeGrace," Quentin said. "Nelson was his first name."

"That's right, I always forgot." Tom licked his lips. "I wonder, ah, if you heard anything about the condition of the body."

Quentin shrugged. "Not really," he said. "I mean, he *did* get run over by a truck, so he can't be in that good shape. Why?"

"Well, it just seems to me that, you know, like that boy they found," Tom said; and he didn't say any more, as if that sentence had made sense.

"I don't know what you're getting at," Quentin said. "Can I finish eating before we discuss this?"

"Oh, sure," Tom said. He retreated back to the stove. Quentin continued eating and reading, and then his little cellular phone burbled. Quentin took out the phone and flipped it open and said, "Hello?"

"Is this Quentin Farmer?"

A woman's voice. Women never called him on his cellular phone, and rarely on his regular phone, either. "Yes," he said. "Who's this?"

"I'd like to arrange a meeting."

"Who is this?"

"I want to talk about your assistant."

"Are you from the paper?" he asked.

"I know what you've been doing," she said.

Quentin found that he had no response to this.

"Hello?" the caller said.

Quentin said: "Who *is* this?"

"Meet me in Selden's Falls Park in two hours," she said, "at the Lost Angels Memorial." She hung up.

He looked at the phone. Back to the memorial, huh? Maybe he was in for another go-round with the blackmailers, although as far as he knew a woman hadn't been involved.

Well, she would find out that he couldn't be trifled with. He had powerful friends.

He left his eggs on the table and went upstairs to call Paul Shockton.

After Florence had been still for several minutes, Henry went back to her side lifted the pillow from her face. Where she had breathed into it the fabric was yellowed, the pattern faded; in her death throes she had sucked the time away from it. It was a fascinating, frightening power, and Henry was afraid he was going to come down with it. Despite what Paige had said about immunity, he wasn't at all sure that this was the sort of thing that you could have antibodies for.

"*Now* what are we going to do with her?" Paige asked.

"Well, we can't take her anywhere, that's for sure," Henry said. She looked like one of those thousand-year-old bodies found buried in the dry desert sand or frozen under a glacier high in the mountains. They'd never be able to explain her condition, short of saying they'd had her in a dehydrator in the basement.

"You could bury her in your yard," Simon suggested.

"Yeah, I guess we can do that," Henry said. But when he went to pick her up, she fell to pieces in his hands, leathery skin and brittle bone and desiccated internal workings all spilling into a heap on the floor. He was left holding scraps of flesh and bone that crumbled like chalk in his grip. Florence's wrinkled, hairless head lay on its side on top of the heap, staring with sightless anthracite eyes across the room.

Henry successfully contained an urge to vomit, but only barely.

Not saying a word, Paige went into the kitchen; she emerged a moment later with a garbage bag, a dustpan, and a broom. She handed the broom to Henry and held the dustpan; Simon held the bag open. Both of them looked at the ceiling as he swept up his mother's remains.

After they were done, and the bag was tied shut, it felt like it weighed less than twenty pounds. Paige came with him when he carried it out of the house. They laid it inside the shed at the edge of the woods. Henry picked up a shovel, but Paige said: "Not now. We can do that later." And he put the shovel down again, and he stood inside the little wooden shed in the already-stifling heat, and he looked at the plastic bag at his feet. That was his mother in there. A pile of scraps, that's what she had turned into; he didn't have any tears for her, and he wondered why.

"Should we say something?" Paige said.

Henry shrugged. "Don't know what."

She stood there a moment longer, then stepped out of the shed. He joined her after a few minutes. He held up his hand and they both looked at it; the red slash was still there, jagged, cutting through the lines of his palm. He knew one of them was called the life line; he didn't know which. Didn't matter. The scar went through all of them.

They walked back to the house, still not speaking. What did you say, after your mother had crumbled to pieces on the dining room floor?

When they got back to the living room, Simon was gone. Freddie had come down while they were out, though; he was sitting in front of the television set, blowing away aliens and cursing every time one of them hit him.

Paige went to the front door and looked out. "Simon's car is gone," she said.

Freddie said: "The buttons are too small."

Paige closed the front door. "What now?" Henry said.

She watched their son for a little while, then looked at Henry and said: "How about a drive up Chicken Hill Road?"

When Simon left the Fontana house, he took the morning paper and left it face-up on the passenger seat of his car so he could look at the headline and keep his anger stoked. It was the only thing keeping him going, really; his supply of courage had run out quite a while ago, and his instinct for self-preservation was screaming at him to blow town, fast. So the only thing keeping him here, driving him on, was fury: over Roland's murder, Shockton's betrayal, the tawdry story in the paper, the sleazy campaign attacks that Karl Castle was sure to come up with in response to the whole situation.

Wanted for questioning. Ha. Wanted for railroading, more likely.

He'd intended to go up into the hills and pay a visit to the Farmhouse bed and breakfast, but after driving for some time he realized that, perhaps subconsciously, he had been heading for the site across the canal from the plaza, the place where the Teller farm had been. So maybe his subconscious knew something he didn't; maybe that was where he had to go.

He didn't need to be recognized and picked up by the police, though. As he entered the city proper, he slipped on a pair of sunglasses that had belonged to Roland. They were black as pitch; maybe they would help disguise him, at least a little. Roland had forgotten them in the glove compartment a few weekends ago, when they had gone to the beach. One last favor, from him to Simon.

He stopped at a light at the foot of the hill. The cross street, Johnson Strip, was major but not very busy yet. Too early for the morning rush. Only a couple of cars went by; none of the drivers even glanced his way. The light turned green and he went on through, following the curve of Marsh Road, past Canal Plaza. He had no idea what he was going to do once he got to the little park. He'd been thinking, and thinking, and hadn't been able to come up with any plausible method for avenging Roland and getting out from under the rap at the same time. It was especially hard since he didn't even know who had killed him; it wasn't Shockton, it wasn't Florence, it wasn't Paige's mysterious Bird Man. Someone else was involved; but who?

He finally reached the gravel road—Bulldozer Boulevard, they called it, in memory of that trailblazing piece of equipment—which led to the spot where the old church had stood. He slowed to a crawl, debating what to do. He really shouldn't go down there, he knew; the police weren't done with the site, there was a sign right at the entrance that said *Restricted area, authorized vehicles only*. Didn't include him, he was sure.

On the other hand, he *was* the mayor.

He started down the long, grey road, to where it had all begun. Right through that copse of trees, where the old church had stood at the edge of the field—

A realization struck him just then, struck him so hard it made him stomp on the brake. The car jerked to a halt; gravel slid beneath the tires.

Who had said it was a church?

He had to think about this very, very carefully. It had been months and months ago, and it had all gotten very confused, what with Jane Trott talking to spirits and Henry getting run over and gunfire across the water. But *who had said it was a church?*

He honestly couldn't remember. Everyone had just sort of assumed. Even after he'd seen the map showing the little cluster of buildings on the Teller farm, he had still been thinking the place was a church, it was so ingrained by now.

But … what if it wasn't?

He started driving again, rumbled along the gravel, hearing bits of it spit against his wheel wells. The land down here belonged to the city; from what he had found out during his initial research back in March, it had been George Selden's property and had gone to the state after he'd died with no heirs; the state, having no use for it, had ceded it to Selden Falls. Simon wondered how crafty old George had acquired it in the two years between 1908—the date on the map, when it had still belonged to the Teller family—and 1910. He had a sneaking suspicion that the rightful owners had been shafted out of it. For all his gilded philanthropy, George Selden had been quite the shark.

But however it all had come to belong to the city—the old building, the access road, the mound of earth that was supposed to be a bank of blossoms, the trees and the swamp and the bodies they dug out of the ground—it was theirs now; and they hadn't even known what it was or where it had come from.

It wasn't a church.

It was the Teller family's damn barn, that's what it was. There had been no masses there; there had been no weddings, there had been no funerals. No faithful flock of worshipers.

That didn't mean, though, that there had been no *rituals*. Did it?

Simon parked behind the wall of flowers, hoping his car would be pretty much out of sight. The embankment was built up against a terraced wall of bricks, like steps, rising fifteen feet out of the ground. He'd been hoping to make a proper park out of it; needed more landscaping, sure, but that could be done. Just look how Farmer had worked the earth like across the water. Tax revenues from the plaza would cover the expense of putting in a more extensive flower garden, and benches, and a footbridge across the canal to the promenade on the other side. Maybe move the Lost Angels memorial over, since nobody went to Selden's Falls Park anymore.

None of that was going to happen now, he thought; he was finished as the mayor of Selden Falls. Besides, if Nelson was right, he was standing on cursed ground anyway. What kind of a park could you build on cursed ground?

He didn't know what he was looking for, but he got out of the car and stood next to the wall of clay blocks. It looked like they hadn't been properly mortared together; there was already leakage from between the bricks, brown streaks and residue left by dirty water. The hole under the old barn had been filled in with a couple of tons of dirt and stone, and this flower bank had been constructed on top of it; but like the structure it had replaced, it seemed to be falling apart.

He touched the warm, damp wall. It seemed to hum slightly under his fingers and he took his hand away, startled. He hesitated, touched it again. There was a definite tingle of power there, a faint electrical current. He flattened his palm on the brick, and was overwhelmed by a sudden rush of images; he plunged into them like a cliff diver into the sea.

The forest around him had vanished; he was stood at the edge of a neat, trim barn, but it was translucent, shimmery at the edges. He could see through it, see other structures nearby: a farmhouse straight ahead, with a well beside it; a smallish stable off to the left; a series of silos alongside the barn. Off to the right, where the canal and the plaza were now, there was only grassy field; he could see a small cemetery, narrow tombstones the color of ivory ringed by black iron fencing, off in the distance, about where the I-90 bridge went over the waterway. The Teller family plot, he thought. Back along the dirt road where Henry's car had gone into the swamp, corn waved in a summer breeze.

Only the sky remained unchanged; it was bright and clear and blue, just like the sky that had been above him before he'd touched the flower wall; but as he looked up at it, he saw that something was creeping through the sky, bruising the azure: a stain of darkness in the shape of a gigantic bird. Circling, circling; coming to rest above the barn, hovering there, just like he'd imagined back in March when he had ventured into the place in search of Jane Trott. The thing hung in space directly over his head, flapping its broad black wings, surveying the area with fat, cruel eyes; and the air was filled up with its thrum and flutter.

Then it was gone, and the sky was clear again, and Simon was lying in a heap some distance from the flowers, as if he'd been thrown by a great shock. He stayed still a little while, until the tingle left his arms and legs; then he staggered to his feet, feeling worn out and groggy, as if he'd awakened from a night of short, nightmare-haunted sleep.

The farmhouse. He had seen where the farmhouse was; he needed to go there, to see if his vision had been true. He had to *know*.

He started into the woods, toward the site of the explosion that had blown Nick Garson's body into the canal. The well had been next to the house; if he found the one, he should find the other. At the edge of the clearing he stopped and looked back at the wall, and hesitated, eyeing the pattern of muddy whorls on the back of the flower bank.

From where he stood, it looked like a gigantic caricature of a vast black bird.

Something had come here when the Tellers had still owned the place, settled in and made itself at home; Jane Trott had been right, knocking down the old barn had produced a backlash. He doubted, though, that things had turned out the way Jane had feared they would. He wished she were still here, so they could discuss it; but she wasn't, was she? She was the thing's first victim in the modern era.

Who would be the last?

He turned away from the wall, pushed into the trees. The cops had made quite a mess out of the place, smashing through the forest with their heavy equipment to create paths. The power company still had some digging equipment on the site, the big Eastern Electric logo— interlocking white and black *E*s—spray-painted on the sides. He wondered if they were done removing the old gas lines. The power company had found the other bodies, he remembered; the old ones that had been shot in the head.

Members of the Teller family, executed like gangsters? Who would've done that? George Selden, maybe?

He passed the spot where the corpses had been discovered. It had been excavated into a pit, twenty feet across, ten feet deep, surrounded by orange plastic fence and police tape. He went over to it, looked inside. Empty. Just dirt and the corroding remains of pipework, running lengthwise along the floor of the hole. The gas line.

He kept going, and soon reached the site of the explosion. He had seen pictures of it, of course, both in the paper and at his office when Shockton had brought them around; somehow he had thought the damage was worse. Looking at it first-hand, it didn't seem too bad. He knew what had happened; he had a report in his office somewhere. Nick Garson had fallen down a well; the well was somehow full of natural gas—leaking pipeline, the power company said—and when a live firework had fallen down it, *boom*! The explosion destroyed the well and it had collapsed onto itself, smothering the fire, leaving the small crater beside which he now stood, a conical depression leading to a hole that went down maybe five feet before being blocked by rocks and dirt. This was also cordoned off by orange plastic mesh, but it didn't look like there had been any activity here for a few days.

He circled around the pit, eyeing it; his foot kicked something hard and it clanked metallically. He knelt and picked it up; it was an iron wheel, like from a valve, blown out of shape by the force of the explosion. He turned it this way and that, wondering where it had come from.

Behind him, through the trees, he heard a car door slam.

Had to be the police; *had* to be. Who else would come down here? He dropped the wheel and moved quickly away from the well, away from the ersatz park, farther into the woods. The farmhouse had to be here somewhere. Scrub branches tugged at him, begging him to stay, scratching at him bitterly when he pushed on through. He couldn't hear anything but the vehicles on the interstate and his own crunching progress through the brambles, and the foundation was so overgrown with vines and weeds that he tripped over it.

Simon fell headlong into a soggy depression that had once been a building. He caught his arm in a thorn bush and it raked his skin, raising tiny bleeding lines. He rolled over and sat up, back against the moist flaky concrete. He smelled dirt and decay; it rose from all around him, up from the ground itself, as if the old Teller farmhouse was made of flesh and was rotting around him, like the tree in the barn the first time he'd suffered a vision.

This confirmed it; what he'd seen when he'd touched the wall—his second vision—had been accurate. He got back to his feet. Still no sound of pursuit; they were probably searching his car first, calling in the plate, identifying it. He crossed to the other side of the foundation, climbed out, kept going.

The farmhouse had been about where he'd thought it was; somewhere nearby, too, there must be the ruins of a stable; somewhere were the graves of the Teller dead. He was beginning to think he knew what had happened here, all those years ago. George Selden had stolen the land somehow; maybe he had had the Tellers killed, bullets in their heads, bang bang bang. Eighty years later, the phantoms had been disturbed, and were exacting revenge on him, Simon Jones, the last of the Seldens. After all, hadn't they said that name, over and over again, when he'd been in the barn?

And now he was in the heart of their territory. How long was he going to last before he ended up like Jane, or Nelson, or Calvin?

Before long, he reached the bank of the canal, right next to the vast grassy embankment that lifted I-90 up above the ground and sent it arching across the water. A hundred yards or so to his right, Quentin Farmer's plaza squatted on the other side of the canal, the three tiers stacked one above the other like the stepped levels of an ancient seaside village. A boat was tied up to the promenade, motionless in the still water. A few shoppers wandered the white concrete, peering into canal-level stores. He noticed a security guard on patrol, a big flabby guy, strutting around the promenade: Jasper Shoemaker. Simon had seen him during the grand opening, but hadn't realized he was actually an employee of the place.

God, that seemed like decades ago.

He moved left, under the bridge, out of the sun. The air was already starting to steam up. The day was rapidly achieving a *small-bathroom-after-a-hot-shower* type of atmosphere, but it was cooler under the overpass, on the dirt, than it had been out in the sun on the slanted, cracked grey rocks of the bank.

He climbed to the top of the earthen slope, up to the concrete bridge piling. He jumped up onto the cement and pressed himself back into the corner. And then he noticed that, of course, a trail of gouged footprints in the earth led right up to him.

Oh, yeah, he thought; good hiding place.

The girders, close above him, seemed to have a lip wide enough for him to perch on. He hesitated, then pulled himself up among them, hoisting himself onto the narrow ledge of steel running across the canal. It was stifling hot between the I-beams, warmth from the highway radiating down through the surface over his head, running through the girders that surrounded him; it stunk of tar and sand and metal.

He began shuffling forward, out over the canal.

Halfway out, he heard a disturbance from below, bubbling and hissing, as if the canal were boiling. He paused where he was, clinging to an angle iron, and looked down the twenty or thirty feet to the roiling surface of the water. The dark liquid was churning, steaming, a witch's brew of rainbow-colored gasoline, dirty foam, bits of flotsam. If he fell into it, he wondered, would it cook him?

Then something erupted from the water, floated in the midst of the turmoil, bobbing left and right but seemingly fixed in its position directly beneath his feet.

A tombstone, floating face-up, so he could read it. It was remarkably well-preserved, in much better shape than the cracked, stained, blackened stumps that years of sun and snow and acid rain produced in the old cemeteries of upstate New York.

Efrem Teller. Born 1804; died 1842.

He clung to the girder, frozen, staring down at the spectacle; and shortly another marker appeared to bob beside the first. Another Teller, even older than the first. And another; and another; and another. Before long there was a veritable graveyard floating in the water below his perch. The rising vapors from the churning water gathered beneath the bridge; a stench like rotten cedar filled his nostrils, made him light-headed. He closed his eyes, gripped the angle-iron, gulped the foul air.

Slowly, slowly, he began to move again, toward the plaza side of the canal.

He felt presences around him, things, spirits, plucking at him with sharp little fingers, like bird's feet. He ignored them, he held on tight, he kept going without daring to open his eyes for fear of what he might see swirling around him.

He didn't know how far he'd gone before they finally went away, left him alone; but when he opened his eyes, he was at the end of the girder, at the opposite side from where he'd started. Somehow he had made it across. Sweating and exhausted, wrists and ankles throbbing, he swung down off the girder; just before dropping out completely, though, he noticed a pistol lying on the lip of steel. The missing gun, he realized; it must have been sitting there since March. He picked it up and brought it with him to the concrete bulwark. Lying on his side in the shadows, he weighed the thing in his hand. Heavy. He found what he thought was the safety; it seemed to be on, so he tucked the gun into the pocket of his pants. They were actually Henry's pants, and were somewhat big on him, but they had nice deep pockets for holding wallets and keys and, as it turned out, weapons.

He eyed the surface of the canal. Perfectly still; perfectly calm. No tombstones, no slabs of rock floating, impossibly, on its surface.

Across the canal, a police officer stood at the edge of the brush, not far from where Simon had come out of the forest. Simon crushed himself against the wall of the abutment, scarcely breathing, watching as the cop stood there on the cracked and tilted flagstones, staring across the water with obsidian eyes. After a moment the man produced a cigarette from somewhere, lit it, and took a few drags. Then he took it out of his mouth, flicked it into the canal, and disappeared back into the forest.

Simon exhaled the breath he'd been holding.

Then he heard grunting, heavy breath nearby; and a moment later Jasper Shoemaker's head appeared only inches from his hiding place. The big man looked right at him and said, "Hello, Mr. Mayor. Comfortable?"

Quentin parked the Jaguar in the same spot he'd put it the last time he came to Selden's Falls Park, the day they had caught the clowns who stole his computer. He checked his watch: nine o'clock. He was a little early for his rendezvous with the unidentified caller. There weren't any other cars in the lot; maybe she wasn't here yet, or maybe she was hiking in from elsewhere.

He got out of the car, wandered over to the information kiosk at the mouth of the trail. There were pictures and descriptions of the flowers that were in bloom; he looked at the photos but didn't read the names. He looked at the plaque about the Lost Angels memorial, but all it said was that the monument and the park were dedicated to *everyone's lost angels,* whatever that was supposed to mean. He remembered that Nelson had been interested in the story behind it, but Quentin couldn't care less. Ancient history, irrelevant to present concerns.

He started down the red clay path, past flowers that grew on stalks, flowers that grew on vines, flowers that snaked up trees and poles and trellises. As the path dipped into the ravine the oppressive combination of heat and humidity eased somewhat. He began to hear the sound of the creek splashing over the rocks that had once formed the waterfall; except for the water and the crunch of his own feet, the ravine was silent. No birds, no buzzing insects, as if they all knew something was wrong and didn't want to draw attention to themselves. He followed the curve of the path as it curled along the wall of the ravine. A low stone wall to his left didn't really do anything to prevent a nasty fifteen-foot fall into the swift, narrow stream.

The path branched near the Lost Angels Memorial, one route crossing the gully via a wooden bridge, the other climbing sharply up and out and away through the trees. He took the left branch. The bridge echoed under his feet. He could see the memorial now; no one was there. He walked along the damp clay, crossed another bridge, and then he was at the promontory on which the monolith stood. He looked around. Nobody. Nothing. No sign of Shockton's people, though they were supposed to be around. He sat down on the foot of the memorial, and waited.

And waited.

And waited.

He finally looked at his watch. Nine-forty. She was half an hour late. Maybe the others had already intercepted her; maybe they were eviscerating her in some quiet glade, just out of sight. Well, either way, he didn't think he needed to wait around any longer. He stood up and trudged back out of the ravine. He dropped a quarter in the donations box in the kiosk as he passed; it hit the wooden bottom with a hollow *clunk*.

He got back into the car, started the engine. He waited a little bit longer, then drove out of the parking lot. He hadn't gone very far when he heard a noise from the back seat; but he didn't even get a chance to look over his shoulder before a dark blade slid in from behind him, right against his throat.

A familiar voice—not the woman's, but one that he recognized— said, "Turn right on O'Malley, then left on Upton, then right into the cemetery, or you're a dead man."

* * *

Jasper Shoemaker hauled Simon down from the concrete wall, holding his arm in a painfully firm grip. They marched down to the blacktop path, then up it toward the plaza. Simon let himself be dragged along. He had a sick, crawly feeling in his stomach, like he'd swallowed a bucket of scorpions.

"We weren't sure you would come," Jasper said. "We've been calling you for hours. But here you are."

Simon said nothing; he didn't have any idea what to say, and sort of hoped being quiet would draw more information out of the man. But no; the only other thing he said, as they entered the sparsely-populated promenade, was: "Keep your head down. I don't want you recognized." Simon ignored this instruction, until Jasper did something with the hand that was gripping his arm and nearly knocked him out with a rush of icy agony. He kept his head down after that.

"What do you people *want?*" he said after a moment.

Jasper shrugged a little, but didn't answer. Up the levels of the plaza to the top. They didn't go all the way to the office door; Jasper led him into an alley to the left of the building. The alley was blocked by a chain link fence and gate, but the gate was unlocked and they went through it. Jasper let go of him briefly to attach a chain and padlock. Simon didn't bother to run, although he did contemplate shooting the man in the back of the head. He decided not to, because it didn't seem likely to help his situation any.

Jasper gripped his arm again—not as tightly this time—and they walked along behind the shops, past the big brown garbage bins, the piles of boxes, the refuse. They stopped at a metallic security door near the opposite end. Jasper punched in a code and opened the door and ushered Simon into a narrow blue hallway that smelled like rotting flesh. The air conditioning was running full-blast, sounded like a plane getting ready to take off. Jasper marched Simon up the hall and into a stairwell that smelled even worse than the hallway. The only way to go was down, into a subterranean chamber decked out like a conference room. It was freezing down there, meat-locker cold; frigid air poured from a vent in the ceiling. Despite the low temperature, though, the room stank of decay. The odor stuck to Simon's hair, his clothes, his skin, clinging like a physical thing, a creeping, crawling film of rot settling over him. Shoemaker marched him to the back of the room and sat him down on top of a desk. On the floor nearby was a heap of thick blankets tied up with yellow cord. The smell was strongest back there; whatever it was seemed to come from under the pile.

Simon noticed that an iron eye-hook had been screwed into the desktop, and thought immediately of the black ring Jane Trott had fastened herself to before she'd been killed by crows in what she had thought to be an old church.

"What are you going to do with me?" Simon asked.

"Just sit tight for a little while, Mr. Mayor, and you'll see," Jasper said. He stretched Simon's arm out to the ring and cuffed him to it. Then he produced a long, sharp knife from somewhere, and cut the nylon cords that bound the blankets into a bundle. That done, he pocketed the knife, stood, and said: "Now, if you'll excuse me, I have to get back to work." He turned and ambled out of the conference room, pausing to disconnect and remove the telephone. After the door closed, Simon heard the click of a lock.

Once his captor had departed, Simon examined the ring. It was big, industrial-strength, and it looked to be screwed down tightly. He tried to turn it but it wouldn't budge; they must have used some kind of tool to put it in. He slid off the desk, back onto his feet, arm stretched nearly to its limit; and that was when he noticed that there was a very large crow in the room with him. The conference chamber had fluorescent lights suspended on wires from the ceiling, and the bird was perched on one of them, looking down at him. Inspecting him, apparently. It had white feathers mixed in with the black, giving it a salt-and-pepper appearance, as if it were starting to go grey.

The crow sidled along the fixture to get into a better position for staring at him. The mayor contemplated shooting it, but decided not to waste the ammunition. He would probably miss anyway, and —he suddenly realized—he didn't even know if the gun had bullets in it.

Then he heard heavy fabric rustling. The blankets were twitching. He moved around to the side of the desk, as far from them as he could get. They were shifting around; whatever was beneath them was slowly pulling them off.

He could feel the gun against his hip. His fingers twitched, wanting the weapon in their grip.

The big crow chuckled softly.

A pallid, mottled, flabby arm thrust out from beneath the covers, flopped around, grabbed hold of the blanket and pulled it off, revealing the missing girls. The missing *dead* girls, he thought; because even though they were moving, they couldn't possibly be alive. Not with their half-rotted faces sloughing off the bone, their skin loose and sagging from their limbs and hanging from their shoulders like draped cloaks, their hair falling out in clumps, leaving gaping red patches in their scalps. Their eyes, white and runny like undercooked eggs, searched the room and found him.

"Simon." They said his name in unison, two gurgling, dead voices. "Simon Selden."

Simon *Selden*. So that *was* it. All this time, they'd been after *him*.

The girls started to stand; he didn't know how they did it when they were so decrepit, liquid flesh shifting beneath the bulging sacs of their skin, but they did. The big crow fluttered down, landed on the shoulder of the one on the right, pecked at her neck and swallowed a tiny scrap of putrid flesh. She reached up with a purple-splotched arm and stroked it, as if it were a favored pet.

The gun was in Simon's hand, and he was firing at them.

And it did have bullets in it.

Lots of them.

Quentin drove into the cemetery, following the instructions coming from the back seat. The place was built on a high, steep hill; waste of a potential ski slope, he thought, but what could you expect from a backward town like this? The markers were densest at the bottom and at the summit, with a broad expanse of tombstone-dotted grass between the two areas. Just inside the entrance he had the option to take four or five different roads; his captor guided him to the leftmost fork, which skirted the edge of the graveyard, then turned to the right and began to climb the bluff.

The route to the top was a steep, narrow asphalt track, the angle of ascent reminiscent of the climb before the first big drop of a rollercoaster. An ocean of monuments stretched out below and to the right. Quentin didn't think he'd ever been in such a big cemetery; who would've thought there were so many dead people in Selden Falls?

Getting to the top must be a bitch in winter, Quentin thought, as his Jaguar churned up the road. Maybe there was a back entrance, some other route with a more reasonable incline. He noticed a side road not far ahead, branching off from this one, held up by an ancient-looking bed of enormous earth-toned blocks. A spidery-looking iron fence, rust visible even from this distance, ran along the edge; something so flimsy would offer no resistance to a car on its way over the edge. Shoddy construction, Quentin thought.

His gaze followed the fence to where it ended, up against a crypt that stood at the edge of its own little promontory, overlooking the graves below like a jealous sentinel. It seemed to be made of marble, and had a large, baroque *S* emblazoned on the wall that faced the world. The inlay flashed gold here and there in the light, but mostly it was tarnished and blackened. Decades of neglect had robbed it of its lustre.

He knew, somehow, that they were going to this mausoleum; he knew what family it must belong to. Who else could that initial represent?

When they reached the access road—a ribbon of crushed gravel and earth, a flat surface chiseled into the side of the hill, narrow and pitted and eroded, washed out here and there—the voice from the back seat said, "Turn right." Unsurprised, Quentin complied. The Jaguar ground slowly along the decaying road, bouncing in the potholes and miniature gullies, until they came at length to the mausoleum.

He'd been right; the place *was* marble, with a green copper roof that had leaked pistachio dribbles down the aging walls and cherubic carvings that time had gnawed at in cunning fashion, reducing the angelic hosts to birdlike figures. Crows, perhaps. Behind the crypt the gravel track ballooned out, cutting into the hill, forming a pocket that seemed big enough to turn around in. It had to be; there was nowhere to go but back, nothing but thin iron rails between the cul-de-sac and the drop.

As the Jaguar edged into this space, the voice behind him said: "Stop here."

Quentin put the car in park but left it running.

"What the hell is this about?" he asked, not turning, wondering where Shockton and his people were, if they had followed him or abandoned him.

"Take off your seat belt."

He took off his seat belt.

The blade slid away and his abductor said, "Get out of the car."

Quentin got out of the car. The air was still and heavy, lying over the town like a mattress; a haze spread over the valley that stretched out beneath his vantage point. The sun was bright and hot and stifling, gauzy through the vapor. He moved into the shadow of the mausoleum, out of the glare, and looked back at the car. There was no one in it that he could see; the rear door on the driver's side was open, though. Whoever it was had snuck out of the vehicle.

The dust he'd raised from the gravel road drifted slowly down the hill.

The old iron door of the mausoleum beckoned, and he finally went to it. Written across it in wrought lettering was a name.

Selden.

So he was right, this *was* the Selden family crypt, up here on a perch overlooking the town that bore the man's name. Appropriate place for it, he thought. The door wasn't solid; it was a sort of mesh, a gate, allowing him to see into the mausoleum. Light filtered through narrow windows high up in the stone walls. These small apertures were also barred; Quentin wondered what they were supposed to be keeping in.

Or maybe they were keeping something out.

It didn't look like the crypt got many visitors; the stone floor was thick with dust, as were the biers to either side of a central aisle and, at the back, what looked like a spiral staircase, leading up into the ceiling. The door wasn't very welcoming, anyway; it sported a black iron padlock the size of his fist. Except the padlock was open, just hanging there.

Was that an invitation?

He looked at the car again. Still empty. He looked at the lock. Still open. He lifted it out of the latch and it fell to pieces in his hand, leaving him holding a curve of rusted metal. He dropped it and opened the door, which swung outward, creaking. He stepped inside. It was cooler within the confines of the thick stone walls; the interior smelled of stone and dust. Quentin went to the spiral staircase. Each step was engraved with a name. George Selden, Matilda Selden,

Catherine Selden. Stairway to heaven, he thought.

He heard the iron door creak, looked away from the stairs toward the entrance.

Tom Teller was coming into the mausoleum.

Henry pulled into the parking lot of the Farmhouse bed and breakfast, where Quentin Farmer was staying. He wasn't sure what he thought of this whole idea—that the owners of this place were descendants of the people who had once owned the land across the canal from the new plaza—but it was worth a look. Paige thought so, anyway, and he wasn't going to argue with her about it. Not when they had a thirty-year-old son at home and no clue how to fix him. Any possibility had to be pursued.

Henry got out of his car, shaded his eyes against the high, hazy, broiling sun, and checked the place out: a big square house on lots of land, porch with narrow colonnades, cupola sticking out of the broad roof. Probably had a great view of the valley on clear days. There were a couple of cars in the lot, but Simon's wasn't there. He must've gone somewhere else. Maybe he had left town.

Henry walked to the front door and went inside, finding himself in a cool, dim foyer. Stairs went up from here, and doors opened from every wall. A little reception desk stood in the corner, unmanned, a sign-in book lying open upon it. He leafed through it; it revealed a steady stream of guests, including Quentin Farmer and Nelson DeGrace, who had checked in last Friday.

"Can I help you?"

He glanced at the doorway in the wall to the left of the front entrance. Beyond it was a kitchen; standing in it was a stout little woman in an apron and a flowered dress.

Henry turned away from the book and said: "Raye Teller?"

"Yes."

"I'd like to talk to you and your husband, if I could."

"I'm not married," she said.

"Oh, I'm sorry. The phone book said Tom and Raye Teller—"

"Everyone makes that mistake," she said. "We're brother and sister." Pause. "Are you a salesman?"

"Actually, no. I just wanted to ask you a few questions."

"Are you from the police?"

"No," he said.

After a moment she said: "I'm making a late breakfast for one of our guests. Come into the kitchen if you want to talk to me." She turned and vanished into the other room; Henry followed.

The kitchen was wide and bright and shiny, brass fixtures and lacquered cabinets warmly glowing in the yellow light. Raye Teller had gone to the big stove and was busily mixing ingredients in a large bowl next to it. "So what were your questions?" she said, not looking at him. "Are you reviewing our inn for the paper, maybe?"

"I'm afraid not," Henry said. "I was just wondering if you were the same Tellers who used to have a farm down where the canal is now."

"That was ages ago," she said.

Holy shit, Henry thought. Paige was right. "You had a house, a barn—"

"All the usual farm buildings," she said.

"The building they knocked down just before the plaza was built —"

"Our old barn. That is to say, my father's barn."

Christ, Henry thought. This was too easy. Just like that, everybody's working assumption about the building, shot to hell. Jane Trott's whole crusade was for an old barn. It would be funny, if a dozen people weren't dead over it.

"Well, I guess that's really what I wanted to know. It was just a barn, huh?"

"That's right," she said, stirring harder. "It was *just* a barn, on what was *just* our farm. And after they diverted the stream for the canal and our fields were flooded, our father sold all the buildings and land to George Selden for peanuts. But who cares? It was *just* our farm."

Oops, Henry thought; got to stuff all those worms back into the can. "Why did he sell it for peanuts?"

"He didn't have a choice. He couldn't make a living off it anymore —he tried, believe me he tried, out there building dikes, putting up sandbags, digging trenches. Didn't do any good. He'd work into the night, and come the morning the water would've washed away what he built, or the sandbags would've ruptured. Finally he gave up." She scowled into her pot. "They *said* the flooding was an accident, but my father didn't think so, and neither do I." Pause. "There was a mock auction, right there in the barn, and George Selden was the only bidder. He wanted the land, wouldn't let anyone else buy it. He had a lot of influence back then."

"What did he do with it after he, ah, bought it?"

"Nothing. I think he planned to drain it and build on it—take advantage of the canal, just like our Mr. Farmer—but he died not long after the auction, before he got a chance to start." She didn't say it, but her tone made it evident that she thought an early death was George Selden's just reward for screwing her family out of their property.

Then she leaned over the stove to turn on the burner, and he caught a reflection of her face in the polished chrome. Her eyes were jet black, like chips of obsidian; and her face looked exactly like his mother's had, up there in the attic.

Henry suddenly felt like she had taken that pot of boiling water and whipped it right into his face.

She glanced at him then, all rosy cheeks and eyes of twinkling blue, and said, "Was that all you wanted to know?" And he realized that she could *turn it off*. She could turn it off, or make it so he couldn't see her for what she was, or something. But as she looked at him, her face slowly changed. The friendly smile flattened, withdrew from the eyes, and she said, in a voice hard as the floor he stood on, yet soft as a feather: "You don't *even* want to get into that with me, sir. You don't even."

Her gaze froze him where he was, pinned him to the floor.

A guest came in, and Raye Teller looked at him, and she was back to the well-scrubbed, elderly cherub she had seemed to be. "You slept late today, Mr. Finch," she said. "But I've got pancakes on for you just the same."

"I was out late last night," the man said. "Just couldn't get going today."

Raye glanced at Henry as she said, "Must be the years catching up with you."

Paige lay on her stomach on the couch and watched her thirty-year-old kindergartner play video games, and her thoughts were of Florence and were utterly black. She couldn't believe the bitch had done this to her own grandson. The old woman was lucky she was dead or Paige would've gone into her room and taken her apart, piece by piece, starting with her toes and working her way up.

After a while, Paige said: "Freddie?"

"What?"

"Do you feel okay?"

"Uh-huh."

"Did it hurt?"

"Did what hurt?"

"What Grandma did to you."

"Oh," he said. "A little bit. It made me throw up. She said later she would show me how to do it, so I could get small again." *Blam!* The screen lit up in a halo of destruction as Frederick took out some sort of mother ship. "When is she gonna show me, Mommy?"

"I don't think she will, honey," she said.

"When'll I be small again, then?" he asked. "The other kids'll laugh at me."

He really didn't understand what had happened to him; he thought he could start school in the fall with all his little friends. Thirty-year-old body, six-year-old mind. If he showed up in the elementary school halls and tried to go to nap-time, they'd call the cops.

"I don't know, Freddie," she said. "We'll figure something out."

An enemy fighter appeared on the television, right in the middle of the display, guns blazing. Freddie's imaginary cockpit shattered; the screen turned red and the game began to play a dirge. Frederick dropped the controls. "My fingers are too big!" he shouted; then he started to cry. "This sucks!" He picked up the controller again, fumbled with it, then threw it to the floor and ran upstairs.

Paige rolled onto her back. Poor Frederick. He thought the worst thing was he couldn't play video games very well anymore. It was probably a good thing that he didn't understand the implications of his condition; if he did, he'd probably be a basket case. Florence had shot him right through grammar and high school, college, grad school, landed him at the far side of his twenties, moved his death up a quarter-century.

Bitch.

Jesus, she wished she knew what to do.

Overhead, she heard the floor creaking as Freddie paced around his room, the movements transmitted to the beams and transformed into noise. She couldn't remember the house creaking before. Maybe it was because of what the old woman had done to the timbers in and around the laundry room, aging and weakening them. Damaged the integrity of the structure. Hell, why stop with the family? Destroy the house too.

Paige went to the stairs, started up them. She was going to have to talk with her son, explain what was going on, even though she didn't have any idea how to do it.

A voice from above her said: "Jane."

Paige froze on the steps, hand clenching on the railing. The smell of age and mucous and rot in the air washed down over her, the sharp odor of aged cedar.

She slowly raised her head.

And saw the Bird Man looking down at her from the top of the stairs.

20

Tom Teller carefully closed the wrought iron door behind him, then leaned against it and looked at Quentin with a mournful expression on the pallid mask of his face. In their deep and shadowed sockets, his eyes never budged, never flickered.

Quentin said, "What the hell are *you* doing here?"

"I brought you," he said.

"*You* brought me? You were the one in the car?"

Tom's head moved in a languid nod.

"So, what, Raye was the one on the phone? She called me from the other room?"

"Yep."

"Why?"

"I think you know that, Mr. Farmer."

"Damn it, Tom, what do you think you're dealing with?" Quentin let the power flow through him, let his fingernails grow into talons, let the mask of humanity fall away from his face. "I could rip you to pieces in a second," he said. He heard the thrum of the wings in the sound of his voice. "I could suck the life right out of you."

Tom Teller said: "Parlor tricks. You're nothing but a shadow of me and mine." He waved his hand and a surge of nausea crashed over Quentin, sent him staggering against the tomb to his left. He felt himself wanting to retch, choked it down, acid burning in his throat.

Tom said, very calmly, "That was five years. Give or take."

Quentin looked at Tom with watery eyes, streaming tears pattering onto the dusty old stone. "You're one … one of us?" he whispered, his voice hoarse.

"Hardly," Tom said. "We've been dragged into that swamp before, by a better man than you." Pause. "Didn't I warn you about that place? Didn't I tell you the ground would swallow you up?"

"You never told me a damn thing, Tom. Not a thing."

"Didn't I? Must've been young Nelson, then. But let's not pretend it would have made a difference, Mr. Farmer. You would've gone ahead with your plans no matter what I said. I could've told you about the wings—"

"You know about them?"

"Of course I do," Tom said. "Haven't you been listening to me? For nearly ninety years, I've been hearing them in my dreams. Every damn night. That's why I brought you here. The wings won't come here. Hallowed ground."

"Why *are* we here? Did you bring me here to kill me?"

"Yes," Tom said.

Quentin pushed himself upright. The sick feeling in his stomach was ebbing away, draining like a sink with its drain unstopped. "Then get it the fuck over with," he said.

"Not yet," Tom said. "Because killing you won't solve anything. You're not the one behind it, and that's what I want to know. Who's leading the flock this time? Is it my father? And who's the target?"

"You already told me you were gonna kill me, you dumb old fart, so you can shove your questions up your—"

Tom didn't move or twitch a muscle—evidently the waving of the hand had merely been for effect, to demonstrate that he was doing something—but Quentin crumpled to the floor in a miasma of pain and vertigo. This time he did retch, vomiting up what he had eaten of the eggs he'd been served in Tom's kitchen.

"Waste of good food," Tom said affably, though his eyes were hard as iron. "That was ten years."

When Quentin could see again—when the spots cleared from his eyes, the dizziness from his head—he slowly straightened up. The old dusty crypt now stank of the puke that was puddled at his feet. Tom Teller lounged against the grillwork, completely at ease, like he was standing at the corner store chatting about the weather.

"What the hell do you want from me?" Quentin rasped. "What's all this got to do with your father?"

Tom stood there, motionless, for a long moment; Quentin gritted his teeth, waited for another rush of sickness, another twist in his gut. But then Tom said, "When George Selden took our land and our livelihood all those years ago, Mr. Farmer, my father prayed and prayed and prayed for vengeance. At first he prayed to God, but I guess God wasn't listening; so he started praying to … other things, and finally one of them answered him. He was crazy by then; he gave my mother and my brothers to it, just handed them over, chained them up in the old barn and let it have them. *I* was the one had to bury them, when it was through, and they were looking up at me with their dead eyes, and I swear they could still see me, and cursed me for what my father had done." Tom trailed off, stared at the wall, obviously replaying in his head that scene from nearly a century earlier. After a few seconds he said: "Once it had its blood, that thing came down on the rest of us, came down with wings like a hurricane and *changed* us. Just like someone changed *you*, Mr. Farmer. Who was it?"

Quentin hesitated; he almost said Jasper's name, but didn't. Tom gave him a disappointed look, the kind a teacher might give a favorite pupil who had become disruptive. Quentin sagged back onto George Selden's sepulcher, waited for Tom to wrench a few more years out of him. His heart felt like a shriveled hunk of leather in his chest, his lungs as hard and dry as plaster.

But instead, Tom Teller just leaned against the wrought iron door, folded his arms, watched him for a while. The old man's face was flaccid and expressionless. "I haven't heard those wings outside of my dreams for *eighty years*, Mr. Farmer. Not until the morning you disappeared. I want to know why they came back. I want to know if they brought my father with them."

"I don't know," Quentin said, his voice barely above a whisper.

"I can't hear you," Tom said.

Then Paul Shockton stepped into view just outside the tomb, shadowed eyes and hook nose for all the world like a rubber mask. Quentin almost said something to the police chief, but caught himself before he did. If Tom Teller knew Shockton was here, he would make short work of both of them; he needed to keep the old man occupied until Shockton could make a move.

"You *knew* what was there," Quentin said. His throat was intolerably dry, like it had cotton growing inside it. "Why didn't you *warn* me before I built, for Christ's sake?"

"And you would've listened to an old man's ramblings?" Tom said. "I don't think so, Mr. Farmer. I don't think you would have listened if God himself had come down and told you to build somewhere else."

"You should've tried," Quentin said.

"No," Tom said. "What I *should* have done was kill you. I don't think your company would survive that, would it? But Raye and I promised each other, after the girls, that there'd be no more killing. Not of normals, anyway." Pause. "You're not a normal anymore, Mr. Farmer."

And then Shockton lunged, flung his arm right through the bars. Three black-bladed fingers popped out of Tom Teller's chest. He looked down at them, wide-eyed, slack-jawed; a few seconds later blood began to dribble from his lips, pattering onto his shirt, lost in the greater flow of red pouring from where the fingers wiggled like polyps sprouting from his lungs.

The fingers slipped back into the holes they'd created, and Tom Teller sagged to the floor and lay there like a crumpled piece of paper. Quentin scuttled across to him.

But apparently, even the likes of Tom Teller could die.

Paul pulled the gate open, stepped delicately over the body, closed the gate behind him. He nudged Tom Teller with his foot; the man didn't move. Quentin sat on the cold stone coffin. He wanted to lie down in it and sleep for at least a year.

"You look like shit," Paul said.

"Thank you."

"Don't mention it." Shockton bent over and grabbed Tom's wrists and dragged him to the phony staircase, laid him on the steps, out of sight of the door.

"How'd you find me?" Quentin said. "I didn't see your people, I thought you bailed out on me."

"I had a 'copter in the area. I told you I would keep an eye on you, didn't I?" Paul looked Quentin over. "Are you up to driving?"

"I think so."

Paul gave Tom's body a kick. "So what'd chuckles here want, anyway?"

"He wanted to know what was going on. He said he wanted to know why the wings came back—what they wanted us to do, I mean."

"How the hell would *he* know about the wings?"

"He said his father called them down originally, to get revenge on George Selden for stealing their land. I asked him if he was like us, and he said we were just shadows of him and his."

"Him and his, huh?" Paul said. "So he's saying there's more like him?" Shockton looked at the corpse with a shade more respect and a thoughtful expression. "He wanted to know why the wings came back?"

Quentin nodded, but said nothing; he was too exhausted to do much more talking. His throat felt dry and raw, his limbs felt wobbly. If he didn't rest soon he was going to collapse.

Paul said: "Why'd he decide to come after *you*?"

"I was staying at his inn. The Farmhouse B-and-B."

"Farmhouse, huh? He run it by himself?"

"No," Quentin said, his voice nothing but a whisper now. "His wife runs it too."

Paul Shockton nodded, rubbed his chin. "Him and his." After a moment he said, "Get back to the plaza. There'll be fresh meat soon. You can get your years back, and then some. Let me worry about the old man's wife."

Quentin nodded in dumb gratitude, and shuffled out of the crypt.

Paige stumbled down the stairs as Calvin Trott glided toward her. His bony arms were outstretched, his hawk-like face a rubber mask of desire and confusion, as if he couldn't quite figure out why his wife kept running away from him.

She crashed through the kitchen door, ran straight to the knife rack, pulled out a big vegetable-chopping blade and turned just as the Bird Man came in. He saw her standing there holding the knife and his dark eyes narrowed and he made a quiet little squawking sound, as if to say: *What are you doing, Jane?*

"I'm not your wife, damn it," she said. "Jane is *dead*, Calvin."

He took a hesitant step forward. His gaze seemed torn between her and the knife in her hand.

The *shiny* knife.

She hesitated, then tossed it into the corner. He went after it and she darted out of the kitchen, back through the living room, up the stairs. "Freddie!" she screamed. "Where are you?"

She heard the kitchen door bang open. She paused at the top of the stairs, looked back as Calvin came swarming up after her. He held the knife like a pinwheel, the silver blade pointing straight up into the air; he had also acquired the roll of twine they used to tie up old newspaper into packages for the recycler. Even maddened by confused lust, he was still stealing items for his nest.

She grabbed the marble-topped trestle table from against the wall of the upstairs hallway—the vase of fake flowers slid off, fell to the floor and bounced on the thick pile rug—and flung it at Calvin. His upward momentum left him no chance to evade it and it smashed into him, sent him tumbling down the steps. He clawed at the banister, trying to check his fall, but his nails just left tan streaks in the wood.

With her pursuer out of commission—at least temporarily—she flung open the door to Freddie's room. He wasn't there. The puppy, confined to his pet box since last night, saw her and whined piteously. She spun and darted into the master bedroom; Freddie wasn't there either. The glass door to the balcony was open, though, letting steamy summer air billow in. Sunlight fell in slants across the floor and the foot of the bed.

Behind her, she felt a rush of wind.

She turned just as the Bird Man blew into the room, soundless but for the air he pushed aside. His face was bruised, blood dribbled from a cut across his forehead. He had impaled himself on the kitchen knife during his tumble down the stairs; she could see the handle sticking out of his abdomen, way to the left. Didn't seem to be slowing him down.

He plowed into her, bore her backwards onto the bed. He was trying to kiss her. The knife handle poked her in the hip; he didn't seem to even feel it.

His lips, dry and cold and leathery, brushed hers, then mashed against them. She squirmed beneath him, trying to break the contact, but his hands shot up and gripped her head like the edges of a vise.

His mouth opened, forcing hers to open, too.

She felt the first clammy, sticky bubbles of slime coming out of his throat, dribbling into hers. Salty mucous, gunk like the stuff that had slurped out of the dashboard of their car after it had died by the side of the road. Her stomach heaved, heaved so hard she thought it should be strong enough to knock him right off her, though of course it wasn't, that was just a desperate fantasy as the stuff choked her. She couldn't breath; he had gummed up her nose with snot, her mouth was full of it. He wanted her to swallow, that was it; swallow and breathe and be like him, and even if she didn't she would pass out from lack of air and then it would just slide right down her throat—

Then Frederick grabbed the Bird Man by the back of his neck, lifted him off her, and flung him across the room.

She rolled over onto her stomach, pushed herself to her hands and knees, and spat out the vile glob of gelatinous shit he'd forced into her mouth. The contents of her stomach followed it. The jiggling heap of glistening slime shivered under the acidic vomit, steamed and shook and shriveled away. She could still taste it inside her mouth, down her throat, under her tongue.

She staggered into the bathroom, filled her mouth with the antiseptic mouthwash Henry used, swished it around and around and around and spat it out, tiny threads of mucous spurting along with the tart green liquid. She wiped her face with a towel, repeated the process twice more, unable to think of anything but getting the taste of that shit out of her mouth.

Until she heard a crash from the bedroom.

Christ! She had left Freddie alone with the Bird Man!

She stumbled out of the bathroom. Calvin Trott stood in front of the balcony doors, bleeding from his nose and a split lip. Frederick had taken him by surprise; but he was really just a six-year-old in a body too big for him, he didn't have the coordination or the control he would have needed to put the Bird Man down. Now he was sprawled across the floor right in the wedge of light, uninjured as far as she could see, but the Bird Man had his claws out and looked ready to eviscerate her son.

Paige charged right at him.

She pushed him through the open door, onto the balcony and into the waist-high railing. He pivoted over it, started to fall; but then one hand shot through the opening between two bars and fixed on her ankle. She went down and her leg slid into the gap, all the way to her hip. He ended up swinging from her leg, which felt like it was just about getting pulled apart at the knee.

So there she was, squashed against the railing, Calvin Trott suspended from one of her major limbs, the taste of his disgusting bubbly spit reasserting itself over the fading influence of the mouthwash, her son lying in a semiconscious heap on the bedroom floor. And as if all that weren't bad enough, the door of the woodshed—the shed where the remains of Henry's mother lay—slowly began to open, all on its own.

What the hell was she going to do now?

The part Henry couldn't figure out was why Raye Teller let him go.

After seeing her face in the chrome, after her threat veiled as a good-natured joke with a guest, he had simply walked out of the kitchen, and she didn't make any move to pursue or impede him. He'd gone into the dim front hallway with its smell of wood polish and old carpeting, then out onto the porch, looking into the sunlight of the front lawn. The parking lot with the cars in it seemed pretty distant, down the flower-lined walk of white gravel. An entire world away.

He noticed a cloud of dust rising from the driveway: a car, coming fast. As it approached he could see flashing blue and red lights within the dust.

Police.

Henry slipped off the porch to the right, behind the shrubs, and picked his way along the cool, narrow, leafy corridor to the end of the house. He heard tires scrape on gravel. The police car, stopping. He should jump from the bushes and tell them what he knew about Raye Teller, he thought; but either they already knew or they would think he was crazy.

He suspected they already knew. Paige had told him about Shockton; who knew how many other police officers were affected by this plague?

The bushes ended before the house did. He stopped at the edge, peeked around at the lot. The cops were striding side-by-side to the house, looking straight ahead. Their faces were rubber masks, birds masquerading as humans. When they were out of sight, Henry sprinted the rest of the way to the end of the house. He took the corner, found a window that looked into the kitchen, and peered inside. The guest, Finch, was at the little table eating his breakfast.

Raye was pouring him some coffee.

The cops entered.

Raye and Finch both looked at them. The policemen had their guns out and one of them shouted something. The sound was muffled but Henry could tell it was a command to freeze. Finch looked like he was shitting his pants; but Raye just straightened up, still holding the carafe of coffee, staring straight down the barrels of the two guns.

The cop on the left said something. Finch got up and fled the room, exiting into the interior of the house. The swinging door swished shut behind him.

Raye carefully put the pot of coffee on the table, and as she did so, both cops suddenly doubled over as if struck in the stomach. They crumpled from Henry's view, sagging to the floor behind the table. Raye took a few steps toward them; Henry crept to the back door and cracked it open, just a fraction of an inch, so he could hear what was going on.

Raye said, "Who sent you?"

"Shockton," one of the cops said, his voice strained and stiff, like he was talking through clenched teeth. "Paul Shockton."

"Why?"

No answer.

There was a momentary pause, followed by a shriek that made Henry recoil from the door; he slipped and nearly fell off the stone steps. The scream was high and thin and desperate, and the click of the door closing cut it off. Henry hesitated, not sure he really wanted to be hearing this; then he thought about Freddie, and opened the door again.

Silence.

Then the other cop's voice, quivering: "Don't, not me, please, don't —"

Raye said, calmly: "Then tell me what I want to know."

"I can't, please, I don't know—"

"What did you people do to my brother?"

Henry saw movement from the corner of his eye, fast movement; and in the glass of the door he caught a reflection of a rubber-mask face. The warning gave him just enough time to twist aside as a set of sharp black claws raked through the air only a whisker to his left.

Whoever was behind the sneak attack reversed in mid-swing, so the back of his arm smashed into Henry's shoulder and sent him sprawling across the grass. He rolled and tumbled and ended up on his side looking back the way he'd come; the person who had tried to slash him in the back was coming after him, his face dusky and mottled, knife-sharp nails growing from his fingertips.

"I didn't come here to kill *you*," Paul Shockton said, "and this has to be quick, so just hold still, okay? That's a police order, son."

By the time Simon realized that the gun had gone from producing nice loud *bangs* to empty *clicks*, the two girls had gotten within a few yards of him and were still coming. The crow was chuckling. And the room stank worse than ever from the voluminous fluids that had exploded out of the corpses with each bullet that tore through them.

The desk was between himself and them, but with his movement restricted by the cuffs it was a useless barrier, especially when the girls split up. The one with the crow went right, the other left. With nowhere else to go he climbed onto the desk, but he had to bend over because the handcuff chain left him hardly any play at all. The girls were on either side of him, smiling at him with what was left of their mouths, oozing something thin and vile—he couldn't say it was *blood* —through their wounds, from the bullet holes and the missing bits of flesh that the crow had taken.

With their decaying hands, they reached for him.

Simon flipped the empty gun around and whacked the nearer one on the wrist with it. Her hand just snapped right off and flew across the room, hit the floor with a wet smacking sound and slid away on a layer of goo, fingers twitching like some weird decrepit crab. But the other girl got hold of his belt and started pulling him toward her. He swept the gun into the side of her head; the butt of the weapon broke through her skull like it was no thicker than an eggshell, and when he withdrew it, sticky greenish slime clung to pistol grip, a quivering streamer that grew thinner and thinner as he pulled the weapon away. The girl let go of him and stepped back a pace, her head cocked at an odd angle, as if she couldn't quite figure out what had happened to her brains.

And then the desk was sliding beneath him, shifting, tilting toward the ceiling. The one-handed girl was lifting it up, those decrepit muscles somehow powerful enough to upend the heavy wooden thing with him standing on top of it. He lost his footing and slipped until the handcuff checked his motion, jerked him to a halt with his arm stretched up over his head. He was half-off the desk now, stretched out and exposed.

Wings fluttered near his head; the big crow settled onto his shoulder. It cawed right in his ear, but it didn't peck at him. It seemed content to just sit there and enjoy the show.

The other girl came toward him, still oozing slime from the hole in her head, dead milky eyes lolling in their sockets, mouth half-open and dripping. When she got close enough, he kicked her in the stomach and sent her reeling away. She fell over the close-packed chairs, went down with much crashing and clattering. The crow squawked appreciatively.

The girl holding the desk gave it a tremendous shove and it flipped over all the way, carrying Simon with it. The bird shot away as the heavy piece of furniture came crashing down. It caught on some of the chairs, smashing them to pieces. Simon scrambled to get out from under the thing, but the handcuff chain was too short, leaving his arm underneath it as it tipped sideways and tumbled to the concrete; but the broken chairs kept it partially off the floor, so it didn't snap his arm off at the elbow.

He heard a faint metallic *clank* from under the desk, and his arm came loose. He jerked it out from under the desk. He was still handcuffed to the eyelet, but it had come out of the wood; the impact must have splintered the desktop. He stood, the long iron corkscrew swinging at the other end of the cuff chain. He snatched it into his hand, held it by the head.

Freed from the desk, he ran to the door and tried the knob. It turned, but the door wouldn't budge. Deadbolt. He put his back to it. The corpses were approaching. Their pursuit of him had left them even more decrepit than when they'd started; the horror of their demolished bodies and the miasmic stench of the room made him light-headed. He heard the crow chuckling, but he couldn't see it.

Suddenly there was a *click* from behind him and the door swung into the stairwell. He tumbled out just as the girls closed in on him, ended up lying on his back looking up at Quentin Farmer, who was looking at the corpses with what looked like a mixture of lust and loathing—self-loathing, maybe, if he had any humanity left to him.

Simon jammed the spiral screw into Quentin's leg, gave it a twist, yanked it out. Quentin howled and dropped to one knee and slashed back at him with clawed fingers, but Simon was ready for that and ducked under the swing and scrambled up the stairs. The twisty thing bounced and jingled at the end of its chain.

At the landing he discovered that the door was locked with an electronic keypad, so he scaled the ladder, pushed open the hatch, and emerged onto the roof in the bright, hot sunshine. He slammed the hatch shut, and ran to the facade at the front of the building. Shoppers walked up and down along the sidewalk, chatting with each other, peering into shop windows, totally oblivious to what was going on under their feet.

Behind him, the hatch crashed open.

Simon whirled. Quentin Farmer was there, though he hardly looked like a man at all; his skin was mottled and scaly, his eyes were wide and black and birdlike. The crow was perched on his shoulder, beating its wings and coughing vehemently. Quentin's hooked fingers slid through the pebbles of the roof as he hauled himself out; his tongue flickered over his lips, dry and rubbery and long as a lizard's.

And Simon was armed with nothing but an oversized corkscrew.

As the creature that had once been Quentin Farmer fluttered across the roof toward him, Simon clambered up onto the facade, and jumped.

Paige watched the wooden door of the shed creak open, half-expecting Florence's disembodied head to swirl out in a cloud of dust and worn-out parts. But when the door reached its full extension it just stopped, and a few seconds later a fat, malignant-looking crow hopped out, its head flicking this way and that, from one angle to another.

The Bird Man let go of her; Paige immediately pushed herself away from the railing, scrambled back against the wall of the house. The leg Calvin had been hanging from felt numb and tingly. She rolled onto her side and started crawling toward the door to the bedroom, only a few yards away.

Then the Bird Man swooped up in a gentle arc, a graceful gymnastic leap that defied both gravity and his apparent age. He flipped over the railing and landed softly near the edge of the balcony, oriented on her, and said: "Jane."

"I'm not Jane!" she shrieked. "Get it through your fucking head!"

But he started walking toward her again, toddling across the balcony toward her. She noted that the knife handle was gone; it must have fallen out somewhere along the line, when he'd fallen or when he'd done that leap. It had left a small rent in his shirt, highlighted by a corona of purplish-red blood, turning brown around the edges.

Paige heard the fluttering of wings, saw a fat crow land on the railing; she thought it was the one that had come out of the shed, but she couldn't be sure. It fluffed itself up and stared at her with tiny, beady, hostile eyes. Then the Bird Man got between her and it and cut off her view.

Paige didn't resist this time. She just lay there, limp and acquiescent, as he fell upon her, crawled slowly up her body. He was grunting and panting, and she realized that he might fly through the air like Superman, but he was still an old man, and tired.

Maybe he'd die of a heart attack and save her a lot of bother.

But he didn't die, he kept creeping up until he got right above her face; then he leaned down toward her, bubbles forming on his lips as he generated more of that goo. She lay there, frozen, staring up at him, at the glistening dribbles of slime he was getting ready to belch at her. Her guts felt like oily ribbons.

He opened his mouth.

The bilious stream came pouring out.

She twisted out of the way and the putrid gunk splattered onto the floor of the balcony, a stinking green pool of mucous. He hadn't been using enough pressure to hold her down; he still thought she was his wife, and when she hadn't struggled, he hadn't pinned her.

She'd hoped he would make that mistake.

Paige grabbed the back of the Bird Man's head and slammed it into the puddle he'd created. She clambered around on top of him, straddling his back, holding his face down as he thrashed and flopped beneath her.

The crow squawked and launched itself at her, tearing with its black claws, stabbing with its long black beak. Paige flailed at it ineffectually with her free hand, but then there was a swirl of white and a rustle of fabric, and Freddie was standing in the doorway with the bedroom curtains clutched in both hands. He was holding it like a sack; it vibrated wildly as the crow thrashed around inside it.

"Ha! Good boy, Freddie!" she said. And then she started laughing, a wild, hysterical laugh that came from finally having what looked like the upper hand against these things.

The Bird Man suddenly went still.

Paige stopped cackling, and looked at the back of his head. He was just lying there now. She stayed on him a moment longer, then slowly stood up. Freddie backed off, into the bedroom. His makeshift bag swung and shivered; the crow was fluttering around inside, issuing squawks that were muffled by the heavy fabric. Paige edged toward the sliding door, keeping an eye on Calvin Trott, waiting for him to move, to breathe, to even twitch; but he didn't. He just lay there.

And then he sat up, so quickly she scarcely had time to gasp. He looked at her, his face a morass of puckered flesh and clinging mucous; and in a shallow, gurgly, bewildered voice, he said: "Jane … why?"

Paige sagged against the door frame. "Just go away," she whispered. "Go away, please."

He got shakily to his feet and stood there trembling. Mucous flowed down his cheeks, dribbled down his neck, soaked into his shirt and putrefied it to a rotten brown, though it didn't seem to have any effect on his skin.

He staggered toward her. The captive crow screeched and shivered in the sack.

"I'm not your wife!" Paige shouted.

The Bird Man stopped, cocked his head at her, as if she were a potentially tasty morsel he had found lying on a questionable floor. "You visited me in the hospital," he said.

And there she stood, struck dumb by the simple fact that he had strung words together into a coherent, understandable sentence. "No," she said softly. "I was there. I saw you. But I didn't visit you."

"You … visited me at the … place. The home."

His voice sounded raw, stiff, unused. His throat was more used to making bird noises than human ones, she thought. "No," she said again. "I was there to visit someone else."

"You *talked* to me."

"Yeah," Paige said. "I did. I talked to you. But that doesn't make me Jane."

The Bird Man stared at her.

She stared back.

Downstairs, the doorbell rang.

"I'll get it," Freddie said.

"No you won't!" Paige said, turning away from Calvin. "Put your grand—uh, the crow in the bathroom and stay up here. I'll see who it is." She glanced at Calvin over her shoulder. "You stay up here too."

He said nothing; but he didn't follow her as she left the bedroom, and he didn't come flying down the stairs at her. Those were both improvements; with her recent luck, though, the person at the door would be a cop looking for Simon, and he'd have a search warrant, and he'd find out about all the weird stuff that was going on in her house today. Maybe he'd even find Florence's head out back. Wouldn't that be peachy?

She went to the front door and looked through the peephole.

It wasn't a cop; it was Karl Castle.

What the hell was *he* doing here?

She opened the door. Karl smiled at her. He looked very natty in his three-piece politician's suit; then again, he always managed to look natty, no matter what he was doing. He was the only person she had ever seen operate heavy machinery while wearing a tie, even if it *was* a clip-on.

"Afternoon, Paige," Karl said. "This a bad time?"

"Well, as a matter of fact—"

"Won't take but a minute." He opened the screen door and stepped inside. "I heard you were out to see Simon last night. I hope I can convince you and your husband not to side with Simon. He's on his way out. I'd hate to see my old friends back a losing horse."

Yeah, he'd probably hate that a whole lot, Paige thought. "Well, Karl, this actually *is* kind of a bad time—"

He closed the door behind himself, pushing it shut, still facing her, still smiling.

"Won't you come in," Paige said.

Still facing her, he reached back and locked the door.

"Karl?"

Then he put on the chain.

She began to get an itchy, icy feeling at the bottom of her stomach.

"What's the matter, Paige?" Karl said. "You look nervous."

"What do you want, Karl?"

"I want to be mayor," he said, grinning. Then he said: "More specifically, I want to ruin Simon. I want to humiliate him. I want him to suffer."

"What did Simon ever do to you? Is this all because you didn't get to work on the plaza? Grow up, for Christ's sake."

"It's got nothing to do with the plaza," Karl said. "Not really, anyway. It's got nothing to do with Quentin Farmer, either, except that he's the one writing the checks." Pause. "It's got *everything* to do with the Selden blood flowing through Simon's veins."

Selden blood.

Oh, God.

The lost angels, all those years ago. The disappearances had stopped with George Selden's only daughter. Had all those girls been murdered just so that when it was Catherine Selden's turn, she didn't seem like the specific target?

"I see what you're thinking," Karl said, "but you're wrong. Let me satisfy your curiosity. George Selden did a lot of fucking around. He was one of those macho types, wanted a son, figured if he scattered enough of his seeds around he'd get one. Unfortunately he was scattering nothing but Xs, but what the hell, at least he had a good time. Every one of those girls was a Selden girl, even though they didn't know it. We wiped out the Selden line." Pause. "At least, we thought we did. Somehow, we missed one."

She didn't need to ask what he was talking about, saying *we* did this and *we* did that. Even though Karl hadn't been around eighty years ago, the force or creature that was behind it all had been, and it was speaking through him.

She said: "You killed a dozen innocent girls, and now you're going to kill an innocent man."

"No one with Selden blood is innocent," Karl said. "But if it makes you feel better, we're not going to kill Simon. We're already confident he's not going to reproduce, so we don't need to kill him, but he might wish we did by the time we're done with him." He ran a hand through his tufted black hair. "I went up to his house last night to kill Roland, not Simon—don't think I couldn't have gotten around that sunroof if I wanted to—and just imagine my surprise to find not one freelancer, but two. What's up with the old lady, Paige? I'm not worried about the old man—him I know about, he's nothing to me—but the woman took me by surprise. Who is she?"

"My mother-in-law," Paige said.

Karl laughed. "Oh, that's rich! Your *mother-in-law*? Talk about taking the old stereotype to an extreme!" After he stopped chuckling, he said: "I know you brought her here. Where is she?"

"She's dead," Paige said.

"Is she? Good, saves me some trouble."

He wasn't here just to find out about Florence, Paige knew; he was here to eliminate a potential threat to his scheme to bring down Simon. Still, she said: "Is that all you wanted?"

"You know the answer to that, I'm afraid," he said. A shiver passed over him. His features, skin and eyes and hair, began to darken. He began to sprout tiny, wispy, downy black feathers. "I need to kill you and Henry and your little boy. It isn't anything personal, you understand. Nothing to do with revenge. I won't make you suffer."

With a faint, wet, mucky sound, his fingernails elongated and blackened into wickedly curved hooks. He was turning into the creature that had killed Roland; ever so much faster, ever so much more dangerous, than the Bird Man she had left upstairs.

He took a step forward. "All I'll do," he said, in a voice that barely clung to intelligibility, "is make you keep quiet."

Henry scrambled to his feet as the police chief approached. "Just hold still, and it'll be over quick as a slash," Shockton said. He grinned at his own joke and, then suddenly lunged and swiped at Henry's gut and cried: "*Get it?*"

Henry jumped back. The flashing claws missed him by inches.

"See, now, that's what I told you *not* to do," Paul said. "You're just making it harder on both of us."

"Go to hell," Henry said.

"Already there, sonny." Shockton leaped, missed again as Henry twisted left and retreated farther from the house, into the broad back yard, with its dry fountain of blue concrete and its rose bushes and its floppy-petaled peonies. "You're a quick one," he said, striding after him. "No wonder Paige hooked up with you. She always liked it fast."

"What the hell do you know about—"

"Fast and hard, yeah, that was her," Paul said. "Liked it up the ass, sometimes. She ever let you do that? Lots of fun. Bet she'd like a twofer. Of course, you'll be dead, so I guess it'll be me and some other guy doing it."

Shockton was trying to rattle him, that was all. Trying to get him to make a mistake.

"Besides, you wouldn't even try that, would you?" Paul said. "You probably never try anything without permission. You're just a little wimp, I bet? Look at you, doing nothing but running away. What Paige is doing with a good little boy, I'll never know."

Henry said: "Shut up."

"Oh, I'm sorry, am I striking a nerve?"

"I said *shut up*, you monster!"

"Monster? Me? I must protest," Shockton said. "I'm just a poor working stiff like you."

"I don't go around *killing people!*" Henry shouted.

"You got your job description," Paul said, slashing again, missing again. "I got mine. Hold still, would you?" He swept his claws in an arc, and Henry stumbled out of the way, then bumped into the fountain. The knee-high concrete rubbed against the backs of his legs. "Oh, this is good," Shockton said. "Something to hold the pieces. Stay right there."

But before Paul could spring at him, Henry lunged and grabbed the man's arm and flung him into the fountain. With an almost comically shocked expression on his face, as if he couldn't believe good little Henry had actually taken the offensive, Paul Shockton tripped over the lip of the basin and smacked head-first into the pedestal from which water had once burbled. Henry jumped in with him, grabbed him by the thin hair on the back of his head, and smashed his face against the edge of the saucer-shaped top of the spout. Again. Again. The aged blue paint chipped away, the weathered concrete beneath it cracked, splintered, broke into flakes, sharp little fragments pattering to the cement floor. Underneath the paint and the grey outer surface, the concrete was white, but only briefly; then it was purplish-red, the color of Paul Shockton's blood.

Henry let go of the hair at last, after he had reduced the man's skull to something approximating an egg that someone had stepped on; Paul collapsed into the fountain, lay curled and still on the cracked blue floor. His wicked black nails were still extended, and when he twitched—he only did it once—they scraped little grey lines through the paint. Henry stood over him until his heart rate dropped to somewhere near normal, until his fingers uncurled from the fists they had made, until he was sure Paul wasn't going to get up again.

Christ. He just killed the chief of police.

No, he told himself. Not the chief of police. Somebody who *looked* like Paul Shockton, who wandered around the police station doing Paul Shockton's job, who maybe went home and screwed Paul Shockton's wife … but not Paul Shockton.

As if that would do him any good when they tried to arrest him.

He looked up the long sloping lawn, to the wall of the Farmhouse. No one was visible, but that didn't mean there wasn't someone—that Finch character, for instance—watching from within the building. One good thing, at least: they probably wouldn't be on the phone to the police, figuring that the police were already here.

He heard a sound from the fountain, a mucky, whisky sound, and looking back he saw that Shockton's body was collapsing into itself, starting at his middle back and spreading out from there, the way sand went through an hourglass, pitting in the center. Pink dust and white dust and red dust all ran together; and then fluids started trickling from the corpse, staining the clothes black, gathering in the basin like a long-stagnant pool. A smell like rotting garbage wafted from the melting cadaver, gagging Henry, forcing him to step away; then he turned from the fountain, and trudged back to the house.

He peeked through the kitchen window; as far as he could see, no one was inside. He opened the door slowly, and entered. The room smelled of the last meal Raye had cooked and which still sat, partially eaten, on the table. But there was another smell underneath the food odor, a pungent, sour smell; the same one he'd noticed in the presence of his mother, and in the car when that slime thing had been there, and on Shockton's breath as he had tried to taunt him into a mistake.

The smell of *them*.

The mixing bowl lay on its side on the counter. He went and looked at it. Drying remnants of pancake batter clung to the stainless steel. The door next to the counter was slightly ajar. He moved away from the bowl and nudged the door open with his foot.

Cellar stairs.

He kicked the door the rest of the way open. The steps went down and to the left; the well consisted of dry wooden beams and plaster walls, hung with ropes of garlic and a variety of dried herbs. He stepped into the stairway. The suspended plants gave off an aromatic and heady odor, but they didn't mask the fact that there was something sour in the basement.

The stairs came down in the middle of the cellar, in the center of a long, narrow space dotted with heavy wooden members to hold up the ceiling. Dim light filtered through small windows situated high along the walls. The foundation was clearly quite old; rather than concrete or cinderblock, it was constructed of odd stones mortared together in a crazy lithic patchwork. The floor consisted of ancient-looking boards, nearly black with age, warped and curled at the edges.

He stepped away from the stairs, into a feeble sunbeam. It didn't do much to warm him up; if anything, it felt like *he* was warming *it*, the little beam stealing his warmth on its way to the damp floorboards. He stood there a moment, then turned his back on the light. The cellar was clogged with wooden shelves arranged parallel to each other and end-on to him. From what he could see they were filled with pickling jars, small boxes, bags of flour and sugar, wine bottles: all the usual stuff that went along with a busy kitchen, but none of the usual junk you found in the basement of a house. The aisles were narrow and dark, running back away from the light.

He heard a noise, a scraping or dragging sound, emanating from one of those dim corridors; and a moment later caught the whisper of a single, labored, scratchy breath. A wheeze; a death rattle.

He hesitated. He knew, even without seeing it, that whatever had made that sound was not going to survive much longer. And he also knew that it was one of the policemen who had arrived to kill Raye Teller and became her prey instead.

Henry heard the hoarse, whispery breath again, and drew a breath of his own; then he went into the malodorous depths of the cellar looking for the source. He walked slowly up the nearest aisle. The warped planks were soft under his feet; old, rotten. The whole floor needed to come out. He would do the job for them cheap, he thought, if only to find out what might be underneath the aged wood.

After about twenty feet, he came to the end of the aisle. The shelf terminated two paces from the back wall of the cellar. A single dungeon-like window admitted the faintest threads of light through the filtering gobs of shrubbery that grew along the front of the house; it lent a shredded illumination to the gap between the storage racks and the jagged wall of uneven stone so that, in the far back corner, he could see the bodies.

It was the cops, all right, piled one on top of the other. The bottom one looked almost mummified, sallow flesh and sunken eye sockets, the way his mother had looked just before she'd fallen to pieces. The other one didn't look much better, but his eyes were open; the dark, piteous orbs were looking right at him.

"Help me," the cop gasped. "Help me."

Henry stayed the hell away from him. "Where'd she go?" he asked.

"Come … come here … and I'll … tell you."

Henry shook his head.

"Please … dying …"

"I can see that," Henry said. "I don't want you to take me with you. Where did Raye Teller go?"

The cop's head lolled to the side, his gaze going to the roof of the cellar, the thick crossbeams, the cobwebs, the sparkling motes of dust that drifted through the pencils of illumination. Was it dust? Or was it something rising from the bodies, particles of decay, liberated by Raye Teller's power?

Henry thought the cop might have expired, but then he said softly: "She went to the plaza."

"The plaza? By the canal?"

"Yes," he said, stretching out the word into a sigh.

"Is that your headquarters? Is that why she went there?"

No answer.

"Is that your nest?"

The cop opened his mouth and said, "Kill the bitch for me." The last word drew out into a sigh, and the sigh turned into a cloud of dust, or something like dust; a puff of smoke rising into the air like the burst of steam from a teapot. Henry stepped back as the dust formed an amorphous blob, then began to disperse. He didn't want to inhale the stuff. He took another look at the cop—he was motionless, eyes still open but no longer seeing, already starting to glaze, like bits of glass going opaque with frost—and then, holding his breath, he went to the body and unsnapped the cop's holster and took his gun. To do so he had to move through the cloud of exhalation, and he felt the tiny particles on his skin, each hot as an ember, tingling, burning their way into him.

He retreated and went quickly up the aisle, climbed out of the basement. He shut the door behind him, put on the latch. He felt like burning his clothes and then taking a good, long, hot shower. But he couldn't.

He didn't have time.

He had to get to Quentin's plaza or he was going to miss the showdown.

21

"You don't have to kill us," Paige said, as Karl advanced on her. He was changing, changing into a man-sized carrion bird, filling up the room with the odor of spoiled meat. "You don't think anyone would believe us if we told them what was going on, do you?"

"People believe all kinds of crazy things," Karl said.

"We'll move away," she said. "We'll pack and leave."

"This is not negotiable," Karl said. "I noticed Henry went out alone, by the way. Where's he off to, leaving you and Freddie here all by yourselves?"

"I don't know."

"Liar, liar," Karl said. He had pushed her all the way back to the kitchen now, up against the swinging door. He wasn't recognizable as Karl anymore, he was something else entirely, a mass of stubby charcoal-colored feathers and gleaming black eyes, thick arms ending in talons, a short, flattened beak that spoke with a ludicrous parody of a human voice. He didn't really look much like a crow; he didn't look like much of anything, except a guy wearing a suit over a cheap, silly costume. She felt an obscene urge to giggle and choked it down, but only with an effort.

The thing that had been Karl Castle said: "You find this situation amusing?" He held up a black-taloned hand. "I can take care of that."

Paige saw movement at the top of the stairs. Karl cocked his head at her; he must have noticed her gaze flick over his shoulder, and he started to turn, but too late.

Calvin Trott came flying down the stairs at him, howling: "Jane!"

The Bird Man plowed right into Karl, and he slammed into Paige, and the three of them tumbled into the kitchen in a tangle of bodies. Paige felt a claw graze her arm but didn't know whose it was. Karl was screeching and coughing and Calvin was shouting gibberish, and both of them were swinging their arms at each other, Calvin trying to rip Karl to shreds and Karl trying to throw off his attacker. Paige scrambled away from them, left them rolling and hissing and screeching on the floor.

She ran out the back door, to the shed.

She tried not to look at the garbage bag that Florence had been in. It was open and empty, except for some soggy shreds of gunk and the weird talc-like dust that had cascaded from her body. Paige figured the rest of the old woman was fluttering around in her upstairs bathroom, but that wasn't the most pressing issue at the moment.

She looked for Henry's axe, spotted it in the cobwebs of the back corner, went for it. Her fingers pierced the webs. They clung to her, and to the axe as she lifted it. The resident of the web, a huge spindly-looking spider, ran along the handle and over her hand and she shook it off.

She turned.

Karl Castle was right outside the shed. His feathers were matted, his suit stained with blood. He slammed the door in her face; as she stood there stupidly, momentarily stunned, she heard him slap the padlock into place. "I'll be back for you in a minute," he called, "after I pay a visit on Frederick."

"No!" she shrieked, and she charged at the door, ran into it shoulder-first. It gave a little, then threw her back. She started whacking it with the axe, right where the latch was on the other side, again and again. The door quickly began to splinter, but not quickly enough; she imagined Karl leaping up to the balcony, just like the Bird Man had done, going into the bedroom where Frederick was hiding, ripping his guts open and smearing them all over the walls—

The wood broke.

She kicked open the door and charged outside.

And a dark arm swept down from the roof; black talons grabbed the axe, ripped it out of her hands, flung it into the forest.

She spun around, and saw Karl on the roof of the shed.

He dropped on her like a stone, smashed her against the wooden ramp. The wood splintered beneath her. She felt pain shoot up and down her back, but if her ribs were breaking she couldn't hear it over the sound of the crunching wood; she had to ignore the pain if she wanted to live, to save Freddie from this maniac.

Paige grabbed a broken chunk of two-by-four and slammed it into the side of Karl's head. His saucer eyes went wide. She hit him again and knocked him off her. He stumbled away, half on his knees. She pursued him and cracked the chunk of wood across the back of his neck and flattened him on the grass. She stood over him, holding the board, ready to hit him again if he moved. It hurt to breathe, and her left arm was starting to get numb; she could still use it, but for how long?

After a few minutes—during which Karl didn't even twitch—Paige dropped the two-by-four and stepped back from the body. Sprawled face-down in the grass with his hairy black feathers, he looked like a dead gorilla, a gorilla in a suit.

She glanced up at the balcony of her bedroom. She thought of the big, aggressive crow she'd locked in the bathroom. That was Florence.

Maybe if you killed them, they came back as birds.

She didn't want this one coming back.

Paige went into the shed. The lawn mower was against the right-hand wall, near the can of fuel. She picked up the red metal container, shook it. Liquid sloshed around inside. She unscrewed the cap, tossed it in the corner, smelled the spout. Definitely gasoline.

Okay, good.

Still carrying the can, she ran into the house to get the matches. Her kitchen floor was a slick of blood and she nearly lost her footing on it. Calvin Trott lay near the swinging door. He looked like he had been run over by one of those soil-tilling machines with all the circular blades; as it happened, he was lying right in front of the cabinet with the matches in it, and she had to gingerly step over him, careful not to slip on the blood and the scuds of flesh scattered around.

She opened the drawer directly above the Bird Man and took out a box of wooden matches and, for good measure, a cigarette lighter. She put them in the pocket of her blouse, then grabbed the Bird Man's wrist with one hand and dragged him toward the back door.

He was heavy, but the blood helped him slide.

The swinging door opened and Frederick came in. He was wearing Henry's clothes; they fit him perfectly. He stopped and looked at the blood on the floor, looked at Calvin, looked at her—she must be a fright, she realized suddenly—and said, in a small, ridiculous voice: "Mommy?"

"Go wait in the living room, Freddie," she said. "Mommy's just cleaning up in here."

He backed out of the kitchen. The door swung shut behind him.

She bent to pick up the Bird Man's wrists again.

Then sharp claws dug into her sides and lifted her right up off the floor.

In her ear, Karl Castle whispered: "Not quite enough, dear Paige. Not quite enough."

The gasoline can clattered from her hand, bounced on the floor, landed on its side. Volatile liquid gurgled out, fanned across the linoleum, softened the blood from crimson to a pale pink. At her feet, the eyes of the eviscerated Bird Man stared up at her. The stink of gasoline made her head swim.

Karl dragged her toward the back door. His scarcely-human voice was right in her ear as he whispered, "We're going for a little ride, you and I." He withdrew one of his claws from her side. She felt a weird, itchy, crawly sensation as the talon slid out; there was a hot rush of blood, but it stopped almost immediately; she could feel her flesh puckering into a welt, sealing up the wound, sealing in whatever weird junk Karl's talon might have put inside her. He reached around in front of her—his hand had become human again—and slipped his fingers into her breast pocket, pulling out the matches. He let go of her then, tossed her into the corner; she slammed into the wall and slid to the floor, pain throbbing from her ribs, her sides, her arm. She tried to get up, but her feet just slid and scrabbled on the slick floor, and the room seemed to spin around her.

Karl struck a match, held it carefully in his human hand, at the end of his inhuman arm. He sidled over to Paige, grasped her ankle, dragged her over to the back door and shoved her into the yard.

Then he dropped the match into the gasoline.

There was a soft *whoosh*, and through the miasma of her pain and the spreading glaze of shock, she saw her kitchen turn into an inferno.

Karl came down from the back step. He was transforming himself back into a man. His clothes were in covered in gore, but he didn't seem to care. He stood over her and said: "Poor Paige, you don't look like you could take another step." He knelt down and scooped her up in his arms easily, as if she weighed no more than a feather; he carried her to the front of the house and laid her gently in the passenger seat of his car. She managed to tip her head so she could watch in the mirror as he puttered in the trunk; when he got into the car himself, he was wearing a clean shirt and a jacket, natty as ever, though he still had a few laces of blood on his grey pants.

He started up the car, then turned and looked at her.

"Seat belt," he said. "Remember, safety first."

As it turned out, Simon was a better jumped than he'd thought he was. Or maybe his muscles, fueled by the adrenaline of panic, just pushed him farther than they normally would. Or maybe God reached down and cradled him in the palm of His hand, to keep him out of the clutches of the flock. Whatever; Simon leaped, and found himself soaring in a gentle arc, above the heads of the shoppers, over the concrete walkway of the plaza, down into the flower bed, where he landed with a *thump* in the soft, spaded earth amid the bushy flowering shrubs.

He pushed himself out of the planter. Moist dirt and crushed petals clung to him. The shoppers had noticed him; they stared as he clambered out of the flower bed, both those who were passing and the pale faces beyond broad glass panels in the dining areas.

He ran left, farther into the plaza, weaving, avoiding the customers when he could, pushing them aside when he couldn't. He reached the steps to the next level, took them three or four at a time, jumped when he was within five of the bottom. The gun bounced heavily against his side in the too-big pocket of his pants.

At the end of the second tier, he found what he was looking for: the sporting goods store. He darted inside, into the cool dimness of the place. It smelled like leather and nylon. Guns were in a bulletproof glass rack along the back wall; ammunition was locked in the display case. There weren't any shoppers present, and the clerk was nowhere to be seen. Simon raced to the counter, took out the pistol, and whacked the glass of the ammunition display with the butt of the gun.

It just bounced off.

Perhaps in response to the sound of the gun beating on the case, the clerk came out of the back. He was tall and scrawny and covered with freckles and orange hair, and he had on a big name tag that said *Ivan*, and when he saw Simon standing there holding the thirty-eight and whaling on the glass he said: "Dude! You in a hurry to hold somebody up?"

Simon looked at him. "Open the case."

"No way, man."

Simon whipped the gun up and pointed it at the kid's face. "Open the fucking case." He noted, with some surprise, that he was holding the weapon perfectly still, that his voice was perfectly calm. To himself, he sounded like one of the icy cool villains in an action flick, the guy who thinks he has the upper hand right until the hero drops out of the suspended ceiling and blows him away.

Except *he* was the hero, right?

The clerk said: "What do you need ammo for if that thing's loaded?"

"You wanna find out if it's loaded?"

"Not really." The kid headed around behind the case. Then he looked over Simon's shoulder and said, "Afternoon, officer."

"Very funny," Simon said, not turning.

Then he heard a sound like an inflated paper bag being popped, and he felt a sudden sharp pain in his left shoulder, and he stumbled forward into the case and slid down it to the floor, leaving a crimson streak along the Plexiglas.

He looked at the door.

It seemed intolerably bright outside, as if the sun had crashed out of the sky and landed right outside the store. He saw the silhouette of the man who'd shot him, saw the points of his hat; thought he saw, faintly, wisps of smoke rising from the muzzle of his weapon, dark spirits against the light outside.

He heard the clerk say: "You *shot* him!"

The cop—it was Grady, the policeman who had interviewed him after he'd found Jane's body—came over and picked up the gun Simon had been carrying. Simon noticed, in a detached, hazy way, that he was wearing black leather gloves.

Grady laid Simon's gun on the counter, then held out his left hand, palm up, and said: "Bullets."

"Huh?" Ivan said.

"Give me bullets for this man's gun." Pause. "*Now!*"

"Okay, Jesus, hold your horses," the kid said. Simon heard him slide the display case open, heard him rummaging around inside.

The front windows were pure sheets of light. No one was looking in.

Why was no one looking in?

They were outside, keeping people away, he thought. They didn't want any witnesses.

Simon knew why Grady wanted to put bullets in his gun.

"Don't do it," he said, as the orange-haired kid lifted a box of bullets out from the display case.

"Shut up," Grady said.

"He'll shoot you," Simon said. The clerk looked down at him, the box of ammunition held in his trembling, freckled hands. "He'll load my gun and he'll shoot you with it."

The clerk looked uneasily at Grady, who said: "You gonna listen to this guy? He pulled a gun on you, for Christ's sake."

"Why *do* you want—" the clerk said.

He never finished the question. Grady slid Simon's gun off the counter and smashed the kid in the face with it, then deftly plucked the box of bullets from his hands before he fell. He then calmly loaded the gun with a single bullet and angled it over the display case, muzzle pointing toward the floor.

Simon could see the kid through the glass. He was sitting up, blood streaming from a split in his face, looking up at the mouth of the weapon that was pointing at him. His eyes were wide and pale; then Grady pulled the trigger, and one of the pale, wide eyes vanished in an explosion of bone and blood, and the kid fell like he'd been slammed with a ten-ton weight.

Grady very carefully laid the gun on Simon's chest, then straightened up and stuck his own gun in its holster. He removed the gloves and stuffed them in on top of the pistol; he snapped it shut, but the leather must have been in the way because the strap popped open after a second. Apparently not noticing this, or just not caring, Grady said: "Mayor Jones, I'm arresting you for, oh, call it first-degree murder. You have the right to remain silent. If you choose to give up this right, blah blah blah." He grinned. "Do you understand these rights?"

"Go to hell," Simon said.

"Already there, pal," Grady said. "Already there."

After Simon jumped, Quentin allowed himself to shrink back into his old human self. The spiny feathers left an itchy, prickly sensation as they shriveled back beneath his skin; the bony protrusions around his mouth left his jaws sore and tender. He didn't recall these unpleasant sensations before, back in the Farmhouse, when he'd been practicing his transformations. Must be a combination of things. What Tom Teller had done to him; his suddenly-advanced age; the big hunk of flesh missing from his leg.

The wound Simon had inflicted didn't hurt all that much, now that he had gotten over the initial shock; it wasn't bleeding a lot, either, but it was gummy and sore, made him limp a bit. It really wasn't any worse than, say, a bad cut or a sprain. One good thing about his condition: he healed like a son-of-a-bitch.

Not from what Tom had done, though. He was still feeling the effects of that; his entire body ached, he felt bloated and sluggish. He had some sort of edema going on, he thought; his prematurely-aged heart wasn't pushing blood around properly. He could feel it, his leathery heart, hammering away in his chest. Yesterday—earlier today, even, before his encounter with Tom—he'd had a strong, firm, trim body, tough, powerful; now he could scarcely walk five yards without sitting down.

He suddenly realized he had never seen the plaza from this perspective before. He had to go take a look at it before he climbed back down. Quentin toddled to the facade, looked out over his shopping center. He allowed himself a sigh at the beauty of it. Like the ruins of ancient Greece, in a thousand years people would still be coming to where Canal Plaza had stood, coming and marveling at a civilization that could produce such architecture. Yes, they would. It was built to last; it was built for the ages.

Something settled onto his shoulder with a fluttering of wings. Tiny claws gripped him through his shirt. He didn't need to look to know it was the big crow from downstairs; it had fluttered away after Simon had jumped, flown out of sight beyond the facade. He wondered what it had seen.

Wait a minute.

He looked at the crow and said: "You son of a bitch, you're Tom Teller's father, aren't you?"

It looked at him and blinked its grey eyelids.

"You understand me perfectly well, don't you? You understand all of us."

The crow burbled at him.

Quentin suddenly felt very tired. Nausea boiled up from his stomach and he choked it down, leaned over and rested his head against the curving crest of the facade. The concrete was hard and hot and pebbly.

He saw Raye Teller walk in under the arch, pause, look around. What was *she* doing here? Shockton had said he was going to take care of her. He watched her wander into the plaza as if she were lost; then she looked at the door to the offices and went over to it, disappearing from his sight. He leaned forward to see if he could get a look at what she was doing, but she wasn't visible anymore.

Shit. He had to get back down, warn the others. If she was anything like Tom, she could handle all of them put together, and this time surprise would be on her side.

A gunshot from deep in the plaza distracted him. His head snapped up, but he couldn't tell where the sound had come from. He stretched on his tiptoes, trying to see. Shoppers were flooding up the stairs to the right; the cops were there, directing them toward the end of the food court. They were clearing the second level of the plaza. Must have Simon cornered down there, Quentin thought. Endgame in progress.

He looked back at the entrance as someone stepped into the plaza. This one seemed to be looking up at him. He was vaguely familiar but Quentin didn't know from where.

Then he realized that the man had a gun, and the gun was pointed at him.

In the second it took his tired brain to register all this, there was another gunshot and a puff of smoke from the man's weapon. Something whistled past Quentin's ear. The dark shape of the crow, which had been occupying his peripheral vision, disappeared in a puff of blood and feathers. He felt his pulse jump a beat or three, like a drummer startled out of his rhythm.

The gun moved an inch to the left. Now it was pointed at Quentin's head.

"You people shouldn't have fucked with my family," the man said.

Quentin ducked down behind the facade. He heard yet another gunshot, but this one was from deeper in the plaza. It seemed to bounce off the sky and echo back down to him, then rumble away like thunder.

He crawled across the gravel to the hatch, passing the remains of the crow. The bullet had torn into it and turned it into what looked like a bloody, feathery, wadded-up rag. The bits of it were spread around, and twitching.

He could feel the heat of the sun, falling on him like sand. He slowly turned himself around, got onto the ladder, started to climb down.

And that was when he felt a sudden, sharp, stabbing pain, right in his chest, like someone had snapped a mousetrap shut on his heart. His arms clenched on the ladder, then went limp. He let go, and fell, and landed on his back, staring up at the hatch. His chest was a morass of fire. He gasped for breath, but it felt as if his lungs had turned to stiff old parchment. He smelled shit, and realized it was coming from him, as his bowels opened up and let loose.

The patch of blue that was visible through the hatch began to turn grey.

Heart attack, he thought. Thirty-seven years old and dying of a heart attack. Except he was really fifty-two now, wasn't he? Once you factored in the fifteen years Tom Teller stole.

Through the roaring in his ears he heard the door groan; through the shadows in his eyes he saw it sag inward, drooping from its bottom hinge like a drunk just barely clinging to a light post. A small dark shape came in, bent down over him and said: "Mr. Farmer?"

Raye Teller.

He tried to lift his arm, but it felt like lead. "Help me," he said.

She swept her hand over him. He felt a wrenching sensation in his guts, like they were being twisted on a fork, big ropy bloody chunks of spaghetti that she was sucking up and eating.

He closed his eyes.

The last thing he heard was Raye Teller's soft voice: "Give my regards to my father when you get to hell."

Henry lowered the gun after the guy on the roof disappeared. He didn't know if he would've shot him, really, although if he hadn't moved it would have been very, very tempting.

He headed for the office. The glass door was ajar; in fact, it looked like the frame had warped and twisted with age, so he couldn't close it even if he wanted to. It creaked loudly as he opened it, crying out for oil. He stepped into the hallway beyond, and immediately knew that he was in the right place; the air was heady with the thick, sour stench he'd become accustomed to. The smell of *them*.

The corridor was painted powder-blue, with ash-grey rugs, indirect lighting, and pastel paintings depicting nothing. Azure doors opened left and right. He tried them one by one. The first was a maintenance closet. The second and third, both on the left, were tiny restrooms. None were occupied.

A bit farther up, just before the corridor banked right, he came to a door on the left that hung open onto a concrete stairwell. It stank even worse in there than in the corridor. A shriveled corpse lay on the floor, dry lips pulled back in a grimace from protruding teeth, sunken eyes and cheeks, wispy threads of hair clinging to the wrinkled skull. It was dressed just like the guy he had almost shot.

Raye Teller had gotten here first.

He left the stairwell, kept going, around the dog-leg. More doors. Offices, small conference rooms, a break room. Empty, all of them. Where the hell *was* everyone?

He reached the end of the hall, a door marked *exit*. He pushed it open, saw the rear of the plaza, the Dumpster area. On the left was a big office, with a nameplate that said *Monroe Parker*. When he opened that door, it snapped off its hinges and fell into the room.

And there was everybody.

A dozen bodies, looking like long-dead mummies: a guy behind the desk in a suit; a withered girl in a miniskirt and sweater, both of which had probably once been tight but now hung loosely on her desiccated frame; a maintenance man in a blue uniform; a security guard with the name *J. Shoemaker* sewn onto his breast pocket. The room smelled like old death, like a crypt unsealed after a hundred years of rot.

Raye Teller had gotten here first, too.

He backed into the hallway, keeping an eye on the corpses, just in case; but none of them twitched. He went out the back way, into the alley behind the building, keeping the door open with his foot. Sirens were approaching from the distance. More cops, he thought. He wondered if they, too, were members of the flock. He couldn't force himself to believe Raye had gotten them all, much as he wanted to. He noticed that some of the wooden slats in the fence had rotted and come loose, leaving an opening big enough to squeeze through. That was probably how she had gotten out of the plaza.

He looked at the gun in his hand. Turned out he didn't really need it after all, apparently. No one to shoot, except a crow. He untucked his shirt and wiped the gun with it—he wasn't sure that would get all the fingerprints off, but what the hell, it was better than doing nothing—and then dropped the pistol into the big Dumpster on the left. There was a scraping noise and a *clang* as it slid to the bottom of the refuse-filled trash bin.

He went back inside and walked slowly through the offices. The place was utterly dead; no one was moving except him, and the only sound was the steady hum of the air conditioners, dumping frigid air over his neck and shoulders.

He pushed open the glass door, stepped out into the heat of the sun. Shoppers milled around aimlessly, in little knots, staring up at the far end of the plaza.

An arm snaked around his shoulder, pulled him off to the side.

Startled, he turned; Karl Castle was standing there, with his other arm around Paige. She looked like shit: battered, smeared and streaked with blood, her face pale and drawn and listless. The two of them smelled like a gas station; and somehow, this spectacle was not attracting attention.

"Henry Fontana," Karl said. "What a surprise."

Henry felt a pricking on the back of his neck, where Karl's fingers were. A flicker crossed Karl's face, and he caught a glimpse of the rubber mask look the members of the flock wore beneath the veneer of humanity; then it was gone.

"What did you do to Paige, you bastard?" Henry said.

"I'm afraid I damaged her a bit," Karl said. "She was uncooperative, to say the least. I actually brought her here for Quentin, but unless my nose deceives me it's too late for that." His shoulders shrugged slightly, as if this were of little consequence to him. Then he nodded toward the interior of the plaza, and said: "Have they brought Simon up yet?"

"What the fuck is going on?" Henry said, afraid to move; that blade at the end of Karl's finger was right on his spinal cord. One little twitch and he was in a wheelchair; one big twitch and he was in a coffin.

"This is checkmate, my friend," Karl said, "and we win."

The cops swarmed through the door of the shop, surrounded Simon. There were at least six of them, though they kept moving around so much that he could hardly keep track of them. They hauled him to his feet, heedless of the fact that he had a bullet in his shoulder, and marched him out of the confines of the sporting goods store, out into the light. Surrounding him like bodyguards, they hustled him through the plaza. Every step sent a bolt of pain down his side, but that was good, in a way. Kept him conscious, kept the shock at bay. Or maybe he was already in shock and just didn't know it.

Up the stairs, hup hup hup, to the top tier of the plaza where the shoppers had been herded like sheep. They slowed their pace on this level, thinned their ranks a bit, making sure everyone could get a good look at who they were escorting off to prison. It was a show, he realized, a game of *parade-the-mayor-past-the-people*. Part of the plot to humiliate and ruin him, a plot that seemed to have succeeded admirably. Karl Castle would be thrilled. He had a thick, icky combination of feelings in his stomach: dread, and despair, and utter defeat.

As they neared the entrance, they slowed down even more. There were three people standing beside the door to the offices, Paige was on the left, looking like a refugee from a slaughterhouse; Henry was on the right, looking ashen and frightened and totally lost. And between them was Karl Castle, his face a leering, triumphant mask. He had one arm around each of them; Simon could see his fingers, and their nails were long and black and wickedly curved.

As Simon approached, Karl raised one hand—the one holding

Paige—and he mouthed a word and wiggled the claws in the air so only Simon could see.

The word he made was a name.

The name was *Roland*.

It took a few seconds for Simon to realize what Karl was saying. Then the lump in his stomach caught fire, and all the other emotions burned up and the only thing left was rage. And as he and his police escort passed Karl, Simon lunged at the cop on his left, Grady, the one who had shot the kid in the sporting goods store, who had put his gun away but hadn't been able to snap the holster shut.

Simon slid the cop's pistol out with his good arm. The leather gloves fluttered to the ground. Simon swung the weapon up and around and pointed it at Karl, and thought:

Pretend it was racquetball.

Pretend Paige and Henry were the walls of the court.

Pretend the gun was the racquet.

And pretend Karl's head was the ball.

Bang.

Henry could've sworn it all happened in slow motion: Simon whipping the gun out of the cop's holster, raising it, firing. He could've sworn he saw the bullet rush out of the cloud of smoke, snapping it into little swirls and eddies with the velocity of its passage. But that was just his imagination, of course; time didn't really slow down, it all happened in the space of a second.

Karl's head flipped back, smacked into the wall of the plaza, left a blotchy crimson stain the size of a beach ball on the brilliant white stucco.

Henry heard the ricochet, heard Paige grunt, saw her body jerk.

Oh, Jesus.

Karl sank to the ground between them; Paige's knees buckled, too. Henry reached across Karl, caught his wife, pulled her to him. She was breathing shallowly, her eyes half-closed. His fingers brushed something, a small hole in the back of her shirt. The spot was sticky and hot. "Jesus, Paige," he said.

"Freddie," she said, her voice barely a whisper. "The house … burning."

The plaza had dissolved into chaos, shoppers screaming and

running every which-way like frightened cattle, police piling on top of Simon, flashbulbs popping near the entrance. Henry hauled Paige into the azure office corridor, knowing full well she shouldn't be moved, but what the hell was he going to do, let the cops take care of her? They would take care of her, all right, exactly the way Karl had been planning to.

Her feet made half-hearted plodding motions as he dragged her through the hallway to the back door. "Got to get you to a hospital," he said.

She shook her head, groaned softly. "No good," she said. "Too late."

"Don't say that," Henry said.

"Back to the house," she said, managing to open one eye, black as coal, though it should've been blue, and fix her gaze on him. "Back to the *house*, Henry."

They went out the back door. The opening in the fence beckoned and he took Paige through it. His car wasn't far away; he helped her into it, and they roared out of the parking lot. Not going to the hospital, where they could maybe help Paige; going home, to the hills.

Henry saw the fire trucks when he came around the corner near their house, three of them, a rescue truck and two tankers; and men in floppy olive coats and broad black hats, too, spraying water on the charred heap visible through the trees where their home should have been. He slowed down as he neared the scene. Paige was sinking deeper into her half-conscious stupor; her skin had turned ashen, and she was shivering despite the fact that he'd turned the heat up full-blast. Still, she roused herself a bit as he pulled to the side, perhaps realizing they were almost home.

Henry stopped some distance away; the fire crews didn't pay any attention to the car. "Jesus," Henry said. "Karl did this?"

Paige nodded, grimaced. "Freddie," she said. "Do you see Freddie?"

Henry scanned the trucks. "No," he said. "No, I don't see anyone but firemen."

She sighed, and said softly: "Too late. No good." She seemed to collapse into herself, sagged back against the seat, as if the only thing keeping her going had been the possibility of rescuing Freddie from the fire.

"Hang on, Paige," Henry said. "Hang on. There's paramedics here, see, there's the van, maybe he's in there—"

"Bad … liar," Paige said. "Couldn't even fool … your mother …"

She was letting herself slip away. He turned to her, and saw someone crouched in the woods near the side of the road, peering out at them, clutching a blue pet box containing a wriggling, whining puppy.

Freddie!

"Hang on," Henry said. "Hang on, Paige, I see him, he's in the woods!"

She smiled fondly at him, and her lips moved, forming the word *liar*.

"No, he's there!" He reached over, turned her head so she could see.

"Too dark," she murmured. "Can't see."

Shit! "Hang on, Paige, I'll get him." He scrambled out of the car, circled around behind it. He shouted, "Frederick!" Freddie's eyes widened and he vanished into the brush. "Stop! It's your father!" Henry shouted, diving into the forest.

He caught up to Frederick not far from the road. Freddie was cowering under a big oak tree, the pet box at his feet. "I'm sorry, Daddy," he said. "I didn't do it!"

"I know you didn't," Henry said. He shouldn't have called him *Frederick*, that was the boy's trouble name, made him think he was being blamed for burning down the house. "I know." He picked up the pet box. "Come back to the car. Your mother needs you." He hauled Frederick to his feet and the two of them stumbled back through the scrub, smashing through the ferns, back to the road. Paige was barely visible through the window, she had slid so far down in her seat.

Henry yanked the door opened, thrust Frederick into view. "Here he is," he said. "See? See? Here's Freddie."

Paige turned, and some focus came back into her eyes. She smiled, and reached out with a trembling hand to touch Freddie's shoulder. "There's my boy," she said. "There's my little boy."

"Are you okay, Mommy? You look sick."

"Mommy's just fine, now," Paige said, an obvious untruth.

Then the nail of her index finger slid out like a black switchblade;

and before Henry could make a move to stop her, she jammed the talon into Freddie's shoulder.

"Paige! No!" Henry shouted.

She was doing the same thing Florence had done to him; except Freddie wasn't getting older.

He was getting *younger*.

Henry watched, astonished, as Freddie shrank, as if Paige were deflating him. And that was exactly what was happening; she was pumping the years out of him, and into herself. As he returned to childhood, she shot through middle age. Flecks of white appeared in her auburn hair; her skin tightened, wrinkled, grew spotted and sallow.

Freddie was shivering and making a sound, a little *uh-uh-uh* sound that made Henry's skin crawl. Paige was silent, until she pulled her finger out and gave a little sigh and said, so softly Henry could barely hear her, "Mommy's little boy."

Then she slumped down in her seat and lay still.

"Mommy?" Freddie said, his voice once again a six-year-old's.

Henry straightened up.

Jesus God. This had to be a nightmare, didn't it?

"Mommy?"

He looked up the street. The firemen had finally noticed them, and one was coming down the road, sternness in every step.

And Freddie shrieked, "*Mommy!*"

Epilogue

As it turned out, Henry met Raye Teller one more time; she turned up in late September, in the graveyard.

Paige had been buried way up on the hill, toward the back corner, near where the clipped grass of the cemetery gave way to the woods. Henry had gone up to collect the big ceramic flowerpot he left by her headstone, only to discover it had been smashed by vandals; so he collected the pieces instead, trying to balance the shards—they were sharp and curving, like his mother's claws—in his hands without cutting himself. He had begun to turn, away from the stone and the woods, toward his car—Paige's car, actually, his own vehicle being nothing but a rusty smear on the road—when, from behind him, a crow coughed loudly.

Henry froze.

In the weeks since everything had happened, he'd heard many crow calls, of course. He could tell, somehow, whether or not they came from a *natural* crow—they nearly always did—or from what he had come to think of as a *spirit* crow, the residue left behind when you killed one of the flock. It didn't seem as if the spirit crows had any special abilities—even the big one, the one with the white flecks, had never to his knowledge demonstrated anything other than unusual intelligence—but he didn't like to hear them, just the same. They were threatening, and they made him remember.

This was not a natural crow.

He turned, scanned the dark, tufted greenery of the forest wall. Pines, scrubbly little ones. The ground was littered with fallen cones, matted with a spongy carpet of brown needles.

A voice said: "Mr. Fontana."

Raye Teller. He couldn't see her, but he'd never forget the voice.

"What do you want?" he asked the forest.

"You killed my father," she said. It was approbation, not accusation. He squinted into the shadows, and thought he could see her, a dim shape out beneath the trees. She seemed to have a large bird perched on her right shoulder.

Henry stood there, and waited.

"Before you shot him, he got what he wanted. He humiliated and ruined Simon. Simon was a Selden, in case you didn't know."

"I knew. Paige told me." Pause. "It's over, then, isn't it?"

"Oh, no, Mr. Fontana," Raye said. "What's called up from the pit is not so easily sent away again. The wings remain. I hear them in the night, flying through the trees. Don't you?" Then, after a moment: "No, I don't suppose you do. You never were one of us. Not really." He heard a sound then, out under the trees, the rustling of spiny branches. "I would leave Selden Falls, if I were you," she said; her voice had become distant, remote, like the wind off a mountain. "It won't be safe, when the wings come again. They're watching you."

He still couldn't see her, but he knew she was gone.

He stood there a little longer, then carried the pottery shards to the car. He dumped them into the trunk, climbed in beside Freddie. "Who were you talking to, Daddy?" Freddie asked.

"No one," Henry said. He started the car. He stared at the sky, where cirrus clouds twined around each other in a lover's embrace.

Dry leaves skittered across the narrow blacktop road.

He wondered what the weather was like in California.

About the Author

James V. Viscosi is the author of several horror and fantasy novels. An expatriate New Yorker, he currently resides with his wife and various finned and furry animals in sunny Southern California, where he spends most of his time hiding beneath a very large hat. Visit him at www.jamesviscosi.com.